THE TOMB OF THE DARK ONES

The DANCING TUATARA PRESS Books from RAMBLE HOUSE

CLASSICS OF HORROR

1. **Beast or Man!** — Sean M'Guire
2. **The Whistling Ancestors** — Richard E. Goddard
3. **The Shadow on the House** — Mark Hansom
4. **Sorcerer's Chessmen** — Mark Hansom
5. **The Wizard of Berner's Abbey** — Mark Hansom
6. **The Border Line** — Walter S. Masterman
7. **The Trail of the Cloven Hoof** — Arlton Eadie
8. **The Curse of Cantire** — Walter S. Masterman
9. **Reunion in Hell and Other Stories** — The Selected Stories of John H. Knox Vol. I
10. **The Ghost of Gaston Revere** — Mark Hansom
11. **The Tongueless Horror And Other Stories** — The Selected Weird Tales of Wyatt Blassingame Vol. I
12. **Master of Souls** — Mark Hansom
13. **Man Out of Hell and Other Stories** — The Selected Stories of John H. Knox Vol. II
14. **Lady of the Yellow Death and Other Stories** — Selected Weird Tales of Wyatt Blassingame Vol. II
15. **Satan's Sin House and Other Stories** — The Weird Tales of Wayne Rogers Vol. I
16. **Hostesses in Hell and Other Stories** — The Weird Tales of Russell Gray Vol. I
17. **Hands Out of Hell and Other Stories** — The Selected Stories of John H. Knox Vol. III
18. **Summer Camp for Corpses and Other Stories** — Weird Tales of Arthur L. Zagat Vol. I
19. **One Dreadful Night** — by Ronald S.L. Harding
20. **The Library of Death** — by Ronald S.L. Harding
21. **The Beautiful Dead and Other Stories** — The Weird Tales of Donald Dale
22. **Death Rocks the Cradle and Other Stories** — Weird Tales of Wayne Rogers Vol. II
23. **The Devil's Night Club and Other Stories** — Nat Schachner
24. **Mark of the Laughing Death and Other Stories** — Francis James
25. **The Strange Thirteen and Other Stories** — Richard B. Gamon
26. **The Unholy Goddess and Other Stories** — The Selected Weird Tales of Wyatt Blassingame Vol. III
27. **House of the Restless Dead and Other Stories** — Hugh B. Cave
28. **Tales of Terror & Torment Vol. 1** — Edited by John Pelan
29. **The Corpse Factory and Other Stories** — Arthur Leo Zagat
30. **The Great Orme Terror and Other Stories** — Garnett Radcliffe
31. **Freak Museum** — R. R. Ryan
32. **The Subjugated Beast** — R. R. Ryan
33. **Towers & Tortures** — Dexter Dayle
34. **The Antlered Man** — Edwy Searles Brooks
35. **When the Batman Thirsts** — Frederick C. Davis
36. **The Sorcery Club** — Elliott O'Donnell
37. **Tales of Terror and Torment Vol. 2** — Edited by John Pelan
38. **Mistress of Terror and Other Stories** — The Selected Weird Tales of Wyatt Blassingame Vol. IV
39. **The Place of Hairy Death and Other Stories** — An Anthony Rud Reader, Volume 1
40. **Dark Sanctuary** — H.B. Gregory
41. **Echo of a Curse** — R.R. Ryan
42. **The Finger of Destiny** — Edmund Snell
43. **The Devil of Pei-Ling** — Herbert Asbury
44. **The Madman** — Mark Hansom
45. **Laughing Death** — Walter C. Brown
46. **The Silent Terror of Chu-Sheng** — Eugene Thomas
47. **Death of a Sadist** — R.R. Ryan
48. **The Crimson Butterfly** — Edmund Snell
49. **Vampire of the Skies** — James Corbett
50. **The Back of Beyond** — Edmund Snell
51. **My Touch Brings Death and Other Stories** — The Weird Tales of Russell Gray Vol. II
52. **The Tomb of the Dark Ones** — A novel of the occult by J.M.A. Mills
53. **Food for the Fungus Lady and Other Stories** — Ralston Shields
54. **The Evil of Li-Sin** — Yellow Peril tales from Gerald Verner writing as Nigel Vane
55. **Cathedral of Horror and Other Stories** — Volume 1 of Arthur J. Burks' weird fiction

CLASSICS OF SCIENCE FICTION AND FANTASY

1. **Chariots of San Fernando and Other Stories** — Malcolm Jameson
2. **The Story Writer and Other Stories** — Richard Wilson
3. **The House That Time Forgot and Other Stories** — Robert F. Young
4. **A Niche in Time and Other Stories** — William F. Temple
5. **Two Suns of Morcali and Other Stories** — Evelyn E. Smith
6. **Old Faithful and Other Stories** — Raymond Z. Gallun
7. **The Alien Envoy and Other Stories** — Malcolm Jameson
8. **The Man without a Planet and Other Stories** — Richard Wilson
9. **The Man Who was Secrett and Other Stories** — John Brunner
10. **The Cloudbuilders** — Colin Kapp
11. **Somewhere In Space** — C.C. MacApp

DAY KEENE IN THE DETECTIVE PULPS

1. **League of the Grateful Dead and Other Stories** — Day Keene in the Detective Pulps Vol. I
2. **We Are the Dead and Other Stories** — Day Keene in the Detective Pulps Vol. II
3. **Death March of the Dancing Dolls and Other Stories** — Day Keene in the Detective Pulps Vol. III
4. **The Case of the Bearded Bride and Other Stories** — Day Keene in the Detective Pulps Vol. IV
5. **A Corpse Walks in Brooklyn and Other Stories** — Day Keene in the Detective Pulps Vol. V
6. **Homicide House and Other Stories** — Day Keene in the Detective Pulps Vol. VI

THE TOMB OF THE DARK ONES

J. M. A. MILLS

Introduced by

John Pelan

RAMBLE HOUSE
2014

Copyright © 1937 by J. M. A. Mills

This edition © 2014 Ramble House

Introduction © 2014 by John Pelan

DEDICATED
WITH MUCH AFFECTION TO
LUCIAN WAINWRIGHT
IN GRATITUDE FOR ALL THE
EXPERT ADVICE AND CRITICISM
GIVEN ME IN MY WORK

ISBN 13: 978-1-60543-775-0

Preparation: Fender Tucker

Cover Art © 2014 Gavin L. O'Keefe

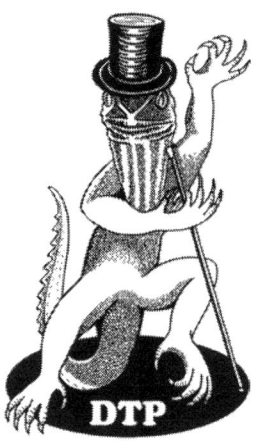

DANCING TUATARA PRESS #52

OPENING THE TOMB

This volume is one that will amply reward the reader with an excellent story and also allow me to expound on one of the facets of collecting that (surprisingly) gets ignored. The British publisher, Rider & Co. is known mainly as a publisher of books on the occult and a good deal of theosophist nonsense. Now, don't get me wrong, with what I do for a living I tend to read lots of books on the occult (I mean really, *lots* and *lots*), many of which were published by Rider or another great imprint, Andrew Dakers & Co., however, something that has served me very well over the years is the advice from one of my mentors in book collecting/selling that "when you encounter the words "Atlantis" and "reincarnation" in the same paragraph, it's time to set the book down and go on to something else . . .) The aforementioned worthies also published a number of tomes that proved the truth of this adage.

What does any of that have to do with J.M.A. Mills? Well, Ms. Mills was apparently a true believer and authored several books on the "truth" of such matters, she also wrote two exceptional novels (the present volume and a loose sequel) that used her vast knowledge on the subject to very good effect. This latter fact has become misquoted over the years as "she wrote two books", this notion can be readily disabused by using any of the book-search engines on the Internet, she actually wrote quite a few, but sadly only two that will be of interest to us.

Mills is an author that I can claim to have discovered in large part on my own, backing up my findings by consulting with George Locke of Ferret Fantasy. One of the things I learned from George is mentioned above as "that facet of collecting that (surprisingly) gets ignored; if you're not interested in this, feel free to skip the next few paragraphs.

One of the very first things we learn as readers or collectors is that if we enjoy a certain book, it is likely that the author wrote other, similar books during their career. However, with the exception of specialty presses whose intent is well known to all, a lot of folks skip over the subjects of time-period and imprint, or even editorial direction. Some exceptions would be in the mass-market paperbacks in the post-WWII years up through the 1960s and 1970s. You would have to be pretty obtuse to not realize that Gold Medal Books was a good place to find crime novels and Ace an excellent place for science-fiction, westerns and mysteries. However, for those of use that grew up in the era of publishing giants, we weren't inclined to apply this logic to seeking out publishers' catalogs; sure there were the occasional smaller publishers such as Ballantine that one could turn to for books on several specific subjects, but for the most part the hardcover publishers weren't given the same sort of scrutiny.

One of my mentors, who was of considerable help in my putting together a complete run of the "Creeps series" (actually, *more* than complete, as there are several related titles that are of interest to collectors of supernatural fiction, after all, Charles Birkin was an editor there in the years prior to WWII and put together the "Creeps series", it only stands to reason that he would acquire similar titles), asked me point-blank if I had researched publishers' catalogues and suggested that in addition to Philip Allan (the "Creeps" publisher), I might look at some other British publishers from that time period, one being Rider & Company.

Well, those of you that have been following DTP books know of Rider as the original publisher of H.B. Gregory's *Dark Sanctuary*, but that's just the tip of the iceberg, I knew of Rider as the publisher of Elliot O'Donnell's excellent supernatural thriller *The Dead Riders* and Warrington Dawson's *The Guardian Demons,* so the suggestion made sense. Using the advanced search feature on abebooks I tried the Internet version of browsing through a used bookstore, I pulled up all titles from 1900-1960. Whoa, way too many to read through so I tweaked the search by adding the keyword "novel". This would certainly miss books that weren't fully described by content and might show only the wares of the priciest dealers that did enter full descriptions of content as well as condition, but after making my original list, I could always go back with titles in hand and search for more inexpensive copies.

Several promising titles showed up, the most intriguing being *Tomb of the Dark Ones* by one J.M.A. Mills. Checking an indispensable reference book, George Locke's *A Spectrum of Fantasy,* I found a listing of the book and its sequel, *Lords of the Earth*. I should perhaps mention that the only copy of the book that turned up was priced at $500.00, a bit rich for my blood, not knowing if the quality was there (recalling spending $150.00 on the Dawson book only to be vastly disappointed, I wasn't about to spend that kind of money if it could be avoided.) As it turns out, I was able to borrow a copy through inter-library loan and make a Xerox of it. My searching under Mills' byline also turned up a book described as a "sequel" to *Tomb of the Dark Ones*, but made no use of the word of the word "novel", this latter I was able to acquire at a far more modest price.

The same methodology when applied to Herbert Jenkins, Modern Publishing Ltd, and others of that era yielded similar worthwhile results. I should mention that "vastly disappointed" in the Warrington Dawson book is perhaps a bit unkind. The book is worth reading, and there are some atmospheric scenes that are as good as anything you could imagine in a supernatural novel. The problem is with the use of the term "novel". As a novel it just doesn't really deliver; it is more a collection of scenes, excellent when depicting supernatural occurrences, fairly weak when it just has characters sitting around talking. Someone should have told Dawson that it's quite possible for people to communicate with each while *doing* something.

Anyway, enough of that, this is supposed to be about Janet Melanie Ailsa Mills. Since much of her work was done for occult publishers even smaller than Rider, I can't be certain that we have a complete bibliography, and I'm not about to try, but I will detail some highlights. Mills also wrote as "H.K. Challoner" and a number of her non-fiction works were being reprinted as recently as last year by the Theosophical Publishing House and similar imprints.

The earliest book that I can locate is *The Way Triumphant*, (Hutchinson, 1927), apparently a novel and because of the publisher, it's on my list to investigate further. Next up was *Marsh Fires* the following year. Then in 1933 one of her most popular works, almost perpetually in print since then, *Watchers of the Seven Spheres*. Her detour into fiction again came with the present book in 1937, with *Lords of Earth* following in 1940 from Andrew Dakers, Ltd. *Tomb of the Dark Ones* went through at least two printings indicating at least some level of success, but the timing of *Lords of the Earth* couldn't possibly have been worse; not only was England at war, but the German bombers destroyed much of London's warehouse district and thousands and thousands of books were destroyed making anything published in 1939-1940 somewhat scarce. In the case of small imprints such as Rider and Dakers, nearly entire print runs were destroyed.

Harry (H.B.) Gregory author of *Dark Sanctuary* told me that only those copies sent out for review to Canada and Australia escaped destruction; in fact, he had to send the publisher one of his three author copies in the hopes of securing a sale to a foreign publisher. While J.M.A. Mills' two novels are by no means that scarce, they are certainly uncommon. Whether it was disappointment at the sales of *Lords of the Earth* or simply a lack of interest, Mills did not revisit the realm of fiction, though she kept writing almost until her death in 1986.

J.M.A. Mills joins Elliott O'Donnell as an author that ably demonstrated a gift for dark fiction, but spent most of their career writing "non-fiction". In the case of both authors, they gave us two wonderful novels and we can only wonder at what might have been had the muse called them in a different direction.

John Pelan
Gallup, NM
2014

PROLOGUE

"I MANAGED to get a paper at last."

Weyland glanced up from the writing-table at the figure framed in the doorway.

"You look rather wet," he remarked.

"Wet!" The young man shook himself like a retriever and struggled out of his mackintosh which was rapidly turning the small paved hall of the cottage into a miniature lake. Weyland thought how blue his eyes looked in the flushed damp face under its unruly thatch of fair hair.

Simon Conningsby drew the folded newspaper from an inner pocket and threw it across to the older man. "There you are—a bit of luck! I met the boy wheeling his bike up the torrent they call a road; I asked him where the devil your *New Statesman* had got to and my *Lancet* and *The Times* on Saturday, to say nothing of yesterday's *Observer*, and he had the cheek to inform me that they had all been ordered by a 'party name of Smith,' so he'd left them there, up the valley. I asked him, did I look like a 'party,' or for that matter, even a Smith, and told him to jolly well get them back. I hope the 'party' is properly edified by our choice of literature, that's all."

Balancing himself on one leg he began to struggle out of his waterlogged boots.

"This isn't ours, either," commented Weyland mildly.

"I know, but I was determined to get you the news of the day somehow, even at the cost of filching somebody else's pet rag. Lord, what a country!" He stripped off a wet sock and hung it on the hat rack. "Old mother Bates will have a great time getting everything dry enough for our afternoon walk. This is your fault, you know," he continued, shaking the wet out of his hair, "you swore the Lake District was at its best in the Spring. Preserve me from it in August, that's all I say!" He made a grimace at the swirling mists pressing against their sitting-room window. "First three days muggy and soaking, then three days icy and drenching, I wonder what's next on the programme? I have a horrid conviction that the only scenery of which I shall take back a vivid memory is that," and he waved his free hand towards the window, "still life: budding fuchsia in a fog." Struggling now with the other boot, he continued his monologue. "I suppose the English mountains do have tops to them? Are they ever seen by visitors? And to think we might have been in the Alps now, skiing down the high slopes in the sun with all the Spring Bowers below us in the valleys."

He looked up at Weyland's prolonged silence. "Well . . .?" But the set expression on the face bent over the newspaper, brought him over to the table. "What's up?" he said, "something happened?"

"Yes." Weyland laid the paper down and sat back, staring before him with narrowed eyes. "Yes, I think so, I'm not sure . . ."

Simon leant over his shoulder. "What is it?"

Weyland's finger tapped a paragraph and Simon gave a startled exclamation. The column was headed: "Disappearance of Famous Specialist."

"No news has been received with regard to the whereabouts of the great alienist, Sir Edwin Hornsley, who disappeared from his clinic a week ago," he read. "Since the broadcast appeal on Friday last, Scotland Yard have taken up the search. It is feared that some ill may have befallen Sir Edwin, as his friends and relations are unanimous in declaring that latterly his behaviour has been distinctly abnormal. It is understood that he was much distressed by the prospect of the impending lawsuit which is being brought against him by one of his ex-patients."

"But Hornsley," Simon cried, "how amazing! Why, I attended a lecture by him before I left London. He seemed all right—a bit *distrait*, perhaps, now I come to think of it. And what's the lawsuit? Do you know anything about all this?"

"Naturally, I know nothing about his disappearance," Anthony Weyland replied after a pause, "it must have been in Saturday's paper, which we missed, but I had heard rumours of a lawsuit."

"Funny I hadn't; a nice, juicy bit of scandal in medical circles isn't usually allowed to languish in obscurity, either."

"It was being kept as quiet as possible in the hopes of averting it, I think." Weyland's voice was remote; he was still sitting, staring before him, with a frown of concentration between his brows.

"I believe you know more than you say, all the same," commented Simon, and went to fetch from the cupboard his shoes which he had forgotten to put on.

"I don't *know* anything." Weyland got up and taking his diary from his despatch-case, began to look carefully through it. It was not a daily list of trivial events, rather a record of ideas, of passing thoughts, of anything, indeed, which had a useful bearing upon his own interests and his particular work.

"I thought so," he said presently, "look at this, Simon." He pushed in front of him a page which had been inserted. It was stuck over with newspaper extracts. They were all records of incidents which had occurred within the past years in connection with public men: disappearances, suicides, sudden illnesses, and in one case, an unsolved murder. Simon noticed that two well-known statesmen of progressive views were included in the list, a doctor or so, the leader of a religious movement which had promised at one time to produce a kind of spiritual revival through all grades and classes of society; an explorer who had made some remarkable discoveries in Ecuador throwing light on one of the earliest known civilizations, and had disappeared from the ship with all his records on his way home; and others more obscure who, for some reason, Weyland had included. It struck Simon that the majority of these fatalities seemed to have befallen scientists, also that the greater number of cases recorded were men of British nationality.

Weyland was carefully cutting out the paragraph which had caught his attention. "Doesn't it look to you rather more than coincidence?" he asked.

"Lumped together like that, it certainly looks a bit sinister, I must say; but aren't you giving the thing rather a spurious importance? I mean there are thousands of cases of disappearance, suicide, madness . . ."

"Certainly; but you see I happen to know that there was a factor common to all these men. Each of them, in his own way, was trying to discover—*one thing.*"

Simon stared uncomprehendingly. "What sort of thing?"

Weyland shook his head. "I'll tell you, but not just now. I want to go and brood over this." He picked up his dispatch-case, nodded to Simon and went out of the room. The young man heard him moving about for a few moments in his bedroom overhead; then there was silence. He was used to these disappearances. Whenever Weyland had a problem, either of his own or of one of his friends, he would take it away with him into solitude, and invariably after an hour, or a day or so according to its complexity, would return with a solution.

Simon settled himself down by the fire with some books he was studying. He had just taken his medical degree with honours and was supposed to be having a complete rest, but his wasn't the type of mind that can rest by lying fallow; he always found his best relaxation in more study, different in kind perhaps, that was all. Now on an impulse he had set himself to learn Arabic, why he hardly knew, but Weyland had given him enthusiastic encouragement, and that was good enough.

He lost touch with time entirely; it might have been an hour later or even more when he was suddenly roused from his work. What it was that had disturbed him, he did not at once know, but he had the feeling that he was being watched, and sharply turning towards the window, was just in time to catch a movement in the fog which swirled outside, as if someone had stepped back, or had just walked past.

He half rose, then thought better of it. There was a mirror opposite the window. He collected a book from the floor and bent his head over it, watching the reflected square of light. At first nothing was to be seen but the slightly swaying branch of fuchsia and the continuous drifting movement of the mist, then something materialized and he saw a face against the pane; it struck a note of vague familiarity in his mind. He rose to his feet, and instantly the man disappeared. In two strides Simon was out of the room and had flung back the front door; the man was standing on the threshold as if the fact that he had been observed had decided his action.

At first sight he looked like a tramp. He had a three-days' growth of beard and was dirty and generally unkempt; but Simon noticed that the hat jammed down over his eyes had once been expensive, and the clothes, crushed, sodden and mud-splashed though they were, still proclaimed an acquaintance with Savile Row. And where had he seen that face before? When the man spoke his voice was also familiar.

"Is a Mr. Weyland staying here?" he asked.

Weyland's voice, coming from the narrow stairway behind them, answered him.

"Hullo, Hornsley! I had a sort of idea you might try to get into touch with me. Come in. This is my adopted son, Simon Conningsby; you've heard me speak of him, I think. This way, there's a fire; you look perished. Simon, go into the kitchen and get a glass and some hot water, will you? Sir Edwin would like a hot whisky, I feel sure."

Now Simon knew the face, but what a difference the beard made—yet there were other differences too—the man seemed to have shrunk. Full of curiosity, he spent an impatient ten minutes over a kettle which refused to boil. When he re-entered the room

Sir Edwin was saying: "I tell you they've got me—got me like that." He shook his clenched fist before him. "I can't believe there's a way out; if it hadn't been that I recalled that conversation we had, and realized you knew something—were trying to warn me"—he shrugged—"if there were the slightest hope of putting things right . . ."

"There's always a way out," came Weyland's calm voice. "Here's your hot water," he held out his hand for the glass and poured out a stiff peg. "This will warm you."

Sir Edwin drank slowly, crouching forward and gazing into the flames. Presently he looked up. "Was it all true what you told me that day, or merely hearsay—imagination?"

"Perfectly true; you'd be safe there."

The other gave a short, bitter laugh. "Would they take me? You've heard about the lawsuit, I suppose—and that's not the worst."

"That would make no difference—none at all; but of course there would be—conditions."

"Conditions? What sort?" He turned back to the fire with a weary gesture, "but what does it matter, I'm in no position to pick and choose, my career's finished, all I've worked for, my wife, too, and the girls—" he broke off.

"You don't know," said Weyland gently, "it may have only just begun. But I'll find out what can be done."

Sir Edward glanced up sharply. "How can you? It'll take days, and every moment . . ." He glanced over his shoulder at the window, "nothing, nowhere is safe," he cried, and there was a note of agony in his voice.

"You are quite safe here. Nor will it take days—I have other methods." He got up. "Won't you try and sleep for a bit? Simon will get anything you want. What about some food first?"

The other shook his head. "I can't eat."

"All right, but do rest, you must be dead-beat; and don't worry." His hand dropped lightly on the bowed shoulder. "We'll find a way out for you somehow."

When he had gone Sir Edwin leaned back in the big arm-chair with a sigh and closed his eyes. Simon fetched a book and settled down to read. Conversation was evidently not indicated. Yet after he had been reading perhaps a quarter of an hour, Sir Edwin's voice disturbed him.

"What's that you've got? Anything good?"

"Jung's *Modern Man in Search of a Soul*."

"Search of a soul? God! He'd better take care! I hear he's on to some very advanced theories now."

"I think he's one of the greatest minds of modern times," said Simon.

The other man ignored the statement. "He'd better take care," he muttered again. There was a short silence; Simon felt somewhat at a loss. He was relieved when the next question touched more normal ground.

"I think I remember Weyland telling me that you were going to take up medicine."

"I've just got my degree."

Sir Edwin sat up abruptly and spoke with emphasis. "Then if you take my advice you'll stick to the beaten track, my boy; don't go experimenting—don't try and delve down below the surface . . ."

"But I always understood, sir," said Simon deferentially, "that you yourself advocated research of all kinds; you once wrote that nothing was to be accepted on its face value, that even so simple seeming a thing as measles—"

He broke off, startled by the expression of excitement and distress upon the great doctor's face.

"I know, I know, but I was wrong—wrong! Research, where does it lead you? You think you are going to find truth, but what do you find? The devil!"

Simon gasped. To hear the scientifically-minded Sir Edwin Hornsley shouting wildly about finding the devil! The man was obviously insane.

"I remember," Sir Edwin continued more calmly, "my parents, who were good orthodox Christians, used to say with a prophetic shake of the head, whenever science discovered anything new, electric light, telephones, flying and such like: 'This can't go on; it's tempting Providence; so far and no further,' I laughed at them, of course; now—I'm not so sure."

"What should prevent us?" Simon asked. Mad the man might be, but somehow he felt impelled to accept the challenge. "You don't surely mean that you think God—a kind of Israelitish, jealous god—steps in and says: 'Here, I can't have you emulating me—this *must* stop!'"

Sir Edwin gave a half-smile. "I almost wish He would! No, it's merely that if we go too far, something happens. Yes, perhaps some power does 'step in,' as you call it; who knows?"

Simon stared at him. It was amazing. "But surely," he argued, "things are there to be discovered and used—if we are willing to pay the price?"

The other leant forward. "That's just it—don't you see? How do we know what the price will be, if we go beyond a certain stage? What is all this knowledge? Isn't it power? And power is a force—don't forget that, my boy, a vital, terrible force. And how can we tell, until we have experimented with that force, what it may do to us? It may destroy us; it may destroy others; it may—yes, it may destroy the world."

He sank back as if exhausted; Simon would have liked to question him further, to discover what he was really driving at, but at that moment Mrs. Bates came in to lay the lunch. Sir Edwin shrank into the depths of his chair as if to escape observation, while Simon engaged in the usual patter which their landlady always expected from her "gentlemen."

He was glad when Weyland returned. The lunch was a very silent one. Sir Edwin hardly touched anything, and seemed anxious to get it over so as to talk to his host. When the meal was at last cleared away, Weyland turned to Simon with a rather placating smile: "Would you go down to the village to get me some stamps? I think it looks more like clearing. I won't be able to have my usual walk after tea, so you'd better take Ruff, otherwise he'll feel we haven't done our duty by him to-day."

Simon accepted his dismissal, and calling the sheepdog which always accompanied them on their walks, set out. He was away for a couple of hours and came back only in time for tea. He found the sitting-room empty, and looking round saw an envelope addressed to him in Weyland's handwriting.

There were only a few words: "So sorry, but had to leave at once, and have taken car, I may be away two or three days, hardly more, I should think. Will give you full explanation when I return. Keep letters. No address possible. A. W."

The following morning the weather began to clear. Still the peaks were swathed in cloud, but at moments shafts of light stabbed downward into the valleys, or travelled like the spears of an invisible army across the slopes. Simon spent the day exploring, with Ruff in ecstasies of joy by his side, and the following day went further afield, tackling some stiffer ground and rejoicing in long periods of warm sunlight which even set the earth steaming and brought the prospect of serious climbing nearer.

Yet all the while when his delight in the glories of hill and dale was not holding both mind and senses in thrall, his thoughts were busy scouting round the mystery of Hornsley's visit, or else dwelling on his own immediate problems. But Hornsley held his attention longer. He puzzled over those few sentences which he was certain constituted some kind of clue. "I tell you they've got me." And Weyland's assurance: "You'd be safe there."

There was also Sir Edwin's strange conversation with him, his outcry about the dangers attending research, his wild talk of finding the devil.

Simon had always been aware of mysteries surrounding the man who had adopted him and had been to him father, mother and friend, from his earliest years. But despite the sympathy and affection which existed between them, deeper than is usual even between most fathers and sons, Weyland remained in many ways still curiously remote, so much so that Simon had at times a faint sensation of awe with regard to him. He had never, for example, in all these years talked to the boy much about his work; yet this work, this research, occupied the major part of his life. For days at a time he would be shut up in his laboratory, or sometimes for weeks he would disappear completely, just as he had done the day before, into the blue, leaving no address. His answers to Simon's earlier questions had always been evasive, and somehow one didn't press Anthony Weyland beyond a certain point. During the last few years, too, they had of necessity been separated a good deal, except for those delightful holidays spent either in the Swiss Alps or in Austria, climbing or ski-ing according to season; for Simon had to be in London for his studies, while Weyland remained working in his country house in Sussex. Now Simon was free, at least until his future movements were definitely decided, and they had joined forces once again.

Still Weyland had not spoken about his work, as the younger man had so much hoped he would do. Chemical research was such a vague word that it conveyed practically nothing. Simon had very much hoped for some startling revelations during this holiday. But now he was confronted with activities of quite another kind, and none of his speculations seemed to lead him to anything very conclusive. That Weyland was deeply interested in the occult, he was well aware. He also, from earliest boyhood, had been drawn towards the study of the mysterious and the unusual. But curiously enough Weyland had never encouraged him in these speculations beyond a certain point, and except for the few books he had found time to read on the subject, he had been too occupied with his medical studies to do more than skim the surface of such questions. That was for the future. About his career his thoughts were much more precise. He had decided to take up a general practice in the slums for a year or so, in order to gain valuable experience—after that, well, it rather depended upon Weyland; but he felt that Weyland would be in entire accord with him when he put forward his ideas. They could wait, however. Everything could wait. He had the power of absorbing to the full every gift that the moment brought him. He was only twenty-five and life opened out to him as fraught with wonder and promise as the country which spread at his feet. He stood now on the summit of his first hill: valleys and mountains lay beyond. Where he went, how high he would have the courage, the tenacity to climb, this depended entirely upon himself.

However, he was very glad when, on approaching the farm that third evening in time for supper, he saw their car standing in the dilapidated barn that served as a garage.

Weyland was stretched in front of the fire and turned to greet him with a smile.

"Just got back; a rather heavy day. Have you been having a good time?"

Simon dropped into the other chair with a sigh of pleasant fatigue. "Marvellous! I got in a tight corner this afternoon; I've never quite believed all the yarns you hear about these mountains, but I can see they're not for amateurs."

"I'm glad you've discovered that, it would be a pity to have such a promising career cut short prematurely. As a matter of fact good climbers never underestimate the powers of even the simplest looking mountain—rashness isn't skill. I'm always telling you so. All the same I'd class you among the safe climbers on the whole, you've got a natural climbing sense."

Simon flushed with pleasure. "From you, that's a very high compliment indeed. As a matter of fact I somehow always feel so much at one with whatever place I'm in. I can't explain; but if what some of your books say is true, and every so-called inanimate thing is ensouled by something higher, more responsive, it may be that I get in touch with that part of it—it feels like it sometimes." He was trying to lure Weyland on to speak of these things of which he seemed to know so much, but he remained uncommunicative. Only his eyes twinkled, as if he were fully aware of the young man's tactics.

"Perhaps," was all he replied.

Simon sighed. He was longing to ask where Weyland had been, but had long ago schooled himself not to question him about anything.

"I'm ravenous," he complained after a pause. "And I do wish these places ran to hot baths."

"I know. A small jug was the most I could raise from Mrs. Bates, and as I've been travelling with hardly a stop from six this morning, I felt it wasn't quite adequate." Weyland yawned. "I shall turn in directly after supper. I was thinking it would be rather pleasant to go to a favourite hill of mine to-morrow to watch the sun rise. There may not be much to see, the clouds are still hanging around, but—well, the place has a particular meaning for me. What do you say? We ought to start soon after five."

"Rather, I'm game."

Weyland looked at him with a smile. "I know quite well that you're aching to ask questions, but I don't want to talk here. I have reasons. So you'll have to curb your impatience for another few hours. And now, I think, supper and bed—don't you?"

~ ~ ~ ~ ~

Weyland spoke very little while they walked through the twilight of the spring morning towards the hill he had chosen as their objective. Even when they reached the summit and he had taken his seat on a rock with Simon stretched upon the ground at his feet, for a long while he was silent, watching the clouds turn rosy and the first shafts of sunlight strike through the mists upon the hills.

At last, looking down affectionately upon the young man, he said: "Well, I suppose I've got to tell you all about it now."

"You don't have to," replied Simon, adding quickly, however, "but that doesn't mean I'm not bursting with curiosity!"

Weyland smiled. "Frankly I did intend to wait a while, but this business of Hornsley has upset a good many of my calculations."

"He said some remarkable things to me when you were out of the room. Do you think the poor chap's going off his head?"

"Not exactly; but it's a very complicated business. I'll have to go back a bit to make it at all clear to you." He paused for a few minutes as if considering his next words, then continued: "Everybody knows something of Hornsley's work, you medical people in particular; but probably nobody quite realized the extraordinary progress he had been making in the last few years; he was always a very secretive man—and he had need to be, for he was following up some strange theories. We met frequently at one time, but even to me he would never disclose the exact line of research upon which he was engaged. Yet there's no doubt in my mind that he was on the right track judging by results, for he seems to have discovered some way, not only of readjusting people's mental balance, but actually of stimulating what you might call their moral sense. Apart from ordinary neurotics and so forth, his greatest successes were with the definitely a-moral types and those with criminal tendencies. I followed up a number of his cases and can vouch for the fact that many left his clinic finer, more spiritual, more capable of living useful lives than even the average man." He sighed. "Yes, at moments he appears to have been able to inculcate almost a fire of genius into some of them. What he might have achieved if he had gone on . . ." He broke off, sinking into a reverie. The memory of Hornsley's words came clearly back to Simon; what tragedy could lie behind this failure?

"What happened?" he ventured to ask at length.

"No one knows exactly, but a man came into Hornsley's life who persuaded him to undertake other kinds of experiments upon his patients," Weyland shrugged his shoulders: "with the results you have already seen."

"But who was he? And what kind of experiments?"

"His name was Zarov. From the little Hornsley let fall he seems to have been almost an adept in his knowledge of the human mind; but he kept himself completely in the background, and although I asked Hornsley several times to arrange a meeting between us, it never came off. Anyhow he so fascinated the poor chap with his theories or perhaps his promises, that in the end he seems to have got him completely under his thumb. I suspect it eventually became a matter of blackmail."

"But don't you know anything of their experiments? Hasn't Hornsley talked about them in the last few days?"

Weyland shook his head. "No; he's a very sick man, worse even than you may have gathered from what you saw of him. He doesn't seem able to talk at present, but later when he has recovered he may be able to tell us something, though I've an idea that Zarov may have hypnotized him and inhibited certain memories. However, if anyone can cure him, they will."

"They? Where have you taken him?"

"Never mind; but he's safe and in the best hands, although whatever happens he's finished, I'm afraid, so far as his work in the outer world is concerned. His name will be mud by the time our sensation-mongering Press has done with him. There seem to have been some terrible things going on in that place towards the end."

"And what of this Zarov fellow?"

"Oh, he's disappeared. But in any case he was safe; he took good care never to be directly implicated—hardly anyone even knew of their association."

Simon sat for a few minutes in silence, revolving the whole queer business in his mind.

"I see now," he said presently, "why it was he warned me against research. He said an odd thing: something about trying to find Truth, and instead finding the devil. The devil, I suppose, in his case, being Zarov." He looked up, his eyes narrowing. "All this explains a good deal, but not everything, not by a long chalk. What about those other men you spoke of, the men on your list? How do they come into the picture? And what did you mean yesterday when you said they were all looking for *one thing?* How could they be? They seemed such a mixed lot!"

"Not fundamentally, only in their lines of approach. Aren't all great scientific minds in reality engaged in an identical quest?"

"Are they? I don't know; I haven't thought about it."

"Well, do think about it. I'm pretty certain you'll end by agreeing with me. Aren't they all trying to discover causes? And what do all causes lead back to, if not to the First Cause of all? Yes, my boy, the real quest is for the solution of that greatest of all mysteries, the mystery of Life itself. We're all following up different clues, of course. Some suspect there's a key to it in Radiation; some try to reach it by bombarding the atom; some attack through chemistry; others think the Ancients held a clue, and search for it in dead cities and sacred writings. Men like Hornsley believe that, since Mind to a large extent controls, and even shapes Matter, the nature of the Life Force will only be discovered when we possess a complete understanding of what Mind really is. And I," he finished with a little smile, "am trying to discover it through the process which used to be called alchemy."

"So that's what you're doing, is it?"

Weyland nodded; after a moment's consideration Simon said with a puzzled frown: "I'm sorry to be so dense, but I seem to have lost the thread somewhere. What's this to do with Zarov, and the fact that all those men were the victims of some kind of fatality?"

"The thread is, that they were all searching for this particular secret; and I happen to have actual evidence that each one of them was on the point of achieving some measure of success when—disaster overtook him."

"You are implying that these disasters were brought about deliberately by an outside agency?" Simon cried. "You think this man, Zarov, had something to do with each separate case?"

"Not necessarily Zarov, he's a tool, no more, albeit an extremely dangerous and able one; but I certainly believe that these men were all the victims of some kind of deliberately planned attack."

Simon shook his head. "Sorry, but it seems to me too far-fetched for words. Granted that they were on the track of some such discovery, why should it be in anyone's interest to stop them? I can't see any object in it at all."

"And yet it ought to be clear enough," said Weyland gravely, "if you consider the nature of the thing they were after, and what it would mean if it were discovered. Can't you see that the man who unveiled the mystery of Life would have the power actually to rule—yes, and to change—the world?"

"Change the world?" echoed Simon rather stupidly.

"Yes." He leant forward and spoke with deep impressiveness, "I can see you haven't really grasped the potentialities of the thing at all. Think carefully now. Whatever this Basic Element is, it must be subject to—or indeed itself represent—an as yet unknown or unrecognized Law of Nature. This Law, being what it is, the primal Creative Mystery, must, therefore, be the Cause whence *all* effects are derived. Now I want you to assimilate what I am about to say, Simon, because it is exceedingly important. First consider the fact that a Law in itself is neither good nor evil, it is merely, if you like, a sequence of Cause and Effect, something inevitable and unchangeable; then try to analyse what exactly the understanding of such a Law as this would imply." He paused for a second while Simon waited—for what he hardly knew. Weyland answered his own question. "Wouldn't it give its discoverer power—unlimited power?" He emphasized the word until its rounded syllables seemed to open out as if to engulf the world. "Power! Not alone the power to prolong life, to turn dross into gold, but power over everything that exists! For he would know how to control and manipulate the all-pervading Energy, the Creative Force—the supreme Word. Yes, he could control all and every manifestation of life, he could transmute and change all forms at will, he could even govern and direct all the minds and actions of mankind." He swung round and struck his clenched list upon the rock at his side. "Simon, I tell you most solemnly that, should it be possible for a man or a group of men to discover the nature of this mystery, they would indeed become masters, not of this world alone, but of all worlds!"

Simon stared at him, spellbound by a conception so vast, so terrifying, yet which, something within him whispered, was not outside the bounds of possibility. Then he remembered once more some words of Hornsley's. He, too, had spoken of power. "How can we tell," he had said, "until we experiment with that force, what it may do to us? It may destroy us, it may destroy others—it may, yes, it may destroy the world."

And he cried out, because he was shaken, afraid: "It would be impossible!"

"Nothing is impossible," said Weyland soberly. "I believe that this knowledge is man's goal, his rightful heritage; and I think the time is drawing near when some part, at least, of this Secret is bound to be discovered. Haven't you noticed how, as the iron filings approach the magnet, its attraction for them increases until they literally hurl themselves upon it? So it is now; man is approaching the portals of the temple of Truth, and the pace is increasing in proportion to that advance. Everything depends upon who discovers it first: those who are genuinely working for the benefit of humanity, or those who desire nothing but their own aggrandisement. If by any chance ruthless selfish and destructive men should seize upon it and, armed with this supernal knowledge, make a bid for world dominion, then indeed the fate of the Race would be sealed." He turned and looked at Simon gravely: "Now do you see why Zarov and those for whom he is working are anxious to check any such advance by men of integrity? They want to be first in the field so that they can dominate mankind." He gave a deep sigh. "God knows what Zarov may have learned from Hornsley's experiments before the end. I only pray he didn't get as far as I imagine."

"But I still don't quite see how a psycho-therapist could get at such a secret."

"My dear boy, as I said just now the potentialities of Mind appear to be almost infinite; you ought, even with your small experience, to have discovered that. As yet we know so little of the laws governing the manipulation of what, for want of a better word, I would call Mind-Matter. But I confess I don't really know what

Zarov and Hornsley were aiming at. I wish I did. It's possible we may be able later to get something out of the poor old chap."

"But can't they be stopped, Zarov and his crowd, I mean?" Simon cried, aghast.

"That's exactly what my friends and I are trying to do," Weyland replied quietly.

"Your *friends?* Who are they?"

"I'm not at liberty at present to tell you much about them; all I can say is that in every age there have always existed secret bands of men pledged to give their lives, if necessary, to save humanity. The method differs, of course, according to the need and the times, but the fundamental principle is the same. Secret Societies are not all bad, I assure you, and the men with whom I am privileged to work are members of such an Organization. Our job is to endeavour to keep the balance between the destructive and the constructive forces in the world adjusted—if no more, and incidentally when it is possible, to guard the innocent from the aggressor."

"A kind of secret moral police force, in fact?"

Weyland smiled. "Put it that way if you like; I would rather call them a group of spiritual physicians who seek to heal the world, to check disease by occult counter-measures as far as is lawful. To develop the analogy: if you think of the world as a Being of which Races and Nations are the arteries, the glands, the ganglia, and individuals the cells, can't you see how a wise physician in possession of some such knowledge as, say, the old alchemists' Elixir of Life—for that is only a term for this self-same 'First Cause' we were discussing—could bring the sick parts back to health and harmony and so stimulate and revivify this ailing body of humanity that the Golden Age itself might return? For human misery only arises through disease, mental or physical, usually both."

"And you believe the Elixir—the Secret, whatever its form—might do that?" Simon asked in a low voice.

His companion inclined his head, but did not at once reply, and the young man's words dropped into the grave and beautiful silence which lay like an enchantment on these remote uplands. It was, he thought, as if he had put his question—not so much to the man at his side, as to something vaster, more impersonal—that Being, perhaps, which in Weyland's phraseology was symbolized by the Earth.

He lay listening to that silence. It had an indefinable quality which only belongs to early mornings and remote places; it was pregnant with promise, quick with life, yet portentous, too, with the burden of past eternities.

Below them stretched Grasmere, its small island rising faintly out of the morning mists like a boat adrift from the shores of dreams. Beyond, even more faint, yet lit by a gleam of sunlight upon their bronze slopes, the hills lay still in the mysterious languor of their awakening. There was an unreality about the whole scene which seemed in keeping with their conversation. Everything looked, somehow, a little impossible. The nearer oaks and larches were too vivid to be real, a-fire with colours which, ranging as they did from sharp yellow through every shade of green to a glowing reddish brown, seemed, already in Spring, to be foreshadowing their autumnal glory; just, he thought, as birth is but a kind of inverted image of death.

Death . . .

A ewe with two queer little black-faced lambs pastured slowly below them, bleating as she moved; a thorn tree flung its branches, like a drift of late snow, across the bleak rocks on which they sat. A cool breeze came rushing over the heights from the newly risen sun, bringing with it bursts of far-flung bird notes, the occasional call of a cuckoo and the barking of dogs from remote farms.

How peaceful it was, and still. And yet—and yet . . . This, if Weyland was to be believed, was only an illusory appearance. Behind it contending forces strove for mastery. Life and death—good and evil . . .

He glanced at Weyland secretly with a feeling which was almost one of awe. Certainly it wasn't that Weyland's exterior was striking, likely to arouse that rare emotion; he was a quiet man with rather rugged features of no specific type. He would have been quite unremarkable in a crowd until you heard him speak or looked into his eyes. Those unfathomable eyes were brooding now, half-closed, gazing at what? Simon wondered; at a dream of a world made beautiful and sane and wise and the forces of Reaction routed forever?

And suddenly an idea stabbed into his mind, like a flash of lightning out of a summer sky. He sat bolt upright.

"But they might attack *you!*" he cried, "You say you are looking for this Elixir or whatever it is!"

Weyland smiled. "My dear boy, they have attacked me—several times."

"You never told me!" There was mingled horror and reproach in the words.

"What would have been the good? It would only have upset your studies and you couldn't have done anything. You needn't worry, anyhow. I'm well protected. You see, I know my danger and can take precautionary measures, the other poor devils like Hornsley don't."

"How can you take precautionary measures against a band of unscrupulous gangsters like this Zarov and Co.?"

"I've got some good allies, you forget them. It's to their advantage that I should succeed in my experiments, and they—and I, too, for that matter—have means of protection which even our enemies would find pretty hard to circumvent."

Simon grunted and looked sceptical, and it was obvious, although he abandoned his protests for the moment, that he had no intention of doing so for very long.

"I want to hear more about this Elixir of yours," he said; "are you certain such a thing can be done? And how will it work?"

Weyland laughed, waving his hand as if to put a stop to the spate of questions he saw threatening him. "Not now, later perhaps; my Elixir is beside the point at the moment. It's Zarov's activities we were discussing." He grew serious again. "There are forces abroad in the world to-day, Simon, which will destroy civilization—the real civilization, all that man has striven for and developed through the ages, freedom and that independence and security which are essential to the development of the higher qualities—unless they are checked. Personally I think this particular manifestation of their activities, this attempt to frustrate the discovery by men of integrity of the secrets I have spoken of, is only one among many others. I think there's something terrific stirring everywhere; I believe soon a gigantic conflict between these Powers of destruction and the evolutionary forces which guide mankind is bound to occur. I don't mean, necessarily, a great war—if it takes that form we're finished; I mean something more inward. I don't know what—I can't see . . . But all we can do at present is to neglect no opening, no chance, no clue which will help us, not only to seize this power for ourselves, but to prevent Zarov or his master obtaining it first."

"But could they? I mean, one feels that there are sort of—well—Forces of Good, and so on, which could step in and prevent it; would it be *allowed* to happen?"

"Why not? The race is to the swift, Simon. As I said before, a Law, an Element is in itself neither good nor evil. It seems to me that as man appears to be the only medium through which the

Consciousness of good and evil can manifest at this present stage of evolution, it follows that it is only man who can prevent his fellow-men from using this greatest of all Laws for their own selfish purposes."

For a little while they were silent again, staring down at Grasmere, as if seeing other reflections in that still dark water than those clear-cut, inverted trees and mountains.

A lark got up suddenly behind them showering them with a vivid rush of song so penetratingly sweet that its abrupt cessation left almost a feeling of pain. Simon rolled over and buried his face in the short, fragrant turf. Beneath his fingers he could feel the earth, immense possibilities formless and vague, seemed rising up through it, enveloping him. His mind was a whirl of conflicting emotions. He was afraid. When he spoke his voice was muffled and hesitant.

"Then I don't see how one can hope to stop them!"

Weyland made no reply to that and Simon sat up abruptly and began to talk at fever heat so that his words almost tumbled over each other. "How can you? The Hornsleys of this world work in the open, comparatively; they're easy prey, but these others—they're too subtle. And who's to know, anyway, on which side anyone is? No, it's hopeless! You can't keep a check on every research worker, nor, even if you could, would it be possible to know what his real motives and his real goal were. Besides, a man's motives might be reasonably pure to begin with, but once he found himself in control of such power—unlimited power—how could you trust him? Even a saint . . ." he broke off with a gesture of despair.

"That's true; but there's one thing you've overlooked. The ordinary research worker, as you call him, might possibly get back to this First Principle, but the test would come when he attempted to *apply* it. It wouldn't be like harnessing the other elements of power we have discovered, nothing so simple; it would need a mastery of higher and more subtle laws altogether, what we call 'occult laws.' It would need a key, a supreme key, to read *that* cipher."

"You mean a kind of code, a glorified Rosetta stone?"

"Yes, obviously there must be something of the sort, but exactly in what form it exists, no one knows. Legends, traditions, not to mention the Secret Doctrines of many races, all seem to point to the fact that something of the sort exists—though what form it takes has always been a mystery. It's given different names by every race; it's been symbolized by the Palladium, by King Solomon's Ring—oh, endless symbols." He gave a slight shrug: "anyway, whatever it is, whether a material object of merely a Power, an element to be attained by study and research, one thing is certain, there have existed in every age men who have actually been able to transcend the ordinary laws that govern physical conditions, making and unmaking forms at will, conquering time and space, and even abolishing the power of death. Obviously, then, such men must have been in possession of at least a part of this supreme knowledge. And what a few men could do, all men can do, *providing they know*."

Simon gave a sigh of relief. "Well, if there's got to be a key found as well, that makes one feel safer—much safer."

Weyland shook his head. "Don't be too sure. It narrows down the field, that's all, and removes the possibility of its full utilization by the ordinary scientific investigator. But there are plenty of men who combine materialistic science with a deep study of what, for want of a better word, I must call occultism. The society to which Zarov belongs is working entirely on such lines."

"Good Lord," Simon groaned. "In that case it is hopeless."

"Nothing's ever hopeless; I think we *can* stop them." He turned and looked full at Simon: "but only if we find men who are knowledgeable and intrepid, who understand how to use the so-called magical powers which these enemies of ours wield so efficiently, so that they can pit themselves against them."

"Whites versus Blacks," murmured Simon with a grin, and Weyland smiled.

"Yes, plenty of risk and adventure for young men who have a taste for that sort of thing; these people will have to be traced and then tackled with their own weapons, it's certainly not a sport for the average man." He paused, then added abruptly: "Well, are you game?"

"Me?" Simon cried ungrammatically, "but I'm a doctor, I couldn't tackle a black magician." He stared at Weyland; little prickles were going up and down his spine. Until this moment it had been just enthralling talk, hardly real; suddenly it had become concrete, close to him. Men like himself, only wiser, more powerful—enemies! A fierce excitement seized upon him; he felt a background of mysterious activities rising behind the ordinary coloured pageant of everyday life. How little one knew of what went on around one! Weyland in his laboratory, intent on his strange experiments; others elsewhere, searching, delving, manipulating the forces governing minds and bodies; mankind the experimental guinea pig, nibbling its fodder, going round and round in its little cage, supremely unaware of everything that was of real importance—the causes of its moods, its elations, its depressions, the powers governing all the activities of its existence; unaware of its dangers—or of its potentialities! He closed his eyes. A G.P. in a slum, a psycho-therapist in Harley Street, touching the fringe only, scratching the surface, patching men up to go on for a little while with the unequal fight before their inevitable defeat—dealing with Effects which would yet be ever generated afresh by unescapable Causes. A hopeless struggle against odds too vast, too profound, too far-reaching. True, he had thought to go a little deeper than most, to heal through more recondite methods, but this ... His mind reeled at the thought! Rightly had Weyland called the mysterious men with whom he worked spiritual physicians, carrying on the tradition of all the great ones of the earth. And he was being asked if he would throw in his lot with them! A wave of humility overcame him.

"How could I help?" he stammered, "how could I?"

"You are young," replied Weyland, "you have your life before you—you have very unusual gifts."

He hesitated, staring down into the valley where the lake lay now, blue as a jacinth in a setting of emeralds. Everything about them was becoming hard and brilliant as the country unveiled itself to the sun.

"I had your horoscope cast before I adopted you," he continued more slowly, "you know enough already of astrology to be aware how perfectly your future would be revealed to me."

Simon smiled. "Yes, I've cast my own map, too, but I can't say I was overwhelmed by my possibilities."

"You probably did it very badly," Weyland commented drily. "You'll have to learn not to be so slap-dash if you're going to use it for diagnoses—which I hope you may. In any case it takes years of study to understand the subtler aspects. But you are wrong, you have got remarkable possibilities, and because of these and that strong link from the past which binds us together, I chose you, my dear boy, and trained you in the hope that you would eventually join us in this work. Of course," he went on, as Simon did not reply, "you will need a far greater variety of knowledge than you now possess. In fact for any work which entails pitting oneself against Zarov and his master you will need, as I said, to be trained in a very specialized way. For, make no mistake, Simon, if you agree to undertake this, it may often be for you a matter of life and death, and only such a type of knowledge and understanding will see you through. It's no mere fighting with revolvers or brute strength; you'll not be able to call in the police or invoke the laws of the land. You may not be able even to see your enemies unless you have learned to develop a subtler sight than that possessed by the majority of mankind; you will find yourself up against the Lords of the Earth, principalities and powers and Rulers of Wickedness in high places of which, at present, you know absolutely nothing; for you will be opposing the schemes of a man—if we are right in our assumption, which I have reason to believe we are—who is possessed of vast and terrible powers, knowing neither pity nor scruple. He is backed, moreover, by untold wealth, and there is no doubt that he exercises an hypnotic influence over many important people who are utterly unconscious even of his existence."

"Good God," muttered Simon, "but who is he?"

"I don't know for certain. We've never succeeded in tracing him, although we know a great deal about his agents, such as Zarov, and their activities. Undoubtedly it is he who is responsible for all the fatalities recorded in my book. He seldom or never acts direct, but using some form of suggestion, employs others as his tools, so that in case of failure they shall bear the brunt. We call him X., for he is indeed very much the unknown quantity; but one thing we do know—he, with all the forces at his command, is out to obtain this Secret, and we, with all the powers at ours, are out to frustrate him. There are, unfortunately, very few men who are fitted to help us. But because you could be trained I have been ordered to offer you this opportunity of joining us in our work for humanity."

Simon shook his head. "I feel—extraordinarily inadequate."

"You are at the moment," Weyland smiled.

"May I ask a few questions?"

"Of course."

"What I want to get clear is, that if this Society to which you belong—these very remarkable men with unusual powers—know about this fellow X., why can't they track him down and do him in? There must be some way. Why think of using a fallible instrument like me, for instance? I've always understood that someone with real occult powers could find out anything, kill at a distance—that sort of thing. Or are these just legends and romantic fancies?"

"Unfortunately not; up to a point they are perfectly accurate. Only those happen to be the methods employed by black magicians and not by white ones. True occultists never use force, only the dark ones interfere with the freedom of the individual. You see, those who really understand the workings of the Law know that eventually the use of force of any kind always reacts upon him who employs it, however careful he may be. It actually is a case of those who draw the sword perishing by the sword. As for killing, no thank you! We are very far from being cranks and sentimentalists, but we know too well that by the same Law whoever kills maliciously is bound to restore that life, usually at great suffering and loss to himself if some later period in his incarnations; sheer common sense would hold one back from violent methods such as you propose, if nothing else."

"A bit hard," commented Simon, "to have to let a fellow gain an advantage which may be absolutely vital to the World and all that, just because you mustn't hit back!"

Weyland gave one of his rare chuckles. "No one suggested that you would have to come all over meek and passive; there are other methods, far more efficacious, believe me, than hitting back. For one thing, force has a kind of boomerang action, if it's diverted from its object it recoils upon the sender. You have a perfect right to divert it from yourself."

"That's interesting."

"Very; and important! That's another good reason why, if one is wise, one always allows the other fellow complete free will. If you try to force him to do anything, and fail, it's you who will suffer from the repercussion. As for self-defence, there are plenty of methods which are legitimate; you will learn those, I hope—that is, if you accept."

Simon was silent for a few moments. "And my medical career?" he asked presently, "will I have to give that up?"

"Of course not. Every man should have a career and yours will be exceptionally useful, inasmuch as you will be more in touch with the minds of different types than is possible to the average man; you can thus gauge what currents of thought are predominating, particularly in the more sensitive and suggestible. Don't imagine, either, that I'm offering you a whole-time job; it is rather something that should run parallel with your normal work. It should help you, of course, teaching you more recondite methods of healing and greater opportunities all round."

He got up and stood still a moment, facing the mountains; he seemed to have forgotten Simon. But presently he turned and laid his hand on the young man's arm.

"You needn't answer now, my boy, you must think it over very carefully. As I told you it isn't going to be easy, nor safe, nor comfortable. You'll never be a really successful practitioner in Harley Street, you may never even be called a successful man; on the contrary, you may end by being despised and mocked at, rejected—yes, and crucified in the modern way, just as a far greater than any of us was crucified when He endeavoured to give the world knowledge and truth for which it was not prepared to pay the price. But all the same I can promise you one thing, it will be a great game, and a man's game, and I have always felt it was your game. I don't think you'll ever regret it if you do throw in your lot with the little band that is working to build up this future for mankind."

As Simon listened to the voice of the man whom he loved so profoundly and admired even more than he loved him, he was swept by a sudden, queer exaltation. This man, these mysterious secrets for which powerful antagonists strove in silence and obscurity with mankind—yes, the very world—for prize, waiting in ignorance of its destiny or its danger; and himself, what had Weyland once said? A cog in the wheel; once more all that was idealistic and romantic, all the youth in him that yearned for excitement and adventure rose up at this fantastic vision. It was a clarion call, to what he did not quite know, but of this he was sure, wherever it led him, to whatever end, it could not be denied.

He smiled at Weyland. "You know my answer. There's no need for me to think—there could only be one answer after what you've told me."

Weyland touched his hand lightly. "I am glad," he said.

CHAPTER I

THE HAND OF THE DESTROYER

"Mr. Weyland, sirr, says will you come to heem at once."

Simon looked up, startled. He had not heard Ahmed come into the room. One never heard Ahmed move. Like a shadow he was there, like a shadow gone. Simon had found this a useful accomplishment more than once, as indeed he found most of Ahmed's peculiarities useful. Now, as he pushed back his chair from the desk piled with correspondence, he wondered, not for the first time, what actual admixture of races, Mongol and Aryan, Egyptian or Nordic, had produced this queer servant of his. The result, at all events, was uncanny: a man who, possessing an astounding faculty for imitation and a subtle, retentive memory, could, with a deft touch of make-up, in a trice impersonate almost any one of the racial types of mankind. Ahmed was, indeed, one of those creatures who, according to the early treatment meted out to them by fate, may become almost anything. Fate, in his case, had decreed that after a career so varied and fantastic as to be well-nigh incredible, he should be saved from a worse end than death—retention in an Eastern madhouse—by Simon Conningsby.

Consequently that young man won the allegiance of a life-long slave, faithful, even fanatical, in his devotion. Simon had trained him in secretarial duties and had succeeded at last in turning him into an apparently civilized piece of humanity. Apparent only— but it was enough. In actual fact he knew himself possessed of a cross between a tame thug, a perfect servant, a true friend, and an invaluable watch-dog.

The servant was at this moment uppermost.

"Are you certain he wants me now?" Simon insisted. It was so unusual for Weyland to send for him while they were both in the middle of their work.

"He sure does, sirr," remarked Ahmed with a grin. "O.K. you go now." For a short time Ahmed had thrown in his lot with gangsters in the States and although Simon had endeavoured to wean him of the additional vocabulary thus acquired, incongruous Americanisms would often decorate the reasonably good English he could speak when he chose.

Simon rose. "Well, I don't know how I'm going to get through this packet to-day," and he indicated the letters neatly arranged on his desk. "I've put a batch in the basket with notes, so you'd better get busy on them at once." He spoke his thoughts aloud. "I wonder what on earth he wants me for at this hour, he knows I haven't usually finished my rounds until eleven."

Ahmed's slim, coffee-coloured fingers were already at work on the letters. He flashed his master a glance.

"Perhaps," he said softly, "Mr. Weyland send us for a leetle holiday."

"What do you mean?" Simon swung round on him, but he was industriously settling himself down to the typewriter.

"Oh, I just think," he remarked affably.

"You think a damned sight too much!" He stared at him. "What have you been up to? Spying as usual?"

"I?" injured innocence was written in every mobile line of Ahmed's face. "I never up—I neh-var spy—I just feel."

Simon grinned. "Well, stop feeling, and get on with my letters; and you'd better not put that bastard pidgin-English of yours over on me either; I always reckon it's a sign of a guilty conscience." He turned at the door, "you might ring up Mr. Saunders and ask him from me kindly to stand by in case anything should happen; he was going out, I think. If he's gone already, tell Matron where I am."

He left by his own private entrance. It led through the ancient walled garden by way of the terrace towards the woods which enfolded the old building as a casket encloses a jewel.

At the furthest gate he paused a moment. He always loved this view of the rambling red-brick house Weyland had bought for their experiments. If any place, he thought, could provide for those broken minds and bodies which it sheltered, an asylum from the world where peace and health might be regained, it was Skilworth Manor with the great mountains behind it and the lake at its feet.

He shut and locked the gate and the quiet of the woods enfolded him. He hardly ever entered here without thinking of that holiday nearly seven years ago when, after the momentous conversation above Grasmere, Weyland had put forward his idea of buying some place in the Lake District where he could work in solitude unobtainable in the more populated South.

After a year's practice in the East End, Simon had gone out to study in India, and when he returned via China and Siberia some three years later it was to find Skilworth Manor already established as a clinic and making a name for itself under the capable charge of Dr. Saunders, a daring and somewhat unorthodox experimenter in the realms of psychotherapy. Since then Simon had led rather a piecemeal existence, a few months of work at Skilworth being inevitably broken by journeys on strange missions for those men whom although he had not yet seen them he obeyed as his superiors. That this summons meant another such adventure he did not doubt.

Well, that was his life! But as he climbed the mossy path he felt a moment of regret. One had such an extraordinary sensation of peace when one entered this ground that Weyland had enclosed as a sanctuary for bird and beast, just as Skilworth was a sanctuary for human beings. Here the hunted fox and otter fled, knowing that hounds might bay after them in vain; here the birds had become so tame that they virtually ignored the few humans who invaded their territory. Below the falls, whose voices filled the silence with a monotonous and muted melody, a family of beaver lived and built their dam. They were quite tame and flourished exceedingly.

The path wound steeply upward amid huge trees, ferns, outcroppings of moss-grown rock. All the fret of the world dropped behind. Colonies of foxgloves tossed their purple bells in the green gloom, and, after the early morning's rain, every separate shrub and tree poured forth its own intoxicating scent.

"The morning of the First Day," Simon said aloud. There were no sinister influences here, no men striving for mastery; but the path went on, out of the silent places, to where one man strove, indeed, but for good and not for evil. The woods were behind him, he was crossing a windblown fell; the path circled a pile of fantastic rock, and there, abruptly revealed, was the house which that man had built himself.

Weyland always said, when its curious shape was commented upon, that it was designed on the model of the houses the Atlanteans had used for alchemical and astrological experiments. When asked how he knew, he would merely laugh, shrug his shoulders, and talk of something else. True or not, it was certainly unique even in this day of experimental architecture. Semicircular in shape, it was built in a series of bays. There were no corners throughout; the main portion had a flat roof and upon one side was a circular tower made almost entirely of glass. The double bronze doors, set between their severe white columns, were open, and Simon went straight upstairs. Weyland, he knew, would be in his laboratory in the tower. He did not knock, afraid lest the jarring sound should cause a disturbance in that atmosphere dedicated to the most profound abstract thought, but passed softly into this room where his friend and mentor worked.

Entering here one's first impression was of whiteness and glitter. Simon always thought it was like stepping into the heart of a diamond. Even the sharp facets of colour were there: liquids, in bottles and containers upon glass shelves, catching and reflecting the light in prismatic flashes of colours brighter, clearer, stranger even than their counterparts which lay in the glass-covered drawers: emeralds, opals, rubies and onward through every kind of precious and semi-precious stone even to rock crystals and coral, iron and copper.

Weyland, clad in a white coat, was seated at a steel and glass table, peering through a microscope at some copper-coloured powder in a crucible. He did not move or look up and Simon, crossing the room, bent over a retort under which burned a small, steady flame. In the container was a gold liquid; the experiment had been in progress three weeks and each time he examined it a significant change had taken place. It was only latterly that he had begun to comprehend something of the magnitude of the task Weyland had set himself.

As Weyland showed no sign of detaching himself from his present work, Simon sat down on the window-seat to wait. Outside, wherever the eye ranged through the transparent walls—save where, upon one side, Weyland had drawn the sheltering blind— the shapes of mountain, fell and dale, unrolled themselves; it was as if he and this man and all this glittering apparatus were poised above the earth in some cloud-supported, aerial laboratory.

Watching his friend at work thus, Simon often got a strange fragment of vision, seeing him in another setting and another age. Always the scientist, the alchemist seeking mysterious transmutations, but working in a dark, shadowed place amid great books full of cabalistic symbols, surrounded by curious and fantastic materials, "tongue of newt and eye of frog," amid mystery and terror; around the walls skeletons, globes and charts, designed more to affright the ignorant than to be of practical use, with a cauldron boiling over a fire of wood which an apprentice kept at even heat, working the bellows rhythmically. Another life? Who could tell? And was he, perhaps that apprentice? He liked to think so. Who, then, was this man who still sought to unravel the greatest secret of the Universe, this modern scientist of repute with his delicate apparatus, his electric furnace, working in a laboratory fitted up with all the latest discoveries and facilities? Paracelsus, perhaps, or Leonardo returned to earth determined to discover that of which the ignorance of a bygone age had cheated him.

Weyland interrupted the flow of his fantasies. He put down the microscope and looked up.

"We're getting on," he said with a half-smile. "I sometimes have a feeling that we're nearer than we think."

"The Elixir of Life," said Simon in a dreamy voice. "Just think what our worthy colleagues, even the most advanced of them, would say if they knew what you were really attempting to discover! They'd consider Skilworth too mild for you!"

"Or if they realized the full extent of their ignorance and what there still *is* to discover, they might begin to think Skilworth was the only place for *them!*"

Simon gave a sigh of satisfaction. "Skilworth is becoming a name to conjure with, all the same. Do you know, Mrs. Welling is going home next week? There's a spectacular cure for you—and quick."

"Yes, she's the type of case Hornsley used to tackle so successfully."

Simon looked up. "Hornsley? We haven't caught up with him yet. What a tragedy that was! I'd like to have got to the bottom of that business."

"Perhaps you will," Weyland spoke quietly. "It's that I want to discuss with you. I heard yesterday—Hornsley has remembered something at last."

That Hornsley had been taken by the Brotherhood, as Weyland's mysterious friends called themselves, Simon knew; but where he had gone and what had been happening during all these years he had never cared to ask, although that strange conversation in the cottage often recurred to him.

"Yes," continued Weyland, "he's just beginning to remember, not much yet—but enough." He gave a short laugh. "People dare to talk of coincidence! Last week I heard, apparently by chance, of Zarov again."

"Zarov! That's interesting. Queer how completely he's managed to cover his tracks all this while."

Weyland grunted. "I've suspected his influence in several recent and rather similar cases. Of course he's probably passed under a dozen different names since then. However, I don't think he has ever suspected that we had an eye on him, even when the whole of the scandal about Hornsley's clinic became public. Anyway he's back again in England now."

"What's his game this time?"

"I wish I knew, and I wish even more I knew what he's been up to in the interval," He shook his head and sighed. "If he's been working on that hypothesis, he may have got anywhere!"

"What hypothesis? Something Hornsley remembered?"

Weyland did not answer at once, but leaning towards the table picked up a small phial which was filled with a translucent liquid, colourless, yet glittering, almost as if it were white fire. He held it up to the light and instantly infinitesimal specks of colour appeared within it, dancing and swirling like motes seen in the rays of the sun. When at last he spoke it seemed more as if he were apostrophizing the spirit imprisoned in this delicate bottle than the man in the window seat.

"What is the secret of Life? It must be everywhere about us, since it is implicit in everything that exists, yet its nature eludes us still. But if we could become consciousfully conscious, I mean, wouldn't we be nearer to elucidating the mystery? At present we only see and study separate parts and, concentrating on them, probably miss their relationship to the whole pattern. For the parts, by the very fact of their inevitable limitations, must be cut off from the possibility, even, of apprehending the significance of the Whole. Therefore it must follow that the closer man can come to identifying himself with the Whole, the more of Its nature he will be able to discover. Supposing, then, there were some way of obliterating, as it were, those barriers which shut one part off from another, the barriers of Form, of Personality, of separate consciousness . . ."

He stopped and Simon made no comment. Weyland never really wandered from the point, even when he appeared to do so; he would reveal presently what all this had to do with Zarov and Hornsley. Simon had not long to wait. Weyland put the phial back with the movement of a man who has made up his mind to something. He twisted his arm-chair round until he was facing Simon, and said in a quiet, almost matter-of-fact voice:

"I believe Zarov may be on the track of the discovery of some very important clue which will perhaps indicate to him how this fusion of the parts with the Whole can be achieved—and that might very possibly lead to the discovery of the Secret itself, if my own deductions are correct."

"Good Lord! But what makes you think that?"

"Partly inference, partly because of something Hornsley admitted. I may be wrong, of course, I hope to God I am. But I am convinced, although at the moment I can't see any real connection between this business and what I got out of Hornsley, that they do hang together, and that there must be some key or something to the mystery in this tomb . . ."

"Tomb?" interrupted Simon. "That's the first I've heard of a tomb!"

Weyland smiled. "It won't be the last," he remarked drily. "In fact this tomb is likely to be the hub of your universe, my boy, for the next six months, at least."

"Well, as you know, excavating's my idea of a holiday; as a matter of fact I've been pining to get back to Egypt. I suppose it is in Egypt, by the way, and not a barrow in the South Downs?"

"It's Egypt right enough, somewhere in the mountains of Lybia. The place has a queer history; although it has attracted various parties of excavators it's never been properly surveyed. One of the reasons seems to be that it has such a bad reputation that it is almost impossible to get any natives to work there at all. It's said to be under a curse, and it certainly is a fact that on the few occasions when work was started in the district it was always brought to a standstill by something unusual and spectacular, an epidemic among the workers, a series of accidents—in two cases fatal ones, I believe—or some trouble which forced the excavators to abandon work and return home. Quite enough to confirm the Egyptians' superstitious fears and make the place practically taboo! For a long time it was left alone, but about three years ago a man named Wortley did succeed in recruiting enough men and began to dig there."

"Wortley?" interrupted Simon, "I seem to know the name; why, he was at Amarna for a bit when I was working there. Didn't something happen to him? I seem to remember hearing him mentioned in connection with an accident of some sort."

"Yes, he was killed and several men with him by a fall of cliff in this valley a short time after they had commenced operations." Weyland leant forward, tapping his fingers on the table. "Now we happen to know that Wortley was in the hands of one of X.'s agents at that time, but I must admit it never occurred to us then to connect these two factors in any way. Last year, however, another man, Thomas Derwent, went up there. As far as I can make out he spent the best part of a season working around, then suddenly went down with a mysterious illness and was invalided home. That wouldn't have registered with us either, if we hadn't heard, a few weeks ago from the archæological society through which he had obtained his concession, that a friend of his, a Dr. Zarov, was arranging to take it over for this season and, for the preliminary work at all events, was putting a quite unknown man in charge. In view of the circumstances of Wortley's death at the same place, and his association with X., I feel there's something here that merits investigation."

"It certainly looks fishy. But they know for certain that there *is* a tomb in the district?"

"Yes; I've been making enquiries and it seems that Derwent had just uncovered what appears to be the beginning of a ramp when he went sick."

Simon nodded. "You said it had a queer history. Are there any legends connected with it, then? Or are you just building a theory on these—accidents?"

"All we've got to go on is the alleged curse, the intense fear of the local inhabitants, and the name." He said the words slowly. "The place is called Wādi al-Zalamah. Does that convey anything to you?"

"Valley of the Oppressors—Evil—Dark Ones," Simon translated slowly. "It might mean black magicians too."

"Yes. To my mind it can only mean that."

Simon grunted.

"Looks as if there *is* a legend. It might give us a clue. If your deductions are right X. probably does know something important about it. I shouldn't think he'd be after the glory of an archæological discovery exactly."

"Quite; it looks as if he is after something—but knowing the power of the curse guarding it has been using these men to pick the chestnuts out of the fire for him. His idea is, I suppose, that the full force of such a curse would be bound to fall on the first offenders—the people who actually opened the tomb; then, the force being expended, he could follow on without incurring so much risk and get whatever it is he's looking for. In which case he'll go on sending people there until someone does succeed."

"Nice!" commented Simon.

"Very! Typical of his methods. I admit, of course, that this is all surmise, but one thing appears to be quite certain, very grave danger threatens anyone attempting to excavate in this valley. Therefore the main thing, as I see it at present, is to dissuade these new people from taking over Derwent's dig. If they do, poor devils, something unpleasant, to put it at its mildest, is bound to happen to them."

There was a pause. "But supposing I can put them off somehow," the younger man said presently, "Zarov'll merely drag someone else along to do the dirty work."

"Undoubtedly. But the next move, if your job succeeds, will be for *us* to try and discover what it is he believes to be buried there, and to take possession ourselves, if needs be."

"Have you any idea what it is?"

"No, not definitely; but some of the things we learned from Hornsley may offer a kind of clue."

"You haven't told me yet what Hornsley did say."

Weyland settled back in his chair, putting the tips of his fingers together and narrowing his eyes, a habit of his when he was working out a problem.

"No," he said slowly, "because it's a little difficult to fit all those isolated remarks, half-memories and so on into any kind of clear pattern. But I will tell you what I've deduced from them, although, mind you, it is only deduction, and I may be quite on the wrong track. That's another thing I hope you'll be able to clear up for us."

Simon nodded, and Weyland continued after another long pause: "So far as we can make out Hornsley and Zarov between them seem to have been conducting some quite extraordinary experiments regarding the *Hinterland* of the human mind—psychoanalysis of a sort, but carried deeper and further than anyone has yet attempted. They must have rather anticipated the hypothesis put forward by Jung not so long ago, that behind what is generally called the individual unconscious there are other layers of memories, national and racial, and ultimately, I imagine, something even vaster, a kind of ocean of Mind-Matter containing a record of every experience of humanity, even perhaps of the Earth itself; a substratum that is common to us all, which colours our actions and thoughts to a greater or lesser degree according to our personal response, our sensitivity to its influence."

Simon nodded. "In fact," he interrupted, "the 'Akashic Records' of occultism."

"Yes, something like that. Jung hints that this may be the true Consciousness; our present state being one of virtual unconsciousness, since hardly any of us have begun to understand, much less to control the causes of even the most apparently simple of our thoughts and actions." He gave his quiet smile. "Interesting to see how our scientists are gradually accepting and adopting the Ancient Wisdom, isn't it! But that's rather by the way. The point that interests us is this: these two men were obviously trying to discover some method whereby, through controlling and directing certain minds that were peculiarly sensitive to the influences emanating from this *Hinterland*—for I must give it some name, call it Race-Consciousness if you like it better—they could, through such minds, make a direct contact with it—as a whole—a mass."

"But would such a thing be possible?"

"I don't know, but admitting the validity of the hypothesis I can't quite see why not, Anyhow it seems to me that this was what they, or rather Zarov—for Hornsley was only his tool—were aiming at. What happened, however, was that one after another the wretched experimental rabbits, people already unbalanced when they came to the clinic—people, you note, exceptionally sensitive, for most neurotics are that—succumbed; several died, and quite a number were rendered incurably insane. But whereas Hornsley recoiled in horror when he found out the results of their attempts, we may reckon that Zarov, naturally, has had no such scruples and has probably been continuing the experiments elsewhere." He made a despairing gesture: "If only we could have discovered this before."

"It's all terribly vague," Simon complained.

"Of course it's vague. We can only draw inferences from what we know of Zarov and of X.'s aims."

"But supposing X. or Zarov should succeed in tapping, as you call it, this Race-Unconscious, what exactly would that imply? What do you suppose would be the next move and, anyway, where does this tomb business come in?"

"Good Lord, use your imagination, man! Don't you appreciate that, if such a thing were possible, nothing," he stressed the word, "nothing that has ever been known or experienced by the human race from the very beginning of time, would be inaccessible? Can't you see that once such a technique were perfected it would merely be a matter of working deeper and deeper, cutting away, as it were, more and more undergrowth, until the very Originating Impulse, the Source of all energy, thought and action were revealed? The Secret, in fact, for which we are all searching!"

Simon looked unconvinced. "Yes, but how do we know that the Secret actually exists in the Race-Unconscious or whatever it is? Even *that* must have its limitations."

Weyland smiled. "Good for you, my boy! It's a very sound objection. But whereas I agree that the whole of Truth could not be found in the Race-Unconscious—since the greater cannot be contained in the lesser—I think the Key might be there. If you postulate that the Whole is One—which practically every system does—then it *must* be. As a matter of fact we have pretty clear proof that at a very early period in the history of this planet there *did* exist a race of men with an infinitely more profound knowledge of natural laws than has ever since been manifested, save in one or two isolated individuals."

"You mean what occultism calls the Initiate Kings of the First Golden Age?"

"Yes; in all the traditions of every race you find mention of such god-like men who not only worked what we would to-day call miracles, but taught their followers a wisdom which has never been surpassed, and has been attained later only by the few, Buddha, Jesus and other saints, yogis and sages who all had powers which make our most advanced efforts look pitifully childish."

Simon whistled. "You're suggesting that it might become possible through the medium of this Race-Consciousness, to establish contact with all those great minds of the past, almost to identify oneself with them and so discover the secret of their power?"

Weyland nodded. "Unfortunately, though, it isn't only that type of highly spiritual mind one would encounter in the process. The other side would be represented in the Race-Consciousness just as accurately, the black magicians with their powers, the knowledge, say, of the Atlanteans, which was so terrible and destructive that in the end it was instrumental in sinking their continent beneath the waves. There are all sorts of possibilities, good and bad. Just to give one instance—think what it would mean if a band of unscrupulous men learned the secret of the transmutation of metals and of how to turn dross into gold! What would happen to the world's markets? And in an age which looks on gold as a god, think of the power such knowledge would give to its possessor! But to my mind there are even worse dangers than this. Sometimes I wonder . . ."

He fell silent, while Simon sat watching his set expression and waiting for what was coming next. But the pause lasted so long that at length the younger man grew impatient.

"What?" he prompted.

Weyland stared at him, but his gaze was remote. "It's only an idea based on one of those fragments that Hornsley let fall; but isn't it a bit strange that in the last few years so many men are arising who appear to be gifted in a superlative degree with the power to sway the minds of ordinarily quite intelligent and independent people?"

"Do you mean you think these leaders have got hold of the knowledge of how to use the Race-Unconscious?"

"I don't think *they* have"—Weyland spoke slowly—"but I was wondering if they weren't being used by someone who has, and who may be manipulating their minds. X., for example."

Simon stared, aghast. "Impossible!"

"Again I don't see why—if you could contact the Race-Unconscious—why couldn't you use it in some such way?" He smiled rather apologetically. "Perhaps I am going a little far, but frankly I am afraid of X. I am convinced he has got on to the track of something vital through Zarov's experiments with Hornsley. I tell you, Simon, most solemnly, that if he does succeed in even half he has set out to accomplish, he will set up such a cancer, such a disruption throughout the whole race, that even we may be powerless to save the life of humanity."

"What beats me," said Simon after a moment, "is that the Brotherhood with all its occult powers as well as its remarkable intelligence, can't trace him or, apparently, do anything to stop him."

Weyland gave a rather grim smile. "If you knew as much as I do you'd realize that X. has powers just as remarkable as our own; but whereas we are handicapped by our respect for the Law—human as well as divine—he knows of no such restrictions. As a matter of fact some of our leaders have, I believe, a shrewd idea who he is; but, as you know, the whole point about our methods is that we never attack persons, not even seek to influence them against their will. When it comes to defending our own secrets, or helping the innocent and the foolish against such aggressors, it is, of course, rather another matter. And that's your job at the moment, leaving all other possibilities and speculations entirely aside."

"That's all very well, but supposing I can't stop them . . ." He leant forward. "Your theories are pretty hair-raising, you know—supposing the tomb is opened, what do you think *could* be hidden there that would help X. with this scheme of his?"

Weyland shrugged. "Don't forget that in every one of the Esoteric Mysteries you find the tradition that the Secrets of Atlantis—whence, mind you, the Race of Initiate Kings I've been talking of originally came—were preserved by those bands of priests and Initiates who sought refuge in Egypt and India before the destruction of their continent. It's obvious, then, that some traces, anyway, of all this forgotten knowledge might well be hidden in an Egyptian tomb."

"But if 'Dark Ones' did mean black magicians, they wouldn't be likely to know such Secrets."

"Just the very people who might! Some of the later High Priests were by no means models of virtue. The fact that it has got such a powerful curse laid on it rather indicates that there may be something there of an unusual and dangerous nature. When the ancient Egyptians wanted to guard their secrets you often find they protected them by invoking some Power to attack intruders and prevent any but the right people from discovering their hiding-place."

"What do you mean by the 'right people'?"

"Well—those who would use the secret in the way it was intended to be used; or again, those who came at the exact moment in time when such power was ordained to be released."

"But if that were so X. would never be able to get at it."

"A man knowledgeable and subtle enough always has a chance of circumventing a curse," said Weyland. "X, seems to have evolved quite an efficacious method. Or perhaps the hour may have struck; I don't know. At any rate, one thing is obvious to my mind, these innocent people can't be left to their fate, nor, for that matter, should X.'s activities remain uninvestigated."

Simon pulled a wry face. "But do you really consider I'm fitted for the job? I've done a few odd things in my time, but tackling a king of black magicians face to face isn't one of them!"

Weyland looked at him. "You have been trained in the Yogas, you have reached a high stage in the science of judo—what has it all been for, if not—this?"

Simon got down from the window-seat and began pacing the room. "You may be right, but when I think of all you've told me I feel a puling babe!"

Weyland stared beyond him, at the mountains. "Of course you can refuse; we have other men, but I was instructed to give you the first opportunity."

Simon laughed shortly. "Can you see me refusing? I suppose I ought to feel flattered, but I can only hope They haven't backed the wrong horse." He dropped into the other armchair. "Well, let's hear a little more about it, anyway."

"I can't tell you any more, except the people's names and the boat on which they sail. The rest you must find out for yourself."

"But isn't this the type of case which would really justify the Brethren using their occult powers to discover a few more useful details?"

"There really isn't anything more to be discovered, so far as you are concerned."

"Oho, isn't there? I'd like to know what the tomb really contains—yes, and the nature of this curse. Don't they know that?"

"Perhaps," he spoke slowly, "the Brethren *do* know; that may be why they are sending you." His piercing gaze was fixed on Simon's face: "But it wouldn't affect the issue. Your business at the moment is to try and stop these people from going at all; that's obviously not a case for the employment of any but ordinary means. Nothing but persuasion, an appeal to their common sense or their fear, in fact a psychological approach can be used there; for again, as you are perfectly well aware, man must always be allowed complete free will, it's only the blacks like X. who dare interfere with individual liberty. Of course if it should come to a direct conflict with X.'s powers, or if you should have to face the Guardian of the Tomb, occult help might, if absolutely necessary, be given you if you prove to be too weak, but that would only be allowed when all normal methods have been tried and failed. You must never count on it. It was for emergencies such as these that you were given your specialized training, you'll have to use your own judgment about the desirability of invoking occult aid—and take the consequences if you invoke it wrongly. I can't emphasize too strongly that we are on the physical plane to conform to and act in accordance with its laws, that's why all this modern interest in what is called 'psychic phenomena' is so dangerous. But you're not likely to get much of that," he paused, "unless . . ."

"Unless?"

"Well, unless the forces up against you should attack you in some materialized form. But there's no need to go into that at present."

Simon grunted. "Thanks for all this reassurance. And now about these people—who and what are they?"

"Arthur Mannering, who has been persuaded by Zarov to take over Granger's concession, is, so far as I can gather, an oldish man with a mania for Egyptology to which he has never before had the opportunity to give active expression. He is the vain, petty type who, because he has been ignored by better men, could easily be lured on to any folly in order to 'show them.' He'll be your first difficulty; he's the kind who'll do anything, even risk the lives of his daughters, to vindicate himself by making a great discovery. I'm not sure that the other man, Nikolai Annerly, isn't one of X.'s agents, at all events it was he who introduced Zarov to Mannering. He may, of course, be just in their toils in some way. He is engaged to one of the daughters. I don't know anything about them."

"Do you mean the daughters are coming, too, then?" cried Simon.

Weyland smiled. "Now don't let your very unreasonable bias against women influence you. When you've had a bit wider experience you'll be more competent to judge them. Your few affairs—at least those I am aware of—show a curious lack of discrimination."

Simon made a grimace. "I'm not so inexperienced as all that, but I'd be happier if I knew there were no women in the party; they always complicate things."

"Well, there are—two of them; and no doubt they will count as quite a big factor in the affair, so you'd better get used to the idea." Smilingly he watched Simon's glum face. "I should think," he went on as he received no reply, "that the fact that two quite innocent young women were being dragged on this expedition to be sacrificed on the altar of X.'s plans through the vanity of the male portion of their family, would be alone sufficient reason for any man to make an effort to save them—even if there were no more vital stake involved."

"They mayn't be as innocent as all that," Simon commented drily.

"Maybe not. Of course you can still refuse to take on the job—if you don't like it."

Simon looked up, grinning. "Would I? Well, well, I suppose I'm fated to pull these females out of the mess, quite in the style of the best Knight-errant. At least I hope I will, but I repeat I feel singularly ill-equipped."

"Better than most people would be; but I don't think you're in for an easy time. By the way, have you looked at the progressed aspects of your horoscope lately?"

"I have; and as nasty a collection of stinkers as I've got coming to me at the end of this year I've seldom seen. I've been wondering what on earth they could indicate. Some kind of unholy smashing up, with Uranus squaring my Mars from the 8th House into the bargain."

"Yes, I know," Weyland answered softly.

"What do you know?"

"No more than you do. But it means danger certainly grave danger." His gaze grew remote. "It will be a smashing-up in every way, I think."

Simon watched his grave face. His eyes were steady as he leant forward a little and asked: "Do you think it means—death?"

Weyland got up abruptly and went to the window, turning his back on the young man he loved as his own son. "I don't think," he said, "I'd rather not; but it's just one of the risks we've all got to run in this game. In this man we are challenging Evil itself and all its powers. This is only the beginning; yet it is a very definite beginning. If we win this first round we will be one step nearer success, but only one step; if we lose"—he shrugged and turned towards Simon, who had also risen—"if *you* lose, that too will he but an episode. You and I are only pawns that the Player uses to capture Kings and Queens, but even the Kings and Queens who think themselves so important are but pieces in a larger game." He broke off, smiling, and patting Simon lightly on the shoulder crossed towards the electric furnace and bent over the retort.

"In any case it is comforting, whatever happens, to believe as firmly as I do that we are on the winning side—ultimately—even if it does take a few thousand years."

Simon burst out laughing. "And while awaiting that propitious date I'll endeavour to do my little part and bring you back in one hand X.'s head on a charger, and in the other the Elixir of Life—I feel they'd make a very pretty combination—"

CHAPTER II

CHANCE OR DESTINY?

"CAN you spare me a moment?" The soft, rather deprecatory voice of Ramage, the ship's doctor, stirred Simon from his contemplation of the pattern of foam swirling back from the swift passage of the keel. He looked up with a smile.

"We won't be in Port Said for five days yet," he remarked.

The little doctor glanced at him, not quite sure whether or not this was intended to be a species of joke. His natural solemnity always made him the butt of other men; but despite, or perhaps because of this characteristic, he was a sound and trustworthy physician, although never likely to become a brilliant one.

By what appeared to be a curious coincidence Simon had discovered, when he came on board the ship that was to take him on his adventure, that Ramage and he were old acquaintances. They had been at the same hospital in their student days, and Ramage, a serious young man even then, had conceived a tremendous admiration for his more brilliant colleague, and had, therefore, been willing to spend hours listening to those strange theories with which Weyland's conversations always filled Simon's mind. They had not met since but the very first evening on board, the apparently matter-of-fact little doctor was cross-questioning Simon with eagerness as to whether he had abandoned his peculiar theories on psychism, or if he were indeed seeking to utilize them in his medical work. His interest in Skilworth was immediate and Simon had been delighted to find unexpected companionship. He was, therefore, all the more ready to listen to whatever Ramage had come to discuss.

"As far as I can see," said Ramage, deciding to take Simon literally, "I'm landed with a problem that'll take me longer than five days to solve."

"What! A case already?"

"Yes; I was wondering . . ." He stuttered nervously and broke off, rubbing his hands together. His sense of inferiority always made him wonder, when he had embarked on a sentence, whether it really was worth finishing; hence half his conversation ended in space. At Simon's sympathetic nod he plunged again. "I feel somehow it may be something rather in your line, but of course perhaps you'd rather not—I mean I feel it's beyond me. As a matter of fact I'll admit I'm completely flummoxed. I was wondering . . . I mean, I know you're on a holiday . . . but I thought perhaps you would . . ."

"My dear chap," Simon hastened to rescue him from his flounderings, "of course I will. Fire away; what's the trouble?"

Reassured, Ramage became more professional and discussed symptoms. He thought it was some form of epilepsy; the girl, who was still quite young, had had strange attacks all her life, now they appeared to be increasing. But there was something unusual, distinctly odd about the case. "She talks, for instance," he said, "in different voices. Something they told me reminded me of those things you used to say about possession—of course I know it's usually put down to dissociation of personality—it may be that . . ." A vague wave of the hand indicated that his confidence had already vanished. "But really I don't feel I have the right—on your holiday, too."

Simon clapped him on the back. "What rot! I'm already panting after my prey. Come on, what's the special trouble at the moment?"

Ramage smiled feebly and heaved a sigh of obvious relief. "Yes, I really am in trouble, or honestly I shouldn't have felt justified in bothering you. The fact is the girl had an attack more violent than usual almost directly we came on board, and has been unconscious ever since; she's in a queer state—I don't like the look of it. Her sister has always dealt with the attacks, but she says—"

"Sister?" Simon broke in sharply. "What's this about a sister? Are these two women alone, or is anyone else with them?"

Ramage blinked at what to him, absorbed in the case, appeared to be quite an irrelevant question.

"No, no; the father's there and another man, engaged to the sick girl, I understand, though to my mind . . ."

But Simon interrupted again with every sign, now, of suppressed excitement. "Not by any chance that party who have kept to their cabins since we left—have had all their meals taken down to them?"

"Yes; why, do you know them?"

Simon recovered himself with an effort. "No—just curiosity—nothing more."

"Well, you seem rather wrought-up over them, I must say."

Simon hedged. "As a matter of fact I had heard something about them from a friend, but nothing that has any bearing at all on this case."

"Oh! Anyway those are the people. What I was wondering was—I mean, I felt . . ."

"D'you want me to come and have a look at her?"

Ramage beamed. "My dear chap, if you would! You see from what you've told me of your work I do feel you may be able to do something."

The other nodded. "Yes," he said slowly, "so do I."

"In that case I'd better go down and tell Mr. Mannering that I have decided to have another opinion. I didn't mention it, in case you didn't want to take it on."

When he had bustled off Simon went back to the rail.

Was this another coincidence? If so, a truly amazing one. He had been racking his brains how to get into touch with these people who appeared so determined to keep themselves isolated from their fellow-passengers. At Liverpool, before they sailed, that last night at the hotel, Weyland had gone through the passenger list with him. "There they are," he had exclaimed, tapping the names with his pencil. "You've got twelve days to get on a sufficiently friendly footing to justify your following them up without arousing undue suspicion. If you can gain their confidence enough to stop them making this attempt at all, so much the better, of course; but if not, then you must be on the spot when it is made. Remember, most of our conclusions are only surmise; we don't know anything for certain. You'll have to check up all my statements from what you can get out of them. And it won't be easy. They are sure to have been warned not to give anything away."

Weyland had been right. When Simon realized, after the first day or so, that they had obviously no intention even of appearing at meals or taking the usual exercise on deck, he had wondered how on earth he was going to break down their defences. Now, it appeared, Fate was about to take a hand in the game.

A light step, pausing behind him, made him turn. A young woman stood there, muffled in a long coat.

His first impression, a sudden one, was that he had seen her before. With lightning rapidity his trained, observant mind searched its archives: innumerable women's faces: patients, friends, faces encountered in hotels, trains, the houses of acquaintances. No, he couldn't place her—and yet . . .

She was speaking. She had a rather deep voice and a brusque manner which made her appear almost unpleasantly mannish. The grey eyes searching his face were hard, challenging; the fair hair, he noticed, was cropped too close. He wondered how accurate his swift summing-up would turn out to be: a woman at odds with life, aggressive because she's fundamentally frightened; masculine because she daren't let her emotional side get control; repressed, bitter, yet gallant. Yes, certainly gallant; that impression remained. All this between the beginning of her first sentence and its end.

"You're Dr. Conningsby, aren't you? I came to speak to you. Dr. Ramage tells us he wants you to see my sister."

Whilst he murmured something appropriate Simon was thinking: "So it's you I've got to pull out of this mess!" Again that queer feeling of familiarity assailed him, then common sense asserted itself. "She's just a type," common sense said. "Nature's turning them out by the hundred at the moment; but she might be worse. At least she's not hysterical and she's got mentality—look at that brow!"

"I'm glad," Simon was saying aloud, "that you've come, as I understand you've always dealt with your sister during previous attacks."

"Oh dear no!" (How aggressive the girl was!) "She's been under dozens of doctors. I'm afraid I've learnt not to put much faith in them."

He began to cross-question her very minutely and was thankful to find her replies terse and to the point. She told him that her sister had been subject to mild attacks since her birth. "We hoped," she admitted, "that when she got engaged to Mr. Annerly—the man who is with us here—she would get better. She has refused to marry him until the attacks ceased; quite rightly—of course."

"And instead they have been getting much worse, with fresh symptoms?"

"Yes; but how do you know that? I didn't tell Dr. Ramage."

"I'm working on an hypothesis, that's all. It fits in."

"Well, I hope it's a right one; it'll be the first time anyone has been right—that's all I can say."

"Let's hope it is," he agreed courteously. "Shall I come down now?"

She hesitated; she evidently had something else to say. "Please; but I must tell you that Mr. Annerly is very much against our having another doctor. Every one she's seen has a different theory and they all make her worse rather than better. She seems to hate strangers. And—I had better warn you—she says queer things."

"What sort of things?"

"Oh, rubbish mostly. Sometimes it is as if she were—well, arguing with someone, fighting them, as if she were afraid . . ." She shrugged her shoulders, "one can't make head or tail of it, like delirium. But sometimes she discusses our affairs." She hesitated, frowning: "I suppose doctors do consider themselves bound never to repeat what they overhear, don't they?"

"Why, certainly. You may rely on my discretion, anyway."

She seemed, he thought, relieved. "Thank you. I'll go down and tell my father you're coming." She turned away and then abruptly, as if on an impulse, swung round towards him. Her air of assurance and self-sufficiency had left her. It was as if suddenly a mask had been displaced to reveal what lay beneath, a frightened, unhappy child. "If you could help—if you could do anything! I—I daren't think how it will end!"

He found himself speaking with such assurance and authority that his words carried conviction even to himself. "It will end happily, both for her and for you."

She stared at him, gave a little gasp as if aware that for a second a perfect stranger had discovered the chink in the armour of her invulnerability, then turning, fled below.

When Simon entered the Mannerings' cabin he found Dr. Ramage and the two men awaiting him. The girl's father struck him as being an obviously futile but quite kindly individual; he was short and thin and had the stooping, peering aspect of the typical scholar-recluse. The other was a man of about thirty-five. There were lines of discontent and bitterness round his thin, determined mouth; his eyes, a little too close-set, were of that reddish brown one sees in things of the wild: sly, quick-moving, as if on the look-out for enemies. Yet the idealistic forehead belied this impression, giving him the dual aspect of the intellectual ever doing battle with the primitive instinctual. Simon felt at the first glance that there was bound to be friction—even enmity—between them; they were like ancient antagonists met in a fresh guise.

Ramage introduced them. Mr. Mannering, the Egyptologist, bustled forward; he had all the important, fussy movements of the ineffectual man.

"How kind, how very kind of you this is, Dr. Conningsby! On your holiday, too, I understand. Dr. Ramage here tells me that the study of epilepsy is your speciality. Ah, dear, dear, a terrible affliction for a poor father to have a daughter like this!" He would have chattered on, but at that moment the door opened softly and the girl to whom Simon had spoken came in. "My daughter, Carol," Mannering said. Evidently she had not spoken of their meeting. Annerly, save for a brief nod, took no further notice of Simon, but seated himself on the other side of the cabin as if to emphasize the fact that he disapproved of Simon's presence there. His first words were indicative of this attitude, for, after the two doctors had discussed the case with Mannering for a few moments and Simon intimated that he would like to examine the patient, Annerly interposed with: "You won't do any good; no one has."

Carol gave him a cold stare, then turned to Simon.

"You must excuse Mr. Annerly's bad manners," she said in a tone of sweetness which yet held an envenomed note, "he really doesn't mean it."

"I quite understand his natural anxiety," smiled Simon. "I'm afraid the medical profession must often appear extremely inefficient to the layman, who perhaps doesn't quite realize the difficulties that confront the doctor at every turn. And now, if you will permit me . . ."

"I'll come with you," said the girl.

"If you don't mind, I think I'd prefer to see her alone."

"Oh, but I must be there. You don't understand, when she wakes from these attacks she's in a dreadful state, so it terrified; sometimes she cries for hours. If she didn't see me—"

Fortunately Ramage came to the rescue. "Dr. Conningsby always insists on being alone with his patients, Miss Mannering."

"Oh, but . . ." she seemed disinclined to give way.

"Don't be silly, Carol," came Annerly's jeering voice, "all doctors have their own methods. Give Dr. Conningsby his chance."

Simon, as he opened the door, heaved a sigh of relief at escaping from that atmosphere of repressed irritation and rancour.

When he had gone, Ramage, who, unsubtle as he was in some ways, could hardly remain unaware of this state of tension, made several quite abortive attempts to set them all talking and at ease; but his remarks dropped into a well of silence and drowned there. Mannering sat at the table nervously drawing hieroglyphics on a blotter; Annerly remained in his corner glowering at the closed door of the cabin where his betrothed lay, while Carol, still in her long coat, a cigarette drooping between her lips, stood against that same door rather with the threatening air of a tigress about to defend its young.

There came no sound from within. The minutes dropped away, like Ramage's efforts at conversation, into a vacuum. At last the door moved softly. Carol sprang aside, the three men half rose. Into the opening came Simon's head. He nodded towards Carol and smiled reassuringly at the old man, then he disappeared while she followed him.

What she expected to see she hardly knew; she had witnessed so many horrors connected with this dearly-loved sister. But what she did see brought a half-cry to her lips. Betty was lying on her back with her eyes open—alive, sane eyes in the haggard face to which already the colour was returning. Her lips were faintly smiling. One hand rested in Simon's, the other, feebly, she stretched out to Carol.

The girl rushed to her side and fell on her knees by the berth, clasping the slim fingers in her own strong, brown ones. "Darling, are you all right?" She looked up into Simon's calm face. "What have you done? She's never been like this!" All her reserve was momentarily quenched in a wave of gratitude. "I can't thank you . . ."

With an involuntary movement her other hand had gone out to him. He touched it lightly. "Don't talk now. She's all right for the present, I think." His fingers smoothed the sick girl's forehead and she smiled as if they brought her some magical gift. Her eyelids fluttered and closed.

"Keep her quiet and let her sleep it off. I'd like to see her tomorrow, or to-night if she wakes and you consider it necessary. And I'd like another talk with you sometime."

She nodded and half rose.

"No, stay here," he said and went out.

It was after dinner that she came to find him.

He saw her as he sat in a deck chair in a dark corner by the bridge. He had succeeded in shaking off the excited Ramage and with some difficulty had also escaped from his fellow-passengers. Unattached males were, as usual, much in demand, particularly now when dancing was in progress. Faintly he could hear the cacophony of jazz above the hissing of the waves and softened by the uncertain wind upon which it came and went. He knew her by her walk, brisk and purposeful. It was strange how clearly all her characteristics were already limned in his consciousness; strange and a little irritating, since he found them already inclined to impinge upon his trains of thought; and the events of that afternoon certainly needed all his attention.

He rose from his chair and softly called her name. He saw her start, glance round, step back. "She's frightened," he thought. "What is she frightened of? That's what I've got to find out." At that moment she saw him and stood still.

"You wanted to speak to me?"

"Yes; how is your sister?"

"Still asleep, but she looks marvellously better." She sat down in the chair he brought forward and drew a deep breath of the keen, salt air. "How did you do it? What did you do?"

"I haven't done it yet," he replied gravely.

"You mean you will—you can cure her?" Her voice shook with eagerness.

"I think so, under certain conditions."

"Conditions? What do you mean?"

"Well, really I'd like to have her under my care, in my own clinic; but if that is impossible I would suggest that her environment should be most carefully studied. For one thing"—he shot at a venture—"that she should on no account go to Egypt."

She stared at him. He saw that her eyes had grown very wide, almost horrified they looked.

"But we were told to go to Egypt," she stammered. "A man in whom Nick—Mr. Annerly—has the greatest faith, the only man who seems, so far, to have done her even temporarily any good, said Egypt was the only place where she might hope to get cured."

"Oh? Who is he; anyone I would know?"

"Probably not; a man called Dr. Zarov."

Simon's eyes narrowed. "So! Dr. Zarov said—Egypt, did he?"

"Well?" Her voice cut sharply into his significant silence.

"I was just wondering; do you know anything about this—doctor? I suppose he has an English degree, by the way?"

"Of course. At least I think so. Mr. Annerly knows him well. Dr. Zarov has been a very good friend to him, he helped him out of some financial difficulties in the past. I must say, in all fairness, he *did* do Betty good. He saw quite a lot of her last year and certainly seemed able to calm her and give her confidence."

"Not with very lasting effects apparently."

"No." She hesitated, then said slowly: "Why did you speak in that tone of voice? Do you know anything against Dr. Zarov?"

Simon hesitated, weighing his words. In this girl he saw a possible ally—his one ally, perhaps. But she was so aggressively inclined that he must proceed with the utmost caution.

"I have heard of him vaguely, as a matter of fact."

"Good or bad?" she shot the words at him.

He shrugged his shoulders. "If you don't mind, I would prefer to suspend judgment until I have had some personal experience of him and of his methods."

"That means it was bad." It was her turn to hesitate now; at last she said slowly: "I'm not surprised. I don't know why, but I never liked him. I wish we didn't have to see him again."

"And must you?"

"Yes, in Egypt."

"Oh. Going to show you the sights, I suppose."

"Yes—oh yes, of course."

He knew she was lying. "That will be very nice. As I said, I don't want to set my opinion up against his, but all the same I repeat I am convinced that Egypt is the one place on earth your sister ought *not* to go to. I think it might even be fatal to her—to all your hopes."

She gave a stifled cry. "Oh, but we can't stop now—"

"Couldn't you persuade them to go on to Palestine, say? Go and see the new Jewish city of Tel Aviv—extraordinarily interesting. "

"Of course not—you don't know how set on it they are." She made a gesture of despair. "This horrible idea! They'll never give it up!"

He leant forward and put his hand over hers; but at the instant movement of withdrawal he shifted his finger to her pulse and spoke in his most professional tone.

"You are frightened about something, Miss Mannering, aren't you?" He only smiled and nodded at her aggressive nature. "You are! I knew it from the first moment." He continued firmly, as she did not reply, "believe me, I'm not merely curious or prying; but when I take on a case it does, inevitably, usurp the place of first importance in my mind. And you see you are part of your sister's case; I can't separate you off. You could throw light, I am convinced, on the cause of her trouble, but I feel you are holding back some information which is vital to a true understanding and diagnosis of her disease. I want to cure her, and incidentally I want very much to help you all; I think, moreover, I can do so, but not if I am forced by your attitude to work in the dark. What's more, I don't consider it worth my while taking it on at all if I am to be treated in this extraordinary way. You will understand this, I am sure." A less formal note crept into his voice. "If I knew why you are so afraid, perhaps . . ."

There was a pause, then she said in a voice which belied her words, so tense was it with the effort at self-control: "I am not afraid; not, that is, except for her."

He smiled and said softly, yet authoritatively: "Don't forget I'm a doctor—*and* my finger is on your pulse."

The bluff worked; she withdrew her hand as if it could reveal the most intimate secret; then she said—and now there was sincerity in her tones: "I think I have honestly told you all there is to tell about Betty; I don't know any more. As for my fears, you are wrong there, they aren't connected in any way with her, just a silly complex of my own."

"Perhaps there is a connection all the same. Can't you tell me?"

"Oh, well, if you like, but it's so stupid. It's merely that I hate the idea of going to Egypt—that's all."

"That's unusual," he remarked judiciously, "most people would give anything for the chance of seeing all the tombs and monuments and things."

He heard the catch in her breath. "It's that," she cried, in a tone of actual distress, "it is the tombs—and the temples! It's quite illogical, but ever since I was a tiny child I've been terrified of anything Egyptian. Why, the first time Father took me into the mummy room at the British Museum for a great treat I was promptly sick and had to be carried out, screaming. They never got me near it again, but later on I went once just to prove to myself that it was a childish fancy; but I had the same feelings exactly—nausea, terror. I can't explain, it was just a nightmarish feeling. And now to have actually to go there, to . . ." She broke off as if aware that she had almost said too much. "But all this is quite beside the point," she added, her voice grown cold and distant again.

"Not so much as you think. Didn't it strike you as odd that I should say, without knowing anything about your 'complex' as you call it, that your sister ought not to go to Egypt—that it might even be fatal?"

"Yes, yes!" She was eager now. "It expressed my own fear exactly."

"Yet you insist that your sister's fiancé and her father will not allow themselves to be persuaded to change the plans for what appears to be merely a holiday undertaken on the rather remote chance of doing her some good? Do you really expect me to believe that? Look here," he continued after a pause, "I must get things straighter if I am to cure her; as I said just now, this won't be possible unless I am in possession of the full facts. It isn't fair on me or on you." He rose and began walking slowly up and down in front of her. As she sat silently, staring at the deck, he stopped before her. "No doctor can do a patient any good if, when he writes out a prescription, the patient's relatives instantly say: 'Oh, she mustn't take that,' but refuse to give valid reasons. If there *are* valid reasons—right! He'll adapt himself to them, find some other prescription; but just to be frustrated—you must admit it makes all work impossible. Come, Miss Mannering," he added as she still remained silent, "you are obviously one of those women who value logic and fair dealing; is it giving me a sporting chance?"

She did not reply at once, but presently said in a low voice: "And you believe you really can cure her?"

"I honestly believe I'm already on the track of the trouble; but I'll get no further if all my clues are deliberately obscured."

"What exactly is it you want to know?"

"What will you tell me?"

She spoke with concentrated passion. "Anything—everything, if I thought you could save her."

"You mean that?"

"Absolutely."

"Good!" He sat down in his chair. "Then we'll start right at the beginning, if you don't mind, but first have a cigarette." While he lit it for her he continued conversationally: "And now, please, I'd like a sketch of your complete family history."

"Oh, it would take ages to tell you all that."

"Hedging already," he thought. Aloud he said: "Never mind, it's not very late—or are you awfully tired? You've had a pretty heavy day."

She gave him a quick glance of gratitude; she was obviously unused to such solicitude. "Of course I'm not, I couldn't sleep if I tried."

She smoked in silence for a few moments. Her close-cropped, fair hair glinted occasionally as the slight roll of the ship caused a distant light to play upon it. Her pose was full of unselfconscious grace and vigour. Although her face was not beautiful, too irregular, too determined, it held promise to him of something infinitely more alluring. "Gallant" was the word that had come to him at first sight of her; now the thought flashed into his mind what a wonderful companion a woman like this might make, with those qualities he divined in her: humour, intelligence, endurance and the hidden passion which the curve of her lips betrayed.

As if aware of his speculations she stirred and faced him swiftly, almost with suspicion.

"I really can't think why you should want to know everything about us, it seems such a waste of time. We're in no way interesting. Dull—dull, that's what we are, all of us, except perhaps Betty."

"Well, I haven't found you that, exactly; but carry on. Don't forget I'm a doctor and your whole family is my 'case' at the moment; you ought to know how vital the study of originating causes, of heredity, etc., is in any attempt to arrive at a correct diagnosis, particularly when one is dealing with a case of this kind."

He proceeded forthwith to ask her various questions of a physiological kind. "Now," he said at last, "we come to the question of environment. I want to know something about your lives. Your father, for instance: has he always been an archæologist?"

"Oh, yes, he's always been mad about it, even in the early days when he had a business and we were fairly well off; now it's become a mania . . ." She paused, blowing smoke slowly into the air. "He never was a good business man, but when my mother died soon after Betty's birth and he was landed with the job of bringing up two young girls he just went to pieces. He got frightened, I think; he always hated any kind of responsibility. He became slack and consequently had some heavy financial losses; then he got the idea into his head that life was treating him rottenly and that everyone had a down on him. After a bit he let everything go, lived on his income and just buried himself more and more in his Egyptology, hiding in the past because the present wasn't to his liking, I suspect; you see he just hadn't got the character to face up to facts." She turned to her companion anxiously: "Don't think I'm being cruel, but I've been forced to analyse things. Father's a dear, but it's no good pretending that he isn't a complete failure. I think, in his heart, he knows it, so he likes to imagine he's a great archæologist, and if he'd only had the chance would have been as famous as Budge or some of the others. All his life it's been his ambition to make some extraordinary discovery, so as to prove to the world what a misunderstood man he really is. Of course there was no hope of that while we were so poor, and naturally things got worse and worse. By the time I was sixteen our income had dwindled to a mere pittance and the responsibility for them both devolved on me. Fortunately I'm rather good at organization and

I'm more a man than a woman, really, so I managed to work my way into quite a well-paid job. Betty, of course, has never been strong enough to earn anything much, although she's very keen on journalism and writes quite well. But with this illness she'll never be able to do more than be a free lance; though her dream is to make a *coup* and get on the regular staff of some big newspaper. Still, things were going along as well as could be expected until Nikolai came."

"Mm; I gather you don't much approve of this gentleman?"

She sat silent for a moment; when at last she spoke it was with care, as one choosing a way over dangerous ground.

"Oh, he's charming really, a most generous man, devoted to Betty, but—well, we don't seem to hit it off, he and I—I expect it's partly my fault. I've never quite trusted him, I've always felt he might let Betty down. And I know he's suspicious of me too. It's one of those things one can't explain—a queer, inward antagonism with apparently no logical cause for it. Perhaps I'm jealous—it may be that. I'm devoted to Betty and have always been the one person she turned to, the one person who ordered the whole household. Now he's taken over the reins and they think everything he says or does must be right . . ." She threw away the stub of her cigarette viciously. "Yes, I expect it is my fault. But it's so odd, we're always trying to be friends, yet never quite bring it off. Now, of course, with this wretched Egyptian business, there's no pretence left. We're just in opposite camps—and I think he hates me. Well, let him! I wouldn't care a damn if it didn't make for unhappiness all round."

"You forget," he reminded her gently, "I don't know yet the real object of this trip, it's obvious that Betty's health is only part of the story."

"The idea did originate because of her health," she said; "as I told you, Dr. Zarov believed the air was right for her, that it would probably cure her."

"Of course, I remember. And he was going to be there just to show you the sights, wasn't he?" said Simon drily.

"Yes, he was going to show us the sights, of course." But she had the grace to blush and he made a mental note that she was one of the most inefficient liars he had ever met.

He leant forward. "Come, be frank with me; you promised, you remember. What exactly are you going to do in Egypt?"

"I—can't tell you; it's a secret. I swore I wouldn't say anything."

"Oh, all right; I wouldn't dream of forcing your confidence; but it's only fair to say I feel that upon this hangs all hope of curing your sister."

She sat up abruptly. "All right, I will tell you. But you must swear to know nothing about it. Zarov made us each promise separately." She glanced uneasily about her, "He's such a strange man."

"You needn't be afraid of him," Simon put in quietly.

"I'm not afraid of anyone." Her voice was so sharp and indignant that he had to repress a smile. "Anyway," she continued, "all this secrecy is absurd, to my mind. In fact I don't understand it. The whole thing is we are going to do some excavating. But Zarov and Nick seem so afraid someone will get wind of it. They think there's something particularly spectacular hidden in this place and, of course, the others, each for his own reasons, have got all wrought up about it. Nick has been promised a large sum of money if we succeed; Father will be hailed as an archæological hero and Betty will make a journalistic map that will give her instant fame."

"And you—will just be sick," he grinned. She grinned back.

"Yes; and now you know why I am the only one who isn't shrieking for joy. I don't get any personal kick out of it anywhere."

"This is going to cost a lot. Who's financing the expedition? Is Annerly rich, then?"

"Oh no, he's only put a comparatively small sum into it, but it represents all his savings, all the money that might go to cure Betty and that they would have to marry on, apart from the moderate income he earns. That's what's so mad to me—but I can understand it in a way. He's a gambler by nature. He's half Russian and had a hellish time during the war; not only lost everything he possessed, but was caught by the Revolution and was in prison for several years, went through every kind of horror; he escaped at last and came to England, very ill, ruined. He met Betty when he was just about to throw up the sponge, he says. Ever since he's been working like a black, trying to build up his business again so that he can get her cured. I genuinely admired him for that. But he worked far too hard and his health gave way—his lungs had been affected in Russia. It was essential for him to get out of England, and as Dr. Zarov was so keen on Egypt for them both, it was decided to pool all our resources and go there for a cruise. We all needed a change almost as much as he did. But even then, when it was merely a question of a trip, nothing more, I couldn't bear the thought of it. I admit I did everything to put them off. I pointed out that it would only tantalize Father if he got out there and couldn't dig, and it wasn't likely we could have got permission to do so, even if we had had enough money; none of us had any influence, and Nick, even though he had done a little work with a friend at Thebes before the war, had no real experience.

"Then, just as we had almost decided to give up the idea and winter in the South of France, Zarov introduced Nick to a man called Derwent who told us about his concession and a ramp he had discovered before he went sick, which, he was convinced, led to a tomb. He had been desperately ill—he looked simply awful; no one could find out exactly what was the matter, but the doctors all said he must on no account go back and rather hinted he wasn't likely to live long. He was in a dreadful state about his discovery, couldn't bear to think of dying before the tomb had been opened, as for some reason he was convinced it had never been plundered. He implored Father to take on the work and was even ready to pay our expenses out. He and Zarov swore us all to secrecy, as I told you, because they seemed to think someone was trying to get the Egyptian Government to cancel the concession and give it to them or something; I really don't know what all the fuss was about, I've no experience of this kind of thing, and anyway I hated the idea so much I really couldn't even pretend an interest. Of course the others jumped at it. You've no idea the amount of hush-hush business there has been going on. Personally I hate all this feeling of intrigue, but I'd promised to say nothing, that's why I kept it up. But now—well, I've told you," she ended; rather, he thought, on a note of bravado.

"And you know nothing more about it at all?"

"Nothing; all the arrangements are being left to Zarov and his agents. He is meeting us in Cairo and everything will be more or less ready for a start up to Lybia, I gather, where the beastly place is."

"He's going with you, I suppose?"

"That's the idea, I believe; why?"

"I just wondered." He sat silent a few moments. "I wish I could get your father to talk to me about it," he said presently. "I quite realize now how difficult it is going to be to dissuade him, but if I could discuss matters openly . . ."

"He'd probably tell you anything if you talked to him enough about his nasty little Ushebtiu or whatever they're called, and were careful to defer to his opinion all the time," she said drily.

He smiled. "Thanks for the hint; but I don't think Nick, as you rather appropriately call him, would be quite so amenable."

"No, he disliked you on sight—said so!" She threw away the end of her third cigarette and rose. "I must go, I don't want to leave my sister for too long."

"I'll see her to-morrow morning and I should like another talk with you. How is it I never see you on deck?"

"We were told to stay in our cabin." She made a face. "I believe Derwent and Zarov between them have spies on the brain."

"Well, I consider it very bad for your sister, in fact for everyone. I'm going to prescribe a lot of fresh air for Miss Betty—and for you, too," he added.

"I think it would be an excellent prescription. Personally I loathe being stuffed up down there."

"To be taken before and after every meal in one hour doses, preferably in the company of the doctor." He called after her softly.

She turned and gave him the first really friendly smile he had seen. "I'll see what we can do," she called back as she disappeared down the gangway.

That evening Simon had a long talk with Ahmed who was travelling steerage, made up to look like an itinerant vendor of carpets from Armenia. It was also arranged with the Captain that he should be put ashore before the rest of the passengers. Simon was armed with many papers which would pave the way for special facilities. He never ceased to be amazed at the authority that Weyland, or those behind him, could wield when they chose.

The next morning he went to see his patient. She was eager to get up and welcomed the suggestion that she should go on deck. Annerly made a slight demur, but it would have presumably looked too suspicious to challenge so sensible a suggestion, so he had perforce to give way, although he insisted on accompanying them.

When they had gone off, Simon began to talk to the old man. Before the others returned he had so won his confidence that he was telling him all about the proposed expedition and had even produced a map showing the site of the concession. When he heard that Simon himself was something of an archæologist, had spent a season at Amarna and knew of some excellent and experienced workmen, his delight knew no bounds.

"Perhaps if you have time, you could come with us? That would be pleasant, very pleasant!" he chattered.

Simon was non-committal. He was too wise to appear eager, and talked vaguely of a trip up the Nile he had planned with a friend. However, from that moment, despite Annerly's antagonism, he was established as *persona grata* with the Mannering family, especially as Betty continued to improve. Even Annerly showed a rather grudging gratitude for this. Whatever sinister mysteries surrounded him, it was obvious that he was genuinely devoted to the girl.

Very gradually, with infinite care and no little skill Simon was day by day consolidating his friendship with Carol. At first he told himself that he was only doing it out of policy; but it was not long before he became aware that her image was obtruding itself more and more into the pattern of his life. He became indignant then, and determined to shut her out. He had learned scientifically to control his mental processes in India, but Carol, her face, her walk, the sound of her voice, was proof against all but the most strenuous forms of exorcism. And one morning, awakening suddenly from some half-remembered, yet vivid and strange dream of seeing her, clad as an Egyptian, fleeing before him between the fearful images of infernal gods, he knew. His hands were stretched out still, the yearnings and agony of the loss of something dearer than life still contracted his heart. No, he had no doubts any more about his feelings for this woman; and he realized that actually from the first sight of her some deep inner part of him had already known. That sense of familiarity—what had it been but an instant recognition of a lost, but still cherished love? To Simon, who accepted, as completely as the average Westerner accepts the tenets of Christianity, the doctrine that again and again the enduring spirit of man casts its reflections upon the mirror that is called physical existence, in order to perfect itself and to finish the work it has begun, this explained the fact that he should have been the man chosen to save this girl and those she loved from a threat of disaster. If they had met before, loved before, perhaps wronged each other before, who else had the right but he? And perhaps, he thought, there was more to it even than the working out of this personal love. This shadow, half-apprehended even by her, which hung over them all, might it not also be projected by some monstrous Egyptian image—for he saw it thus—which had been generated also in that mutual past of theirs—something which belonged to all of them?

What, then, did this Mr. X. stand for, that he should have the power to menace these apparently innocent lives? No effect without its cause—he believed that; and he believed moreover that the Law of Causation held good for all forms and in all dimensions. The thing was to discover the originating cause through which he and this group of people had been drawn into the net of this unknown man.

In the light of such a realization, his mission itself became filled with a deeper and more far-reaching significance. All of them—even X. and Zarov—were no longer strangers to be used or combated and then abandoned, but intrinsic parts of the very pattern and texture of his own existence. He felt rather like a man who is doing a jig-saw puzzle and glimpses suddenly the relation of some parts to the whole. He locked his cabin door and spent the rest of the morning in an endeavour to analyse each piece more thoroughly. He took them one by one, studying the potentialities of each.

Carol and the old man had, comparatively speaking, few complexities, Zarov and X. were, at the moment, outside his range. But Betty was another matter. Here was an hysteric, probably also a medium, a perfect subject for hypnotism, who had come under the influence of a man who was—what had Weyland once said?—"an adept in the knowledge and control of the human mind!" From several strange sentences which had fallen from her lips when she was returning to consciousness he was convinced that Zarov still had her, in some way, in his power. Yet he had succeeded in bringing her back from her trance; it was, he felt, as if in so doing, he had won the first round.

As for Annerly, he could not make up his mind about him. How much did he know? To what extent was he cognisant of Zarov's true purpose? In any case it was probable that either Derwent or Zarov had, so to speak, a thumb on him. Simon wished he knew more of that financial deal about which Carol had spoken so vaguely. One thing was certain, of them all, Annerly was the only one who might be in a position to tell him a little more about the expedition, but he was also the only one who could be relied upon not to do so. Simon saw clearly that his influence would counteract any efforts he himself might make to stop them carrying out their present intentions. On the other hand, he thought, if to stop them were impossible, perhaps it might not be such a bad thing if they did carry on, so long as he could contrive to be with them when they opened the tomb. For supposing there were a secret in this place, or the clue to other secrets, to procure them for Weyland would be the surest way of preventing X. from ever using them in the way they feared.

"If only I knew what it was I'm supposed to be looking for," he groaned, "or if only I could see what is likely to happen so as to be prepared . . ."

Then, suddenly, an idea struck him. He jumped up from the bunk on which he had been lying and went on deck.

Fortunately he found the two girls alone. Betty greeted him vivaciously. She was a queer, puckish-looking little thing, with a mop of black hair and strange greeny-blue eyes. No one looking at her there, gay and flushed, would have imagined she could be subject to such attacks, those long periods of coma, those frenzies which bordered on madness.

"I'm terribly thrilled," she announced, "at the idea that we'll be in to-morrow. We won't lose sight of you, will we? You've been so marvellous with me."

"You'll have Dr. Zarov," he said, smiling.

"I know." Her brows drew together. "It's funny, when I'm away from him I somehow never want to see him."

"But when you do see him?"

"Oh, then he's so kind—I forget . . ." She broke off, shivering suddenly, while her eyes grew vague. He saw fear written on Carol's face.

"I hope I shall meet him," he said briskly, "he certainly sounds must remarkable. By the way, Miss Betty, have you ever had your horoscope cast?"

She was all eagerness. "Oh, no, can you do it? I'd love to have it done!"

"I wouldn't," put in Carol sharply. "I think it's very dangerous monkeying about with the future, and anyway it's all rubbish—superstition."

Simon raised his brows. "Oh—have you studied astrology, then?"

"Well—no; but one reads such a lot of piffle nowadays in papers and things."

He smiled. "So you do about other forms of science when they are watered down to suit the public palate; it doesn't invalidate them, all the same."

"But this isn't a science."

"A most exact—and exacting—science, believe me."

"Anyway," she parried, "I still think it's very dangerous to know the future—does more harm than good," and she glanced towards her sister.

"I see you've got the usual idea that astrology is a kind of glorified fortune telling," he said, "which, if I may say so, proves your complete ignorance. Any scientific knowledge can be abused, vulgarised and employed for debased ends; in proof of which you've only got to look at the way we are using our knowledge now, creating weapons of destruction which may end in abolishing us altogether! Astrology isn't immune from this kind of treatment, but that's not its true aim. I, for instance, find it invaluable in diagnosis. It shows me to what diseases patients are most susceptible, what tendencies in mind and body are most pronounced; I can delve deeper than an X-ray or a scalpel—yes, than the most acute psychologist also. I tell you, medical astrology is one of the most neglected, yet greatest aids to the relief of human ills."

Carol stared at this outburst of enthusiasm from one whom she had always considered admirably detached and calm.

"But on the face of it," she said rather scornfully, "how can stars millions of miles away affect human lives?"

He smiled. "Well, what should we do without the sun? Don't its rays play an all-important part in our lives, both physical and mental? The moon, too: the tides answer to its pull; dogs, lunatics, all sensitives in fact react definitely to its influence, and certain bodily functions are regulated by its cycles. Why then should only the sun and moon affect us and not the other planets? You'll probably say 'because they are nearer,' but when you think of the speed with which light travels, really, distance is only a relative matter; their influence isn't so obvious, that's all. Even the scientists are turning their attention to the action of the so-called Cosmic rays upon the earth and its inhabitants. There are millions of rays impinging upon our bodies all the while of which we are unaware and the influence of which we ignore completely."

"But I always feel," Carol complained, "that a belief in astrology would do away with free will."

He laughed. "I'm not going to start arguing about free will; but I would like you to try to think of one single action in your life which has been dictated by complete free will, quite uninfluenced by outside pressure. Personally I'd like to know how free will is possible while we are such slaves to circumstances, to our emotions, our desires, our antecedents, environment, heredity! Whatever we do, if you dare to be really honest, is the result of causes far more remote than people will readily admit. The psychoanalyst will prove that to you—but to my mind he, even, doesn't go back far enough," he hesitated; "chance—free will—do you think it's due to either we are on this ship—on our way to Egypt now?"

Carol gave him a swift, half-puzzled glance, but did not reply. A short silence fell which Simon broke by returning to his subject. He was speaking with a two-fold purpose and even at the risk of sounding rather didactic, had no intention of abandoning it.

"But as a matter of fact," he continued more lightly, "neurology doesn't necessarily imply predestination. The stars are influences in the life—no more. The Chaldeans used to teach that a strong man could rule his stars and only the weak were governed by them."

"Most of us are weak," said Betty rather sadly.

"Granted; but only through knowing our weaknesses can we discover how to conquer them. That's where astrology comes in. Of course it's not a thing to be broadcast, put into the hands of the unwary and ignorant; it can injure, it can be a poison, but its value is curative if it is understood. That's why I use it." He leant forward and laid his hand gently on Betty's frail, claw-like little hand. "If I could cast your map, it would reveal more about you and the sources of your illness than I could discover after weeks, perhaps months and years of research."

"Have you proved that?" asked Carol. She had been listening intently to his words; he knew that her critical yet receptive mind had seized upon the information he was flinging out with such apparent casualness, and he was perfectly aware that she would put him through a gruelling third degree later on. But he always liked minds that didn't accept new things too readily; a healthy scepticism was a good corrective to all the sentimental pseudo-mystical tosh which passed for occultism nowadays.

"Give me the details of the birth of a perfect stranger—without even a name attached—and I'll present you with an accurate reading of his character, a short sketch of the main currents of his life, also any tendencies to disease or constitutional weakness, within twenty-four hours," he said lightly.

"I wish I could! But aren't you supposed to know the exact hour or something?"

"Yes, exact moment and place, but of course it can be done without, only it's the devil of a job."

"Well, I can tell you Betty's; I remember it. Mother died then, you see. But it wouldn't be quite a fair test," she added judiciously.

"Never mind, but I'd like to have it, all the same; yours, too if I may."

"'Oh, mine! Father might have some idea, but I doubt it; he'd sure to be a few hours, if not a few days out."

"That's a pity. If you'll give me your sister's now, I'll work it out and bring it along when you are settled in your hotel. Luckily I carry my astrologer's Bible with me wherever I go."

"What's that?" asked Betty.

"An ephemeris—I've got a collection of them bound, dating back about fifty years."

"What is it, though, a tome on magic or something?"

"Nothing so exciting, just a table of planetary movements published every year in London—I told you it was an exact science!"

While he was writing down the details, Carol got up and started collecting their cushions and rugs.

"This is the last evening," she said in a low voice, "tomorrow—Egypt."

Betty had jumped up and gone to join Annerly who had appeared lower down the deck.

Gently Simon took the rug from Carol's hand. "Need you go yet?"

For once she made no demur, but followed him to the rail and leant there by his side without speaking. At last she said, half below her breath: "Why do things have to end?"

He drew so near that his arm was touching hers. "So that others may begin," he answered in the same tone.

She looked up. "But you don't understand how I dread—this beginning." She was silent again, staring out into the darkness which hid the land they were now so rapidly approaching. "Do you believe in dreams?" she asked presently.

"That's rather my profession," he remarked.

She made a grimace. "Oh, Freud, and that kind of thing! True for some people up to a point, no doubt; but I wasn't meaning that; I meant—premonitions."

"Of course; I think our inner self, the part of us that knows so much more than the conscious mind which is governed and restricted by the brain, puts many things over by means of dreams."

"You really believe that?" Her voice sounded frightened, yet eager.

"Most certainly." She shuddered. "That makes it worse."

"What is your dream?"

"It's about this place we're going to. It's a horrible dream; I can't give you any details, I just see huge rocks, cliffs, and a moon looking down at me; and I'm running and running in sheer terror; and then suddenly everything gets dark, and I wake up choking. But it really isn't as definite as that, it's sensations rather than things to cause sensations." Her hands were clutching the rail now, the knuckles showed white. "And to-morrow it begins. I've got to go forward alone, into that—dream. Here I'm safe, protected, there's the sea and the air and—" she broke off, turning away with a short laugh, "what an hysterical fool you must think I am!"

"I don't," he said, "I don't."

She straightened herself with a sigh. "I really must go below, I've got to pack for everyone. Please forget my stupid fancies."

"I've no intention of forgetting them." He put his hand on her arm and, surprisingly, she let it rest there. "Listen," he continued firmly. "I want you to realize one thing, perhaps it may help you a little: whatever happens you won't be alone when you come to those rocks."

She looked up, startled: "What do you mean?"

"Just this: that you won't be alone because I shall be there, too; it's no good your protesting, somehow I shall be there." Suddenly he gave her his impish, schoolboy grin, "it's written in the stars, fatally, irrevocably—no free will! Now off you go to bed and sleep well. There's no need to dream to-night, but if you should, just think, when you run down that valley under the moon, that I shall be running with you." He took her by the shoulders and smiled into her wide eyes. "No nightmares, do you understand? And to-morrow is a beginning, the beginning of a fight perhaps—but of other things as well, happier things. I have a sort of feeling you rather like a fight, anyway."

She gave a laugh which sounded rather more like a sob. "Perhaps," she whispered, then breaking from him suddenly, as if she didn't trust herself to stay, ran forward after Betty and Annerly.

Simon, smiling, went below.

CHAPTER III

THE DARK GENTLEMAN

SIMON made a point of absenting himself when the time came for them to go on shore. He did not want to be seen by anyone who might meet the Mannerings, but Ahmed was there, metamorphosed now into an unmistakable Egyptian idler on the quayside; he would get all the information necessary.

On arriving in Cairo Simon spent a very busy day. He had a number of friends in the city both among the native and European population, for he had been several times to Egypt on missions for Weyland, apart from that season spent in America.

It was growing late when he got back. He had put up at one of the larger hotels near the Nile where he had personal friends among the staff. It was a good centre, besides being near the unpretentious hotel in which Zarov had booked rooms for the Mannerings.

He settled down to study the information he had collected; as far as it went it was not particularly valuable. However, it was all he could hope to glean from such sources as were at his disposal, but he knew Ahmed would supplement it through his friends among men regularly engaged by the various parties of excavators.

He went through his notes with care, memorizing addresses and data, then burned them. After that he settled down to Betty's horoscope.

He worked on and on; the little jotted calculations grew, were checked, checked again. Once he sat up with an exclamation; his face was set and grave—grave as a doctor's face might be when his diagnosis reveals an incurable disease. Then he rose, rummaged among his papers and brought out his own horoscope. More calculations; at last he flung his pen down and sat back staring into space.

"They tally," he whispered, "but what can it mean death? . . ." He rose and began pacing the room, sucking at his pipe, long since grown cold.

~ ~ ~ ~ ~

Next morning early he went to the Mannerings' hotel. He found Betty in the lounge idly turning over illustrated papers. She looked ill and drawn, but her whole expression changed when she caught sight of him.

"Oh, my dear doctor!" she exclaimed with her usual spontaneity, "how nice of you to have come so soon!"

He sat down next to her. "And how are you?"

She shrugged. "I had a ghastly night; you know, dreams, half-awake. I'm feeling fagged out."

"What does Dr. Zarov think of you?"

"Oh, he didn't meet us after all." (Simon had known that.) "He sent a message to say he'd been called away, but a friend of his, a very nice man, is going to take us round and show us the ropes."

"I'm sorry, I should like to have met him," he said casually.

She made a grimace. "*I* met him—in my dreams. Once I actually thought he was in the room—so odd."

His eyes narrowed. "I'll give you something harmless to get you off to-night. Where is your sister?" he added, looking round.

"In the smoking-room, over there."

"I'd like a few words with her, if I may."

Her rather monkey-like little face screwed up in a mischievous grin. "Only a few? I should have thought . . ."

"And you'd be right." He looked at her gravely; another ally was just what he wanted. "Do you think, in the language of the novelettes, that I have a chance?"

"How should I know? Carol is such a man hater."

"Oh, that's a phase that can be outgrown fairly easily, I believe," he laughed.

"I do hope so, but she's never liked anyone; men have been attracted, of course, but she has always spoilt things by jeering at them or snapping their heads off." She sighed, "if she only knew . . ."

"Well, my head's screwed on pretty tightly, so I think I'll take a chance on it—if you'll forgive me—"

Just as he was about to enter the smoking-room she called after him: "Oh, but my horoscope!" He stopped in frown just in time; that was the last thing he wished broadcast in the lounge of an hotel, but it was obvious one could never hope for much discretion from Betty Mannering.

"I haven't nearly finished it yet," he replied lightly. "I'll tell you when it's ready."

On the threshold of the smoking-room he paused, glancing swiftly round. Carol he saw at once, writing in the window. A few other English people were scattered about and in one corner was a dark man, obviously an Egyptian, entrenched behind a newspaper; but Simon saw more than this, for he had caught a swift, searching glance before the paper was raised to hide the face.

He strolled across the room; his voice when he spoke was clear and very casual. "Well, well, Miss Mannering! And how do you like Egypt? I've brought those photos I promised you—your sister thinks they're first-rate."

The girl looked up startled. Betty would have said: "What photos? I don't remember any photos," but Carol, as if her receptive mind had instantly registered the warning he sent her, after that first puzzled glance, merely smiled and said graciously: "How kind of you to have bothered to come all this way."

"Not a bit, a pleasure! Pooh," he added, looking round, "you have chosen a hot place, I must say—all this smoke! What about a little stroll outside while you look at them. Have you seen the terrace and garden? It's really not bad for its size, and you do get a breath of air."

"But my letters—"

"Oh, come, can't they wait?"

"Perhaps they can." She got up, putting some loose sheets into her handbag; as they reached the door he continued loudly: "And what about showing you a few sights? I don't know much about it, but I've had a good guide promised me." The moment they got into the lounge he dropped his voice. "We're watched. I must talk to you alone."

Betty had tactfully disappeared, but this was no place to escape observation.

"I hope the garden is all right," he had raised his voice again, for the dark gentleman was sauntering out of the smoking-room. "It's through here to the left"—and in a whisper, *"don't look behind."*

The garden consisted merely of a paved square with a few palms and tubs of flowers, where tables stood under striped awnings; but in one corner there was a seat so situated that it would be practically impossible for an eavesdropper to approach unseen.

"I hope I've got something that'll look like photos if our friend comes along," he murmured, searching in his case. "Yes, here, visiting-cards from people on board: Hiram O. Rusington—the

Misses Ennerly-Smith—charming, don't you think? So like them!"

"Have you gone mad, or what?" she asked, half-angry, half-amused. "What is all this play-acting?"

"A grim necessity, unfortunately. Do you mind if I sit rather nearer you and we keep our heads together?" Again his voice changed. "How stupid, I've dropped one."

As the card fluttered to the ground, he swung round abruptly as if to pick it up. "Thought so—our dark gentleman just come to look at the view through that french window. Well, good luck to him—he's going to have a busy time! Do you mind if presently I make a pretence of carrying on a mild flirtation with you?"

"Not particularly, but I don't see the object . . ."

"That's what I've got to explain to you, but I don't want to rouse any suspicions; as a matter of fact I think I've been a bit of a fool coming here at all."

"But what's it all about?"

"It's going to take a lot of explaining, I'm afraid. I wish we could get out of here."

"But why can't you say what you've got to say now?"

"I'd rather not; you don't know Egypt, there are ears on every bush and in every grain of sand. The best thing would be for us to go for a drive. I've got my servant outside made up as a taxi-driver—it will look quite normal if I hail him. We could go to the Pyramids—I'd like to be the first to show them to you, and I know a spot there where I defy anyone to listen. Will you come?"

"It all seems rather melodramatic," she said doubtfully, "but I will if you really think it's necessary."

"Right! Run up and get your hat and I'll get the taxi."

He found Ahmed in violent altercation with an American who was endeavouring to hire him. Ahmed's price, in desperation, was rising to fantastic heights, but the man seemed quite unaware of these flights of fancy till Simon offered his services in the dispute, and after pointing out that the driver was a thief and a bandit, got him another at a reasonable fee, and started in to haggle with his servant till Carol appeared. Then Ahmed suddenly gave way with a final wail, and taking Allah to witness that he was a poor man and that the Effendi was taking bread out of the mouths of his fourteen children, started to drive off at breakneck speed. The decrepit car flung them from side to side with such violence that conversation was impossible until, having shot down narrow alleys and through sun-baked squares, they came out by this circuitous route on to the Rue Gézirah.

Presently Carol said: "I do believe we *are* followed, there is the same boy on a bike who was in front of the hotel—I happened to notice him."

"I know; pal of Ahmed's, hotel tout. He's just following to see that no one else does, though that first spurt of ours should have given anyone the slip."

She gave him a despairing look. "Really—"

"Yes, I know, but I'm not taking chances. Anyone who does get on our track will be set upon by that young man who's guaranteed to stick to him like a leech and spoil any game he may have on hand for the rest of the day."

She gave a sigh and resigned herself to wait, in the meantime drinking in the beauty and strangeness of this road which led on and on towards those mighty shapes that appeared now and again ahead, glimpsed like a mysterious goal, sublime, absolutely simple, dwarfing everything about them, not by their height, but by some other quality which she felt, but could not define. Even when at last the Pyramids towered close at hand, they remained infinitely remote from the rushing, modern world with its ephemeral activities which, tossed up at their feet like driftwood upon the waves of Time, would soon be engulfed in that Immensity in which alone, it seemed, they dwelt immutable.

"I will take you," said Simon, when their car stopped at last, "where you can't see the trippers or hear their wretched babble. It's amazing how the desert manages, somehow, to obliterate it all in a few moments."

They walked on, side by side. She was silent. Already, as he had said, the finger of the desert had touched her. They were cut off, he and she; here was only silence, heat and a strange feeling of unreality.

They passed under a broken pylon doorway into a space of sand where the remains of a wall cast an oblong of shade. He flung down a rug he had brought from the car.

"This is a favourite place of mine," he said at last in a low voice; "it has no particular archæological value, so tourists don't bother about it; that's why it has retained, I think, something of its mystery and its remoteness." He touched her hand lightly: "Do you hate this, too?"

"No," she murmured, "no—not this."

He sighed. "I wish we could just sit here and give ourselves up to it, but we mustn't. I've simply got to talk to you."

She turned, frowning, looking a little dazed like one awakened from sleep. "What is it? About Betty?"

"Partly, but it's about this tomb, too, this place where you are going—or rather, are *not* going, if I can prevent it."

He paused, staring through the pylon doorway to the empty rim of the desert against the sky. "I'll have to say a lot of things that'll probably seem absolute rubbish to you," he continued presently, "but I want you to try and get away for a little while from the modern, hard, competitive world you're used to. Look at all this!" He waved his hand round. "Our ordinary values and standards mean nothing here. This is a different world. We are always in such a hurry that we forget things, but the East retains everything, knowledge, experience—that's why anything can happen in the East."

She made no comment. His voice, the atmosphere, even those faint, distant sounds of guides and tourists which somehow did not seem incongruous any more in the vaster silence which encompassed everything here, were beginning to cast a kind of spell over her. But he was speaking again.

"If what I say sounds too fantastic don't veto it at once, put in on a shelf, as it were, for future consideration. Will you do that?"

"I'll try."

"Thanks. Well, first I'll tell you all I've found out about this tomb, for I've been doing quite a bit of investigating. It looks as if your dream were a direct foreshadowing of events." He proceeded to give her a short *résumé* of the stories Weyland had told him about the tomb, which he had since confirmed on every count. She listened without interruption and when he had finished sat for a little while smoking thoughtfully.

"Can one," she asked at length, "take those superstitious stories of the natives seriously? Surely most tombs have got a bad name."

"Not a bit; there's usually no difficulty at all in getting workmen. But they won't work here, and don't forget fatalities *have* actually occurred."

"But that might be coincidence. How could a tomb injure anyone? It's preposterous."

"It's not the tomb, but what's in it." At her puzzled stare, he added: "I told you the place was called the Valley of the Dark Ones."

"Dark ones?" She repeated the words, frowning. "I don't see."

"You've heard of black magicians, surely, haven't you?"

"But you really don't believe there were such people, witches with familiars, and all that sort of thing?"

"I believe there were—and *are*—such people," he asserted quietly.

She made a gesture of irritation. "You must be joking; those old superstitions have been exploded centuries ago."

He shook his head. "I can assure you that there are, all over the world, numbers of very intelligent people who not only believe in black magic, but still practise it. I could even give you addresses in respectable London streets where the Black Mass is celebrated quite regularly, to say nothing of even more dangerous practices."

She shook her head in bewilderment. "But they must be pathological cases, self-deluded, hysterical . . ."

"A good many are that, certainly; but the genuinely dangerous kind—no. You need as much intelligence and self-control to be a really efficient black magician as you do to succeed in any other form of mental activity, good or bad. Success and failure depend upon certain fundamental laws, you know."

"But magic is just that," she cried triumphantly, "a claim to be able to transcend natural laws. That's why no enlightened, modern person can be expected to believe in it."

He smiled rather wryly. "I suppose you believe in the miracles of Jesus—or don't you?"

"Well—" she hesitated and hedged, "a lot of people don't."

"No, because some people measure everything by their own limitations. But there *is* plenty of evidence for cures just as spectacular even in our day. However, supposing one says that Jesus, Buddha—all their followers, the Christian and Eastern saints—were hysterics, fakes, what you will, even then one is still up against the fact that man's mind, as it advances into the unknown, is learning increasingly how to control elements which hitherto have been considered outside its jurisdiction. Just think for a moment," he continued as she made no reply, "what our ancestors would have said if a man, by touching a button, illuminated a room; of invisible rays that could ring bells, of music coming from a disk and voices singing from a box—oh, a hundred things that we take for granted! Why, the perpetrators of such devilish activities would have been burned at the stake at once." He leant forward as if determined to drive his meaning through the barrier of her scepticism. "*We* don't call this magic, merely knowledge; and there's your answer! Magic, black or white, miracles, even prophecies are nothing more than an understanding and control of laws which have existed since the beginning of time, but have not yet been discovered. Your magician does not transcend or break laws, no—nor did Jesus—he understands and uses them, that's all."

"Do you mean to say if I liked I could become a magician?"

"Certainly; black or white, according to choice."

She shuddered. "Why is it that talk of magic always upsets me? I want to say: 'No, no!' and run away. All you've said is very plausible, I suppose, but there's something inside me that doesn't want to believe."

"I expect you've been a big, bad, black magician in past lives," he said half-jokingly, "and the memory of its results has remained so firmly in your make-up that you revolt even from the idea of it."

"So you believe in reincarnation, too?"

"Yes; it appeals to my sense of justice among other things, but I *have* more valid reasons. And now I've explained magic to you, we'll come back to our tomb. There's usually some truth in legends that stick to places through the ages, and if there are such gentry buried there, then it's decidedly a place to steer clear of."

"Supposing there were," she objected, "I really don't see how they could affect us, not after all these years."

"My dear girl, an Elemental continues to exist until it's destroyed; time doesn't affect it at all. I suppose you have heard of Elementals, haven't you?"

"Vaguely, I think; but I don't really know what they are."

"Well, you've read about djinn and familiars in your fairy tales, and I expect you've heard of the poem of the Sorcerer's Apprentice. I always think that's an excellent illustration, besides providing a nice little moral lesson for prospective magicians. He got the magic word, you know, which made the broom fetch water for him when the sorcerer was out; but forgot the counter-word and was nearly drowned because he couldn't make the thing stop. It was an Elemental that worked the broom and that's the way they behave; they go on doing whatever you've told them to do until you—or someone else—puts a stop to them. And *that's* not as easy as it sounds."

"But what are they, anyhow?"

"Natural forces, temporarily ensouling—or imprisoned in—a form; or semi-intelligent beings from the lower astral world. And what is the lower astral world? It's that realm of the fourth dimension which the Christian Church adopted as a suitable place to which it could relegate everybody it didn't like—with such ghastly results on the mentality of its followers!"

Her eyes opened wider. "Then you believe in hell, too?"

He burst out laughing. "Not in their utilitarian sense. I can't explain it all now, we haven't time; but the point is that the trained magician can conjure up elemental forces by using certain formulæ, and bind them to perform specific tasks. Needless to say it's usually something disagreeable, and the fact that there have been all these fatalities in connection with a place that has got the reputation of housing black magicians seems to me proof enough that some such malign influence must be on guard there still."

But he could see she was by no means prepared to accept his statements without a further struggle. "But why should they have put such a thing 'on guard,' as you call it?" she objected.

"To keep people out, I suppose. On the other hand, of course, it may not be anything as definite as an Elemental, merely an evil influence emanating from the mummies themselves. The Egyptians, you see, believed that the spirit, or *Ka*, remained with the body as long as it was preserved; and let me tell you, the ancient Egyptians knew more of magic and the unseen realms than anyone has ever known since. If that idea is right, then such *Kas* would be quite powerful enough to do any amount of damage."

She shook her head with a sigh. "It all sounds so fantastic; but of course that theory would explain hauntings, lots of those seem to have been pretty well authenticated."

"Yes, you see, thought and will are really terrific energies when they are rightly understood; if you'd ever been in the vicinity of a really evil man—which I don't suppose you have—you'd know what I mean."

She looked thoughtful. "I wonder," she began, then broke off.

"What? Have you, by any chance?"

"Oh, it's fancy, I suppose; but I would say, if it didn't sound too absurd, that Dr. Zarov gave out a sort of evil emanation, as you call it. He always gives me the creeps. When I've shaken hands with him, I want to go away and have a good wash."

"You're probably quite right. Don't you think it's rather significant that it is he who's so keen on your opening up this tomb or whatever it is?"

"I don't see why he should want to do us any harm?"

"Perhaps merely on the principle of the fox making the monkey pick the chestnuts out of the fire for him. Supposing there should be anything destructive haunting this place, don't you see that it's the people who first open it, or attempt to do so, who will get the full impact? And it's my opinion, in view of what has already happened to Derwent and the others, that something is bound to happen to you, too, if you make this attempt—something horrible."

"But after all, that can only be surmise," she said in a low, troubled voice, after a long pause, "one can't prove that there really is any connection."

"Unfortunately one can—up to a point." He drew out some papers from his pocket. "Here is your sister's horoscope. To start with it explains her illness absolutely. A very badly afflicted Moon and Neptune in the Twelfth House," he shrugged his shoulders, "it can only mean that the person in question is exceptionally mediumistic, an excellent subject for hypnosis, and consequently open to all kinds of obsession. It proves what I guessed at once, that these attacks are due to some kind of possession."

"Possession!" she cried, "what do you mean? Betty possessed—what a horrible idea!" She was trembling with indignation, in fact her reaction was so violent that he felt sure the idea was one which must have secretly come to her before and had been pushed down below the level of her conscious mind.

"I'm sorry if it shocks you, but that's my opinion, particularly in view of her horoscope."

"But possession—and Betty! You don't know her, or you couldn't suggest such a thing. No one could be sweeter, more good, more patient."

"Unfortunately that would only be effective up to a point, if, through having given way to excesses of some kind in a past life, she had brought over a weakened physical body that could be easily influenced by evil powers. But I can't see back; I wish I could, it would explain a lot."

She stared at him, bewildered; but despite the still feebly protesting voice of common sense, she was impressed by the calm conviction of his voice.

"But that isn't, at the moment, the most important thing," he went on. "It's something else in her horoscope."

He paused so long that she broke in. "Well?"

He hesitated, then turned and faced her. "You are a brave woman, you'd better know the worst. The fact is, there are aspects which indicate some kind of catastrophe in the very near future, something so bad that it might mean—death."

She drew a long breath, as if attempting to steady herself. "Can't you tell for certain?"

"One seldom can. As I told you, a horoscope only shows tendencies, dangers, possibilities; one may say that the aspects are so bad that it doesn't look as if escape were possible; but on the other hand people *do* escape from the most appalling dangers."

"Do you think, perhaps, it might just be an extra bad attack?"

"No; you wouldn't understand the technicalities, but an aspect like this indicates something striking, as it were, from the outside; an accident, say."

"Can't you see what kind of accident?"

He stared ahead with drawn brows. "Up to a point; and that's just what worries me. It comes from an Earthy Sign, therefore one would say that the danger will be from the element of Earth."

She gave a gasp. "The Tomb!" she cried.

"Yes, the tomb; and there's something else which is—queer."

She only nodded. He was amazed and thankful for her self-restraint.

"The same danger is indicated in my horoscope, too."

"In yours?" She leant forward intently. "Do you mean yours is the same as hers?"

He smiled. "Only so far as this one progressed aspect is concerned. Mine also shows the possibility of an accident about this time and curiously enough it also comes from the element of Earth. I wouldn't mind betting," he added, "that I'd find the same thing in yours and your father's and Annerly's too, if I could cast them."

She made a gesture of despair. "But if this is true, then we can't escape!"

"We can. It's only a warning, I tell you, a possibility. If you do go to this tomb I'm convinced something *will* happen. But you've got free will, you needn't do it; you can refuse."

"But that's just it! I can't, I'm not free. The others would never believe you, and anyway they wouldn't give it up." She sat in silence for a little while, then looked at him with a puzzled frown. "But yours? Why should it show in yours?"

He grinned. "Probably because if you persist in doing this insane thing, I shall feel called upon to come along too, if only to have the satisfaction of saying: 'I told you so' when I pull you out!"

"Oh, but why? If you really believe in this danger it would be madness."

"Well," he began, "if you must know..." then abruptly stopped. His expression changed, became intent as if he were straining all his senses to catch some distant sound. His gaze searched the ruins among which they were seated; there was nothing in sight, nor any sound save the buzzing of flies.

He rose and cautiously circled all the fallen blocks of masonry; yet he had examined them when they arrived, and she knew that no one could have approached unseen by Ahmed stationed outside. He disappeared at last through the pylon doorway and she heard him talking to Ahmed in low tones. She sat waiting, and found herself thinking of Betty; but it was a strangely vivid and urgent thought, accompanied by a clear mental image of her sister, as she was wont to lie during her attacks, prone upon the bed. She, too, began to feel anxious, frightened. She was glad when Simon returned. But he did not sit down, only stood there with that same puzzled, worried expression on his face.

"What's the matter?" she asked.

"I could have sworn we were being observed—overheard."

"Was there anyone there?"

"No, no one that I could *see*."

"Oh, come, you're not suggesting . . ."

"I'm not saying anything for certain, because I don't know; but I'm pretty sure someone—somewhere—was making an effort to 'wire-in' to our conversation."

She looked round the silent, sun-drenched ruin and despite the heat a shudder caught her, travelling down her spine, bringing out gooseflesh on her skin. "But that's fantastic . . ."

"It's not." His voice was rather sharp. "Haven't you heard of telepathy? Why, even the most sceptical admits the possibility of that, in fact they put everything down to it, *ad lib*."

"You mean someone could listen from a distance to what we were saying?"

"Yes, if they knew how. They might do it by looking in a crystal, or by projecting the astral body through hypnosis." He paused and added in a different voice: "Hypnosis . . ." For a few seconds he stood staring unseeingly at her. Then he nodded as if he had come to some satisfactory conclusion. "Yes, the subject under hypnotic control is told to go off to a certain place and report on what they see—and *hear*. Experiments like that have been often carried out by ordinary practitioners; it can be done through a medium in trance, too." He stretched out his hand to help her to her feet. "I think we'd better be getting back. By the way, have you a watch? Do you mind making a note of the time?"

"Just about five past eleven."

He verified it on his. "Right. We'll get another talk to-morrow somehow; it's absolutely essential."

He said very little on the trip back. When they reached the hotel Annerly was pacing up and down the lounge; he rushed to meet them.

"My God, where have you been, Carol? Betty's bad again. Will you come up, Conningsby?"

As they entered the lift Simon asked: "What time was she taken bad—did you notice?"

"Yes, I did; I was just going up to suggest a walk. It was about ten to eleven or a little after. Why?"

"Nothing, I only wondered how long the attack had been going on," but the glance he threw at Carol was full of significance.

CHAPTER IV

"IN THE EAST ANYTHING CAN HAPPEN"

BETTY'S attack was of short duration. In an hour or so she was her normal self except for a certain mental haziness and languor. Simon had no further opportunity to speak alone with Carol as her sister clung to her persistently and would hardly let her out of the room.

He managed, however, to have a short talk with their father. The old man was full of plans which, quite obviously, he had no intention of abandoning despite Simon's grave warning about Betty's condition and the dangers she would run if she went up country, or even stayed much longer in Egypt.

Zarov had arranged everything with regard to the expedition, even to hiring the workers who were awaiting their arrival at a village about ten miles from the scene of operations.

"We have only to join them—only to join them," Mannering clucked excitedly, "and the most wonderful discovery of the century will be ours!"

"But you don't know for certain that there *is* a tomb," objected Simon. "I understand Derwent never actually uncovered anything definite except a bit of ramp."

Old Mannering dropped his voice, glancing round and rubbing his hands. "He did—he did! But no one knows. He got to the wall at the end of the ramp; that has only to be broken open and we're inside! Only we promised not to speak of it. It was filled in again. Of course it is a dead secret! You must repeat nothing; we were all actually sworn to silence, but I feel that I am justified in telling you, only you must be discreet, it's a serious matter, people are after it, you know!" He reminded Simon of a small boy playing at gangsters.

"But the men who worked for him must have known," Simon pointed out, "you can't hide a thing like that!"

"But he did; I confess I don't quite know how it was done. Zarov assures me that no one knew; that was why there was no need to place the usual guards when the place was left. The men all thought it was a failure."

Simon said no more, there was no point in arguing; the old chap had been well primed by Zarov who, counting on his ignorance of conditions, could put across anything he wished. Simon had a shrewd idea why guards had not been necessary; after that last failure even the most avaricious of natives would not have dared to approach the accursed spot. They would be a pretty villainous and hardened lot indeed who could be persuaded to work at all in such a place.

He only permitted himself to say, in order to test the old man's reaction: "Of course the place is quite well known; it's alleged to be haunted, has a very nasty reputation. Derwent wasn't the first man who nearly lost his life there. You know that, I suppose?"

"My dear sir, my dear sir, you really don't believe all that nonsense!" Mannering replied with his shrill cackle.

Simon gave a non-committal smile. "Egypt's a queer place; there are such things as tombs with a curse on them." But he saw that he would get no further with Mannering. His greed and ignorance were proof against anything but a charge of dynamite.

At that moment Annerly came in and Simon took his leave.

He was deeply troubled. He did not think he had been mistaken in that sensation which had assailed him when he was talking to Carol among the ruins.

In India his mind had been trained to register the impingement upon it of any powerfully directed thoughts, and it was this sixth sense which had warned him instantly that someone was attempting to listen-in to his conversation with Carol. The fact that Betty's seizure had taken place at exactly the same moment, confirmed all his earlier suspicions.

Zarov by treating her had, without doubt, obtained control over her mind and her body. Whereas, before he came into her life, her mediumistic tendencies laid her open to obsessions and attacks by any entities that could influence her from the Astral Plane, since his ascendency over her had become firmly established, he alone was using her. Simon knew that in such cases as this, the fact that the practitioner was not present in person made little or no difference. Zarov had only to attune his mind to hers and issue a command to her, for her to obey him. Having thrown the girl into a state of trance, he could thus quite easily, through the affinity existing between the two sisters, send her spirit to contact Carol and report to him again on all that had taken place.

It was, therefore, more than likely that Zarov, by now, was in full possession of all the facts about Simon known to any member of the Mannering family.

If he was correct, what then? Zarov was warned, and once Zarov knew him to be his enemy he would stop at nothing. It was not a pleasant thought. For no single instant now might Simon consider himself safe. If Zarov were indeed the mysterious Mr. X., as Simon sometimes thought very possible, then the powers he could release against his enemy were manifold and redoubtable. Simon could not help a momentary shiver of dread, although he instantly controlled it. Fear was the open door through which the forces of evil could most easily penetrate. He told himself that, although Zarov launched against him the legions of hell itself, still there was no need for panic; he also had legions behind him; he was not alone. But at that moment, as he went upstairs to his hotel bedroom, he had to admit that the legions of Heaven did seem a little remote.

"Anyway," he argued, "supposing he does get me, and I've got to reckon with that, it may still be possible to save the others—to stop them opening up the tomb. That's the main point. I've got to keep them independent of me, so that whatever happens they'll be protected from Zarov somehow."

Ahmed was his one hope. Ahmed of the fifty-nine disguises, as he had once been called, would not be so easy to keep under observation as Simon. In any case Zarov was probably still ignorant of their association. From the moment of their arrival Ahmed had been swallowed up in the teeming coloured population of the city. He was usually a vague figure in a *galibiah* wandering about the square outside the hotel; occasionally he was made up as a purveyor of postcards and dubious information, a tout, a taxi-driver, or just one of that multitude whose chief object in life appears to be the acquisition of a few feet of shade in which to drowse.

Now Simon opened his window and drew up the sun-blind; then let it down again.

Five minutes later a native with a small parcel announced at the desk that he had come from a dealer in antiquities to show some curios to Conningsby Effendi, and was duly shown up to Simon's room. The moment the door had closed behind him he came forward eagerly.

"I have found out somfeeng; the foreman of the expedition he ees a ver' old friend of mine." The half-closed eyes and cunning smile rather gave the lie to this assertion.

"Oh," said Simon lightly, "one of the kind of old friends that you can blackmail, I suppose?"

"Oh, not blackmail..." Ahmed always appeared intensely shocked at any suggestion that he should dream of departing from the strict path of rectitude, "but influence a leetle—yes? There is no harm in that?"

"Don't ask me! You'll have to work out the *Karma* of your unutterable iniquities, and from what I know of them it'll take you a long time, so whatever I said would make precious little difference."

Ahmed only grinned, apparently undisturbed by this gruesome threat. His religious beliefs, like his ancestry, had become a little mixed by time and alien influences.

"Anyway," Simon continued, "you'd better keep your eye on this chap, he may be useful."

Ahmed smiled meaningly. "More than my eye—my thumb." And he pressed that member firmly down upon the desk in illustration of his intention.

"Well, I've no objection to that either." Simon leaned forward: "Could you, if necessary, *stop him from carrying on the work at this place altogether?*"

Ahmed bowed his head. "No doubt, no doubt, if Allah wills."

"I think Allah might," murmured Simon; "in this case you certainly are on the side of the angels, O worker of iniquity!" Then his tone changed abruptly. "Now listen, Ahmed; we're up against a dangerous crowd. They're determined to force these people to open up this tomb; we've got to stop it. If you can bribe, persuade or otherwise suborn this chap into refusing to continue the work, to strike or anything you like, so much the better for everyone. I'm afraid there isn't a hope of my being able to stop them making the attempt, although I shan't give up. But the point now is this: these people, Zarov, or whoever is behind him, have got their eye on me. I'm the fly in their ointment at the moment and they'll do me in or incapacitate me if they can."

At his words Ahmed made a quick step forward, his eyes were blazing, his whole body tensed: "I will stay with you, always, you shall nevah be alone..."

Simon shook his head. "No, my friend, that won't do. I'll take care of myself, but I want you to swear that if anything should happen to me you'll do everything in your power to stop this tomb being opened. That's the main thing, nothing else matters."

Ahmed made a gesture of scorn. "What is this tomb?"

"Everything," Simon answered, giving his servant a significant look. "Everything to *them*."

The other capitulated then, but with an ill grace. "You say so, Master. But if we can't stop, what then?"

"I don't know; it depends upon what does happen when—or let us say if—they do open it. But I want you to realize one thing; no, two. First, Miss Carol, the elder girl, is the most important person to save if there's fighting or," he shrugged his shoulders, "any kind of danger. I put her in your charge, your sacred charge, you understand?"

Ahmed grinned. "And *how* I understand! She is safe, safe in my heart." And he pressed his slim hand ardently upon his breast.

Simon nodded. There was no need for him to say any more; Ahmed would henceforth constitute himself Carol's guardian unto death.

"And secondly," he continued, "if they do succeed in opening the tomb, someone—possibly Zarov—will put in an appearance and have a shot at getting down; at all costs he must he stopped. No one, not a beggar, not a high Government official, English or Egyptian, not even a dog must be allowed to follow them in; rather you must blow the whole tomb or cache or whatever it is sky-high. Understand?"

"I will do it."

"These are your instructions in case anything happens to me. And if it should, don't let yourself be lured away from them by any message or any apparent chance of saving me. But I don't think anything will happen."

"Then you will go with them, eh?"

"Yes, O my familiar spirit. After all, I do know a certain amount about exorcism—and other things; I might be able to avert a disaster, or protect them somehow."

Ahmed made a grimace. "Veree bad place," he remarked with a shake of his head.

"Don't I know it! That's why I'm going to make every effort to keep them away. Well, they won't be going for a week or so yet, so something may be done. By the way, have you any more of your friends among that low-caste gang that's been recruited for them?"

"Four of them went veree sick yesterday," Ahmed stated, raising his eyes to the ceiling and counting on his fingers. "Most strange coincidence! It is difficult to replace them, ordinary workers afraid to go there, but Abdullah—that is my chief friend, as you might say—will find four others."

"Most convenient! but how will Miss Carol be able to pick our men out? Any distinguishing marks? She'll never remember their names."

"True, true, they are a low, commonplace lot, as you might say! But if she want to pick them out Ali will show her. Ali is easy—he has one eye."

"So many of the wretched fellows have lost an eye in this country with that cursed sand . . ."

"Yes, yes, but he is different, he lost it quite different—gouged out, as you might call it. Moreover, he has lost two fingers of his left hand and has only one tooth, a side one and rather long—also half an ear; a lot of trouble he has had, poor Ali!" He opened out his arms in a large gesture: "Oh, quite, quite unmistakable!"

"He must be," laughed Simon, "even among the sort of riff-raff they would have been forced to accept for a show of this kind. But is he reliable?"

"Ab-so-lutlee! Is he not a sort of relation of my own? But one, you will understand, of whom I am not so proud. However," he added casually, "he is faithful—he will die for me."

"That's something anyway. We'll be needing all the fidelity we can get, I'm thinking."

Ahmed frowned. "But, Master, couldn't you get the Government to cancel permission for them to go?" He jingled some coins together significantly: "It should be easy."

"That's just where you're wrong. There's some very powerful influence at work behind this business. I did everything I could the moment I arrived. You've no idea how inaccessible some of the gentlemen had become. I'm pretty good at wangling but it was like beating on an iron door. Besides, don't forget I had absolutely no valid reason for my interference. Everything had been done in the proper manner, through the proper authorities, there wasn't a slip anywhere. No, we've got to work alone, we're not going to get any help from anyone; you can rule that out at once."

"All ways open to the Controller of Ways," said Ahmed confidently.

"Not all; there's something even more omnipotent—fear! I suspect this Zarov has a very accurate *dossier* of the private affairs of some of these good gentlemen."

Ahmed sighed, shaking his head sadly over the frailty of Government officials. "Too true! Ah well, perhaps a nice leetle strike..."

"That's up to you and your honourable friends. As a matter of fact I think it would be quite a good idea if you had a personal interview with this Abdullah as soon as possible and ran over to the dig to get the lie of the land at the same time. I understand the working party's encamped at a village only ten miles from the site."

"That is correct."

"Good. You clear off, then. You can be back long before we are likely to start. Make out a careful report, you'll probably learn far more on the spot. If we do go earlier I'll pick you up there."

"But you will be alone," said Ahmed doubtfully.

"That's all right, don't you worry. If you can get back in a few days so much the better. You'd better go off by to-night's train, so as not to waste time. Send reports in the usual code to me here. And remember, play on their fears, a strike's our best card; do everything you can to work them up."

"It will be easy with the Opener of Ways." And with a flashing smile Ahmed stretched out his hand palm upward. Simon filled it with a thick wad of notes.

"Don't be too dashing, will you? But there *is* more where that came from."

"Your purse is as safe in my hands as a guest in the tent of a True Believer."

Simon's sarcastic comment was interrupted by the entrance of one of the hotel servants. Ahmed instantly became the shopkeeper and backed out clutching the money, with a rain of blessings and praise for the generous Effendi, and a secret grimace at the servant in the doorway.

Simon picked up the note which had just arrived. The handwriting was strange, but he knew, without opening it, whom it was from.

The message, however, startled him out of his pleasant moment of anticipation.

"We are starting to-morrow, I don't know why; I would like to see you, but I think someone has roused Nick's suspicions about you. He won't let you see B. again. I can't get away as she gets in a dreadful state if I leave her. My only chance is to-night, when she's asleep, but then I can't leave the hotel. I think I pointed out to you where my room was; there's a balcony running along that side of the house. Could you possibly get on to it lower down from the corridor, and we might have a few moments' talk. I am frightened about B., otherwise I wouldn't dream of asking you to do such a thing. I'll pretend to be tired and turn in early, so any time after nine I will be in our room, and shall keep a look-out. If you don't turn up I shall understand perfectly, so please don't bother if it is too much trouble or you are engaged.

C. M."

He struck his fist on the desk. "Damn! so we *were* overheard!" He began pacing up and down. "To-morrow already, before we can make any plans. Clever devil! Thank goodness Ahmed's been at work, and is off to-night, that'll short-circuit our friend Zarov a bit, anyway. Not much hope of stopping them now, unless I abducted Carol. I wonder . . ." He shook his head. "She's obviously not sure of me; don't blame her, and she's one of those women with a super-public-school sense of honour—what a handicap that is."

At about a quarter past nine Carol, who had been standing just outside her window beyond the square of light from the room, became aware of a figure moving towards her along the balconies which were divided from each other by a slanting iron railing. When she saw that it was a tall, bearded Arab, she shrank back with a sharp pang of disappointment, but as he gathered his burnous dexterously together and prepared to negotiate the last barrier she heard Simon's voice:

"It's all right, I'm not a marauding Sheik come to abduct you in the best style of some of our lady novelists. I wish I were." He spoke very softly, looking down at her. "You didn't think I'd fail you? But this disguise took a little while to get. Don't you think I look rather smart in a beard?"

The relief was so great she could almost have cried. Until that moment she had not realized what his coming meant to her. "Oh, it is good of you," she stammered.

"I mustn't stay long. Is she all right, sound asleep?"

"Yes, I gave her two of those cachets, instead of only one; you said . . ."

"Good girl. Is this inevitable about to-morrow? Can't you get it put off somehow for a day or so, play sick or something?"

She turned on him almost indignantly. "How could I do that, with Betty ill and so easily upset, it wouldn't be fair."

He had known that was coming, and countered it quickly with: "More than fair, if it meant keeping them out of danger."

"But you can't really be sure!" She shook her head. "Anyway, if I did, it would make no difference. Betty's suddenly got extraordinarily keen on going, and as for Nick and Father they can think of nothing else; and now they've heard from Zarov that another party is trying to get the Government to rescind our rights by heavy bribes; he also said that he had certain evidence now that it *is* a royal tomb and absolutely untouched—like the Tut-Ankh-Amen one, perhaps—but if we could get there before anything more was done they'd have to leave us in possession. Can you see Father giving it up after that? If I went sick they'd just leave me behind, that's all."

"Well, let them, then," he cried, for a moment carried away by the imminence of disaster to the woman he loved. "If you were safe . . ."

"And leave Betty! How can you suggest such a thing?" He sighed.

"I know, I don't really: forgive me." Abruptly he laid his hand upon hers. Her natural reaction would have been to move it sharply away, but rather to her own surprise she did not do so; only turned her head and looked at him questioningly.

He was smiling at her with great tenderness. "I expect you've heard all sorts of tales about me," he said, "good and bad—mostly bad."

It was true. Particularly since they arrived in Cairo she had been surprised at the number of casual acquaintances who had spoken disparagingly of him.

He took her silence and the sudden flutter of her eyelids for assent. "But I want you to forget it all and merely trust to your own judgment—your own intuition." He stared for a few moments at the tips of the palm trees below them. "I've got to speak to you before you leave, it's so difficult, because I realize that most of what I say must sound such fantastic nonsense to anyone like yourself who takes such pride in common sense." His eyes twinkled and he pressed her hand. "But everything depends upon whether you really feel you can trust me—do you?"

Once again they looked each other straight in the eyes; once again, as if at some inner compulsion, she found herself doing the unexpected thing. "Yes, I do," she said.

He nodded. "Good; then I can go ahead, but first you've got to realize that everything I'm going to say or do is the result of what I feel for you personally." He laughed then, throwing back his head: "You'd better have it straight, my dear, and digest it later. The fact is, I love you. I knew the moment I saw you that our meeting was one of those inevitable things. I hoped you'd recognize it too; perhaps it's a bit soon, but you will—in time. No, don't start talking at me—I won't listen. Even if you still refuse to believe in all my peculiar shibboleths you must admit that there is such a thing as Destiny. It just happens that you and I are bound together by that little scarlet thread the Chinese believe to be fastened at birth round the ankles of those who are fated to meet and love. I think the thread is bound there before birth, in previous lives, but that doesn't matter. The point is, I love you and I'm going to marry you; and now that's settled we'll talk of something else."

"But it's not settled," she said, half laughing, half angry.

"It is, but I haven't time to prove it to you at the moment. I mustn't stay much longer, and I'm afraid Betty may be disturbed if we go on talking."

"She can't hear, I've closed the communicating door."

He shrugged. "You never know." He spoke more urgently now. "Listen, Carol, by hook or by crook I shall get along and join you. I'm dead serious when I say that I know you're all heading for disaster. I intended taking you into my confidence and explaining the whole plot to you, but it's too late now, you've got to believe that Zarov is your enemy, he's tricked you. Somehow the tomb must *not* be opened, and I'm going to stop it. I'll give you a couple of days' start and then turn up on some excuse or other. We can't plan further than that." He hesitated a moment, then added in a lower voice: "One thing more; just supposing anything did stop me and you want help, there's a man among the workers called Ali." He proceeded to give her a minute description of that gentleman's outstanding features. "If you are in any trouble go to him or to the head man, Abdullah, and have Ali sent off at once to fetch his cousin Ahmed, who is my servant. Tell them I gave the order and if you like show them this and they'll obey you implicitly."

He pulled a ring from his little finger. "Keep it for me until we meet; there's a story attached to it, I'll tell you some day. You see, it's a scarab. I've been told it belonged to me once, perhaps you gave it me." His voice became speculative, then he smiled and, lifting her left hand, before she could stop him, slipped it on the third finger. "How it fits! And it was too big for my little one." He broke off and leant over the balcony: "Was that someone, down there?"

"Only a shadow, it's just a little yard, no door even, no one could hide there."

He shrugged. "Oh, couldn't they! Is your sister still asleep, I wonder?"

Carol tiptoed into the room behind them and returned in a few moments. "Yes, sound asleep. Oh, it's about her I wanted to tell you, she's been so odd since this last attack, sort of dazed all the while, never quite *there*, she says everything seems unreal, just out of focus."

His face was grave. "Mm, I'm afraid I can't do much. I could, if I were allowed complete control, but Annerly's antagonism to one surrounds her with a positive barrier. I can't tackle anything as complex as her case in such conditions." He sighed. "Well, I daren't stay; remember if I shouldn't come—and I'll raise hell to do it, you may be sure of that—an S.O.S. to Ahmed will always bring help. You may trust him absolutely, he has my instructions, he'll die for you." His voice changed; he picked up her hand and pressed it to his lips. "And don't forget, I love you and I'm going to marry you whatever you may think to the contrary at the moment."

And with that he swung himself back over the railing and disappeared, leaving her shaken, bewildered, yet with a queer feeling of exultation which, try as she might, she could neither explain away nor root out of her heart.

~ ~ ~ ~ ~

Back in his hotel Simon sat down at his desk and prepared to write his report to Weyland. He wrote in a code, a code so hidden in ordinary and harmless-looking phrases that no one reading the long, intricate description of some jewels he had found in the bazaar and a little excursion he had made into the desert could have imagined this chatty letter conveyed anything of more intimate matters. Yet it was a difficult code to use, and needed intense concentration since Simon was careful to have no key written anywhere, all letters, combinations and numbers being only engraved upon the tablets of his trained memory.

The night wore on. The desk was so placed that anyone writing at it would have his back to the window. It was hot, and both windows were open. Occasionally a faint breeze stole in, billowing out the curtains and fluttering the papers on the desk.

Simon, his head bent, pen industriously scratching, took no notice of these slight stirrings, nor of the whirr of the electric fan, nor of the distant noises of the street. His reading lamp cast a soft aura of clear light upon his hand and upon the paper before him, the rest of the room was in obscurity.

Therefore he was not aware of anything unusual when the curtain, billowing out further than before, was swiftly caught back by a brown hand. He did not see the deepening of the shadows as they materialized into a man's form which slipped, as quiet as any shadow, over the window-sill into the room. Nor did he hear the faint whisper of bare feet upon the heavy carpet.

He only knew suddenly an agonizing, blinding pain around his throat, saw a flash of lights, a rush of scarlet, heard a thrumming in his ears, before he fell backwards unconscious from his chair.

CHAPTER V

THE HOUSE OF ZAROV

THE FIRST DEFINITE sensation of which Simon was aware, as he struggled back through mists of pain and discomfort to consciousness, was that of having been warned against some imminent danger; it was as if his spirit, returning from those realms to which he had been so summarily despatched by the attack in the hotel, brought back with it a message to the body: "Be careful: you are in danger, you are under observation; be careful, *careful*, CAREFUL!"

The word loomed enormous in his mind. He lay rigid, his eyes closed, collecting his forces, arming himself for whatever this awakening would bring. His hands were tied; probably, he thought, to the sides of the divan on which he lay; his feet were likewise bound. That did not worry him unduly. Provided he were left alone long enough he could free himself without much difficulty. During the time he had spent in India he had acquired many unusual accomplishments to aid him in the work he was preparing to undertake. A knowledge of some of the secret methods used by Houdini was among them. "We should always know," the Swami who was instructing him had remarked once with his bland smile, "how to release ourselves from the bonds of any restrictions, physical as well as mental, since all are *Maya*. How ignoble, for instance, that a man should be controlled by so poor a thing as a few strands of hemp!"

Imperceptibly, at last, when he was more sure of his self-control and the buzzing in his head had a little abated, he raised his lids. This had to be risked. How he wished now he had acquired, among those other powers taught by the masters of Hatha Yoga, that ability to see with any part of the body called in the West "eyeless sight"; but time had been too short. Yet, for all he knew, this movement of the eyelids might be his undoing.

The room was in darkness save for a small oil lamp on a shelf above him. To a watcher it would reveal his slightest movement. "Well," he thought, "it's too late now," so he opened his eyes completely and turned his head.

Nothing stirred, and in a few moments he became accustomed to the gloom and saw that he was alone in a small room in what, to judge by the rugs and general decoration, was, evidently, the house of a well-to-do Egyptian. So far as he could make out there was no window; but above the massive door that faced him was a *grille* of ornamental ironwork. It was certainly too small even for a boy to squeeze through, let alone a full-grown man, so he must look elsewhere for any chance of escape.

An electric fan whirred in a corner. On a small coffee table was a tray holding a carafe and a glass. He would have given a great deal for a drink, for his throat was parched and sore, while his neck was still stiff and swollen from the thug's attack.

What did they want with him, he wondered. They must intend to use him in some way, or else, surely, they would have found it more convenient to murder him out of hand. He could not repress a shudder. Who was the owner of this house? Perhaps Zarov or even X. himself—if Zarov and X. were not one and the same. At any rate it undoubtedly belonged to the Brotherhood of darkness, and therefore to those who would have a deep knowledge of esoteric secrets, and possess redoubtable powers. It would take more than ordinary knowledge and cunning to outwit such men, and he would need all his specialized training now if he were to escape. But even that might not be enough.

He must learn their intentions somehow. There was only one chance of doing this, to remain "unconscious" and hope that, when they came to have a look at him, as they were bound to do sooner or later, they would talk.

In the meanwhile he must collect all his strength, physical, mental and spiritual, to protect him against what he knew, without doubt, was going to be a terrible ordeal.

But it was not easy, with the tormenting knowledge that his mission was unaccomplished, and that Carol was alone with only Ahmed to rely upon, and perhaps not even him. Where was she by now? He had no idea how long he had been unconscious; it would probably be days before he could join them, in any case. They might be already on their way to that cursed place, or have even begun digging. Perhaps . . . Firmly he shut off that line of thought. He mustn't waste energy speculating on possibilities. It was something, at least, to be thankful for that he had put her in Ahmed's charge and made some provision for their safety. Foresight? Rather, surely, a premonition.

He was aware of a slight sound outside the door. Instantly he relaxed and closed his eyes. He heard the door open and slippered feet falling, almost soundlessly, upon the thick rugs. Then he was conscious of scrutiny, but one which was compact of such force that it became almost a physical sensation. The attention of an ordinary man directed casually towards a prisoner could not have affected him thus; he knew now that his fears were well grounded, he was in the hands of a magician.

Then came a sibilant voice, speaking rapid Arabic.

"So this is the interfering fool!" A finger touched his forehead; it was like a sharp, burning stab. It needed all the self-control he possessed not to flinch or shrink away.

"I think he has not yet returned," continued the voice; there was a pause, while again Simon was conscious of that probing of an alien mind seeking to penetrate his own, seeking to discover the mysteries of his spirit. He put up no resistance; that would have been fatal, would have proved him conscious and aware; instead, he cut off the image-making faculty of definite thought. His mind went blank, receded into the nebulous half-world of dreams: a few pictures, Carol's face, the hotel lounge, vignettes of Cairo, the life on shipboard, a few confused symbols, these that X-ray vision might perceive.

"There is such a confusion in his aura that I can see nothing; strange . . . but I think it would be safer if a few tests were applied. I am not entirely satisfied with your report."

Another pair of hands took charge. Simon's eyelids were skilfully lifted, but his eyes were already rolled slightly sideways and back. He nerved himself to exercise the utmost control. A finger touched the cornea of his eye lightly, but not by a tremor did he respond. Hatha Yoga certainly had its uses! The eyelids were dropped again. "No Western fool could have stood that, I think," the same voice said.

"I am sure, O Master, that is all he is," answered the other man, "a mere blundering meddler. He is in love with the older girl, my man believes, at least he behaved thus in the hotel."

"And then your man lost them," the voice was a cross between a purr and a snarl.

"There seemed no reason, lord—"

"Seemed! No. But there was. That was obvious from the little I ascertained when I used the sister to report their speech to me. I am not yet satisfied that this man *is* a fool, else why did he break off that conversation as soon as I began to listen?"

"Did you not perceive the cause?"

"No, something went wrong and my medium returned."

"It may have been chance."

There was a pause which seemed to Simon endlessly protracted. He lay there feeling extraordinarily vulnerable. If only he could have opened his eyes, known what was happening in that silence, or dared even tense himself in readiness; but at all costs he must remain relaxed, as if indifferent.

Then, suddenly, a gnat bite started to irritate furiously on his arm; with an effort he tried to remove his consciousness to another part of his body; it was not very successful, for a tickling began in his throat which nearly choked him. Then a nerve started twitching in his leg, followed immediately by a cramp which gripped his feet till he could have screamed. And at that he realized that it was possible the man at his side might be testing him. Instantly exerting all his knowledge he began mentally wrapping himself in an aura of white light, and as he did so the minor tortures faded away.

Well, that test was over! The powers of evil, he decided, had really very little sense of proportion and no humour, or they could never stimulate a gnat bite to annoy you. Then it struck him that it is, after all, through the smallest things in life that our vulnerability is proved; most men can nerve themselves to support spectacular pains and blows, but it is the little irritations which end by wearing down the will.

"You may be right," said the voice of him who had been called "master."

"But how is it, then, that he has shaken my power over the girl? Whose voice was it that called her spirit back to her body if not the voice of One-Who-Knows?"

"He is a doctor, he may be one of those natural healers who have brought over an instinctive knowledge of certain types of magic from past lives."

"If that is so, and it may be possible, then it should not be difficult to use him as I hoped," came the reply in a speculative tone, "and if we learn the Secret," the voice took on a note of exultation so that it seemed to swell, to fill the room, "a doctor will be of great service; we shall need more and more slaves from among these Westerners. If this one has powers, conscious or unconscious, so much the better. They will be mine!"

"Will It not create Its own servants?" asked the other voice.

The first man laughed softly: "It will, Hafiz, it will. It will enter all minds, even as breath enters bodies; it will permeate all thought with such subtlety that men will not be aware of what has befallen, calling black, white, and distinguishing not between the sun and the moon. This is the true alchemy, the power of the Philosopher's Stone, to change all values and confuse all standards. Dross indeed shall become gold at our command, but gold shall also become dross and no man shall know any more the false from the true—only we, we and those who follow us!"

He seemed, for the moment, to have forgotten his prisoner in this vision of power; now the man called Hafiz, who had probably heard too many of such pronouncements to be any longer so impressed by them, reminded him of his opening words.

"But you have not got the secret yet; until you have, would it not be better to put such men as this out of the way? There are so many already on whom you experiment."

"Fool! Will we not need many messengers? Will we not need slaves who can carry our power so that the repercussion of any failure may not fall on us? And do you not perceive that a doctor will be doubly useful to us, since such a one has more influence over the minds and bodies of the masses than ordinary men?"

Evidently Hafiz did see, so also did Simon, and he went cold at the thought. So Weyland had been right! Simon remembered that talk they had had about the Race-Unconscious and the possibility of its control. But even Weyland had felt it to be rather a fantastic theory. Yet it was not fantastic at all—it *was* this man's goal.

Now he knew what he was up against, not a man who was seeking alone how he might shatter humanity with the crude weapons of war, rule from thrones, take his place upon the pinnacles of worldly power from which he might be cast down, but one who intended ruling from within, subjugating the mind of man, sapping his pride, destroying individual free will, that gift which was the source of experience and hence of every possibility of development. With subtle poison he and those behind him intended gradually to penetrate the mentality of each man and woman, perverting it, twisting it, until no one would know "black from white, nor the sun from the moon."

Nor, as he had said, would they guess what was happening to them, they would have no possibility of putting up a defence; they would go carelessly forward, thinking that what they chose to do was their own choice, never perceiving that every action was dictated by an alien will.

Were the times not ripe for just such an infiltration of evil? Or was it, as Weyland had hinted, the other way about? Had X. and his Brotherhood already begun their work? Surely it must be so. Even now in many countries this man's unconscious agents, were they not at work, creating a robot people who, from childhood up, were taught to believe only what the Press or the bombastic speeches of their leaders chose to dictate? Simon was convinced now that this man, or those he represented, *were* already using humanity; and if he acquired still greater powers who should gainsay him, save perhaps those rare souls whose integrity was too great for his dominion? Yet would even they be proof against so subtle an attack? The full horror of it nearly overwhelmed him. His mind went to Carol. Was she not X.'s slave too, she and the others on their way even now to work for him like ants directed by the Group Will, driving into the earth for him, to discover, at the cost of their very lives, the Secret which would give him illimitable power?

Whilst these thoughts flashed in lightning sequence through his mind the man called the "master" had picked up Simon's hand and seemed to be examining the palm.

"Ha, do you see, a most sensitive instrument! A natural psychic and healer, as you said. But look at that, he has a strong will, too strong a will; it is going to make it difficult, yet it may be worth the effort. It is either that or death, but a living slave is more valuable to my mind than a dead enemy. If, as you say, he is in love with this girl, so much the better; we can use him through it. These Westerners with their uncontrolled and sentimental passions for women deliver themselves into our hands."

"No, I do not think he will be easy to hypnotize," said Hafiz, who by this time was also examining Simon's hands.

"Have we not other methods? There are more ways, are there not, of breaking the will and enslaving the mind? Loose him now; when he awakes he must feel confidence, not have his mind set against us before we appear."

The bonds dropped away, Simon heard footsteps, then the door closed.

For a little while he lay listening, sensing with every nerve strained to discover whether both men had gone, then slowly he opened his eyes. He was alone. He stretched, relaxed. What next? What had those words meant: "There are more ways of breaking the will and enslaving the mind"? What ways? He could not keep back the cold shiver of apprehension which went like ice down his spine, and yet he must not fear. Fear was the one point of vulnerability through which most easily the dark forces could launch their attacks. Hypnosis he might resist; he had, possibly, sufficient control over his mind. But even this was not certain. It was generally believed to be impossible to hypnotize anyone against his will, but Simon knew differently. To the ordinary practitioner, yes, it would be a superhuman task; but to the black magician who could bring so many other and more subtle factors to bear, it was by no means impossible. And those "other ways"—what magic forces had he at his command of which most probably Simon knew nothing?

But idle speculation would avail him nothing. He was thankful at least that he had a certain time in which to prepare himself. He would need every ounce of strength that he could command. His mind kept straying to Carol. He felt his chin and decided that he must have been here twenty-four hours or more; there would still be time to reach her before anything serious could happen provided only that he could escape at once.

He had already decided upon his rôle: the outraged Briton, rather dense and rather choleric, threatening the weight and prestige of the Empire. It was evident that Zarov had not heard as much of that conversation with Carol as he had feared, and hence was still ignorant of his power. He must remain so, for the more they were deceived as to his real knowledge the greater would be the likelihood of escape, As for making plans it must be a matter of opportunity, but already a kind of half-formulated scheme was at the back of his mind.

When Hafiz returned Simon pretended to be just recovering; he stirred, half sat up, then fell back with a groan.

"Who are you?" he muttered, "and where the devil am I, anyway?"

He thrust aside the glass Hafiz held to his lips and struggled into a sitting position. In a few minutes he was behaving as any indignant Briton finding himself in the clutches of a foreigner after an attack upon his person might be expected to behave. Hafiz was all bows and smiles and full of explanations, which, although not too convincing, were evidently considered good enough for anyone of the Effendi's obvious mentality. The Effendi did not disillusion Hafiz. He had been found in Mahomed Effendi's garden, had he? Robbed? All right, ring up the proper authorities, and get him a taxi or something, at once!

That was impossible, he had been ill two weeks; there had been trouble in Cairo, didn't he know? Mahomed Effendi had kept him there for safety.

Two weeks? Simon rubbed his chin and smiled. What fools they must think the English were! Very well, he'd believe it if that was their tale—or appear to half-believe it, anyway.

Who was this Mahomed Effendi, he demanded to know.

"Bring him along here," he ended grimly. "I'd like a word with the gentleman myself."

"Excellency, he wishes you first to eat, to bathe, to be rested; that is, if you are strong enough to move?"

"Marvellously strong after two weeks' unconsciousness," said Simon drily, swinging his feet to the floor.

Hafiz bowed. Ah, these English! What physique, what endurance! A bath would be prepared for His Excellency at once, and no doubt a shave? He also offered breakfast, ham and eggs? Simon repudiated ham and eggs; *he* wasn't going to eat any of their food until full explanations had been forthcoming. But a bath and a shave, certainly; then he was leaving—at once.

Hafiz pattered out. "Lord," thought Simon, "they can't really think all English are such fools, they *can't*. But perhaps it's just as well."

His head was still dizzy. He sat still and did some deep breathing till it cleared. After that Hafiz appeared with servants, formidable-looking negroes. Everyone was very polite, but he noticed that, when he was escorted out, he was closely guarded. Perhaps they didn't think him such a fool as they pretended. They went down a passage into a modern and well-equipped bathroom; it was good to shave and lie in that scented water—or wasn't it a bit too scented? No, that insidious and cloying perfume arose from a brazier in the corner. Simon recognized the scent now for a drug; he dropped a sponge on it, and when Hafiz entered, he pointed to it, wrinkling his nose.

"Don't like your Eastern scents—give me a headache. Well, I'm ready, and now?"

"Food," smiled Hafiz.

"Haven't time to waste eating. There's a business appointment waiting. If it's true there's been some trouble in the town, the sooner I see to my interests the better. I've got some friends here, too; they'll need looking after."

"But first His Excellency awaits you."

"Righto, but tell him to be quick about it. I'll give him five minutes, no more; understand?"

He was ushered into a beautifully furnished room which combined the luxuries of the East with those of the West.

At his entrance a man, who had been seated at a table, rose and advanced towards him.

Simon recognized him at once from Carol's description. This, undoubtedly, was Zarov. At first glance he appeared to be merely a moderately good-looking, well-tailored Europeanized Egyptian of about forty years of age. There was nothing remarkable in the face until you looked at the eyes; then, as with Weyland's eyes, it was these which revealed to you the man's true quality. They were fixed now upon Simon; deep, smouldering, so dark that they seemed to hold abysmal night in their depths; but they were absolutely cold, without sympathy or pity, radiating knowledge, power, nothing more. Through this focus the man's will flowed out; it was like being in a pool and feeling the tentacles of some monstrous squid touching one's body, here, there, preparing for a death grip.

Simon took charge of the situation by launching an immediate attack. He refused to shake hands, refused to sit down, refused the coffee that was so courteously offered him. He also refused to believe the story of the riots in Cairo.

"I don't know what your game is," he stormed, "but I have influential friends in Cairo, and if you don't let me go immediately it'll be the worse for you."

His adversary made a graceful gesture.

"I am sorry you are taking it like this."

"How the hell do you expect me to take it?" exploded Simon.

The other smiled. "I see you are too astute; you want truth. You are British, yes? Always the plain, unvarnished truth, is it not? A square deal—yes? You shall have it, then; all cards on the table." He went back to his chair and negligently picked up a long, curiously-shaped paperknife, toying with it as he spoke. As Simon watched that beautiful hand moving up and down, almost as if beating time to an unseen orchestra, a feeling of acute repulsion for this suave, feline man began to assail him. It was with difficulty that he controlled himself and listened to what he was saying.

"The truth is, Mr. Conningsby, that you have been kidnapped. You are a doctor, a very fine doctor. Oh, do not ask how we know; we know many things." He smiled ingratiatingly. "Now I have a relation who is ill, very ill, we must have a doctor at once—"

"In my country," Simon interrupted drily, "we don't have to kidnap doctors in order to get them to a case; quite the contrary, some need kidnapping to get them to leave a case alone."

The other laughed. "You jest with me, but this is different. No doctor would come." He proceeded to go into a long, circumstantial account regarding an alleged relation who had got into trouble with the Government. He was very ill and needed the best medical attention, but it would not be safe to ask a doctor to go to him. "Only thus," he finished with a wave of his hand, "can we give him what he must have. When he is cured you will be well rewarded and go free."

He had risen again and was now quite close to Simon, the unblinking eyes fixed upon his. Simon did not look at them.

"It's an odd business, I must say," he complained, staring at the carpet, yet every nerve tense and alert.

"In the East you will find much that is odd, Mr. Conningsby. If you would come to him now?"

"All right, where is he?"

"Aha, that you must not know. You must not see or feel where we take you. You understand it is too dangerous. But I want it all to be as agreeable as possible for you. I could bind you and bandage your eyes, but even then—one never knows. Or I could give you just a little tap on the head and render you unconscious as before, but the rules of hospitality forbid it."

"Pity you didn't think of them in my hotel," Simon commented. There was something he wanted to find out, so he added in a more friendly tone: "By the way, as a matter of interest, how did you get me out of there?"

"So simple," smiled Zarov. "Your room looked on to the garden, like a parcel you were trussed and lowered to my men below."

"But hasn't it occurred to you that there'll be a hue and cry over this? Important guests can't just disappear, whatever happens you're bound to be traced and get into trouble."

"You underrate my intelligence. You were writing, were you not? What more simple than for a clever man of mine to copy your writing and to address a note to the proprietor saying you were leaving for a week, begging him to keep your room and your things. We even packed a small case—you may take it back when you return. A little trouble was made later outside which called all the employees from their posts; it will be thought that you passed out then, since you were not seen!"

"Most ingenious!" commented Simon bitterly. Once again he felt this tide of anger welling up within him; he kept control over himself however, although he would have liked to jump at Zarov's throat.

"But we waste precious time," Zarov said more briskly. "As I said I would not incommode you or hurt you, so I have thought of a so simple way, whereby we will all be satisfied." He paused, but Simon said nothing, only allowed himself an ironical smile. "If you would let us use on you a little hypnotism you will forget where you go, whom you have seen, and have no after-effects at all."

Simon laughed. "You're a fool. Do you really think I'd allow myself to be hypnotized by you?"

"It would be wiser—Oh, much wiser—if you complied."

Simon replied in a very soft voice: "A threat, eh? All right, what you say may be true, but whether it is or not, your precious friend can die. Nothing you can do will make me attend him, and that's flat."

"I said, Mr. Conningsby, that it would be wiser if you were amenable; I have tried to treat you reasonably, fairly," the smooth voice took on an edge; "if you do not agree to my suggestions, I have methods whereby I can *force* you to obey. Does it not occur to you that I could inject a drug, for example?"

"You probably could, but I wouldn't be much use to you until I came to, and I'd like to see you force any doctor to use his medical skill and knowledge against his will."

"I do not want to have to use them, but there *are* methods; you, as a doctor, should know . . ."

"I don't know. You can't force anyone to be hypnotized against his will either."

The other smiled. "Do you think so? All right; it is a bargain. If I fail to hypnotize you . . ."

"I'll go free," snapped Simon.

"Ah no, and my poor friend, must he die? If I cannot do it, then I will pay you double and I will not coerce; you shall see what you do and I must trust to your honour—but you must submit to the attempt."

All this time Simon had grimly kept his eyes away, but something, it may have been the close proximity of the other, was affecting him increasingly, setting his nerves on edge, stimulating some primitive and forgotten part of his nature to wave after wave of blind hatred and rage. It was that last phrase which was the final goad; the very thought of submission to the man who had broken Hornsley, had enslaved Betty and so many others, and whose goal was to enslave the world in his devilish net, caused so violent a revulsion within him that he cried out: "I do not agree, I will never submit! I'll see you damned first!"

They were face to face, now, eye to eye. Simon saw a smile which seemed to be one of satisfaction pass like a shadow over those delicate features. And at the same instant he was acutely conscious that he had made a mistake. Exactly what he should have done he did not know, but it was as if something within himself recognized failure and deplored it.

"Seize him!" Zarov rapped out. Instantly the two Nubians who had been standing behind him grabbed him by the arms. He did not resist. It would have been idle waste of force.

At another word of command he was thrust into a chair and his arms bound to its back. Zarov clapped his hands, and, rather to Simon's surprise, a man entered carrying what appeared to be one of those shepherd's bagpipes, which are as old, probably, as the Pyramids themselves. The man seated himself cross-legged on the floor, while Hafiz threw some powder into a brazier. Almost at once the familiar suffocating scent began to fill the room. Then the musician began to play. Two notes—no more, but these went on and on, deflecting his power to think clearly, just as the perfume insidiously dulled his capacity for concentration.

Light fingers rolled back his eyelids. There was no escape, he had to gaze into those other eyes, enormous, compelling, which were now looking down into his.

Supposing this man did succeed . . . but that thought must not come, must not be allowed to come. Of all things the subtle suggestion of failure must be repulsed. Zarov was making passes now, and intoning some *mantram* over and over again. It was not in any language Simon understood, but that made no difference, it was the sound that mattered, it was the purpose behind that sound which must be combated. This man was indeed no ordinary practitioner.

The passes increased, the eyes, too, seemed to be increasing in size, until there was nothing left but these enormous pools into which he felt himself being drawn. And he was tired, desperately tired; he wanted to slip away upon this dark tide, to escape from that devastating music which was wearing down his nerves. Once, indeed, he was almost gone, when he was jerked back by a clear vision of Carol's face, quite close to his. He was horrified at the realization of how near he had been to defeat. He must do something, must turn his mind away, occupy it with some intense mental concentration which would counteract the spell; he must inhibit his senses, since it was through these that his enemy could breach the defences of his mind and enter his citadel. And yet, at the same time as he attempted to do this, he must remain alert and aware. There was only one hope. Slowly, then, he began to form about him a mental barrier, wrapping himself, even as he had done before, as in a cocoon, in the pure, glittering white light of the higher planes; drawing to himself through the power of will and imagination linked, atom after atom of finer and yet finer matter and vibrating them against the dense force with which Zarov's will was bombarding his. It needed such concentration, such mental effort, that soon he actually ceased to see the passes, ceased to be aware of the music or the voice, ceased even to smell the cloying and dangerous perfume. He did not know how long he remained thus, but he was jerked back by a question. Zarov thought he had got him, did he? He drew a long breath and grinned rather feebly.

"Nothing doing," he muttered, his own voice seeming to come from an infinite distance; "you see, you were wrong."

His enemy gave a furious exclamation and the man behind him let go of his eyelids. With a sigh of relief he closed them over his burning eyes. When he opened them he could focus properly again, and he saw the livid face of the Egyptian bent over him.

"You defy me, then? You fool! You think yourself very clever, but let me tell you, this was nothing, mere child's play!"

He thrust his face, distorted and evil as some horrible mask, close to Simon's: "I shall not rest till I have broken you, do you hear? You'll see how strong you are when I crush you to pulp."

"Why," said Simon gently, "all this violence? You won't get your friend cured, you know, by breaking me, as you so charmingly put it."

"My friend?" the other seemed to spit on the word; then, as if remembering himself, altered his tone. "That is where you are wrong. I shall get him cured, for do you know what I shall do? I shall drive you out of your body. You think I am threatening you with death perhaps, but it is not so; Oh, no! You ignorant Western fools do not understand the powers we wield; you do not understand your own bodies, so how could you know what can be done to them? Listen then! You—your spirit, soul, what you call it—shall, by my power, be cast out of its dwelling place, which will become for a time an empty shell, what you name 'mad.' *Then* I will put one of my servants in possession of that shell, one I can control. He will use your brain cells, your memories, all you have, in this life, made your own. You do not believe me, but what do you doctors understand of possession, of dual control, or how it is brought about? It will be interesting for you to have a little—what do you call it?—scientific practical demonstration! For you will see it all, you, who will be an outcast, helplessly watching your body being used for my purpose. Believe me, there will be so little outward difference at first that even to your closest friends it will seem to be the man they knew; but later, well, they may find you a little changed in character." He laughed softly: "Oh, yes, Dr. Simon Conningsby, the well-known psycho-therapist, will be *very* useful to me; and that little girl you are in love with, she will also be useful. Well, what do you think of my plan?"

"Rot," said Simon, "that's what I think of it"; but he knew only too well that such things could be done—had been done.

"You defy me, then?"

"No, I just say you can't frighten me, that's all."

"We shall see whether I cannot frighten you, cannot frighten you so much that you will run away—run out of your body and leave it to me. In a few days, a few weeks at most, since you are so stubborn, you will learn to obey my will. In the meantime I think we will begin by a little test. You will not sleep nor eat nor drink until I so desire. Perhaps that will teach you to be more amenable."

After that they took Simon to a small, bare room. The ceiling and walls were curved and were made of what appeared to be jointed sheets of metal.

The couch on which they laid him was in the middle of the floor just out of reach of a table on which stood a jug of water, fruit, cakes and wine. He was bound down, but in such a way that a bell-push was under his right hand.

"If the ordeal becomes too much," said Zarov with one of his flashing smiles, "you have only to press the bell and instantly you may have all you ask—water, wine, fruit. You will be under observation from that little grille you perceive there in the door, so if you should attempt to get free from your bonds you will be prevented before you can eat or drink."

"I wouldn't touch your food," said Simon. "I don't want to be drugged, thanks."

The other shrugged and smiled. "I do not wish to drug you—now. We will see how you feel about food in three, four days' time."

Three—four days; and Carol was no doubt already at the dig, waiting for him, wondering why he had broken his word; soon they would be beginning work, in a few days . . . better not think of that.

When they had left him, he reviewed the situation; it looked more desperate than ever. How, weak as he already it was, could he hope to break through this guarded room, evade these ever-vigilant eyes, defy the powers of darkness which these men could and would evoke against him? Hunger and thirst would weaken his body still further and subtler methods would be employed to weaken his mind— the perfume, the music. True, he had managed to shut them out once, but how long would he be strong enough to employ his methods of defence? The mind was so terribly dependent upon the body. It was the music he feared most. He knew its power. He had used sound himself to heal nervous disorders; but it could be used to destroy, to disintegrate as well as to build up atomic structures. Well, thank heaven, at least for the moment there was quiet, but at any time he might expect some fresh attack.

He had pretended to scorn Zarov's words, but he knew that what he suggested doing was by no means impossible. It was not sheer physical courage, no—nor sheer will-power alone, that would count in the end. Simon might hold out a long while against torture, against suggestion, or any other kind of attempt to get behind his guard, but eventually there comes a time when the human brain, like the human body, touches breaking-point; and supposing his brain did give way, what would it mean? Undoubtedly that Zarov would carry out his threat, and thrust some other entity into his body. It was the final abomination, this violation of the sanctity of the human personality, but it was a commonplace in Eastern magic, yes, and even in the West it was more common than those who actually were in charge of the insane would have believed. Zarov's words came back to him, and he shuddered. If this did happen he would not even appear to be insane. He would go about among his patients, working who knew what havoc on their minds and their bodies . . . And suddenly he pulled himself up short. No; Weyland would find out, Weyland would destroy his body to prevent such a disaster. At the same moment he realized how dangerous it was even to allow such negative, fear-ridden thoughts as these to occupy his mind. He must stick to Weyland, there was safety.

But at the thought of Weyland he had again that uncomfortable feeling of implied failure, as if at a given moment he had abandoned Weyland's teaching and advice. His mind quested back. It had come to him first, this feeling, while he was having his conversation with Zarov. How could he have failed? He had a sudden vision of Zarov's hands holding that paper-knife, and at the same instant that dark sensation of anger and hate welled up within him; but this time he was on the alert. Something had gone wrong, then; before, he had been calm, detached, master of the situation, hiding his own powers beneath the exterior of a fool, but from the moment he had hurled defiance at his enemy, he had lost this advantage and had raised against himself a greater opposition than he might be able to withstand.

He groaned aloud. "Call yourself an occultist! That paper-knife was magnetized, he was using it like a magician's wand, stirring up all the evil and uncontrolled forces in your own nature. Fool, swollen-headed, vain fool to be caught like that!" Hadn't Weyland warned him a hundred times against this cocksureness and this lack of control? What used he to say? "The man who can be made to lose his temper becomes the ally of his adversary." He had thrown away his trump card in showing Zarov his strength and his weakness. "I'm for it now, and no mistake," he muttered. "Well, it's my own fault, but that's not going to help Carol—if it were only my own mess, it wouldn't be so bad."

His one hope lay in his sure knowledge that behind him, for all his weakness, were forces stronger than those which had marked him down for destruction; he had been trained by men who worked with these forces, and he must tackle the situation now as a Yogi would tackle it. There was no other way.

A great deal could be done, for instance, through certain forms of breathing. In the East these men could go for weeks without food or even drink. Although he, half-trained as he was, could not hope to accomplish such a feat as that, he might be greatly helped by what he did know. As for sleeping it would be too risky, in any case. For, in that half-world which the spirit traverses on its way to and from the body, such a man as Zarov had his main field of operations, Well, he could manage without sleep, no doubt, for there was a form of trance, obtainable also through the control of breath, which vivified and strengthened the body sufficiently to keep one going a long time.

So he settled down to work mentally. The hours slipped away. He did not know night from day in this dark place, and could only judge the passage of time by his increasing hunger and thirst. Once or twice the man called Hafiz came in and looked at him. Simon only prayed that they would abandon these tactics before his strength went, but feared it was improbable.

After what seemed to be a day or so at least he became suddenly aware that the temperature of the room was rising uncomfortably. Disturbed from his almost trancelike condition he opened his eyes, straining them in the semi-darkness. Wasn't that a movement close to the door? Surely it was a wreath of smoke. He sniffed anxiously; there did seem to be a faint smell of burning. Could the house be on fire? It was getting hotter every moment. That was a curl of smoke rising from the floor close to his side. He strained over, and at that moment a streak of flame licked up and was gone.

The house *was* on fire! For a minute then, he knew sheer stark panic. To be burned alive! All his artificial calm evaporated at the thought. And as he lost that control he had so far managed to maintain over his senses, the agony of thirst and hunger flared up: the mad thirst of the man wandering in the desert, the hunger which is like the gnawing tooth of a beast of prey.

The room was rapidly becoming a veritable inferno. Bright flames were running the length of the walls, licking at the end of his couch, flickering and leaping everywhere. He began to writhe, struggling with his bonds, but they held firmly. In his terror he forgot that he knew how to free himself. Then, as he fought, rolling from side to side, his fingers came in contact with the bell.

"Ring!" a voice seemed to say, "ring for help! Give in!"

Instantly he was sobered. He lay back panting, gasping from the heat, yet making an effort now to control his panic-stricken senses; if he rang, would they come, supposing the house were really on fire? And if not . . . if not . . .

His eyes wandered round the room which was alive with leaping flame. Soon, surely the couch must catch fire. *Why wasn't it burning already?* For that matter, what about him? He ought to be dead or suffocated by now, but although he was half-choked and his skin was cracking and blistering with the heat, he was not actually burned. And suddenly he realized something: *these flames did not consume!* He gave a broken sigh, dropped back, closed his eyes. Illusion! The whole thing was nothing but a picture projected into his mind from that of the magician. But his already parched tongue had responded to the suggestion, it was so swollen that he could hardly close his mouth; his calm had been broken to such an extent that it would be an almost superhuman task to regain it. The heat was—or seemed, for he hardly felt sure of anything by this time—real enough.

There must be something one could do. If his body had reacted so instantly to this illusion put over by Zarov, wouldn't it also to illusions of a different nature? Could he not, too, create them? Here, surely, was one way out of his ordeal!

Deep inward he turned then, struggling to shut out the terror the agony, the heat. How long he battled there with the pain hunger gripping his entrails, agony of thirst burning, it seemed, into his very brain, he never knew; but suddenly before his eyes, as vivid as the flames had been before, he saw a long range of glittering mountain peaks; he heard the splashing of a waterfall, smelt the indescribable and well remembered perfume of all those early mornings in India when he had walked through the awakening forest to his teacher's *Ashram*. As he walked he ate: fruit and little honey cakes, and he stooped over the ice-cold water and drank his fill. Fear, hunger and thirst were allayed; he was beyond them, in a place where they existed not.

Brief or long the vision may have been, but when he opened his eyes again there were no more flames, only the dark face of his enemy staring down at him.

"I did not ring," said Simon faintly, a little surprised to find that his tongue had become normal once more.

The dark face came nearer. "Who are you?" cried the man, and there was an undercurrent of alarm in his voice, "no one could defy the power of the fire!"

"Water can extinguish Fire, Oh, Worker of Illusion," Simon replied with a faint smile. But he knew, even as he spoke, that this last effort had exhausted him almost to breaking-point. How much longer? How much more?

"What do you know?" said the other fiercely. "More than you have revealed." He swung round to Hafiz and pointed to Simon with a long, slender finger. "This man has power, he must be broken—or die." He leant nearer. "I do not know how you gained your knowledge, but however wise you may be, you will not succeed in thwarting me. I could kill you, but since you have defied me I will keep you alive until I have driven out your spirit, until I have broken your will. If it takes me a year I will do it."

Simon said nothing. What was there to say?

"Listen," said the other, leaning so close that his eyes looked straight down into Simon's. "You may be able to make yourself immune from hunger and thirst, aye, even from me, but from fear no man is quite immune." He stepped back. "You see these walls? They are so made that they can contract. I said I would not kill you, yet perhaps, if you do not submit to my will, I shall do so—in the end. When you see these walls contracting upon you, growing narrower, closer; when they close down on your body, when the air ceases, when their weight presses on your chest, perhaps you will submit, perhaps you *may* ring for me! Then I will spare you. But if you do not, why then you can die. I shall perhaps capture your spirit as it struggles from your crushed body; I have done that to others. In any case I will tell you, so that you have something to think about as these walls converge, that this girl you love and the girl you thought to cure, will both soon be completely in my hands. I see you do not believe it, so l will explain, for I would not have you miss anything, through lack of understanding. Know then that the tomb they are about to open contains a force so terrible that on its release it will fasten upon them all; as bees swarm upon the stick held out to them, so will these forces seize upon the sacrifice and cling there. They will go mad, my friend, or die; and when this happens I shall enter in and take what was hidden there ages ago—the amulet of power which came from Atlantis—the Crystal wherein all can be seen and known. Small it is, they say, so small that it can lie in the palm of the hand, but within it is imprisoned the Soul of the planet Earth. You have not heard of it? You do not understand? Let me explain. This Crystal is the mysterious Womb whence all life on the earth first proceeded, the Primary impulse, the true Philosopher's Stone. Before the Earth was born It existed, radiating life to another world, but when this planet was ready to produce form, it was projected hither to become the focus for all the life forces of this Being within whose body we dwell. Each living thing has within it an atom corresponding to the nature of this mysterious Crystal, therefore It is the key to all that here exists. And wherever this Stone finds Its resting place, there, until It is moved elsewhere, is the centre of the earth whence absolute power proceeds. At first It dwelt in the great temple of Atlantis, but when the hour of destruction came, It was brought by magic means to Egypt, that the Mysteries, the spiritual nourishment of man, might continue through another age to be vitalized by Its force. But another Cycle is at hand—the Age of Aquarius, and It must move again. Whither, then, shall It be moved, but into the hands of those who understand Its nature and are courageous enough to draw It to them! So It shall come to us, and we shall be Lords of Earth, knowing the secret of eternal life, wielding eternal dominion!"

His eyes blazed; he seemed already half-divine, standing there, exalted by this vision. He laughed, looking down at his captive. "Do you still refuse to believe me? It does not matter, for dead or alive, you will be there in that hour, when we become conquerors of you all!"

He leant forward. "Think upon this, while you wait for death; think upon it, and judge whether you would not be wiser to come in with us, to put your will voluntarily in our hands, and so share in our triumph. The bell is still here, you have only to touch it and I will come. I have seen the strength of your resolve, and will take you as my pupil if you are willing. Consider my offer well. Is not life better than death?"

He placed a clock on the table, moving it so that Simon could see the face from where he lay.

"It is now just four o'clock," he continued, "in half an hour you will see the first movement along there above the door as the walls begin to close. I shall not tell you how long it takes for them to crush you, but very, very long. And I will bid the players sit without and play to you; the note they will play this time is the note of madness, of disintegration; so powerful is it that the ears of the musicians must be bound. It is a sound which breaks apart and shatters the unity of the physical atoms; it shivers the cohesion of the brain-cells. We shall see how long you can endure!"

How long indeed? Simon wondered. The hideous threats went round and round in his weary mind. It seemed to him already an age since he had lain in this room. His body, half-starved, clamouring for refreshment and for rest, could no longer be ignored. Yet if he was to hold out it must somehow be ignored.

Then the music started; pulsing softly at first from somewhere behind the grille over the door, it grew louder, more insistent. He had never heard such sounds, nor known they could exist; a sequence of notes each one of which was like a stab tearing its way through his whole nervous system. Then a pause, then a repetition of the same theme. Soon, in these exactly calculated pauses, he found himself tensed up in agonized expectation of the return of the fine, shrill notes which, when they did come, nearly made him scream aloud.

Then he remembered the other threat and glanced apprehensively at the clock. It was only ten minutes past four. His eyes went to the walls; he tried to switch his mind on to something else, but found his eyes straying to the clock again. Yes, this way undoubtedly madness lay. But he mustn't go mad. There was Carol and Betty and more, far more important, the Secret. He knew at last—too late. What a monstrous thought that such a man as X. might seize upon this Sacred Thing, guarded so jealously through the ages! But would it be allowed? Wouldn't it be guarded somehow? What had Weyland said about that? He couldn't remember, he couldn't think any more. He groaned at his own impotence, his failure. Whatever happened now, life, death, madness, he could see nothing but disaster ahead, not only for his friends, but for the world.

Then his eyes were drawn to the clock face. It was four thirty. Instinctively he glanced up at those bare dome-like walls. Was there a movement? Hardly—and yet . . . Yes, surely, surely the sheets of metal were beginning to slide together, they were closer than before.

He shut his eyes, then opened them again. There *was* a movement; the walls were definitely closing in. He had one moment of hope; was this illusion, perhaps, like the flames? He watched the grille high up over the door in horrible fascination. Yes, slowly, like an eyelid closing, a shutter was covering it. Thank God, the music would be shut out! That was the only consolation, he would not need to use so much force resisting the impact of those vibrations.

H shot a rapid glance round. How near the walls were! Nausea seized him; for one moment he was in the grip of claustrophobia, a panic grip, uncontrollable. Then once again by a prodigious effort he asserted control over his shaking body.

"I shall go mad if I give way to this," he told himself sternly. "I must do something."

And suddenly the thought came to him: "What would Weyland do? There *must* be a way out."

A way out . . . As he watched again the slow, dreadfully inevitable movement of those sliding walls, he knew that, in this life, there could be no way out. Death or madness, no alternative. All right, he chose death; but until the very end, the very last second, he would remain master of his own soul.

He lay back, relaxed, closed his eyes. He was helpless, so far as his body was concerned, but he had been taught that the body mattered so little in the scheme of things. Up to this moment he had had the idea that it was imperative that he should live so as to help Carol and stop Zarov entering the tomb; he had seen himself as a bulwark against all the powers of evil; it had been necessary while there was active work to do, a spur to achievement; but now that he had accepted the inevitable end, this attitude seemed ludicrously conceited. Surely if he failed those greater Forces which had used him up to now, could find another agent, and could accomplish Their own work.

Zarov had spoken of fear; of what need to be afraid? There was only death left; no need to be afraid of that. Foolish to worry; could harm really come to Carol, or even to the world, since they were all—yes, even the man who had set himself up in opposition to the Good—an inseparable part of that Good by virtue of which the whole universe existed and from which all things drew their life?

Words flowed in upon him, words he had learned long ago, the exquisite music of the Gita, music which swelled and grew, absorbing those other devilish cadences. A great calm descended on him. He lost all memory of fear; all thought of the possible disintegration of that part of Life he had called his body.

Vaguely he was aware that the walls were still approaching, that they had come very near now, almost touching him; that the air was growing unbreathable; but it meant nothing; he saw it all, walls and air and bodies, as but whirling particles of Life, in which Consciousness moved at will.

There was really, then, no space at all, no part could be separate from any other part; he became preoccupied by this thought. He seemed to be speaking to Weyland about it.

"I can't do anything more, but then in reality the separate 'I' doesn't exist; therefore 'I' must be 'you'—so why don't 'you' take a hand and do something, if you want anything done—"

Weyland was speaking. Simon strained to catch the words, but they were indistinguishable. He leant forward in the effort to approach his friend—got up; there was a faint sound, a kind of click, then without any warning at all Simon found himself free, out of his body, floating above it. He could see that which was called Simon Conningsby lying strapped to a narrow couch. He could also see that the walls had converged now so closely that the space surrounding him was almost obliterated. For a second he wondered if he were dead, then realized that it was not so, for a narrow thread of light, the silver cord of life, still bound him to the unconscious body. He was aware of himself now only as a form of light. Yes, he was free; and| he understood at last that true freedom from the flesh to which the Will can identify itself with any form and perceive and know anything upon which it may choose to project its consciousness.

A thought flashed upon him; it came from without; it was a thought of fear, but also a thought of love—a call. And in the same instant the room disappeared, and he found himself identified with the mind of a frightened girl, seated on a rock gazing out over the desert by some dark cliffs. He *was* that girl. She was afraid and she wanted him. He experienced all her emotions and yet, while participating in them, he was still himself, enough apart to know his own strength and power and to be able to radiate out love from the centre of his being into that of the one with whom, through love, he had become united.

"I will come, in or out of the body, I will save you, I will save us—for we are one; all things are one, and the parts have but to be invoked through love for them to rush together as quicksilver rushes together when it is plunged in water. Fear separates—love unites. Remember this; draw me and I must come. That is the Law." Into her receptive mind his reassurances flowed, and even as the contact faded, he knew that she was comforted. He had made a promise. It would be kept.

It was very bright and clear here; even he, a point of light, was aware of a brighter light in which he moved. It was Weyland's laboratory, but not quite the laboratory he knew, for in this place all the problems with which Weyland was struggling, were already solved. Everything was solved, immersed, as it was, in the Absolute Solvent, the all-embracing Light. But of course it would be hard to bring this knowledge down, it had to percolate through so many layers of dense matter before it could be apprehended even by such a brain as Weyland's; Simon understood that.

And Weyland was there, too; as Simon penetrated into the radiance, he saw this different image of Weyland—a younger, more magnificent, more perfected image—talking to another man whom Simon had never seen before. Yet both these seemed, somehow, a part of himself, of his own light. It was very curious. He was surely a little beam coming from them, and they a beam emanating from a Light even greater than themselves. He was brooding over this, attempting to expand into that wider consciousness, in order to understand it, when Weyland looked at him.

Instantly he was aware of a sense of separation, of "himself" as an entity, it was almost a pain.

"You must go back," came the thought from Weyland's mind, or whatever it now was that made Weyland separate from him.

"But I don't want to go back." His refusal seemed to increase that sense of separation, to drive him apart from these two with whom he desired to be.

"You," said Weyland and smiled, "that which is 'you' on the physical plane must go on living, it has work to do."

"Can't I do it like this—here?"

"No, no; physical plane objects must be dealt with in their own terms—that is why we have bodies—"

"And in the terms of the Workers of Illusion," came from that other tall and resplendent being who stood by Weyland and who seemed, in some curious way, Simon thought, to be part both of himself and of the man he loved.

"But my body is tied up down there, how can I get it free? What must I do?"

He again felt himself losing the consciousness of form, merging into that greater mind. Words were flowing out to him; what were those words? He couldn't remember them. Suddenly he felt that something was going wrong; the light began to fade, he struggled to reach up to it, but like a fish caught in a net, felt himself being drawn away; now he was in a half-world with strange, grotesque forms moving about him. Then he became aware of a room; no, it was a tomb in which his body lay writhing, choking to death. He looked at it indifferently. The walls were pressing on the man's chest, his face was suffused, almost black, certainly in a few moments now he would be dead.

But they had said he must not die. What else had they said? Something about submission, acquiescence. No, surely he had got it wrong, hadn't he been refusing to acquiesce, been fighting for his own integrity, been sacrificing his life to hold the citadel of his mind inviolate? What could those words mean? To capitulate would be to deliver himself to the enemy, body and soul. Yet he could think of nothing else. He was aware of thick darkness, of a huge form which seemed towering above him: Zarov? Then had Zarov perhaps put those words into his mind, for this was his territory, this dense region close to the earth. Had Zarov won after all? He had a moment of confusion, of panic; he must remember, must get it clear before he was forced back. Acquiescence? Yes, that was the word. He saw the fingers of the man on the couch clutch and stretch convulsively. They grasped the bell in a kind of blind agony; they pressed it down. He heard its sound, sharp and clear. He saw that awful constricting movement of the walls cease, somewhere a shutter was lifted and fresh air blew in; now the walls were receding. It was over, the fight, the struggle.

The next thing he knew was a glass being pressed to his lips. Drugged? It didn't matter any more. He drank deeply.

A pair of enormous dark eyes gazed into his. He must obey those eyes, whatever they commanded he must do: *the terms of the Workers of Illusion* . . . Who had said that? He heard a cracked whisper—his own voice—say: "To the greater I submit."

CHAPTER VI

THE VALLEY OF THE SHADOW

IT WAS NIGHT. Silence, absolute and profound, lay over the desert. In the desolation of rock, of cliff, of illimitable sand which faded into the sky like a nebulous cloud, only the stars moved, scintillating points of light.

To Carol, seated alone, facing this immensity, it seemed as if all life had ceased to be and she only was left in a dead and empty world.

With a slight shiver she twisted round towards the gap in the rocks behind her which led to their camping-ground. It was impossible to believe that within two or three hundred yards were her friends with their band of native workers—a little vortex of passions, fears and conflicts.

She strained her ears, but could hear nothing save the blood thrumming in her head and the beating of her heart. This loneliness was such that it did violence to one's reason. Above her the towering cliffs with their gigantic shadows held a brooding menace; before her the desert, if she strained her eyes long enough, became peopled with vaporous movement, as if the guardians of the dead were gathering there to avenge themselves upon the Violator of their tombs.

To-night, indeed, she seemed to feel these dead very close. From their secret burying places, the rocks—the very rock, perhaps, upon which she sat—from the tomb where her own party had been working, from the sand beneath her feet, they crowded, they arose, they spoke. So real was their presence, she found that she was defending herself and her friends against their silent indictment.

"I never wanted to come," she whispered, "I've always hated it, but they don't understand—Oh, if I could stop them now."

She sat upright and laughed shortly. "Stop them? Nothing'll stop them. If he was right . . . but I *know* now that he was. Oh, if only he were here! But even he wouldn't be able to stop them, this tomb's got them like—like an obsession. They wouldn't listen—they're blind to the risks, to everything . . ."

At the thought of those last weeks she made a savage grimace and swinging herself from her perch began walking up and down. She pulled out her cigarette case, and as she did so the faint light caught a reflection from the ring which she was still wearing, but which she had transferred to her right hand to avoid questions.

Instantly her restless movements ceased; she stared at it for a moment, then raised her head with that characteristic defiant jerk. "Yes," she muttered, "l was right to send Ali; Simon" (she called him that now to herself) "is the only one who might be able to tackle them."

She lit her cigarette and sat down again, her mind sweeping back over all those queer events which revolved about this man who so recently a stranger, now seemed to have become the most important figure in her life.

She had always prided herself upon her level-headedness, her common sense, and other such masculine qualities. She had deliberately encouraged this side of her nature because with her unpractical family, so unable to face up to the difficulties of life, she had felt, as she had told Simon, that it was her job to play the man's part in their affairs. But from the moment they had arrived at their destination she had been forced to realize, much to her anger and disgust, that her strength was not adequate to deal with the situation which had arisen, and that someone was needed upon whom they could all rely. Bitterly now she admitted to herself that she was only a woman after all, and not so exceptional a one at that, else she would not have been sitting, as she now was, like some forlorn heroine of a Victorian poem, gazing out towards the direction whence the man she had summoned might eventually be expected to arrive.

Would he answer her call? Had he ever really intended to come? That doubt was like a perpetually nagging moth, a barb festering in her pride. He had sworn he would follow them in two or three days, hadn't he? Yet they had been at work now for over two weeks and he had not come, had not even sent a message. Oh, how she had suffered at first, what absurd agonies of hope and disappointment! Serve her right for being a fool—probably he hadn't meant anything he had said, after all.

And yet . . . She stared hard at the ring. It was a large scarab carved from some strange stone which gleamed as if with a hidden fire. Well, even if he had thrust it upon her at parting, after that preposterous conversation which how had the unreality of those conversations one has in dreams, had she the right to expect him instantly to answer her call? Didn't that prove her all the more a romantic little fool?

Queer! She had had no doubts at the time; all her natural scepticism had been quieted, yes, stifled entirely, by his personality. But since then, as it became increasingly obvious that he was not a man of his word, this sceptical side of her had taken control once more and persisted in reminding her of all those strange, unpleasant things people said of him. She had even been told by an Egyptian in their hotel that he was a secret agent and known to have been mixed up in some dubious company promotion scandal. This same Egyptian had warned the others, too, not to be taken in by him, as he was known to be one of those people who travel around fleecing the unsuspecting tourist. Nick reminded her of this triumphantly, whenever she brought up Simon's name, and though she refuted these suggestions with great violence, she could not quite ignore them; in fact they increasingly filled her mind to the exclusion of the good things which Ramage and several other men she had met reported of him. Was it just due to hurt pride because he had failed her? Or was it something to do with that insidious atmosphere of evil which she felt somehow haunted this whole valley? Could it possibly be warping her judgment, and affecting her sense of justice?

Frowning, she got to her feet and again began pacing up and down. There *was* something wrong. It wasn't only that she had been predisposed by Simon's warnings to discover evil here; that alone wouldn't have infected the others with the curious canker of bitterness and unrest which was making their mutual relationships almost impossible. It was this—this increasing tendency to suspicion, to quarrels, to open conflict, that had at length broken her resolve. Fear had been stronger than pride. Each evening, when she escaped from the atmosphere at the camp to this particular spot that she had made her own, and tried here to gather calm and reassurance to enable her to face with at least a semblance of equanimity the friction with her family, she had struggled with herself and gone over the same arguments again and again. One night, when the fear became too much so that she cried aloud into the darkness for guidance and for strength, she had had the strange feeling that Simon was quite near. It was then she decided on an impulse to send Ali back to Cairo for his servant; but that was days and days ago; she had heard nothing, and since then things had got even worse, but it was her doubt of Simon which made her suffer most of all.

"I'm getting hysterical," she muttered, "I don't suppose there's anything wrong really—if I hadn't heard those stories about the tomb, I'd never have noticed anything. As for the trouble among the men, that's hysteria too. I really must take myself in hand. I won't put up any more opposition, I'll just try and work with the others and help instead of hindering them."

She turned slowly towards the *coulée* which led to their camping-ground. Yet as she began to descend the sandy ramp she looked round and shivered, peering into the black well of shadow before her. Simon had certainly been right when he had said once that the place to which they were going was the most desolate spot on earth. This brooding silence—this immensity of tumbled rock ... could there be something in the stories after all, in their overseer Abdullah's ravings yesterday, and the natives' abject fears? Weren't the men perhaps wise in refusing to continue work on the tomb? She walked on a couple of steps, then stopped. Surely the aspect of the rocks before her was changing, taking on new shapes, deeper shadows, menacing gulfs of blackness whence anything might appear? She looked up, and as she did so, the moon gradually swam out from behind the rocks, flooding the cliffs, the valley, the sand, with a livid radiance. At the same instant, as if through the powerful alchemy of this dead light, she was aware that a change was sweeping also over her own perceptions. She saw, indeed, with new eyes; everything took on shapes of dreadful familiarity. Horror gripped her, rising from within herself in wave upon wave of darkness. She felt as if something appalling were approaching, as if, in an instant, veils would he torn from her subconscious mind and she would know some dreadful, forbidden thing.

She leant against a rock, fighting for control, cold sweat pearling her face and neck, her eyes focused blindly before her. With her reason she knew that never in her life had she seen this particular aspect of the valley before, with the moonlight slanting thus upon the looming rocks and the menace of some unknown danger paralysing her; yet the experience was intimately real, a very part of her life. Then, in a flash, she remembered: she *had* seen it before. In dreams, as a child, she had fled screaming down this very valley to awake trembling in the dark. A dream—nothing more.

Gradually the first acute terror passed; but it did not wholly leave her. Even now she wanted to run, but instead she forced herself to stand still, then presently to walk very slowly down the steep, sandy road. Yet she could not help heaving a sigh of relief when she saw the tents from which the light flowed out in a warm, reassuring glow.

She paused outside. Of course they were arguing. At the thought of the fresh storm her entrance would cause, she felt that she almost preferred the dangerous silence of the night.

And as she listened to her father's falsetto whine punctuated by Nikolai's occasional bass, a surge of blind anger rose within her. Why had this man come into their lives and, for all his eagerness to help them, his genuine love for Betty, upset everything she had so laboriously built up? It was his fault they were here; his fault that she had been forced to throw up a safe job for this will-o'-the-wisp, this dream that had become a nightmare. Oh, he meant well enough, she admitted that; there was absolutely nothing tangible she could hold against him; only within herself was a deep suspicion and a deeper distrust which she knew he reciprocated.

With a gesture of irritation she drew back the flap of the tent and entered.

They were all grouped about Nikolai, who lay upon the camp bed with Betty seated on its edge, holding his hand, and beside him her father at the table, upon which were scattered most of their discoveries to date. These represented nothing of the slightest importance save to so keen an archæologist as himself: a few ostraca, some rather damaged late Ushebtiu figures, a couple of common scarabs, and some shards of what might have been a canopic jar. Even these had been found in a small *cache* outside the entrance to the tomb. They had broken through the wall at the bottom of the ramp very soon after their arrival, but disappointment had awaited them. Through passages bare of inscriptions and of any sign of treasure, they had come at last to what might have been the antechamber; but this, which they had expected to be full of marvels, was bare also save for brilliant wall-paintings and a number of inscriptions that completely baffled old Mannering and had led to hours of argument and much irritation all round. Always this irritation and conflict! So far, certainly, Simon's grimmest warnings had not been justified, but Carol was convinced that it was not merely imagination which insisted that, ever since that first wall had been pierced, a more than usually acute nervous tension had made itself felt among them; tempers were brittle, quarrels arose like sudden sand-storms, dangerous and inexplicable, obscuring all their real affection for each other.

And now, to make matters worse, the men had struck. She was glad—anything for delay, anything to stop them opening that last door and entering what must surely be the tomb itself! This strike seemed to her like the hand of some kindly Fate stretched out to guard them from the result of their own stupidity and blindness.

As she crossed to the table, Betty looked up, smiling. "Hullo, where have you been all this while—communing with the *Kas* of the dead?"

"No, I've been communing with the living," said Carol drily, "they're much more articulate at the moment."

Mannering frowned at her, pulling at his shaggy eyebrows so that they stood out like antennae—a habit which had irritated Carol all her life.

"Now, my dear child," he said in his thin, complaining voice, "I do wish you would leave those natives alone; we've got them well in hand, I promise you. It's for us men to tackle that wretch, Abdullah, not for my little daughter. I don't like to think of you mixing with them, I don't indeed. Now if you'd just type out this little list for me," he waved about twenty sheets of crabbed manuscript at her, "it would be so much more useful. Neither Nick nor Betty type as well as you do."

She shrugged her shoulders, ignoring the papers: "If you imagine you've got them in hand you're very much mistaken. They're almost hysterical. Their English is so rotten I can't make out much about it all; but they won't go near the tomb again, that's quite clear."

Nikolai sat up. "They will," he said grimly. "I wish you wouldn't interfere, Carol; your father's quite right. This is a man's job and we've got the situation well in hand. I spent nearly an hour reasoning with them; when I left they were quite calm—"

Carol laughed rudely. "Yes, I could see you'd been with them. As for being calm, they were about as calm as a nest of fighting ants when you've been prodding it with a stick." Her eyes flashed: "If you think riding the high horse and ignoring all their prejudices is the way to get them calm, you're going to learn your mistake. I tell you, you won't get a man of them to do another stroke of work on this place—and a damn good job too," she ended beneath her breath.

"But they must—they must," piped Mannering, jumping to his feet and pulling at his eyebrows with such force that his whole face became wrinkled and distorted like a comic mask. "They can't leave me in the lurch like this, with only a few slabs between us and the mummies. they can't! It's outrageous! I shall complain to the Government—"

Carol turned away impatiently. "Oh, what's the good of bleating about the Government—a lot they care! No one believes in this blasted tomb, anyway."

Then Betty joined in the fray. "Carol, how can you speak to poor Father like that? Can't you see he's worried to death?"

"I'm sorry," Carol said wearily, "but what is the good of fooling ourselves? We've got no control over the men, any of us, we can't make them work. We'll have to give it up. It's a horrible place, anyway."

"Give it up?" cried Nikolai. "Don't be so absurd! If they won't work, then we'll open the tomb ourselves."

She looked at him with narrowed eyes. "From what I gathered, they wouldn't let us do that, if we wanted to. They're terrified of something—something inside that tomb. I don't know what, but you were there when the panic began. You saw the way they just threw down their tools and bolted screeching like parrots. There *must* have been something to cause it. I don't know what—"

Nikolai laughed shortly. "Nor do I, and I'd like them to try and stop me. We'd see what shooting a few of the blighters would do."

"And get ourselves all massacred—so helpful!" Carol said scornfully. "Really, I should have thought you had more sense. You're in a civilized country, not in the wilds of Tzarist Russia!"

At that moment she became aware of Betty's eyes fixed upon her with an expression of pain and pleading. Her face was drawn and white. Sharp words, sarcasm, quarrelling, always upset her. Carol's anger was swept away by the love and pity which she always felt for those weaker than herself, but more especially for this sister who depended upon her for strength and stability. She recalled her secret message to Simon. All this bickering was waste of time and energy in view of the fact that he might soon be here to deal with the natives as only he could do, and she felt ashamed that, once more, she had allowed herself to be swept into the usual maelstrom of arguments and recriminations. Out there on the rock she had made up her mind to go to her tent without seeing them at all; but she had been frightened and rushed in for shelter. This was the result of cowardice.

Impulsively she went across to Betty and kissed her.

"Darling, I'm sorry; it's this place, I think, upsets us."

But Betty turned aside. "It isn't that, it's you who are behaving so funnily. Don't you see *I* want this tomb opened. I *must* have it opened! It's going to cure me; I know it, I feel it." Her voice became high, a little hysterical. "This is my last chance, if we don't get it open, if we don't get the money we've been promised so that we can get me cured—I shall die." She jumped up, she was quivering from head to foot. "Yes, I shall die—or else go mad. Do you *want* to feel you've helped to drive me mad, Carol?"

Carol gave a horrified cry. "Betty! What's come over you? What a *horrible* thing to say."

She stared at her sister, unable to contend with this sudden, unexpected attack. It was incredible that Betty should take such an attitude. Even in her worst seizures she never turned against Carol. How odd she looked, too. Her eyes—strange, hard eyes—dilated, pools of blackness; her lips drawn back a little, showing her teeth. Yes, she did look a little mad. Carol remembered what Simon had said, and shuddered. Possessed ... She wanted to rush away. Could he have been right? Indeed this was not Betty, not the Betty she knew.

Even Nick looked startled. He went across to her and put his arms round her. "All right, darling, don't get upset; I swear we'll open it somehow."

She gave a little shuddering sigh, and her head sank on his shoulder. "You swear, Nick?"

"Of course, of course. And Carol will help too, when it comes to the point."

Carol dared not contradict. "It will be all right, Betty," she said vaguely. "We'll hold a council of war to-morrow when we've slept on it. I'm going to turn in now."

She kissed Betty, receiving a rather vague kiss in return, said good-night to her father who, having apparently forgotten all their difficulties, was peering with rapture at a tiny shard of pottery, and went out again into the night.

As she paced up and down trying to calm herself, Nick joined her.

"Look here, Carol," he said abruptly, "what is your game? Why are you being such an obstructionist? Why don't you want this tomb opened? After all it's as much to your advantage as it is to ours."

"I've told you why; but anyhow, I'm not an obstructionist. *I* haven't struck work."

"No, but you raise difficulties the moment I suggest that we should open it ourselves—absurd difficulties!"

"Well, I happen to care for Betty's safety, if you don't."

"You know I do. But her safety isn't in question—on the contrary."

"It is. They won't let us open it, I tell you. There'll only be trouble if we try."

He thought for a moment. "Look here, what about doing it at night? The tomb's easy for us to get at and out of sight of the men's camp. They wouldn't know."

"They've probably got spies," she suggested rather feebly, for she didn't believe they had.

"Not at all likely. Anyhow if they don't agree to get back on the job soon, I'm determined to have a shot at it. I'll give them another week—a week exactly, that's fair. Then I'll tackle it at night. Yes, that was a great idea of mine! And I hope they won't have spies, because I shan't hesitate to use violence if they interfere."

His look said: Take that as a warning, if you're thinking till double-crossing me. "And if, when the time comes, you won't help," he continued, "you'll just have to stay outside, that's all. But make no mistake about it, Carol, this tomb is going to be opened." He smiled at her sullen look, and patted her arm. "Cheer up, old girl, you'll be us pleased as any of us when you handle those jewels and get your share of the kudos for the most wonderful discovery of the age."

When he had gone, she continued her pacing in the silence of the starlit night.

What was going to happen? She knew Nikolai. Nothing would stop him, once he had made up his mind. The men, she was certain, would continue to refuse their help, nor would they let them proceed with the excavations—Abdullah had made that clear. It could, then, only end in a fight.

Was this what Simon had foreseen in Betty's horoscope—blood, conflict, death? Then, suddenly, she remembered something else. He had said that the disaster was marked in his, also; if this were true, then it could only mean that he would be there. But was there truth in these things? the voice of her sceptical self argued . . . Yet hadn't there been truth in his prophecies up till now? Except that he had said he would follow them in two days' time—and hadn't followed them.

She suddenly felt so insignificant, small, afraid, that her very soul seemed to shrivel within her. She was snared in a net of mysteries, of horror and menace; Simon was the only one who could understand these mysteries, dissipate the horror, avert the menace.

She bent her face over the ring in an ecstasy of supplication, pressing her lips to it, whispering his name, and it seemed to her, after a moment, that thrilling up from the cold stone through her lips, through every vein in her body came a warmth, a soothing vibration of reassurance, an unmistakable response.

She got slowly to her feet, she was unaware that she had fallen upon her knees.

When she went to her tent, it was with her head high and a firmer step. "I know he will come," she said.

CHAPTER VII

THE MINDLESS ONE

M<small>EANWHILE</small> the man for whom Carol waited, lay stretched limply on a divan with hanging arms and mouth and eyes half-open.

Occasionally Zarov, writing on the other side of the room, would glance across at him with a gleam of triumph in his heavy-lidded eyes. The Englishman was his. There had been no more revolt. There was indeed little to revolt in this half-empty shell that moved—when it did move—like an automaton, with blank eyes and sagging lips from which occasionally senseless words came.

After that spectacular collapse, when, his nerve broken, half-mad with the horror of the ordeal to which he had been subjected, he had clung, babbling, to Zarov's arm, muttering over and over again: "I submit—I submit," there had been occasional flashes of reason. But these, as the result of several "treatments," had grown less. A few more of such treatments when, with all the arts at his disposal, Zarov set himself to drive out the last remnants of that personality which had been called Simon Conningsby, and there would be literally nothing left but a healthy body (he was being carefully fed now) and a set of habits, mechanical reflexes and the like. There would also be at his disposal, of course, all the man's knowledge, the memories he had gathered in the course of his life. These remained so long as the body endured, stored up in its subtle, etheric counterpart, even though the brain might no longer be able to tap them at will.

Zarov had not been particularly surprised at Simon's collapse. He had seen that happen quite often. It was amazing how a man could hold out through ordeal after ordeal and then suddenly let go and fall mentally to pieces. The ordeal of the Closing Room was always effective. Simon, indeed, had held out longer than anyone he had ever known. It was quite obvious that he must be a man of some power. All the better; the more intelligent, the more advanced the man, the greater the potentialities that Zarov acquired, once the Will was given over to him. Yet, for this reason, Zarov had his prisoner under continual supervision during that first week, for it was conceivable that the true personality might endeavour to fight its way back before the exorcism was absolutely complete. Now, however, he was satisfied that all danger of this was over. Simon obeyed him like a puppet and when not controlled by Zarov's will, was in a state bordering on idiocy.

And the poor fool had thought to defy him! Zarov laughed softly and a faint animal-like moan came from the supine figure on the couch. The other man instantly rose and stood over him.

"Get up!" he commanded.

The prisoner raised his head, gave him a blank, stupid look and swaying a little, rose to his feet. Instantly Zarov's arm shot out and felled him to the ground. Again Zarov ordered him to rise. The performance was repeated several times. Then Zarov leant over him. "Who am I?" he asked the crouching man. The reply came almost inaudibly: "Master—master," Zarov laughed. It gave him infinite satisfaction to see one of these accursed Englishmen at his feet. He thrust out his hand and the other bent his head over it, kissing it abjectly. Zarov sneered and pushed him aside with his foot. He fell across the divan and lay there, gazing blankly at the ceiling.

At that moment Hafiz entered. He looked at the prostrate figure and laughed, rubbing his hands.

"May all those who set themselves against our power end thus, Oh, lord," he said softly.

"They will," answered Zarov, "have you any doubt of it?" He moved back to the table, "and in a few days—in a few hours perhaps—I shall hold the Key." He sat down and began tidying the papers on his desk. "Last night I used the girl again and looking through her eyes saw that they have cleared the entrance to the tomb and have entered the antechamber. But there is some trouble with the men—I think it is a strike, but she is stupid and her mind confused; now if I had the other as my medium . . ."

"A strike?" repeated Hafiz, "that is strange—they are your men."

"They are not my men, fool. They have free will; they are but bought men, and who can trust those who serve for wealth? They are superstitious, and no doubt many of them are sensitives; who knows what they may not have seen in that place?"

"Then work is stopped completely?"

"Only for a time, for I can use the girl so to play on the cupidity of her own people and lure them on that they will force it open themselves rather than abandon it. I am sending such thoughts to them continually, bombarding their minds with my suggestions, and just because of their vanity and greed they easily respond to my power. No, it will not be long now, and when they open the tomb itself I must not be far off."

"Are you armed against all danger that may possibly befall when they do this?"

Zarov laughed. "Are you afraid? Have I not said it is they who will receive the full force of the curse with which the tomb is guarded? I can protect myself from any aftermath. Moreover, you forget there are Others behind me."

The man on the couch moved slightly, turning his head from the cushions in which it had been buried.

Hafiz glanced at him swiftly. "Is it safe to talk?"

"Must I bind the ears of my dog," sneered Zarov, "when I would speak? He is even less than that!"

Hafiz sighed. "Ah, if I but had your powers! And do you go to-morrow? Is it settled?"

"I do not go to the tomb, but shall camp close by—close enough so that when it is opened I shall be at hand. I shall use the girl, and through her shall perceive in what form the curse has operated; thus shall I know what rites of exorcism I must employ to make it safe for me to enter there. I can also learn how I may bind That which guards the Secret to my Will."

"And He," Hafiz spoke in a low voice full of awe, "will He be there?"

"That is not for you to know."

There was a short silence, then Zarov spoke again. "I leave you in control here. You know enough to guard this English dog, I hope. Let him wander at will in these rooms and the inner courts, and feed him well. A man of his type needs exercise and food to keep his body in good condition; we must build up this shell that I shall later use. You need not fear a return of the personality, no one could withstand the exorcisms I have used. There will be nothing to resist your orders, for I will treat him once again to-night and put a command upon him to obey you as he has hitherto obeyed me." He smiled: "You may amuse yourself how you will, Hafiz, with this proud Englishman, I give you full permission. It will be good practice for you. He is your toy until I return."

Hafiz laughed and bowed. "My thanks, Lord. And by what means will you communicate with your servant, that I may know all progresses satisfactorily?"

"Look in the dark pool at the hour of midnight. Eat of the drug, and when the Power grows within you, project your spirit towards the tomb; thus you will see. It is a pity you are as yet so uninstructed, else you could summon to you the spirit of the girl. It is a surer method, needing less effort, exhausting the mind and body less than the way of personal projection; but you are slow, Hafiz, I had hoped greater things of you than this."

The next day Zarov departed, leaving Hafiz in charge of his house and his prisoner.

Hafiz, like all men thrust into a position of power to which they are unaccustomed, lost no opportunity to exercise his will on the hapless victim of Zarov's magic. He left the "mindless one," as he had nicknamed Simon, no peace, making his life a veritable torment, but despite all his cruelties, the Englishman almost at once took to trailing after him. In fact he soon constituted himself Hafiz's shadow and would not even be driven from the door of the room where he slept, but lay across the threshold all night like a devoted dog. Hafiz began to think this queer obsession on the part of the Mindless One must be due entirely to his own remarkable magnetism and magical powers. The idea pleased and flattered him. Supposing it was he and not Zarov who eventually became master of his body and mind?

The second night after Zarov's departure he went into the chamber sacred to the mysteries of the black Arts. Here, even, the prisoner sought to follow him, but he struck him to the ground. However, when later he emerged, exhausted and still a little dizzy from the effects of the drug which he was forced to use to facilitate this type of clairvoyance, he almost stumbled over the man's body as it crouched in a corner by the door rocking itself from side to side and whimpering. The moment Hafiz stopped, it crawled forward with little animal noises and clung to his feet.

It was then that an idea occurred to Hafiz. Why shouldn't he use this man as Zarov used Betty? It would only need a little practice, for it would be infinitely easier to control an empty shell than a body over which the personality still held dominion. It was, as Zarov had truly said, an exhausting business leaving one's body in full consciousness; it needed tremendous concentration, an effort greater than Hafiz cared to make. Supposing it were possible to employ some easier method?

As he stared down at that grovelling form, it was almost as if a voice spoke to him: "Use this man, make him your slave, so you may gain greater power. Zarov despises you—you could be as mighty as he if you had such a servant."

All that day, while the Englishman abjectly followed him round, the idea grew, taking an increasing hold over him. Why not? Why not? But he must be cautious.

He tested the Mindless One continually; he seemed to obey him almost before he spoke. How easy it would be to use this medium to discover some of those secrets Zarov still withheld from him! He would do it; he would start practising on him to-night, after he had got in touch with Zarov in the Room of Magic.

So at midnight, when the household slept, he entered the chamber, but instead of shutting the prisoner out, he bade him follow.

They entered a room which seemed as if cut out of black marble. The eight sides and the floor gleamed darkly in the light of red lamps which hung from the pointed ceiling. In the centre was a small eight-sided tank containing water so dark, with those red lights shining therein like drowned eyes, that it seemed to descend into the centre of the earth. On one side of this, set within a pentagram containing many curious symbols, was a kind of little divan made of piled skins. At first these appeared to be of ordinary leather, but a closer inspection would have shown that they were the dried skins of human beings. Standing against six of the eight walls were tall braziers, the seventh being occupied by the door through which they entered, and the one directly opposite this, by a large chair rather like an elaborate throne. Above the chair was the semblance of a great snake and shining dimly on the wall behind, a circle set about with what appeared to be astrological symbols.

Hafiz having, by means of certain passes, commanded the Englishman to become deaf and blind to all that would happen and to remain unmoving to the end, proceeded to light the braziers, each of which gave out a different perfume. The smoke curled forward as if drawn towards the pointed roof above the pool. Soon a haze obscured the corners of the room and dimmed the red lights to a faint glow. Meanwhile the Egyptian had divested himself of his *galibiah* and proceeded to utter invocations in an unknown tongue, making great gestures, and intoning Words of Power. He then seated himself cross-legged upon the little divan of skins, and slowly, between the enunciations of more resounding Names, began to masticate the drug which would give him strength to perform the Ceremony of Projection.

The smoke from the braziers grew more dense. A strange, heavy silence had descended upon the room. Hafiz's eyes were closing; the drug was beginning to take effect. At first its result would be to dim all the perceptions, and to induce a profound indifference and drowsiness; later, however, an extraordinary clarity and strength would come upon the addict, giving him the power to perform feats of endurance greater than those possible to ordinary men.

Meanwhile the Englishman remained as he had been commanded, crouching a little, his blank eyes staring ahead, his hands hanging limply by his side.

Hafiz's eyes were closed now, his breathing had become imperceptible; but had he not been in this quiescent state, he might have noticed that a change had come over his prisoner. Slowly the body became tensed; now the eyes were no longer blank; the crouch became purposeful, like that of a tiger about to leap upon its prey. A moment he stayed thus, watching the figure of Hafiz, then he sprang. His hands closed upon the entranced Egyptian, with a swift movement he had caught and thrown him. He fell at the loot of one of the braziers and lay still.

Simon straightened himself and drew a deep breath. The terrific strain which these days of feigned madness had put upon him, had come very near to breaking his nerve; the relief of being able to behave normally again was almost ecstasy. He stooped over Hafiz, he was still breathing faintly; probably, then, he would survive the shock which such an attack must inevitably cause a man in trance. At any rate he was not likely to recover consciousness for several hours.

In those long days when, as the "Mindless One," Simon had wandered behind his masters, and particularly since Zarov left and he enjoyed increasing freedom, he had learned a great deal which would be useful now. He knew, for instance, that Hafiz kept the keys of one, at least, of the outer doors in the pocket of his *galibiah*. He picked up the garment and slipped it on, then he took the fez from Hafiz's head and, although he could hardly suppress a shudder, put it upon his own. He had nothing wherewith to darken his face. That could not be helped. It was comforting to feel the short and evil knife which had been hidden in Hafiz's sash beneath his hand, although he did not want to use it. Then he trussed up the Egyptian and gagged him, for safety's sake.

Before leaving this evil place, he examined it carefully, but could find nothing of any magical value. Had it not been for the helpless man and all those other people asleep in the rambling house, he would have liked to have set it on fire; it was the only way it could be cleansed. But that was impossible. It will have to wait, he thought.

Fortunately he had learned something of the geography of the house which was built, like all Eastern houses, round a central courtyard.

This room, with a positive rabbit warren of others, used no doubt by Zarov for his mysterious activities, was situated underground. It was approached by two stairways. One led by a secret door into Zarov's library, and the other Simon had not been able to investigate.

But he struck out boldly enough, and after one or two false starts, found the stairs and proceeded cautiously to ascend them. There was no light and they twisted in the thickness of a smooth wall.

Quite suddenly, on turning a corner, he almost stumbled over a huge Nubian who was stretched across the top step before a richly ornamented door. Fortunately the man appeared to be dozing, and Simon shrank swiftly back. This must be the hareem guard, if indeed the door led to the women's quarters and not to some part of the house kept for other magical abominations. Obviously it was not the exit he was looking for. Like a shadow he glided down the stairs again, thanking Allah for his slippers and the thick carpets. He was back once more in the maze of shadowy rooms, brushing against hangings, feeling his way along walls, opening doors leading into he knew not what dangers. It was like one of those nightmares in which one wanders through a haunted house, knowing that at some turn, from some silent chamber, some horrible thing will appear.

Moreover, every minute was precious, for he must be out of the house before dawn, or he would be lost.

At last, after, it seemed, hours of search, he came to stairs again. He hoped feverishly they were not the same stairs. At each turn he half expected to come across that huge, dark form barring his way, but at last he found himself up against a closed door. He had seen Hafiz manipulate the secret lock. It took him but a moment to find the trick of it, and he was standing in Zarov's library.

There was a window here, a rather larger window than was usual in Oriental houses, and through the elaborate tracery Simon saw, to his alarm, the first pale signs of approaching dawn. He had a few moments only, now.

This room led directly into the courtyard. As he opened it he realized that the household was already astir. A servant passed carrying a basket on his head; someone was singing in the shadows, and he heard the swish of water upon the paving. There was nothing for it, he must be bold. Perhaps they would not take any notice of him. Sending up a wordless appeal for help, he stepped out into the growing light and sauntered across to a passage which he knew led to one of the doors into the street.

Whether the key in his possession opened this one, or the main door upon the other side of the courtyard, he did not know. If no porter guarded it, then it would be easy to try the key and if it did not fit, saunter back. He had, by this time, traversed the courtyard in safety; but as he was about to draw aside the hanging which screened the passage, a servant came through and glanced at him. Simon stooped to knock some imaginary insect off his leg, and the servant passed by without a word.

With a sigh of relief he followed the passage. Yes, there was the door. Then he saw that another Nubian was sprawling on a low seat beside it. There was a light suspended over the man's head. It would be far too dangerous to attempt to get by. Simon was about to turn, when the man looked up. Quickly as Simon swung round, he was not quick enough. The man sprang to his feet. He was a giant with great, bulging muscles, and Simon could see the whites of the eyes glittering in the dark face. He said no word, but in a flash drew a knife and leapt forward. In that second the thought went through Simon's mind: "So after all Zarov didn't quite trust Hafiz—wasn't sure of me, this man was set to watch."

He retreated before the swift, panther-like approach. The passage was narrow; once in the courtyard he would be surrounded. He backed slowly, his eyes on those rolling eyes coming at him. Could he do it? If only there were more space! Then the man sprang; Simon collapsed before him, and the next instant the surprised giant was hurtling through the air over the Englishman's shoulder. He struck the ceiling, as Simon had feared, but he couldn't help that; in such a restricted space this throw could not be perfectly achieved. Simon hoped he had not injured him fatally, as he sprinted for the door. The crash of his fall would have disturbed the whole household; already there were cries and shouts and the running of feet. Thank God there was a key in the lock. As he turned it, thrusting back a heavy bolt, a servant dashed out of a room. Simon tripped him and hurled him backwards simultaneously, another Judo trick; the door swung back, and in a flash he was through and running madly down a narrow street. On either side were high white walls, pierced only here and there with slits. He feared that the wall of the house he had just left continued for some distance; if so, there might well be another door lower down into a garden. He was right. As he turned a corner a man sprang out. Simon took a flying leap and as they met twisted the knife out of the man's hand and sent him after the knife ricochetting against the opposite wall. It all took a second. He was past the door. The street widened. There were other houses, turnings to right and left. Then, just as he felt freedom within reach, there was a shot behind him. Something struck him in the ribs. He swayed, then righted himself. To fall now would mean death. Another bullet sang past his ear. He ducked and, exerting all his power, added to his speed and swung into the alley on his right. He did not dare slacken, for he could hear feet pattering behind. As he ran he put his hand to his side and it came away wet and sticky. It can't be much, he thought; but all the same the searing pain was making him faint. He would need all his strength to outpace his enemies. He was now in the confusion of narrow streets with which old Cairo is honeycombed. Houses touching overhead, awnings swung across the road alleys and doorways mysterious and shadowed, some with points of light shining out of the gloom, some shuttered and silent. Life would only awake in half an hour with the sun. Already at the end of a close-packed street the sky was gloriously rose, and the silhouettes of jutting houses seemed, for a moment, darker in that burst of radiance. A milkman rattled by on his donkey. He did not bother himself about the man who, swaying a little, ran slowly past him. Simon's head was beginning to swim. He had not yet had a chance to recover properly from all those ordeals, mental and physical, to which he had been so recently subjected.

Now, at last, he could look back. There were no more footsteps, only the receding form of the man on his donkey was in sight. He must rest. He looked to right and left. He might claim sanctuary in one of these houses, hide for a while in some dark corner. But Zarov, no doubt, had his spies and creatures everywhere. Simon knew how quickly, and by what amazing and incomprehensible ways, information travels in the East.

He came at length into a square. Before him a mosque rose like a dream of beauty, its minarets and domes silhouetted against a now flaming sky. He knew that mosque. His head was swimming now. Things were beginning to go round. He must stop soon, must rest, must have this wound attended to. But he couldn't rest long. Carol needed him. How long would it be before they opened the tomb? Zarov might have already arrived. It was far away, it would take four days at least. No, then Zarov was not there yet. But when could he hope to reach them, with this wound? . . .

He sank down upon the steps of the mosque. He must get help. He couldn't hope to walk to his hotel, or even to the Europeanized quarter. If only he could get hold of Ahmed!

He staggered up again. This wouldn't do. He must get on.

Doors were opening now, shutters swinging back. Children ran out from the alleys, and women, black, shrouded silhouettes, no more, were beginning to emerge from the darkness on mysterious errands.

Then into Simon's dazed and weary mind came a picture of the interior of the shop of one Abdul Gamil, the vendor of strange curios and jewels, silks and charms, a true friend of his, whose hospitality and kindness had never failed; Abdul Gamil, who, it was said, knew all the secrets of Cairo, yet never opened his lips to let them forth. Surely his house was but a little way from here—down that alley on the right? It was worth trying. Somehow he reached the place; the shop was still shuttered, but with the little strength left him he banged upon the door.

A window opened above and a head, only half visible in the darkness which lingered still in this narrow place, appeared rather furtively.

"Abdul," Simon called softly, "it is I, the doctor, your friend. I am hurt, let me in!"

There was an exclamation. The window shut. A minute later the door opened and eager hands drew him into the shop. He collapsed on a bale of silk.

"Send for Ahmed," he muttered, then fainted in Abdul's arms.

CHAPTER VIII

THE EDICT OF THE STARS

THE TIME LIMIT was up. That very night Nikolai and her father were determined to make the attempt.

This was bad enough, but what had been worrying Carol even more during those last few days was Betty's behaviour. Although Carol was ready to put quite a lot down to the influence of this valley, still, surely no mere place could change a person so completely as Betty seemed to have been changed.

For, from a shy, sensitive and rather childish creature, she had suddenly become a forceful and determined personality. Her rage with Abdullah, who still refused to disturb what he called the *Afreet* of the valley by continuing work on the tomb, was terrible to see. Even Nikolai became shaken and anxious. Thereafter she left neither him nor her father any peace, nagging at them perpetually to open the place up themselves, plotting how they could circumvent the natives. When these phases of excessive energy passed she would sit mournfully staring at nothing in particular or reiterating parrot-like: "I want to get well, I want to get well. I *know* I shall get well if we open the tomb." She seemed, too, to have developed a queer antagonism to Carol, which hurt the elder sister terribly. Never, in all their life together, had she known Betty anything but affectionate and kind.

This attitude emphasized her feeling of loneliness and isolation. She was separated from her family by a gulf of misunderstandings; she had no friends. There had been no reply from Simon to her S.O.S. It was obvious that he had only been playing with her.

She became increasingly certain of this, and the fact that she had stooped to send him an appeal for aid in spite of his first failure to keep his word and join them immediately, filled her with shame and humiliation.

Well, it was too late now, in any case. Without a doubt the others would open the tomb. She was powerless to avert it, but she was convinced some horrible fate threatened them all.

For the last few days she had given up all attempt to dissuade them; she no longer cared to sit with them in the big tent where they had their meals. Instead she spent hours aimlessly strolling about the rocks, exploring the *Wadi* or following the base of the high cliffs which cut into the desert like a barrier defying the sand. Sometimes towards sundown she walked for miles among these arid rocks, away, always as far away as possible, from that haunted valley.

This last evening, driven onward by the terror which every passing hour accentuated, she wandered even further than usual. Ever responsive to beauty, she did succeed in finding a few moments' peace in the flaming glory of a sunset so pure, so incredibly lovely, that the colours surpassed anything human tongue might hope to describe. Sitting there, she lost herself for a little while in this sea of glory. No wonder, she thought, the ancient Egyptians believed in a Celestial Nile, with such vivid greens, clear, pure, a river of light indeed, stretching across the rim of the world, wherein the fiery Boat of Ra sank slowly through wave after wave of ever-changing light to meet and conquer in the underworld the uprushing darkness. Music, the sublime music of Bach, triumphant and translucent, must look like this to eyes which could perceive in colour the vibrations of sound. Even the desert, the rocks behind her, flushed for a little while into glowing response as if the earth joined in this triumphant rhapsody. Words came into her mind, whence she knew not: "When Thou risest we live. When Thou settest, we die." And as the colours faded and a uniformity of grey, like a pall of death, enfolded the desert, borne on a chill wind like a veritable breath from the Underworld, she understood to the full the poignant meaning of that cry.

Death . . . Simon had warned them of that possibility. Death . . . to-night—already . . . was this the last sunset she would see?

She jumped up, shivering, and looked round. She was a long way from their encampment. A spur of jagged cliff rose behind her like an arm thrust outward. Its outlines were obscure now; later it would become clear and hard again, sharp-etched in black against a sky patterned with bright stars. But no, to-night, she remembered, the moon was full. Why did that thought add to her fears? It was like a half-comprehended threat. It seemed to make the danger more imminent.

Well, she must get back and have supper. After supper . . . But no, somehow, she had not the courage even to consider that contingency. She was beginning to pick her way slowly back when she came to an abrupt halt. What was that sound? Was it an aftermath of the music she had imagined the sunset to give forth, that soft, strange humming? Absurd fantasy! This was no music, but an approaching aeroplane.

"It must be," she whispered, "nothing else sounds like that."

Her heart gave a great thump. A wild surge of exultation surged through her. He had come, he had come! She stood still, listening. The droning increased. It was so near it must be almost overhead. Now it was growing fainter—louder. Where was it going, was it circling somewhere just out of sight? It seemed to be landing, or was it merely that sound carried far in this stillness? Now it had ceased. She strained her ears—all her senses—nothing.

A feeling of empty misery descended upon her. She sank down on a little rock, battling with ridiculous tears. Aeroplanes, of course, often crossed the desert . . . absurd of her to get so excited about such a commonplace sound! Besides, why should he fly? With burning eyes she stared out into the hazy immensity, towards the vague point whence she had hoped against hope that Simon would come to her. The 'plane had been travelling from that direction, certainly; but that meant nothing. How stupid she had been!

Why, perhaps . . . She sat up, frowning. What made the thought of Zarov enter her mind? Nick had sent a message to the man called Hafiz when the trouble first began, asking for advice, but if, in the interval, Zarov had returned from his trip and was back in Cairo he might answer the appeal in person. Supposing he did come, and not Simon, what irony! Yet at the idea she gave an involuntary shudder. Zarov and Simon! Queer, how alike in some ways those two were. Both gave one that impression of immense power, of determination, of drive. She had the feeling that both of them would be capable of achieving almost miracles to gain their ends; and how fundamentally opposed those ends were! What would happen if they met in conflict, face to face? Who would ultimately gain the upper hand? She wanted to believe that it would be Simon, but something told her it was more likely to be Zarov.

Well, it was Zarov who wanted the tomb opened, and to-night Nick would obey him—Simon had proved himself a broken reed.

There was no sound now, only the vast enfolding silence which was so profound that one's own existence seemed itself to constitute an impertinent interruption. She didn't want to go back; she couldn't face that tent and the talk and arguments. The thought of food made her sick. She would stay here a little longer. They wouldn't worry about her absence, they had accepted at last her nocturnal wanderings and her passion for solitude.

So she sat on, no longer aware of time, brooding so deeply that she herself seemed to be absorbed into the surrounding immensity. But gradually she became aware of a sensation of discomfort; she felt she was being observed, that she was no longer alone. Immediately she was alert. She got up, staring round. Wasn't that something, or someone, materializing over there out of the half-light? For an instant she had a thrill of terror and made an instinctive movement towards flight, then she realized that the moving shadow had already defined itself into the approaching figure of a man.

It was no good running now, he had seen her, anyway. Was it Zarov? A wandering Arab, perhaps? Certainly it was no one from their camp, for he was coming from the opposite direction. How slowly he walked! She had an impression that he was sick, or in pain. She made a few steps forward. Surely that was Simon's build . . . could it possibly be . . . ?

Then, suddenly, she knew. With a little cry she ran to meet him. The next moment she found herself holding both his hands and saying, stupidly: "You've come!"

He smiled down on her. "Of course I've come. Didn't I say I would?"

"Oh, yes, but I thought—I hardly hoped . . ."

"To see me after all this time? I only got your S.O.S. yesterday. I flew. My man's over there with the 'plane. We landed beyond that spur of cliff as I didn't want to disturb the men or let your people know I was here until I managed to see you alone somehow. I was just going to scout around and try to attract your attention. This is a bit of luck."

She felt suddenly weak. She wanted to cry. Instead she sat down rather abruptly on a rock. "You don't know how glad I am," she murmured. "It's been awful here, there's been a strike—they've stopped work altogether now."

"Yes, I know."

"How do you know? They were back at work when I left."

"Because I sent Ahmed to bribe them to stop in the first place; but he returned to Cairo after a couple of days, and when Ali saw him there he told him the men were too frightened to go on, anyhow. But I hear you've got as far as the antechamber."

"Ali couldn't have told you that!"

"No, I heard it from Zarov."

"Zarov?" she echoed.

He grinned mischievously. "Yes, I've been his guest of honour for the last fortnight, otherwise I'd have followed you at once as I promised. Zarov isn't here now, by any chance, is he?"

"No, thank goodness. But what makes you ask? I was only thinking of him a moment ago. I had the feeling that he was somewhere about, but instead—it was you," she ended happily. "As a matter of fact, though, that Hafiz man might easily turn up, Nick sent for him when the men became troublesome, just before I sent Ali for you."

Simon laughed shortly. "I think not. I've every reason to believe that friend Hafiz is still suffering from the effects of a sudden application of the honourable art of Judo which, fortunately for me, I studied in Japan. This particular trick's guaranteed to lay you out for two days at least, but in the circumstances it may have put him out of action for keeps."

"What's been happening to you, then?" she cried.

"I'll tell you in a minute; just wait till I light my pipe." He sat down beside her, and as the match flared up she saw his face clearly. The change in him was startling; he looked, she thought, as if he had recently been on the point of death.

"You've been ill!" The distress in her voice compensated him, in that one moment, for everything he had been through.

"Ill?" He laughed. "Well, not exactly, I wouldn't call it that. Can we stay out here for a bit, or ought you to get back? I don't want a search party to find us."

"They won't bother, I often don't turn up for meals."

"Good. Before I tell you my story I'd like to hear yours, and in detail, please. Have you found anything interesting? And what's the place like? I want to know the position of your dig and everything about it."

"It's under that big cliff, half buried in a sort of landslide; it looks as if the cliff had fallen and blocked it at some time. First there's the ramp, then a wall. After that there's a short, steep passage which leads into a big space—"

"Any inscriptions, any objects at all?"

"Nothing, it seems just hewn out of the rock, anyhow. There are shafts leading off; we explored those, but there was nothing in them but a few bones—"

"Bones? Are you sure? Sounds rather peculiar."

"Yes, holes in the rock with human bones—nothing else."

"Very odd—go on."

"The blocked-in doorway leading to the tomb itself is facing the entrance. It was sealed with a royal cartouche; Father couldn't make it out, but he was sure it was very early. And it was when we wanted to break through this door that the men, who had been getting restless, suddenly struck and refused to go on. Abdullah seems to have been the moving spirit, he said the place was cursed and there were *Afreet* or something there—whatever they are."

"Evil spirits. What happened then?"

"We were held up for a few days, but Nick and Betty (I must talk to you about her) tackled them and bribed them to go on. When we got through there we found another very narrow passage and then—the antechamber—"

"Anything in that?"

"No; quite bare, but there are marvellous paintings round the walls in brilliant colours and another slab closing the burial chamber itself, Nick thinks—which is sealed again with the same cartouche. It has gods painted on either side and a lot of inscriptions—" She suddenly shivered. "I don't know why, but it gave me the horrors, I could hardly stay near it—and they were all so excited; every time I've been down there I've nearly repeated my star performance of the British Museum."

He nodded. "Yes, and then?" His voice was tense.

"Well, we were just preparing to move the slab when one of the men screamed and they all flung down their tools and scuttled out like rabbits. They held a sort of palaver outside and sent a deputation to Father to say that on no account must that place be opened and that they wouldn't go near it again. Abdullah even went so far as to threaten us if we attempted to do anything. You can imagine that put Nick's back up properly."

"Yes, Abdullah's a fool; still, I don't blame him. Now it's up to me, I suppose, to try and persuade your father to leave it alone. Thank God the men struck when they did."

She shook her head. "You'll never be able to do that. Don't you see, having got so far, right up to the very entrance, nothing would stop them with so much involved: their hopes, their ambitions, their money—and more than that—Betty; she'd be the deciding factor, I think."

He grunted. "You say she's been egging them on?"

"She never lets anyone alone! If you knew how queer she is, there's something about her that frightens me; I'd rather, really, she had one of her old attacks." She made a hopeless gesture. "I wish I hadn't sent for you, it's only dragging you into danger. I'm convinced nothing but force would stop Nick having a go at it to-night."

Simon jumped to his feet. "Did you say to-night?"

"Yes." She covered her face with her hands. "Oh, I'm really terrified. I know you are right about this curse."

"I am right," he said rather grimly. "I'm glad you've come round to my point of view, anyway; you may be less inclined to think I'm mad when I tell you what's been happening to me in the interval."

She said with rather a wan smile: "I expect you'll find I'm willing to accept a lot of things I'd have laughed at a week ago. I had an experience . . . but perhaps that was just an attack of nerves, it has been rather nerve-racking here, you know."

"What was it?"

"Oh, you'll laugh . . ."

He shook his head gently. "No, my dear."

She gave him a grateful glance. "All right, then. Well, I was walking back one evening not far from the tomb, when—it's hard to explain—but I seemed to see the whole scene quite differently, almost as if I were another person. I *was* another person for a moment. I was simply paralysed with fear. Everything was familiar. I felt as if I'd been here before, but not as I am now. It was as if all the cruelty and evil in the world surrounded me. Oh, it's hopeless to try and explain—but it was like a dream I used to have." She turned on him sharply, "Why, I told you about it, I remember; and you said it was a premonition."

He sat bolt upright. "This—is interesting. Go on."

"Nothing more. It just passed—like a cloud. I suppose I was just tired or something, the strain—"

He shook his head. "Don't you believe it. This has given me an idea, but never mind. Has it happened again? Has anything else happened?"

"No, I think I've told you everything, except about Betty."

"Well, fire away."

When she had finished he nodded thoughtfully, sucking at his empty pipe. "That doesn't surprise me, in fact it confirms what Zarov said."

"What is this about Zarov and Hafiz?" she cried.

"All in good time." He looked at his watch, "When did you say your people are going to have a shot at the tomb?"

"As soon as they're certain the men have turned in for the night, but you know how late the natives here sit up, they never seem to sleep until the morning. It'll be about midnight, I expect."

"That gives us five hours. I'm going to have a busy time, I can see that, if I've got to talk over your crowd before then. I'd like a word with that prize idiot, Abdullah, first, if possible."

"You're not to tell him Nick's plan," she cried, "if he and his men came to stop us I know there'd be trouble. Nick's in such a state I honestly believe he'd do something rash. They all seem to have gone a bit mad," she added miserably.

"Don't worry, I'm not out to precipitate trouble of that sort. I'm opposed to force on principle; if it can be avoided persuasion's my line—as you may have noticed," and he gave her a swift smile.

"It won't be any use," she said, shaking her head.

"Well then, we'll have to think of something else. If I had a charge of dynamite, I'd blow the whole darned place sky-high," he added savagely, "but I haven't, so it's no use thinking about it. Come on, we'd better be getting back now."

As they went he recounted what had happened to him in those last weeks. She listened incredulously, but when he mentioned the fact that he had been wounded, she cried out in alarm.

"But you shouldn't be here, you shouldn't have come! Oh, why did I send for you?"

"I'd be here, anyway. There's nothing to be worried about. It only grazed me, luckily, and old Gamil had it attended to at once. He found Ahmed as well, so after a bit of a rest we borrowed an aeroplane. Both Ahmed and I are certified pilots, so fortunately there was no need to let a stranger into the business. Zarov, no doubt, has found out about my escape by now. But he suffers from the weakness of so many of his type—vanity and over-confidence. I wouldn't mind betting that will be his undoing in the end. He's too cocksure and despises everyone else to such an extent that he never considers it possible they may know as much as he does. If he hadn't been so certain of his own infallibility, he'd have taken the trouble to observe me more closely, and not been quite so pleased when I crawled around kissing his lordship's hands. However, it was lucky for me, otherwise I'd be there still."

"They might have shot you dead all the same."

"They might," he laughed, "but that evidently wasn't my *Karma*; if I'd been meant to die, believe me, I'd have done it in that Contracting Room."

She shuddered. "That awful room! Like—like Edgar Allan Poe's story."

"Just what I thought. I don't mind telling you I *was* scared of going off my nut at one moment."

She walked on for a little while in silence, then said suddenly: "I only wish you hadn't had to grovel to him; I can't bear the thought of your kissing his beastly hands, it seems so—so—" she broke off with a helpless gesture and he smiled at her a little quizzically.

"I know; you believe in the 'I will not bend, although I break,' school of thought," he laid his hand on her arm, "but doesn't it strike you that there are things more important than personal pride and an 'attitude'? What's it matter if I had to grovel, as you call it? He couldn't touch my inner self, and even if he had been able to do that, what would it have mattered either, compared to the issues at stake? At this game, my dear, you've got to learn to distinguish between essentials and non-essentials. I'll admit that if I'd been alone, with nothing particular to live for, neither this work, nor you, well, I might have come all over heroic." He shrugged, "As a matter of fact, when I was having that extraordinary experience that I've told you about very inadequately, I didn't in the least want to come back. Life on that side—because it *was* life, life a hundred times more vivid and more intense—was much more alluring than the prospect of being tied down to this tiny little bit of consciousness that I call myself." He laughed, "In fact I have a feeling that poor old Weyland had the devil's own job to induce me to face Zarov and get on with what I was supposed to be doing down here!" He came to a stop. "Hello! isn't that the light of the camp? I mustn't come any further, I don't want them to know I've arrived like this—they mustn't guess there's any collusion between us. I'll just stroll in later and tell them that I'm starting work at a dig on the other side of the hills and flew over to prospect before my men turned up. I'll see if I can't get some sense into your Nick's head."

She sighed, "I haven't any hope, unless you could perhaps try explaining things to him scientifically. Of course if you told him about Zarov it might do the trick."

"It wouldn't sound real, you know, to a man like Nikolai who only believes what's absolutely shoved in front of his nose; I'm afraid it'll need personal experience to convince him. And he'll get it, too," he added grimly, staring at the black mass of cliffs ahead of them, "unless I'm greatly mistaken, but then it may be too late." He straightened himself with a sigh. "Well, I can only do my best. Now you'd better get along and have some food. I fear we're in for a hectic night, whatever happens."

"But what about you?" she cried, "your wound—you oughtn't to be walking around like this, and you must have some food, too."

"Oh, I'm all right; I can go without food and rest for quite a while. You don't know me and my idiosyncrasies." He looked down at her with his swift grin which transformed his face into an impish mask. "When we're married you'll have to get used to them, so you'd better start practising now."

"But I never said I was going to marry you!" she cried, laughing indulgently.

"No, but you've thought about it, admit you have!" He took her by the shoulders and bent down till his eyes were level with hers, "And in your heart you know you will, quite soon, too, when we get out of this jam. It's time your family stood on its own feet, anyway; you've dry-nursed them long enough. I was thinking as I came here, what about a little expedition into Thibet by way of a honeymoon? I've got some good pals among the Lamas, and I feel somehow it's rather your line of country." Before she could reply he drew her against him: "Carol," he murmured, "there's no escape for you, as I told you in Cairo; it's written in the stars this time. You don't want to escape either—and you know it."

He stepped back as if with an effort. "Now do get your supper whilst I go on with my sleuth-like activities. I'll give you half an hour, then I'll come along; if I can do nothing more, I may be able to get them to postpone it for to-night. But whatever happens I'll drift off again fairly soon, so as to give them a chance to make up their minds. When you know, one way or the other, slip across down the *Wadi*, you'll find me waiting here and we can talk over last-minute plans. Thank the Lord I can trust you to do the right thing in any emergency!" He pressed her hand: "Sure you're all right? If you're scared I'll come further with you, but I do think it would be better if I had my talk with Abdullah first."

She looked up at him: "No, I'm not afraid—now."

It was true, all fear had left her. As she walked back, what he had said kept ringing in her head: "It is written in the stars—this time." And that talk about Thibet, how could he have known that such a journey had always been her secret dream? Then the old bitterness surged up in her. A dream? Yes, and nothing more. How could she marry with this family of hers? Could she condemn Betty to have no prop to lean on in her times of terror and distress, when even Nikolai was no good to her? No, she had long ago put all thought of marriage from her. Certainly such a decision had been easy enough while no man attracted her; but now she must just be doubly strong. She must not allow herself to drift beneath the spell of idle, romantic fancies.

The others had finished their meal when she got back. She ate in silence. They were talking about the approaching attempt. There was a feeling of expectancy, excitement; the rather guilty excitement, she thought, of small boys setting out to break the law. It seemed a long time before she heard the step she was waiting for outside. It was followed by Simon's voice, hailing them. They all jumped to their feet, and Carol played up at once.

"Whoever's that?" she asked. Betty, who was closest to the flap, peered out. "Why, it's Dr. Conningsby!"

At the name, their father, who had apparently already forgotten all Hafiz's warnings, precipitated himself out of the tent.

"Conningsby! How fortunate, how fortunate!" He grasped Simon by the hand, not listening to any of his explanations. "This is a real stroke of luck. We've made the most amazing find, yes, most amazing! The extraordinary part is that the inscriptions quite baffle me—I'd very much value your advice; I've been told your knowledge of hieroglyphics is quite exceptional—well, so is mine, so is mine; indeed, I may say, without vanity, that there are few people, very few people indeed, who have gone so deeply into the mysteries of early hieratic script; but this baffles me—yes, yes, baffles me. I am certain that it must be very ancient—unknown perhaps! Yes, yes, it may well turn out to be an epoch-making discovery. Yes, I am almost ready to believe that we are making history," he prattled on, his face wrinkled with excitement, his short-sighted eyes glinting, with every word drawing Simon nearer to the cliff where the tomb was situated. It was with the utmost difficulty that the other freed himself to greet the rest of the party.

"It does sound amazing," he said soothingly, "I shall be most interested; but I'm afraid you're having a little trouble with the men, I passed through their camp on my way from my own dig and Abdullah insisted on pouring out a tale of woe; I thought it just as well to listen, as I could see at once they were wrought up about something."

"So far as we can make out," Nikolai broke in, "the whole pack of them seem to have gone dotty; their lingo's impossible, but I think I've got to the bottom of it, they'll come to heel now."

Simon sat down on a packing-case outside the tent and pulled out his pipe. "I'm afraid," he said slowly, "things are a little more serious than you may have realized. These men are fanatical and superstitious to a degree, they think the place is cursed and when they get an idea like that into their heads it's difficult to move it."

"But they can't stop us! They can't stop us!" shrilled Mannering, "it's an outrage!"

"Don't worry," put in Nikolai, "it'll take more than a few fanatical natives to stop me. A curse, indeed!"

"But supposing," Carol said, "there *were* a curse—"

"Don't be so childish, Carol."

"But one does hear of such things—there's that Priestess in the British Museum."

"Just advertisement—no sensible person believes in it."

Carol turned to Simon. "What is your real opinion, Dr. Conningsby? You know a good deal more about Egypt than we do."

Simon looked round at their intent faces, and when he spoke it was with great gravity. "I think the natives are probably right; they know the potentialities of their country, you don't. But what's the good of my talking, you'll merely think I'm as mad as they are."

"Oh, go ahead," said Nikolai, half laughing, "let's hear the worst."

Simon re-lit his pipe, which had gone out, before he answered. Carol, from her vantage post behind the others, against the tent entrance, watched his abnormally long, slender hands as he pressed the tobacco down; she felt they must be strong as steel, yet sensitive as a woman's. For a few moments he remained silent, looking in the direction of the tomb. Seeing him thus, between her and the moon which was floating now high above the cliff, his upright, seated silhouette reminded her of one of those calm statues of ancient Pharaohs who appear to hold all power and all knowledge within their clenched hands.

As if aware of her thoughts he glanced round. Their eyes met in a look of such intimacy that a wave of happiness enveloped her, sweeping away all her previous resolutions. She no longer felt afraid of anything.

"Since you left Cairo I have received some quite interesting information about this place," he began slowly, "and in view of what I know about the ancient Egyptians and their powers, I can't help thinking the men may have a certain amount of reason for their behaviour." He thereupon repeated all he had previously said to Carol in respect of Egyptian magic, but with far greater restraint.

She admired the way he played up to his audience and the cautious manner in which he spoke of magic, comparing it to certain scientific processes known to-day. She felt that he succeeded in making his warning extremely impressive.

Nikolai, however, reacted in just the way she had anticipated. "You mean to tell me that you, a sensible Englishman, believe in these wild stories of curses and whatnot? I really can't credit it."

Simon rose to his feet: "Yes," he replied, "I do; and if you'd knocked about in the East as long as I have, you'd believe in them, too; such things have been known to happen again and again."

Here Mannering broke in. "It's impossible," he cried, "you don't understand what's at stake for us, Dr. Conningsby. Our money, everything, is sunk in this and it's the find of the century, I tell you!" He pranced up and down tearing at his eyebrows and looking for all the world like a demented fowl, "I won't give it up—I can't! I never heard such preposterous advice—never!"

Simon shrugged his shoulders. "All right, have it your own way. If you get the men to do it—go ahead, but you'll have your work cut out. Old Abdullah, when I saw him, was sweating with funk, and could do nothing but gibber about black magic and an *Afreet* one of his men actually saw in the tomb. Argument will be quite hopeless, might just as well try to reason with a dancing dervish. I strongly advise you not to attempt to do any digging on your own, either; the men might very well turn nasty."

"They'll not be the only ones, then. D'you think I'm going to be baulked by a lot of lousy *fellaheen*," snapped Nikolai.

"Of course not—there can't be any question of that," replied Simon in a conciliatory tone, "something will have to be done, but I do beg you not to do anything provocative just at the moment; I know the men, they're not safe when they're panic-stricken like this. They may calm down in a day or so; I may be able to talk them over to-morrow, I'm fairly used to dealing with the Eastern mentality. On the other hand if I fail, I might get some of my own men to come along—they'll do anything for me. It's not much good wrecking all your chances straight away by bringing things to a head when it might be managed by a little patience and diplomacy—don't you agree, Mr. Mannering?"

"Quite, quite," said the old man, taking, as usual, the line of least resistance, "but I must say their whole attitude is quite incomprehensible to me. Such a find would surely be worth any risk—they must realize that it's of world importance. I explained that to them—two or three times—and still they haven't grasped it—curious people! But I'd like you to see those inscriptions."

But Nikolai interrupted, as if afraid the garrulous old man would give away their intentions. "You can't show him now, I hope I shall have mended the electric plant by to-morrow." He turned to Simon: "It went wrong two days ago. I think the men must have been monkeying with it, unfortunately I'm not much of an engineer. Abdullah's supposed to be in charge of that, but of course he won't come near it. We don't want to use up our hand torches, though we're pretty well supplied. It's late, anyway, now. Come along after breakfast, and we'll all go down."

Suddenly Betty spoke. All this while she had been standing staring rather blankly before her; and her voice, feverish, excited, bursting shrilly in upon them, startled them all.

"Yes, to-morrow," she cried, "we'll see it to-morrow! We'll open it, and I'll be cured!" She turned to Simon, grasping his arm: "Do you know I've had wonderful dreams since we came here; sometimes I'm an Egyptian, it's so strange and lovely; I'm rich and powerful," her eyes gleamed. "What do those men matter? Aren't we stronger than they? I know everything is coming right, once we get it open. Think of the fame! Think of the publicity, and the money! We'll all be rich and powerful then." She gave a high, excited laugh and began moving about with a kind of dancing motion, her mop of black hair and puckish face making her resemble some small djinn. Carol had not exaggerated when she spoke of the curious magneticism that emanated from her at these times. She caught Nikolai and whirled him round with her. "I feel so happy! Darling, you will open it, won't you? It would just break my heart if you didn't." She flung her arms round him. "I'll make you so proud of me! I've written the beginning of the article to-day, it came quite suddenly. Can't you see the headlines: *Explorers enter tomb of black magician. Ancient curse defied by Mr. Edwin Mannering and his Intrepid Daughters?*"

Simon laughed. "You be careful, young lady; don't talk too soon. 'They' may be listening, you know."

She raised her impish face eagerly. "They? Who do you mean?"

"Oh, the *Kas* of the dead, the Guardians of the Tomb—and so on."

"How thrilling! Do they really exist? Shall we see them?"

"I sincerely trust not—for your sake," he answered grimly; "if you do, there won't be any article about Mr. Mannering and his intrepid daughters, I can guarantee that!"

"Now, now," interrupted Mannering, "don't get overexcited, Betty, my dear." He laid an urgent hand on Simon's arm, "I want you to give me your opinion on some hieroglyphics, and some of the ostraca are very interesting." Still chattering, he drew Simon into the tent, but the others did not immediately follow them.

Nikolai looked after them with a frown, his thin lips pursed meditatively. "I don't trust that fellow," he remarked, "what is he doing here? D'you remember those yarns we heard about him in Cairo? Fishy, some of them. I wish your father wouldn't be so darned confiding. My opinion is that Conningsby got wind that there's something really important here and wants to have a finger in the pie—if nothing more. I don't believe this story of his about a dig—it's a blind. Why, of course!" he struck one palm on the other triumphantly, "Don't you remember Hafiz telling us, when he rushed us off here, that there was some dirty work going on behind the scenes with a view to interfering with our rights? I'll bet you anything our fine doctor's at the bottom of that, and now we've been too quick for him, he's come along hoping to scare us off so that he can have a go at it on his own. It's as clear as daylight."

"Yes," cried Betty, "of course! Oh, Nick, what can we do about it! We must open the tomb."

"We're going to, my dear," replied the other grimly, "this settles it. For all we know, those men he so generously offered us may be a band of marauding Arabs he's bribed to do us in."

"What rot you are talking," said Carol sharply. "Really, you sound like someone in a Victorian melodrama. Things like that don't happen nowadays. You're getting more hysterical than the natives; I shall soon begin to believe there really is something in this curse business. And as for you, Betty, for goodness sake be careful what you write in your articles; you don't want to get yourself mixed up in a libel case or have your chances spoiled once and for all by sending them such tosh that they won't believe anything more you say." Turning away, with a gesture of irritation, she marched into the tent.

Simon was just saying good night. "I'll come round to-morrow morning if I may," he said, "to see how things are shaping. Perhaps we may be able to do something with the men; but I do seriously advise you, Mr. Mannering, to reconsider this business. I know you don't believe a word I say, but I've seen so many of these haunted tombs bring disaster on people. The game simply isn't worth the candle. Old Derwent's blood-poisoning always did look very suspicious to me."

When he had disappeared in the shadow of the rocks Nikolai, who had overheard his last remark, laughed scornfully. "If it weren't so irritating it'd be funny," he remarked. "That's the worst of these people who dabble in psychic things, they usually go gaga in the end. Look at some of those tales he told us quite solemnly on the boat about mummies and rings and so forth—rankest superstition!" He broke off with a shrug. "Well, he's gone, anyway. Now we can get down to business."

"Do you really mean to have a shot at it after all he's said?" asked Carol. "Why not wait until to-morrow? It would be so much better if we could get our men to agree, or even if his men gave us a hand."

"Thanks! And have his men backing ours up! I tell you I don't trust him. No, it's now or never. I've noticed our chaps are keeping very much to their side of the rocks; they won't get wind of it until it's all over. I'll bet my last dollar that when they see a place packed with jewels to-morrow morning, they'll forget all about their spooks. There's nothing like a bit of gold to lay the most persistent black magician. Betty's game, aren't you, darling? You can join us or not, as you choose, Carol."

For a moment Carol did not answer. She remembered Simon's warning to be clever, but it wasn't easy with terror surging up in her at the thought of her sister going down into that haunted place.

"The idea's all right," she said at last, "but I simply couldn't do it, Nick. I'm far too frightened; I've always been scared of the place, as you know; even in the day-time with the sound of the men's spades, their voices and their singing I've hardly been able to bear it sometimes—but now—in the dark and the silence . . ." She gave a quite genuine shudder. "Supposing Something did attack us, supposing one saw Something . . . think of all those black passages and those bones and the rock so close above us . . ."

"Carol, don't!" cried Betty.

"I can't help it, I can feel it all so clearly." She continued to enlarge on the theme, bringing all her histrionic powers to bear, and watched with satisfaction Betty's courage slowly evaporating beneath her attack. Nikolai, however, soon thought fit to interrupt.

"You're behaving like a silly child, Carol. There's no need for you to go down if you feel like that about it. In fact, for that matter, there's no need for either of you girls to come; your father and I can manage it quite well alone, and we're not afraid of the dark.

Personally, neither natives nor spooks, nor even black magicians, will stop me from finding out what's behind that slab. Don't you agree, Mr. Mannering?"

"Of course I shall come down, of course. I wouldn't dream of letting any of you go alone without my supervision, you'd probably do irreparable damage with your clumsy methods. Look at the way you cut that Ushebtiu figure in half with a spade the other day! Disgraceful carelessness! Now, where are my glasses? Is everything ready? Have you the torches? It really is most provoking about the electric light."

"I've put everything we'll need ready behind the tent on the left," said Nikolai. "We'd better start soon if we're going. I don't think that slab will take long to move. It looks to me as if it might be on a sort of pivot; it's only a matter of loosening stone, but I did quite a lot before those fools took fright, in fact it would have been free in another minute or so." He looked at Betty and Carol: "Well, are you coming, or shall I brave the curse with your father and rely on you to exorcise it if it blasts us?"

"Of course I'm coming, Nick darling," cried Betty with a sudden, renewed burst of excitement. "I'd never let you go alone." She gave a high-pitched laugh. "Oh, I wouldn't miss it for worlds. If we're all together we'll be quite safe."

"And you, Carol?"

Carol hesitated: "I'll stay outside, I think, in case the natives got wind of it—someone ought to be here to warn you."

Nikolai's smile had a touch of derision. "Right! Come along then, you two; gently now and no talking, we don't want them to hear and send someone to investigate."

They stepped out of the shelter of the tent and for a moment paused, looking at the scene before them.

All around, empty, soundless, void of life, lay the chaos of rock. Above the towering cliffs the great circle of the moon was riding, dimming the stars and etching fantastic shapes in ebony and silver. Once more Carol had the feeling that the shadowy places were filled with Presences, inimical and menacing.

Even Betty now seemed affected by the vast silence of the night. She shivered and glanced apprehensively at that cleft among the rocks where the dead had rested so long undisturbed.

"Do the *Kas* he spoke of know we're coming?" she whispered. "I feel as if it's all alive—as if something were happening down there."

"Don't go, Betty," Carol cried.

Betty passed her hand across her forehead. "I—I don't want to, somehow—and yet I do. I feel funny, as if I wasn't here, quite." For a moment she clung to Carol, as she used to, then abruptly she straightened herself, and looked after Nikolai and her father who were already walking rapidly across the moonlit space which divided them from the mouth of the tomb. "But I can't leave him, I couldn't bear it!" And shaking off Carol's detaining hand, she turned and ran after them.

Carol waited until they were lost to sight among the rocks, then she ran down the *coulée* to the place where Simon had said he would wait for her.

He was walking up and down and came to meet her: "Well?" he asked anxiously.

"They're opening it, they're at it already. I couldn't stop them, they simply wouldn't listen."

"I knew it; I was sure that was Annerly's game—the damn' fool."

She was really frightened now, and clung to his arm. "What can we do? Can't you stop them somehow?"

"How can I? I might rouse the men, but that wouldn't help; there'd only be a stand-up fight, with goodness knows what unpleasant consequences; there's nothing to be done with people like that when they get obsessed by an idea. But I can't bear to think of them down there alone—with That."

"Oh, Simon, don't!" she cried, and did not notice that for the first time she had used his name.

He turned to her and took her hands: "Darling, forgive me, I shouldn't have told you, but I had to; what's the good of fooling you?"

"But can't you do something drastic? Those powers you told me you learnt in India—can't you use them? Can't you hypnotize Nikolai into giving it up? He's the leader."

He laughed at that. "My dear, hypnotism isn't one of my accomplishments; besides, as I told you before, I don't believe anyone has the right to force another to do things against his will—that's black magic."

"But to help, to save them?"

"Not even then, unless you know they *want* to be saved. I've warned them, I've done everything legitimate to stop them; if they won't listen they must take the consequences. I know it sounds hard—but there's no other way."

She pressed her hand across her eyes. She had a vision of her beloved Betty, her father, Nikolai, going at that very moment, in their ignorance, down that dreadful passage to the place where that Elemental Guardian awaited them. She seemed to see it quite clearly, bat-like, with outstretched wings and its eyes, pin-points of fire. So vivid was the vision that she cried aloud: "Oh, it's too horrible, we must do something—we *must!*"

"We can't—unless . . ." He paused and looked at her, then said slowly: "Carol, if you like I'll go down after them, I might be able to do something in a crisis; I don't quite know what, but one never does know how much power one has over these elemental things until one's had a shot at tackling them. As you quite rightly reminded me I have got some knowledge that other people haven't, so I suppose it's up to me to try and use it. As a matter of fact—I was told to, but—" He broke with a shrug: "I'm afraid I was thinking more of you. I'd better be getting along."

"But if anything did happen you'd be—caught, too!"

"Oh, nothing may happen after all. Anyhow, one can't have them down there, unprotected." They were already walking back towards the dig. "You can stay outside and fetch help if it's wanted. My man, Ahmed, is camped shout half a mile beyond the place where I found you this afternoon. He's capable of coping with almost anything; it wouldn't be the first time he'd got me out of a mess."

They were now among the rocks at the base of the cliff. She turned and faced him. "I—stay outside? You're mad! I'd be frightened to death. I'm going, if you are. Besides, how could your man help against something even you couldn't tackle?"

"Oh, he might. But that's not the point; I don't want you down there—there's no need for you to run into this."

She smiled, but said nothing more until they stood at the entrance of the tomb. The others had disappeared; absolute silence reigned.

He pressed her hand, then abruptly stooped and kissed it. "Don't worry, I won't be long."

Deliberately she came close to him, looking up into his face. "Do you think that if anything happened to you I should want to go on living—alone?"

He drew a quick breath. "Do you mean that, Carol?"

"Yes," she replied quietly, "I do mean it." And before he could move she had slipped in front of him and had disappeared into the darkness.

But for an instant he paused. He stood upright, staring round, as a man might who looks his last upon the earth he loves. The moon was now at its highest point in the heavens. The stillness seemed to have deepened, as if intensified by the increasing light. A trickle of earth from the unstable rocks went past his face with a stealthy hiss. His glance travelled over the landslide, a huge mass of rock which hung as if suspended above him in a block of darkness. All around the shadows brooded, expectant and alert.

He shook his head and with a sigh he also stooped and entered into the darkness.

The shallow ramp led into a passage which brought him into the first large chamber.

Here Carol was waiting for him. She gave a sigh of relief as he joined her and took hold of his arm.

"It's so still," she whispered. "Awful—I feel I'm being choked."

For a moment they stood listening. The absolute silence, the darkness, the pressure of the unseen walls on every side, gave them a sense of helpless isolation.

"A curse . . ." she murmured, shivering. "I can feel it. What *is* there in this place, Simon?"

"Nothing here; one always gets this kind of feeling in old tombs."

He flashed his torch round to reassure her, but its light was infinitely feeble in this vast place. The roof was a retreat for a legion of shadows which deepened over the mouths of the shafts leading to the tombs of those who had died without the rites of burial, and whose spirits, according to Egyptian beliefs, must be crying for ever in their soundless voices for pity and for vengeance.

Carol could feel them, those spirits of the dead, formless yet filling the darkness with their presence. A wave of terror swept her; she gave a choking sound and stretched out her hand blindly.

"What's the matter?" Simon asked.

"I feel—I don't know—horrible!"

"You'd better turn back."

But she knew she could not; they must go on. "No, no," she muttered.

He put his arm about her. "You'll be better when we've joined the others."

She pulled herself up and smiled at him. "Sorry! I'm all right really—just stupid nerves."

Simon kept his hand upon her arm as they walked down the final shaft, their light making a narrow path before them. At last the passage ended in a gaping hole. As they emerged into the antechamber they saw the faces and hands of their companions picked out of the darkness, sharply white, unreal in the luminous circles from the moving torches. They were examining the large slab of stone which closed the entrance to the tomb. Above them, on either side, loomed the gigantic figures of Maat, Goddess of justice, and the Monster—the Devourer of the Dead.

Simon flashed his torch round, and instantly from the walls bright and terrible figures leapt out at them. Here was Amenti, the Underworld, where the two-and-forty gods torture and devour the souls of the damned. Two women and two men were depicted facing the justice of Osiris, being weighed, condemned and sent writhing to eternal pains. For an instant the animal faces of these infernal gods took on a semblance of malicious life; then the torch-light moved and they were swept into darkness—but the menace of their unseen presence remained.

Nikolai looked up. "Hullo! You here, Conningsby? I thought you'd gone back."

"So I had, but I found I'd left my pipe behind. On my way to your tent I met Miss Mannering, and she told me you were down here. I couldn't resist having a look at those inscriptions Mr. Mannering was talking about."

"Yes, yes," cried the old man, "over here; do you see? All round the slab."

The other two were engrossed in their task. The slab was already free upon one side; it seemed, as Nikolai had said, to be made of one block of stone, and they could see now that it was so balanced that it would eventually fall inward. Betty was holding the torch while her fiancé worked. The pale light circles were still, save that from the torch held by Simon who was moving it up and down. Behind them thick darkness crowded. Carol looked round nervously, wondering what the apparent emptiness concealed. What had the men seen here? She felt icy cold and shivers, impossible to control, ran through her limbs. Where was this Thing? Could they be standing actually in Its mighty shadow? She looked at Simon. Had he seen It? If so, how could he remain so calm? Or might It, possibly, have gone?

Simon was immersed in studying the hieroglyphics round the slab. After a few moments' work, however, he stood back brooding, his brows drawn together.

"Good Lord," he muttered, "this is very odd."

He looked up and his eyes met Carol's; he nodded towards the writing. "The customary ritual confession from the Book of the Dead—but it's reversed. Here the souls are made to say:

"I have done evil against every man,
I have caused my kinsfolk to be put to death,
I have done that which is hated by the gods,
I am a worker of wickedness . . ."

and so on, instead of denying all these things in the usual way—extraordinary! Never seen that before."

He leant forward again. The light from his torch travelled slowly down, drawing line after line from its age-long obscurity. As he read, the torch trembled in his hand; his face came closer to the stone, as if striving to tear its secret from it.

Beside him the others worked in absolute silence, save for their heavy breathing and the sharp noise made by their picks which echoed up and down as if unseen workmen were mocking them from the darkness.

Suddenly the stone shifted; a narrow cavity appeared above it. Nikolai gave a grunt of satisfaction. "That's got it . . ."

He raised his pick, but before it could descend, Simon swung round, seized his arm and thrust him aside.

"Stop! for God's sake, stop!" he cried, and stepping in front of the slab, flung his arms wide across it, as if to defend it from them. His face was white, his eyes full of fear. He pointed to the passage behind them. "Get out—quick—before it's too late!"

"What's happened? What's the matter?" cried Mannering.

"Matter?" Simon struck the rock with the back of his hand, "there *are* black magicians buried there; it's clear in the inscriptions. The place is under an appalling curse. There's something buried with them that's been shut up here deliberately. Something so dangerous—so evil, I suppose—that the High Priest of that day had the place closed up and by his own magic created an Elemental to guard it, so that no one would ever be able to release it. Now do you understand what I was warning you against? Everyone who has tried to open this place has been done in; your men *saw* the Elemental, and ran for their lives." He looked round at their bewildered faces, "You've got to believe me! If that slab is opened, it will destroy us all. We've got a chance—just one chance. I beg you, don't go on. Clear out now." Suddenly he drew himself up, his arms dropped to his sides; to Carol he seemed to grow taller, more impressive. When he spoke again, his very tones were a menace. "It is here," he said slowly, "I—tell—you, It is standing over us now!"

Instinctively they all glanced round and bunched together like frightened cattle. Betty gave a stifled cry, but Nikolai, after that first movement of recoil, came a step nearer, until he stood facing Simon by the slab.

"And you expect us to believe," he drawled, "that this curse could really affect us—after all these thousands of years? You can't bluff me with that, Dr. Conningsby!"

Simon looked at him; their eyes met. A tense stillness fell—a pause in which their wills met in conflict. Then Simon spoke.

"I'm not bluffing. I've got no purpose but to save you. There's no time-limit to such powers as the Egyptians used. I don't know what form it will take, but I do know that if you defy this curse, the result will be more terrible than you or I—or any of us—can imagine. Don't risk it, man! Think of the others! You're not alone in this."

"But we can't leave it like this," old Mannering chartered, "we can't!"

Simon swung round on him. "Would you prefer to see your daughters killed, or driven mad perhaps, rather than forgo your silly little triumph? And much good it will do you anyhow when you've released *that* power!"

"Oh, let's go back," cried Carol, and Betty actually echoed her words. But Nikolai did not stir, only his smile of derision grew.

Carol took him by the arm. "Listen to him, Nikolai; don't go on with it. He does know. If you aren't afraid, we are; think of what might happen—think of Betty! Oh," she flung up her hand and pressed it across her eyes, "it's true, I can feel it—there's something terrible here!"

Still Nikolai remained unheeding. Like one under a hypnotic spell he stared fixedly at the narrow cavity just visible above the great stone, while the others waited in a tense silence.

Then, after a moment, he looked up; his face had taken on an expression so stubborn that it was almost devilish. "A curse!" he echoed, and laughed aloud. "What fools you both are! A curse! I'm not so easily taken in. I've seen through your little game all along, Conningsby, I knew we were in for trouble when you turned up. You believe that there's some treasure inside here, and you've been trying to scare us off so that you'll have a clear run yourself! Priests and magicians! They're not going to cheat us of this—nor are you! Clear out! Let me pass!"

But Simon stood unmoved. "That's a lie, and you're not going to touch this stone."

"We'll see about that," said the other grimly, and gripped his pick.

Carol flung herself between the two men. "Nick, Nick, wait! Don't do anything rash, think it over first!"

"Stand back, Carol," he said sharply, "I don't want you hurt."

But she gripped his hand tighter. "I won't let you," she cried.

He twisted round sharply to free himself, and as he jerked back, the pick swung against the slab, the point catching in the edge of the stone. Simon instinctively sidestepped to avoid being struck and as he did so, Betty gave at shrill cry:

"Look," she screamed, "the slab—it's moving—Father! Nikolai!"

Simon sprang forward, clutching Carol by the arm.

"The shaft!" he cried, "quick, run, run for your lives!"

At his words sudden panic seized them all. They turned and made for the entrance. As she ran, Carol glanced back. She saw a formless cloud, a darkness within darkness, rising from before the slab which was slipping backward unto the gaping cavity—the cloud grew, it rushed upon them; it struck them like a blast from a furnace mouth. The earth rocked. Before their eyes, the walls of the narrow passage caved inward. They turned in terror; the roof cracked and split across; with a roar like thunder, stones and earth crashed about them. The torches were torn from their hands as they were flung upon the ground. In a chaos of darkness, bruised, stifled, stupefied by the tumultuous reverberations of a thousand imprisoned echoes, for a few moments they struggled pitifully against the forces which had been unleashed against them, then gradually they ceased no move.

Slowly the sounds of the catastrophe lessened; soon only the occasional rattle of a stone or the whisper of falling earth could be heard. Then silence and darkness reigned once more, as they had done for untold centuries, in the tomb under the cliff.

CHAPTER IX

AS IT WAS IN THE BEGINNING . . .

Carol put out her hand. Her fingers came in contact with smooth stone. She felt dazed, confused. Words lingered at the back of her mind: "Run, run!" She tried to remember who had spoken them and why; but just as when one awakes, one's dreams for a moment only are clear, but upon the effort to recall them fade instantly into a confusion of chaotic and unrelated happenings, so now, at this attempt to bring into focus these memories and to render concrete the indefinable sensation of terror, of disaster, everything became the more nebulous and intangible.

"I must have fallen," she thought. She listened. No one was pursuing her. She was certain no one was even aware of her movements. *He* was asleep. At the thought of Senhu-re, once more that sense of bewilderment swept over her. Was his name not Simon? And his face—why did she see him differently, think of him differently? The face she saw for a moment was not that of Senhu-re, her lover, High Priest of Ra, God of Gods. These features were calm, strong in their perfect self-control, different indeed from those others, lined with the agony of months of mental conflict. But now that other face, even as she tried to visualize it afresh, slipped from her memory and was gone.

She paused and leant against the wall, attempting to recover from the strange attack of dizziness. "I must have struck my head," but she had no memory of that either. It was very curious, this sense of dislocation; doubtless it was due to the excitement and exhilaration which any dangerous enterprise roused within her.

Already the sense of unreality was passing. She must not linger here. It was dark in the passage, but as she hurried forward, keeping her hand upon the stone for guidance, suddenly, at the turn of a corner, she saw below her the glitter of water in the moonlight, and the prow of a barge drawn up against the step. So the Priest of Sutekh had not failed her! She drew her cloak closer, as she emerged into the clear, cold light. A man who had been crouching among the shadows rose and peered upward.

He gave the word and she answered by raising her right hand whereupon shone the great scarab of the Priesthood of Ra.

She seated herself in the boat, and as it shot forward into midstream she glanced back at the walls of the city and the towering pylons of the Temple where her lover lay in a drugged slumber. Was this episode also finished? Looking back she saw her life as a series of stages, an advance from one setting to another. Up and up from nothing she had climbed. She had been born a slave in the household of a merchant, but since earliest childhood her ambition had been some day to rule. There were no limits to her dreams of domination; her objective was the very throne of Pharaoh, and unswervingly, without rest, without scruple, she had set herself to attain her ends. Each rung of this ladder had perforce been the body of some man, yet none of them had she loved until she met Senhu-re. It was strange how, the moment they met, something had melted within her. They had come together as naturally as wave flows into wave. She experienced then a passion which wiped out even her ambitious dreams; and for a little while she was as one purged in the white flame of his love, his idealism, his wisdom. But as, when the inundation declines, earth appears again amid the waters, so her passion, having run its course, in its ebb revealed once more the original bedrock of her insatiable ambition. She began to tire of his ideals, of his talk of service to the gods, but chiefly of the discipline which, as chosen wife of the High Priest, was an unavoidable part of the Temple service.

Soon she began to plan how she might use Senhu-re also as another stepping-stone to power. To be wife to the High Priest of Egypt's most powerful God was, indeed, to have placed one foot upon the throne, for Egypt was riven by internecine war; Pharaoh was a weakling, and actually it was the Priesthood of Osiris-Ra that ruled in his name.

But although Senhu-re was certainly powerful there was one who bade fair to outrival him. This was Nut-Feru, a mighty chieftain who had risen in the North and with his armies was slowly sweeping forward, consolidating a kingdom as he went. Of him terrible tales were told. With a woman, said to be a sorceress, Anf-Kaseth, he delighted to plan orgies of death, razing whole towns to the ground in holocausts of destruction, while she urged him on to ever-greater enormities, and openly declared that they would soon sit upon the throne of Pharaoh.

When Cheosri listened to these tales she was filled with misgivings. Had she, after all, chosen wrongly in throwing in her lot with Senhu-re?

Something within her thrilled in sympathy with Nut-Feru's ruthless deeds. So would she act when Egypt was at her feet. But to accomplish this either he must become her ally or be overthrown.

To this latter end she worked upon Senhu-re, using his love of Egypt, his desire to see once again a strong ruler on the throne and security and peace in her borders. But Senhu-re, who was essentially a mystic, was not made for battles. He hated war, and always believed that the priesthood should rule by virtue of its spiritual powers alone. He was prepared to pray, to invoke the Gods, but not to draw the sword himself. Cheosri would have none of such feeble measures. Persuasively she lured him from his faith. Was Nut-Feru not the very embodiment of evil? What, then, must evil not be overthrown? Who better than Senhu-re to cleanse the country of this scourge since Pharaoh's generals were of no account? Was it not indolence rather than idealism which held him back from—yes, fear, perhaps? Had he the right to remain in the Sanctuary while blood and fire and pestilence swept the land?

All that there was in his own nature of unsuspected ambition she used with such subtlety that at length he began to waver. It was true he was of the line of priestly Kings of the XIV Dynasty; the saviour of Egypt might indeed be himself; it might be possible that he was more fitted than the weakling Pharaoh to wear the double Crown.

So at last he also drew the sword and joined forces with the Royal armies. In remote temples priests already acclaimed Senhu-re as Pharaoh, and the prestige of his name brought many who before had hesitated into the Royal camp.

Cheosri was jubilant, but to Senhu-re these activities brought no peace of mind, and when he found himself dealing death and confusion where he desired to pour out life and healing, bitterness filled his spirit. Before Cheosri's coming he had always been able, by retiring into the silence of the Sanctuary, to contact One who was above him, and learn the way of wisdom, but now his mind was darkened and he strode blindly forward with the armies of Cheosri who was far more, in truth, their leader than he. Yet he could deny her nothing, even though he grew old and worn and his sleep was full of evil dreams and omens.

Cheosri was well aware of the price he had paid for her love, but it left her untroubled. What continued to torture her was the thought that, after all, Senhu-re might fail. At first she had believed him to be great—great enough to share with her the throne of Egypt; but latterly she had begun to realize that he was much weaker than she, and with this knowledge came contempt, and with contempt the longing increased to be free of the restrictions which this union laid upon her. In the midst of her perplexities, almost indeed as if in answer to the cry for guidance which she had formulated many times in those secret rites to the Powers of Darkness which she performed, unknown to Senhu-re, even in the most sacred precincts of the God of Light, she received a message from Apepa, the High Priest of Sutekh, the Evil One, that Night Serpent who leads his worshippers by short cuts and dark ways into mysterious bliss. What Apepa desired with her she did not know, but she had no hesitation in responding to his call.

It was for his temple that she was now bound, and as the boat slid forward her mind dwelt no more on Senhu-re and the past, but reached out towards this unknown man who might, through his powers, reveal to her how the goal of her ambitions could be attained.

~ ~ ~ ~ ~

The face of Apepa . . . Strangely familiar it seemed. Once again, as she looked upon it, she experienced that feeling of uncertainty, that sensation of being in two worlds. It was not that she had ever actually seen that dark countenance, but rather as if she had met him in another guise long ago—in another life, perhaps. Sternly she shook these idle fancies from her. "I must be alert, strong, very subtle," was her thought, "if I am to match myself against this man with success."

He began without preliminaries. "My daughter, I must be brief, for your absence must not be observed. For long I have watched you; I know your ambition, but I am also aware of your limitations. You are not a great magician, but you might become one; you *must* become one if you are to succeed, for without magic, without the secret knowledge which can command the Lesser Gods, no man may hope to retain, even if he could seize, the ultimate power. At the moment the Egyptians worship Osiris-Ra, but even as Osiris was slain by Set, so I am determined that Sutekh, who is greater even than Set himself, shall cast down the power of the Sun. If you are willing to help me to accomplish this I will make of you, not Pharaoh's wife, but Pharaoh himself, Lord of the Two Lands, with all Egypt at your feet."

He paused, looking at her. Cheosri smiled. "If you know my mind as you have declared there is no need for this question, O priest of Sutekh. There is nothing I will not do to gain the ultimate power."

"It is well." The priest eyed her keenly. "What you have to do is this: deliver Senhu-re into the power of Nut-Feru."

She cried aloud, then. "This is a trick! Senhu-re is my strength; if Nut-Feru seizes On, I, too, will be destroyed!"

"Did I not say you had grave limitations? Can you not see beyond the obvious? But since you are blind I will open your eyes, then you will not suspect me of trickery. Know, then, that Nut-Feru is my brother. He was my tool, I thought to use him to crush Pharaoh and the Priesthood of the Sun. But I had a daughter, Anf-Kaseth, whom I used as a medium for power. She has mighty gifts. I intended, when I had trained her fully and initiated her into the Mysteries of the Underworld, to use her so that I might be enabled to discover something—" He hesitated and looked at Cheosri again with that piercing glance: "Something," he continued, "without which I know I shall never achieve my full ambition. But Nut-Feru took her from me; she betrayed me, desiring, because she was enamoured of him, to put into his hands the secrets which I had been forced, of necessity, to reveal to her. She fled with him, and from that hour I have sworn to accomplish their destruction—but I shall use them first."

"How can I believe this?" she asked scornfully.

He smiled. "I will not ask you to believe it, but I will give you information which, if you can use it aright, will satisfy you that I do not deceive those who are prepared to be my co-workers."

"So be it." She leant back against the cushions of the couch, aware of her beauty, using it already to ensnare him. But he did not seem aware of it at all, moving backwards and forwards as he spoke, his gaze fixed ahead. What power there was in him, what ruthless determination! Her whole being responded. With such a man, indeed, she might rule the world.

He seemed to have read her thought. "To rule the world," he murmured. "But to do so one must have greater power, greater knowledge than even I possess. One must possess the Power of Those who came from other Worlds and other Spheres, the Creators of this planet of which we are a part; the God-Kings who ruled for æons perfecting the body of our Lord the Earth, Those from whose Cosmic substance the very Soul of Earth was invoked and given form."

He raised both arms above his head as if invoking these ancient Powers. His voice dropped to a murmur and ceased, but he continued to move up and down. Yet presently he seemed once more to become aware of Cheosri and stopped before her.

"You gape at me," he said, "and wonder, but I tell you that were it possible for a man to discover the hiding-place of this Soul of the Earth, this Germ of Creation, this primal Fount of the Energy that we call Life, he would become lord absolute of far more than this planet and the realms we know."

He paused, as if exhausted. While he had been speaking all languor passed from her attitude. Now she was leaning forward, tense, alert.

"Who holds this secret?" she cried. "I must possess it! I, too, must make it mine!"

"You!" he echoed, and laughed scornfully. Then his eyes narrowed. "You?" he repeated more slowly. He began to pace up and down again, plunged in profound meditation. "Why not?" he said presently. "Perhaps, since as-yet neither sex is complete, in itself symbolizing the positive and negative polarity without which nothing can be brought to perfection here, it may be necessary for them to join in order that the magical forces may be balanced and my dream materialize. Anf-Kaseth might have served, but would you be strong enough? It would need absolute ruthlessness, absolute courage."

"Have I not both?" she asked proudly.

"I think you may have," he replied, and fell into another long silence.

It was she who broke it, impatiently. "But does anyone hold the Secret now, or know where it may be hidden? Perhaps it is lost, or removed beyond the stars."

He shook his head. "How can that which is of the Soul of the Earth be lost or removed to any other sphere? Do you not know, moreover, that it is the Law that nothing that has once existed on the earth plane can ever depart utterly from its Aura until the End? Hidden it may be, obscured for a time because of the ignorance or the unfitness of men to discover or to use it, but never lost. Therefore I have hope, since I am well assured that there is nothing in all the worlds or the Heavens that man cannot attain to if he will. It is our lack of desire alone that prevents us from becoming gods."

"This, indeed, hath Senhu-re said unto me," she mused.

He made a scornful gesture. "The Priests of the Sun seek to attain the powers and attributes of the Divine Ones in a different manner and for a far different purpose. They would be slaves, obeying, worshipping, seeking to lose themselves in union with the Divine Will; this takes ages to accomplish, many weary lives of self-abnegation. But our way is swift and sure, Oh Cheosri, We control by destruction, we use all and are used by none."

"Who, then, can reveal it to you?" she asked despairingly. "Not the priests of Osiris; they can know nought of it, else we should see godlike men among them—but they are no different from the rest."

"They would not dare to use it," he said sharply, "they would be vowed to abstention. But I believe that there are men, men of whom the vulgar never hear, who do know this secret, yes, and use it still."

"What proof have you?"

He laughed. "None, save perhaps that the world of men still exists, and that all the folly and stupidity of our race, yes, even the divine madness of the Atlanteans, hath not brought about our entire destruction. No, there is a Power that ever protects mankind, protects it even from such as myself, who would control and use it for my purposes. Sometimes in my magical practices, I find myself suddenly opposed by a Force, an Intelligence greater than mine, one that might even destroy me if I persisted in ignoring it."

"It comes from the Gods, perhaps."

"No, through a human agency, that much I can observe; but whence or how I know not. If I am to attain my goal these hidden magicians who thwart me must be destroyed. But I know well that only by possessing myself of the power of the Secret, can I hope to destroy them. Yet spells, enchantments, invocations to the Infernal Gods have so far revealed nothing; but it has come to me that these hidden Adepts must somehow be linked with their servants, the priests of Osiris, therefore some knowledge of their whereabouts and of the Secret itself should be in possession of the Initiates of the innermost Mysteries."

"Senhu-re!" she whispered.

He nodded. "Yes—your lover, Oh Cheosri."

After a long pause she asked softly, "What do you want me to do?"

He drew closer, looking into her face with a smile which for a moment filled her with dread.

"Contrive to draw from him all he knows, then with the power that will be ours, cast him aside, set me up in his place, and between us we will overthrow Nut-Feru and rule Egypt and the world."

"I fear that would be impossible even for me," she said and sighed deeply.

He shrugged his shoulders and turned away. "Very well; I shall help Nut-Feru with my magical powers and you will both be overthrown."

She sprang to her feet. "But you would not then discover the Secret!"

"Do you think you are my only link with the Priesthood of the Sun?" he said scornfully. "I have given you your opportunity. The world is yours if you can but take it; but if you are too small, too afraid—"

At the vision of defeat her last faint scruple was swept away. "I will do it, I will succeed!"

"Be swift, then, for until you have played your part and delivered to me all the knowledge that the Priesthood has in its keeping about this thing you will have to rely alone upon the powers of the great Senhu-re to aid you against Nut-Feru."

She had reason to think much upon Apepa's words in the months that followed; for Nut-Feru was drawing ever nearer and nothing seemed to stay his advance. Moreover, strange pestilences, which she was convinced had no natural cause, swept their ranks, and many times they were prevented from victory by mysterious ill-fortune. Was Apepa already, perhaps, using his magic against them, since she had not yet been successful in obtaining the knowledge he sought?

More and more she looked askance at Senhu-re, scorning him for what she considered his weakness in refusing to use his own magical powers against Nut-Feru. Soon, indeed, she became desperate, for she could find no way of forcing Senhu-re to disclose the secrets of the Inner Mysteries.

Then, quite suddenly, she knew what she must do.

That night she awoke him, trembling, to tell him that she had had a vision in which one of the Great Ones, doubtless Ra Himself, stood by her bed and disclosed to her that Egypt could only be saved from the domination of Nut-Feru and the Powers of Evil if the Priests of the Sun made use of the Great Secret and defeated him with the Powers contained therein. As many of her dreams in the past had proved correct Senhu-re dared not doubt the truth of this one. But he was much troubled. Why had the vision not been given to him? Strange that to one who was not even an Initiate the God should have spoken! Blinded by his passion for her it never occurred to him that she should be other than a chaste and virtuous woman, for none of his associates dared repeat to him the vague suspicions and rumours that were whispered about her, since no one had actual proof of her treacheries nor her evil practices.

From that night she left him no peace, pressing him continually to reveal to her what this Secret was, and to use it as he had been commanded.

When he still hesitated she became fired with righteous indignation. Did he not believe her? If so, dared he disobey the command of the God? At last she declared that if he would not open his heart to her, who had been so favoured of Osiris, she would go to Pharaoh and declare to him how he was served by his High Priest. "Nor will I love one who defies and despises the words of Osiris-Ra," she cried and thereafter shut herself away from him in her own apartments. For a day or so he endured the enforced separation from the woman who was more to him still than life or even honour, then he broke down.

It was true, he admitted, there did exist some great Talisman of Power against which nothing could prevail. But the knowledge that it was hidden in Egypt was only revealed to certain grades of Temple Initiates. "Yet even we do not know where it is concealed," he said. "And if I did know I would not dare invoke Its powers, and those of the dread Guardians who are Its protectors."

"But if the Gods have ordained that you should use this Power to save Egypt then there must be some way of discovering Its hiding place. Surely it could be discovered through the magical powers which you, as High Priest, have learned to wield?"

He turned to her angrily then. "Shall I commune with the dead, bind the spirits of those who on earth have been mighty in magic and send them throughout the land to search for this sacred spot? Shall I command the winds that blow from the four corners of the world, or the eyes of the eternal stars that look down upon the earth and know all that passes therein? And if I could do these things, I tell you it would be forbidden, and would but bring disaster upon myself and upon my cause, unless I were armed with greater authority than could be given through a vision, and unless the Great Ones themselves worked with me and used me as their instrument."

"Who is greater than Osiris-Ra?" she cried.

He answered her evasively, and she realized that still he was concealing something from her. Yet in the end she wrung this secret also from him. His passion betrayed him, even as it had done before. "Perhaps," he said wearily, to justify himself for his weakness, "it is better that you should know the whole truth, then you will understand my reluctance. If Osiris-Ra had wished you to remain in ignorance, could he not have sent the Vision to me?"

"He knew," was her reply, "that without my will to strengthen yours you would never have had the courage to carry out His commands."

"That may be so, but when I have revealed to you the inner truth of this matter you will the better understand." Then, having vowed her to silence by terrible oaths which might not be broken save on pain of penalties for untold ages both in this world and in the next, he told her all.

"Such a vision is not authority enough, Cheosri. I need a further confirmation of the God's decrees. Know then, that although I am High Priest in name, above me there are Hierophants of greater Mysteries. These are the true, although invisible, rulers of Egypt, Whose august existence may not even be known save to the few elect. They live in a secret place apart, and save in certain Ceremonies remain unseen and even unapprehended by us. We are only permitted to attempt to contact or make appeal to Them in moments of utmost necessity. They alone could reveal to me the hiding place of this Talisman, and only with Their sanction and aid might Its invocation be undertaken, Therefore you will see that if this is to be done, They will first communicate with me. It is because no such command has come that I wait and hesitate."

"But why do you not seek Them out and confirm the truth of my vision?" she asked.

"You do not understand the dangers and difficulties of such a presumptuous act. Moreover, I have not the right to leave my duties here until I am bidden to do so. It would necessitate a long journey to a certain Oracular Shrine. Here I would have to stay in the underground temple without food or drink or speech or light for seven days; then a state of trance would fall upon me and in this trance I would be lifted up into the very mind of the Great Ones and could hear Their speech. If this secret were to be revealed to me I would doubtless be shown the place where It is hidden and the methods of invocation to be employed. But this I dare not attempt unless I am commanded into Their presence."

"You said you were permitted to make appeal in moments of dire necessity," she argued; "surely the triumphs of Nut-Feru are necessity enough."

"Nut-Feru may yet be conquered by prayer and by force of arms," he said firmly, and with this, for a little while, she had to pretend to be content.

"So these are the Magicians who have defied me!" said Apepa when she told him what she had learned. "Now I understand the nature of my enemies I will be better equipped to wage war upon them. It is a good thing you have done, Cheosri, but the half of your work only is accomplished. You must persuade Senhu-re to undertake this journey; then, while he is absent, we will strike and once the power is in our hands we will see what these mysterious Priests can contrive against us!"

So she continued unceasingly to work upon his mind, giving him no rest night or day. And events were her allies in this, for Nut-Feru's armies were advancing like locusts for number and for rapacity; spies reported that he was boasting of how easily he would conquer On, and that he would put every priest of Osiris-Ra to the sword and set up a statue of Sutekh even in the innermost sanctuary of the Temple.

"Do you believe that the Gods wish Nut-Feru to conquer Egypt?" Cheosri cried. "Is Nut-Feru to sit upon the throne of Pharaoh with the sorceress by his side, and shall the abominations of red Sutekh become the daily worship of the children of the Nile?"

There was schism now in On and in Pharaoh's household and his army. This was also due to the intrigues of Cheosri, for, as wife of the High Priest, she held an important position at Court. Pharaoh's wife suddenly died, and, yearning now after the beauty of Cheosri, he began to look askance at Senhu-re, wondering how he might conveniently get rid of the High Priest whose wife he coveted.

Senhu-re, aware only that he was falling from favour, that the army was unreliable, and that the unity of their common purpose was being gradually disrupted by intrigues, the origin of which he could not discover, began to waver in his attitude towards the warnings and exhortations of Cheosri, He walked, indeed, in darkness. For the oracles were silent and the Omens obscure, nor could he find as of old illumination and wisdom in the silent hours he spent in invocations to the Gods.

At last he made his decision. He would brave the wrath of the Great Ones, and appeal to Them to give him material advice and assistance.

He called Cheosri to him. "I will go forth," he said; "perhaps I may be permitted to illuminate the night of darkness that has fallen over our land with the supernal light, and strike the enemies of the High Gods, even as the lightning strikes, to burn and destroy them utterly."

That same night he prepared for his departure. Cheosri accompanied him to the water's edge where his barge waited. There he took her in his arms. "Beloved," he said, "you know full well that there is a great danger in what I am about to do. If in any way I have failed the Gods and done what is evil in Their sight, then it may be that I shall be slain through this invocation of the pure Spirit of Truth. If so it be that I return no more, I beseech you, stand firm against Pharaoh if he talks of any capitulation. Better death than that. You have power, I think, over his weak mind, therefore upon you will rest the greater responsibility for his policy. Let Khefri who is next to me be made High Priest, and continue to obey him in all spiritual things. But you, Oh Cheosri, have in you qualities of leadership which I know that I have ever lacked, therefore throw your force and influence upon the side of the Priesthood of Osiris-Ra. Whether I live or die my love will be with you; act only for my honour and for the glory of the Gods."

Then, strangely, for a brief moment, she was shaken. This was the end. Love and yearning swept over her for what had been; she was once more the woman who had first given herself in the full tide of passion to Senhu-re. She clung to him, hiding her face against his cheek, and almost, as he caressed her, she had implored him not to set out upon this fruitless journey. For what would the Great Ones give him but negation? And what would they reveal to him but the faithlessness of the woman he loved and the trick which she and the Priest of the Evil One had played upon him? Was not such love as theirs a more precious thing even than the uttermost power and glory, not so lightly to be cast aside for what, after all, might be but a dream?

But the moment passed; sweeping in like a great tide, drowning the little flicker of divine light, came the returning flood of her insatiable desire for supremacy, for domination, for knowledge. If she held him back she would be defeated, she would be obscure, she would never learn this Secret which was to give her and Apepa lordship, not alone of the whole world, but of worlds now beyond their ken. What madness to think of throwing all this aside for love of a man!

Her mouth sought his, clung to it. "You will return," her lips said, "fear nothing, we will meet again."

A strange prophetic look came over his face. "Yes, I will return to you. We will meet again. Nothing, nor change, nor death, nay, nor the permutations of Time can keep me from you."

Knowing what she did, shaken once more by his faith, she could find no words; her lips refused to shape the lies she sought to speak. So, lest her silence might seem strange to him, she slipped from her finger the great scarab he had given her upon their wedding night, and put it upon his, whence it had come to her.

"This was our pledge of love," she murmured, "wear it again, for my sake."

He bent over it. Upon his face was still that rapt, unearthly look. "Our pledge," he repeated, "into which the power of our mutual love has entered—yes, I will wear it faithfully. May it bind us together, holding our souls captive within the magic circle of the Divine Flame, until that hour when we meet again in love. And when I put it again upon your finger, Oh joy of my Heart, the flame will leap up and fuse us together in the perfection of union, and there will be no separation any more for ever."

~ ~ ~ ~ ~

An intense drowsiness pressed upon Cheosri's eyelids, mists swam before her eyes. For a few moments she lost touch with reality, and felt herself like a disembodied thing borne away on a rhythm that was as the rocking of a boat upon water, the thin piping of the wind among dry leaves of palm. This was followed by a sense of oppression and darkness which weighed upon her like a nightmare. Yet she had only to open her eyes to see the sun beating down on her barge beyond the shadow of her awning, to see her men-at-arms, her slaves . . .

But she could not open them.

Confused visions and thoughts passed within this womb of darkness which held her. Her consciousness of herself was curiously divided. A part she recognised as Cheosri, sole ruler of the Two Lands, Pharaoh, who, even now, was being carried in triumph to On where the captives, Nut-Feru and Anf-Kaseth, awaited what lingering death it should please her to mete out to them.

Everything was hers at last! All earthly success, all earthly glory.

Yet, at the same time, there was this other part of herself: a detached observer, whose mind and outlook were as different from those of Cheosri as day from night. Strange! It was as if she were seeing Cheosri and her triumphs as Senhu-re might have seen them, as things of no account, after all. She struggled to readjust the two points of view, the natural elation of Cheosri, with the loathing and scorn of this horrified stranger. Then Nut-Feru's face appeared, but he, too, seemed changed. Who or what was he, in reality? Now he seemed to be someone close to her heart—a man kindly in the main, a little arrogant, perhaps, and rather obtuse about something that was very important. A danger to her still—and yet a friend. And Anf-Kaseth? Why could she only see her as a child, dear and tender, a suffering girl who smiled at her out of dark, troubled eyes, demanding her protection as a right. Why as a right? Because she had killed her? But of course she must kill her, was Anf-Kaseth not her bitterest enemy? Their faces dissolved, changed into the weak face of Pharaoh whom she had betrayed also to his death in the end. But this other image which now superimposed itself upon his, this was the face of one she had never betrayed, had served rather, protected all her days at the cost of her own youth and freedom.

A sudden feeling of intense panic swept over her. She must escape from them, from any connection with their lives—she must not touch them or injure them; but had she not done so already or was she about to commit some inescapable act of madness? She tried to move, to escape from the toils of this mental confusion. Two worlds? Yet both were surely one world, one existence; two facets of one and the same jewel. But it was a flawed jewel. Were there not, perhaps, other facets of this jewel—flawed also? Oh, she must not look, she could not bear to know. Backwards or forwards, it was the same. "Art thou indeed Cheosri?" a voice within her cried, "or art thou another—a hundred others? Or did these others arise from what thou wert? Only by knowing what seed was cast into the field, can one foretell what grain the harvester will reap!" Confusion, confusion! She was drifting now in a dimension, timeless, ever expanding, thus she would lose herself or would she find another self, another harvest? She must know, she must understand! "Go back, go back," something whispered now. "Light-hearted is the sowing, for him who cares not what seed he scatters. Go back, go back; cling to one, gaze at one, hold fast to what thou hast, lest the realization of illusion madden thee."

Cheosri! The name—the name, that was the key. Swiftly now, like a leaf caught in the current, she was being drawn towards that image—faster—faster . . .

Now pictures were forming before her eyes of events which had occurred in those years since she had, by betraying Senhu-re, gained the allegiance of Apepa. They had been years of bitter intrigue, of battles lost and won, but of ever increasing power. For she had, with the magical aid of the Priest of Sutekh who had taken Senhu-re's place as High Priest of Egypt, been able at last to defeat Nut-Feru. With Nut-Feru a fugitive and Pharaoh dead by her hand, it had been an easy matter to seize the throne.

Yet as her power grew so also grew her ambition. Nothing satisfied her any more, not even these triumphs she had once coveted, while the Secret remained beyond her grasp. It obsessed her, even as it obsessed Apepa, this desire to extend her dominion beyond the bournes set for ordinary men.

From the moment their power was assured, he and she set themselves to search for the dwelling-place of those Secret Rulers of Egypt of whom Senhu-re had spoken. Senhu-re had never returned from that mysterious underground Temple to which he had gone to invoke the Guardians, but if he had known of its existence, it was probable that other priests also knew of it. To discover this they systematically persecuted the whole of the Priesthood. Hundreds were tortured that they might reveal what they knew. Some died raving, some lied, but the secret remained inviolate. Defeated here, they razed temples to the ground in the hope of revealing crypts and hiding-places, they sent expeditions to every shrine, to every hermit's cave, but without avail.

Apepa, leaving Cheosri to consolidate their gains and to make war on the remnants of Nut-Feru's army, had given himself up increasingly to his magical experiments. He had no fear of ultimate failure, but an insidious doubt began to invade Cheosri's mind as the years slipped by. It became like a poisonous growth invading her life. Supposing the Secret should remain inviolate? Supposing they never learned where it was hidden? What then? What were her triumphs if they were to end with her body? What was Egypt? What was the present? A little strip of land—a few short years. There were vaster lands—there was the untold and unimaginable future; of these also she must be sure; these she must hold firmly, not in hands that would drop to dust, but by some other binding power, the power that the Talisman would give her, making her Lord over life and death—the eternal Power which is imperishable.

Besides, while the threatening presence of those unknown Rulers of Egypt remained, whilst the secret fear remained that, perhaps, after all, Senhu-re was not dead, how could either he or she find security? How did one know that at any moment "They" might not arise and smite their enemies with the lightning flame of Power?

She moved wearily on her cushions. She was going down to On; the strange sense of duality had left her, but the sense of frustration, the sense of some unexpressed yet very definite threat remained. Supposing Apepa failed? Or supposing—which was worse—that he succeeded, and instead of revealing the Secret to her, swept her aside? Both were possible, and both would mean ultimate annihilation. The thought of death began to obsess her, she did not feel strong enough to die. She had neither Apepa's power nor his daring, for he could envisage death and failure in this life, unshaken.

He laughed when she spoke of what might befall them if the Gods struck before they were strong enough to defend themselves, before they had gained possession of the Source of the power of the Gods.

"If I do not find the Secret in this life," he said, "I shall find it in other lives, for by magical rites I have dedicated my soul to this search for ever. When I succeed and make the world mine, who then could annihilate me? To destroy is also to create, Oh Cheosri. If I destroy the Universe will not *I* remain? And if ultimately I should be destroyed what will that matter to Unknowingness?"

But for her it was not enough. Her fear, and consequently her hatred, of Apepa grew. And because he was the one being left in the world who could still dominate and command her, she knew that somehow it must be she who discovered the Secret, she who must conquer him—or perish.

And at these times when her fear of him gave her almost sufficient courage to betray him, she remembered certain words that Senhu-re had spoken, words which she had never repeated to Apepa, but had hidden in her heart against the time when she might need a weapon to defeat her master. "Shall I commune with the dead, bind the spirits of those who on earth have been mighty in magic and send them throughout the land to search for this sacred spot?" The true significance of these words still escaped her, yet she felt convinced that therein lay a key, could she but find the lock that it would fit.

A blare of instruments, the roar of thousands of voices roused her from this strange, introspective trance into which she had fallen.

The mists which still clouded her perceptions were dispersed. She sat upright and looked about her. Her great barge was entering the purlieus of the holy city of On. The palaces and temples rose glittering from amid groves and gardens. Crowds lined the banks of the Nile, waving branches and flowers. The sacred barge itself, with serried ranks of priests, was sweeping forward to meet her with the holy Emblems.

Yes, she knew herself again as Cheosri—Pharaoh—absolute Lord. Away with these idle doubts and fears! She sat rigid, a smile of triumph on her lips, as the royal barge with its dazzling escort flashed through the water towards the Temple.

When all the ceremonies were over Cheosri, disguised in a dark cloak, followed a priest into the underground torture chamber.

For seven days and seven nights the torturers had inflicted agonies indescribable upon Nut-Feru and Anf-Kaseth, reviving them with skill when they seemed likely to die under the penalties.

Now the end was near. In the dark shadows where the light of the braziers could not penetrate, Cheosri sat contemplating the victims. She had thought to find pleasure at least in this act of vengeance, but it left her strangely indifferent. It was not this she wanted—not this . . .

Presently she stepped across to where the captives lay. She looked upon that which had once been a woman famous for her beauty, but was now a mass of broken bones and riven flesh. Anf-Kaseth was beyond her derision—but not yet quite beyond the possibility of suffering. With Nut-Feru it was very different; as she stooped over him, he raised himself and cursed her.

"You think," he cried, "that you have conquered us; you can break our bodies, but our spirits you cannot touch. In death we escape you, Oh Cheosri. Aye, and in death and in after-lives will we repay you for this; but for the sufferings of her whom I love *I* will repay you through a thousand lives. You think to rule, to become a god. I tell you, I who die, that it is we who will rule you. I will drag you into the tomb, and my gods will curse you. You shall serve us, and we will destroy your hopes, we will bring schism into your work, we will hurl you into darkness and eternal slavery." He fell back, fainting from the effort he had made, blood and foam on his torn lips.

She said nothing, but looked at him. Her eyes, hard as agate, gave no sign either of anger or of fear. Only they narrowed slightly as if to hide some thought too subtle to be divulged.

Then she turned to the men beside her. "Take these two prisoners, bid my physicians attend them. Save their lives at all cost. When they are stronger, take them to the house of the Embalmers; let them there be embalmed alive, as is the custom with traitors. Bid the priests use potent magic that they die not until they have been many hours in the tomb. Let them be buried in the tomb of the outcasts deep in the rock. Let the passage thereto remain unsealed, and bring me word when all is done."

She came and stood once more close to Nut-Feru. She stooped over him and spoke low that none might hear.

"You have defied me, you have threatened me. I accept your challenge. You were a fool. Oh, Nut-Feru, do you not know, you who, it is said, are so well versed in great magic, that there is a way whereby even the dead may be made slaves unto the living? Whereby they can be held for ever from seeking new bodies, and will be forced to serve, for ages of time, as earth-bound spirits the one who knoweth the manner whereby they can be so enslaved? I have learned the secrets of this magic; but until you spoke I did not realize that in you I had found the door to which I hold a key. I thank you, Oh Nut-Feru, for showing me the way. For to accomplish my desires I must have slaves in the spirit worlds, slaves who see where I cannot see; who will pass like the wind into the places where no living man may go, and upon the threshold of which even the trained magician must needs stay his feet. You and this woman, after death, shall serve me thus. I will command you, and you shall be sent back and forth upon the earth; aye, you shall draw for me the very secrets of Amenti; into the elements of Air, Fire and Water shall you pass and force their Guardians to serve me. I will call you back from death; I will utter your Names; I, alone, will command you. Your magic shall be added unto mine, and between us we will defeat all the Powers that would gainsay us." She raised her arms exultantly: "Through you shall I discover at last THAT which for so long I have sought."

~ ~ ~ ~ ~

It was blacker than Duat in the Valley of the Stones, where outcasts and criminals were buried. The moonlight made patterns there of white, unearthly silence, and the shapes of the rocks seemed as the shapes of watching demons.

A short time before midnight Cheosri appeared, walking with haste and glancing warily about her. Under her arm she carried a bundle and in her hand was a little lamp.

When she came to the entrance of the tomb she sought, she lit the lamp and boldly stepped into the opening, following without hesitation the narrow passage which led to the central chamber.

Here, for a moment, she hesitated. The silence was absolute; the air was furnace-hot and heavy with fœtid and sickly odours. The lamp gave only a faint gleam. The roof was a retreat for a legion of strange shadows which deepened over the entrances of the closed shafts leading to the other graves of those who had died in shame without the rites of burial and whose *Kas* cried aloud day and night in their soundless voices for pity and for vengeance.

She began to search the walls until she came to the entrance she sought. Proceeding down a short passage she emerged into the antechamber. Before her was a dark, gaping hole, the entrance to that place where the bodies of her enemies waited upon her will.

For a moment, then, she was shaken by the significance of the deed she was about to undertake, and by the appalling consequences of failure. What these consequences would be, she could not know, but she did know that she was about to pit herself against Death, that she was going to wrestle with Forces which had even given Apepa pause; that this was the apex of her whole existence, and that if she succeeded—if she lived . . .

She shuddered; even she could not conceive what this success might mean. Suddenly, brought face to face with such a possibility, infinitely beyond even the mighty span of her imagination, she was aware, for a fleeting second, of her own insignificance, her weakness, her fallibility. Fear assailed her, swift and terrible. Cold shivers ran down her spine, her blood seemed to turn to water. She glanced swiftly about her, aware that the place was full of Presences, the air heavy with expectancy. Might not the dead be more potent than the living? What might they not do to her—those two?

And Apepa? Did he know anything of this attempt? She had thought it almost miraculously fortunate that he should have allowed her her triumph alone, and have chosen this time to withdraw himself into far distant mountains where he had a special temple only used for certain mysterious ceremonies; now she began to wonder if he might not have done it purposely, in order to lure her into any treachery she might contemplate.

But the thought passed. Each year at this time he departed for the mountains. No, surely it meant rather that Sutekh himself was on her side. But the memory of Apepa had brought with it a resurgence of her hate. She armed herself now with this hatred, remembering that any breath of doubt or fear was fatal to achievement, and so, fearless once more, she stooped and entered the tomb.

~ ~ ~ ~ ~

Dark was the burial chamber now. One lamp alone sent a thin shaft of light through a gloom so intense, so weighted with horror that it pulsed as if with sentient life.

Upon the floor the two open mummy cases lay crookedly, as if displaced by the victims in the agony of their death-throes; but they formed the two sides of a triangle at the base of which stood Cheosri. In the centre was a tripod whence the light fell upon the shrunken faces of the dead, awful in their distortion and their decay, staring up, as if drinking in the obscene chromatics of Cheosri's voice.

Naked she stood there, upright, rigid, her arms raised, her eyes unseeing. Yet her mind was fixed, unwavering, holding the power in check, governing the secret forces which now filled the chamber, which crowded close upon the participants, drawn hither by the compulsion of NUMBER and of SOUND.

Up from the dead, up from Amenti, past the grim guardians of the Underworld, through her knowledge and her might Cheosri drew the reluctant spirits of her enemies. Now they approached. The vibrations quickened; the air pulsed, quivered; the very rocks seemed to tremble as if soon, unable to contain the dynamic forces which still drove in upon them, they would split asunder.

Now Cheosri was herself caught within the vortex; she was being drawn towards its centre. From her throat strange sounds welled up, words to her unknown. She saw a quiver pass through the semi-mummified forms. The flame of the lamp shot suddenly upward and at the same instant the two bodies shook more violently, swayed and began to rise, impelled by the increasing vibrations of the sounds which were now pouring from her mouth. Towards the apex of the flame and her pointed fingers the two bodies strained. A livid light flickered over them, and from their putrescent lips thin sounds arose.

Now the infernal cadences became higher, fuller, throbbing in a crescendo of abominable sound. The rhythm increased, unbearable, devastating. Upright now, the two dead figures swayed nearer and nearer, one on either side; the breath of their corruption hung like a cloud about them.

Two? But was there not a third—a shadowy form rising by her side, uniting with her in the Ritual? More distinct now, moving with her in the mystic circumambulations; she looked into the face—Apepa!

She had invoked to her aid all the powers of evil, all the forces of destruction, how could he not have heard and responded?

But she feared him no more, no, nor the Guardians of Egypt themselves. Must they not all obey her summons? Exultation thrilled through her. She had conquered. Lord was she now of life and death! Her limbs were flame, power flowed into them, more power, a million particles vibrating to her will. Dead and living together moved now in participation of the Rites, their forces and their knowledge fused in one mighty uprush of will.

Deeper, wider became the sweep of Cheosri's consciousness, as into the mighty vortex, invoked and drawn thither by the increasing strength of this transcendental magic, the Powers of the Elements were drawn. There would soon be nothing that could remain hidden in the Earth, in the Waters, or in the Air. All knowledge, all power these lesser gods would attain for her, they would reveal to her where was hidden the Soul of the World.

Soon—soon! Only one thing was needful now, to bind all these Forces, to make them wholly hers: the Word, the Word of Power which sounded the Note of the Lord of the World; the WORD which would tear the veil from the hidden places of Truth.

It would come to her, in all life it was implicit—of Death it was the Overtone; now she, who had made herself Lord of Life and of Death, would draw It out from latency by her will, and sounding It forth, would bring the Guardians of the very Soul of the Earth Itself to serve her.

It was coming. She waited, her whole being poised in expectancy. She felt It, the WORD, welling up through veil after veil of consciousness, like a flood-tide that nothing can withstand nor control. It grew. Immense, ever expanding, It rushed now from out the caverns of the Timeless Ones, and all that she was rushed to meet it—the Note—THE WORD OF POWER.

Then, even as her mouth gaped open, even as the first faint, yet terrible vibration struck upon the expectant darkness, another Note, shattering, transcendent, broke, with a white and blinding light, into its very heart.

Sound against Sound. Power against Power. Light against Darkness.

Cheosri was hurled backwards. Writhing helplessly in the icy heat of this dazzling flame, she felt within her body each nerve, each muscle, each cell shivered and torn by the clash of this supernal discord.

At the same instant the form of Apepa vanished and the dead bodies collapsed and disintegrated suddenly, so that nothing was left but a few dry bones and wrappings upon the floor.

Yet even in the throes of the dissolution which now assailed her also, still the woman sought to combat the Will which had struck her down, still she endeavoured to use her own will that had ever served her so well, The Talisman! The Crystal! It dominated her still, this obsession. She must know where It was hidden, somehow she must live for this; she dared not die until she had made this knowledge a part of herself for ever!

Then, in a blinding flash of realization, she knew that it was the Crystal which had destroyed her. Invoked by her magic, a Ray from its Centre had responded. How clear her mind had become! Was not the Whole implicit in all its Parts? Therefore the Spirit was Here, now, in this very place. She knew it, indubitably. But she must see it with her mortal eyes, perceive it with her whole being, thus she would be enabled to carry the vision of it with her, down all the ages, until once more she gained power great enough to seize it and make it wholly and for ever hers.

She forced her body from the ground, she raised her dying head, and with mighty, unconquerable will, opened her blood-filled eyes.

Before her stood Senhu-re. His arms were widespread, his head thrown back, but his eyes were upon her own and within them burned a flame which neither Life nor Death could quench.

A flame! What flame was this, mighty and all-encompassing? What Light—supreme, divine, creative? Something within her awoke then, stirred in response, and in that brief instant between life and death, she knew.

Senhu-re and the Power were one. To attain to a knowledge and an understanding of Its nature, she must become one with him who came, a messenger from the Great Ones to defeat her who had sought to transcend the limits imposed upon man by the High Gods.

Until this union had been consummated, until she, too could carry a spark of this flame into the darkness of the tomb, she might search for it, invoke it, in vain.

Was it already too late? She strained towards that still, shining figure, struggled to unite her consciousness with the Mystery of which he was now a part.

She would conquer—even now, she would conquer!

And suddenly, as if her thought had galvanized all evil latent within this place into renewed life, she was caught up into a maelstrom of malignant force. She and it and all the powers of darkness were hurled against that upright figure. Once more the Sound which had shattered her before, pealed forth. Then Senhu-re's body broke and he too, sank writhing to the ground.

And as he fell, she also fell, and went whirling out into darkness and into silence . . .

CHAPTER X

INTO THE DARK

DARKNESS . . . SILENCE. They were no more a part of her; she was separate—alive. She was aware of smooth stone under her hand. Words lingered in her consciousness together with an unreasoning terror. "Run—run . . ." But that was a long time ago. She was lying on her face upon the ground; she could hear her heart thumping. She tried not to think, she did not want to remember. Still in her nostrils was an aromatic scent—an odour of corruption; if she moved, if she even acknowledged her own existence, might she not be instantly precipitated back into the body of that woman who was somehow still an integral part of herself? Might she not once again be rent, destroyed by that blinding light? Might she not see those two dead things swaying towards her, nearer, nearer; hear those forbidden words which still resounded like dying thunder in her brain?

Like this she was safe, wrapped in her little shell of silence, secret—alone. But even here the agony of defeat, of failure could still penetrate. Tears fell from her eyes. Defeat? Failure? These were personal losses, but what of those others whom she had dragged down with her? What of him she loved, who stood, it seemed, still with out-flung hands, seeking to draw and transmute all evil into the flame of his own love?

She found that she was whispering a name over and over again, but the name was "Simon," not "Senhu-re."

Was it imagination, or did a voice murmur:

"It's all right, Carol, that was ages—æons ago."

Carol? Cheosri? Ages ago? Now, it was NOW, eternally now that these women lived. Which was she? She hardly knew. All that had happened to her who was called Carol was so completely overshadowed by the actions of Cheosri, that she felt it would never be possible to readjust the balance between the two.

But that way lay madness; somehow it must be done. She tried to cling to memories of this present life, but all that came to her was a memory of that experience in the *coulée*, the wall paintings of four souls being led before the judges of the Underworld with the gigantic figure of Maat guarding the entrance to their tomb. Then, suddenly once more her mind was swept into the past. She was looking into the tomb itself; there were the overturned mummy cases, but there should be something more. Already the picture was fading, becoming confused, like a dream. What was it that she had forgotten? Why was it that the thought of this tomb brought up blind fear and those words again—"Run—run . . ." Then in a flash she remembered everything, the curse, the shadow she had seen leaping from the entrance to the burial chamber, the crashing rocks, the confusion, the terror.

She tried to move and her body became very much her own again, signalling to her by a stab of pain. She was aware that she was aching and bruised, that there was a burning agony in her head. Her senses became alert now. How still it was! Suddenly she was terrified of this heavy silence; it was worse than the memory of that catastrophe which had overwhelmed them all. Supposing she were the only one left alive!

With an effort which caused fresh jabs of pain in her arm and head, she rolled over and opened her eyes fearfully. At first she could make out nothing but a shadowy confusion, then, as she twisted round, she gave a half-stifled cry of alarm, for there, illuminated by a pale gleam which appeared to fall from nowhere and only revealed his feet clearly, was the vague shape of a man standing rigid, apparently staring at the wall.

But at the first sound she made, he turned; and she saw that it was no magical figure materialized from her past, but Simon who, she realized a moment later, was gazing at the figure of Maat which she could now vaguely distinguish, still undamaged, looming above them.

Simon dropped on his knees beside her and took her in his arms. "All right, darling?" he whispered reassuringly. "You began to come to, a few moments ago, then went off again. I saw you weren't hurt, so left you alone."

"No, I'm not hurt really." She found herself clinging to him. "What about you—and the others?"

"I don't know about them. I was knocked silly myself for a few minutes, I've only just come to."

"A few minutes?" she frowned in bewilderment. She was still feeling dizzy and unreal. "What were you doing over there? I thought . . ."

"I was trying to get back," he said gravely.

"Get back?" She passed her hand over her eyes. "I had such a queer dream."

"I know." His hand was on her forehead, stroking it rhythmically. How did he know? Quite suddenly everything clicked back into focus. "Betty!" she gasped, "Father!" and struggled to her knees.

A groan out of the darkness answered her. Simon snatched up the electric torch which had been lying at his feet upon the ground and flashed it beyond her. It picked out a form, haggard, dishevelled, dragging himself up from a little pile of *débris*. It was Nick, holding Betty in his arms. Carol sprang to his side.

"She's killed, oh, she's killed," she moaned.

Simon took Betty from the other man who seemed too dazed to protest. He laid her down gently and examined her. "No, she's all right, I think; either fainted or in a trance. Leave her for a bit, then I'll see what can be done." He looked round as he swung the light up and down; it revealed Mannering lying a few yards away without movement. Simon knelt by him and rose after a minute or so, nodding at Carol. "Nothing serious, either; heart's quite sound." He looked at Nick who was still standing over Betty. "Are you all right, Annerly? Sure you're not hurt anywhere?"

Nick shook his head. "No—my arm's pretty sore, but there's nothing broken," he moved it up and down and looked about him rather stupidly. "God, what a narrow shave! Absolute miracle none of us was killed! What's the extent of the damage? Have you had a look? Hullo, my torch is working, that's a bit of luck. We'd better get out quick before some more roof comes down."

He flashed the torch rapidly round. Three sides of the antechamber were practically undamaged save for ominous looking cracks, but the side where the entrance had been was a mass of stones and *débris*. It was obvious that the actual collapse had taken place lower down in the passage, but the doorway had either caved in or was blocked up with rubble. In this darkness with only the thin white spears of torch-light to guide them it was difficult at first to see exactly what had happened.

"Where's the entrance?" Carol cried. "It must be behind those stones, Simon—more to the left."

Simon's light followed her directions. It stopped and remained like an ironical finger pointing behind a pile of fallen masonry, at an aperture, about a foot wide.

"There!" he said in a low voice.

For a few dreadful seconds they stared at it, bereft of speech, then his hand slowly dropped. Nikolai turned, and their eyes met. Carol saw that glance and understood.

"We're buried," she whispered, "buried alive!" As they neither of them replied, she clutched Simon's arm. "Is it true?" She clung to him: "Simon!"

Nikolai swung round. "Where are those picks?" He pushed past her and began groping about among the *débris* which was scattered all over the floor. Simon joined him, flashing the torch as he went. Carol remained rigid against the wall. To die like this! Suddenly she was seized with a frenzy of blind rage. She began tearing at the rocks with her bare hands; pieces of stone came away, clattering about her feet. Blood from a scratch on her forehead mingled with sweat ran into her eyes. Above her, as she worked, she felt the low roof, pressing nearer and nearer; around her the walls already seemed converging as they had done on Simon in that room. She could feel the solid rock upon all sides, indifferent, immovable, crushing her in.

Then she was aware of a restraining hand on her arm. "Don't, darling, don't!" came Simon's voice.

She stopped, sinking against him, staring at the rock.

"You mean—it's no good?"

He shook his head. "The picks are smashed. But anyhow it wouldn't be any use." He flashed the light again upon that dark crack. "Do you see those great chunks of rock? It looks to me as if the whole roof of the passage has fallen in—it would take a gang of men to move it . . ."

"But our men—won't they . . .?"

"Yes, I expect they'll have a shot at it."

She looked at him. "You're lying—you don't really think they will!"

He returned her gaze thoughtfully, as if calculating her strength; at that moment Nikolai flung down the haft of a spade with which he was attempting to lever up a rock. "Not a hope! Well, Conningsby, what do you make of it?"

"My real opinion? I think it's a hundred to one against our getting out." His hand closed upon Carol's as if to give her courage. "A lot depends on the men, of course, but I'm afraid Abdullah and his crowd will never tackle it; if they were scared stiff before, what will they be like now that they've been proved right? Ahmed may be able to get them to work, when he discovers what's happened, or he'll go for help. I do feel that if it is possible to dig us out at all, he or Zarov will do it."

"Zarov?" echoed Nikolai.

Simon nodded. "Yes, he's in the neighbourhood. The point is, will they be able to get through before the air gives out?"

"Good God, the air!" Nikolai cried. "How long will it last us?"

"It's difficult to tell, because we can't know for certain whether or not there's a complete block in the passage. If there is any air coming through, then we might last for days; if not, it'll be a question of hours before we actually lose consciousness."

Nikolai passed his hand across his brow, then glanced at the other two lying behind them. "Thank goodness they don't know. A matter of hours . . . I wonder how long we've been here already since the smash?"

"I don't suppose we were unconscious more than a few minutes."

"Oh come, it's not possible! I mean—I thought it was much longer than that."

Simon gave him a sharp look. "Did you have a—dream, too, by any chance?"

"I did have a dream—but what d'you mean by *did I have a dream, too?*" The other man did not reply, but knelt over Betty, and Nikolai stared at him rather with the expression of a frightened and bewildered child.

Simon had risen again and stood looking down at the unconscious girl. A silence fell which none of them was inclined to break. Carol's eyes were fixed upon Simon. She loved him, Soon, in a few hours, perhaps less, they would die and she would never taste this marvellous joy which she had been hungering for all the lonely and bitter years of her life. The devilish irony of it was more than she could bear. She turned away and sank down on a piece of stone. At her movement Simon came to her side; she clung to his hand and bent her head over it. "Why did this happen?" she whispered, "it's cruel—it's hateful. Why couldn't we have all been killed at once—decently?"

He shook his head. "There's some sort of purpose behind it. I suppose—"

But she wouldn't let him finish. "How can there be? What have any of us done to deserve such a horrible end? And you—who only came here to help us! And it was I—I who dragged you into it . . ." She broke off and lifted her eyes miserably to his face. She could only see it dimly, but something in its expression startled her, so that for a moment she forgot her self-accusations. "What is it?" she whispered, "have you thought of something—of a way out?"

The remote expression slowly left his eyes, he heaved a long sigh rather as one who returns from a dream. "I don't know," he said slowly, "I'm not sure—yet. Something you said gave me a clue." He smiled. "But one thing I can tell you, that injustice you've been complaining about simply doesn't exist."

"You mean," she began hotly, but he caught her by both arms, pulled her to her feet and kissed her on the lips.

"I mean—wait. We're not dead yet, not by a long chalk. We've got several hours, a whole lot of things can happen in several hours. But before we do anything I want to get your sister out of her trance. It's most important; more so than you realize."

Still a little dazed by his kiss, she watched him take Betty gently from Nick's arms and, kneeling beside her, prop her head on his lap. Expertly his hands made swift, rhythmical passes above her, sometimes touching her face lightly, sometimes appearing as if they sought to draw her up or to bring down invisible strength.

Meantime Nikolai was eyeing him morosely. "Better to have left her," he muttered; "what's the good?"

"No; this isn't a natural faint; whatever happens she must be free of him."

"Of *him?*" Nick echoed. "Who do you mean?"

At that moment Betty moved and gave a low moan. Simon leant over her, and began to speak in a sing-song voice in a language neither of the others understood. Presently she moaned again, her eyelids fluttered, and they heard her say: "No—no! I can't bear any more." Pearls of sweat dewed her forehead and she began to struggle weakly: "Let me go! Let me go!"

Simon spoke. "You are safe, Betty, with Nick, with Carol. We love you; we will protect you. You are free."

A long shudder passed through her, her eyes opened. They were blank at first, then slowly understanding dawned in them, but terror was there also, pitiful to see.

She tried to sit up. "We'll die," she cried, "die here and Zarov will come! He'll take me—hold me afterwards. I know he will. Oh, save me from him, save me! Don't let him get me again, don't let him send me back!"

She clung to Simon, sobbing, but grew calmer at the gentle touch of his hand on her brow.

"He can't get at you now," he reassured her, "never again, child, unless you let him."

She sat up, then, staring round. She was suddenly quite sane, but more than that, she seemed to have grown curiously mature.

"He can," she said, "I know. You don't understand; he'll come here—when we are dead."

"We won't be dead," put in Nikolai sharply. "They'll dig us out."

She looked at him with pity, smiling wanly. "Do you really believe that?" she asked.

"I don't see why not. Conningsby's man will make them; it's only a matter of time." But he did not meet her eyes.

"Time? Yes. But supposing they can't get through. Or—something else happens."

"What else should happen? Don't be frightened, darling, of course it'll be all right." He took her hand and tried to draw her towards him, but she turned her head aside. She was shivering and tears were pouring down her face. "No, no, it's too late; we're in here for ever. I know. Someone—told—me—so; I don't remember any more who it was, but I know. We'll just die . . ." Her voice trailed off.

Simon, who had been listening intently to her words as if to extract some inner meaning from them, got to his feet. "Come on, now," he said, "pull yourself together, my dear. Let's look facts in the face. Supposing we do die, what's there to be frightened of in that? We'll be really free then, not Zarov nor anyone else could touch us. You may be quite sure of that."

"I can't think why the idea of Zarov's turning up scares you so, though I don't see why he should," said Nikolai wearily, sitting down by Betty's side and searching for a cigarette. "But personally there's no one I should like to see better!"

Betty gave a sharp cry. "No, no, Nick, don't say that!"

"But my dear girl, what *is* all this about? It's your fault, Conningsby, I remember now you suggested it." He looked at the other man with a suspicious frown: "What do you know about Zarov's movements, anyway? There's something here I don't understand?"

"Quite a lot," said Simon drily, and waved aside the cigarette-case Nikolai had automatically held out to him.

Nikolai grunted. "As we seem to have a certain amount of spare time on our hands and precious little to do with it, perhaps you'd explain. A number of things have been puzzling me about you lately."

Simon shook his head. "You're wrong, Annerly. We've got precious little time, and the devil of a lot to do in it, so far as I can see; that is, if we are going to make an effort to get out of here. I, for one, have no intention of dying if I can avoid it."

"What do you suggest, digging through there with your fingers, or whistling for Zarov to come through the roof?"

Simon grinned. "Neither; I've got other ideas, but I *shall* have to do a bit of explaining, you're right there; as a matter of fact that's an essential part of my plan, we'll have to give up half an hour to it."

"Fire ahead, then. It'll keep our thoughts occupied, anyway."

For a moment Simon stared in silence at the figure of Maat which seemed to hold a curious fascination for him. Then he turned and looked down at Nikolai. "You wanted to know something about Zarov. Right, you shall. Does the name 'Apepa' convey anything to you?"

"Apepa?" Nikolai frowned. "Yes, I do know the name; where the deuce have I heard it?" He repeated it several times, shaking his head. "No," he said at length, "it's familiar, and yet it just seems to escape me."

But Carol gave a sharp exclamation. Until that moment she had forgotten her dream—if dream it were. It had been erased from her conscious mind by the discovery of their danger, by her fear for Betty, by all the emotional stress of that last half-hour. But this name recalled it. Although the memory was blurred now and confused, she felt that it had not vanished completely as so many dreams do on waking; it was there still, she only had to have a few moments' quiet, or some clue, some associated train of thought, for the whole thing to return.

But Simon was speaking. "Apepa. Think back; what about that dream you said you had, just now?"

"Dream?" Nikolai stared at him, then slowly his expression changed. "God!" he whispered, "yes, that dream! It was foul . . . queer, too . . ." He sat with his head bent, evidently beginning to recapture fleeting memories. "I was an Egyptian." He gave a short laugh: "Nasty bit of work; seem to have been fighting most of the time when I wasn't engaged in—well, in less savoury pastimes." He shuddered: "The least said of that the better. Let's see, I was fighting some Pharaoh or other, and a woman . . ."

"Cheosri," Carol breathed.

He jumped round on her, "Yes, that was the name. How the hell do you know?"

"Because I was Cheosri—I was that woman."

"How could you be? Someone in *my* dream. You? I must have called it out or something. Well, tell me my name, then."

"Nut-Feru."

"Good Lord . . ." He made a helpless gesture and stared from Carol to Simon who was watching him with a smile. "Am I mad or what? Don't tell me you had my dream, too!"

Simon nodded. "Only it wasn't a dream, Annerly, it was a memory." He picked up Carol's hand and kissed the finger upon which was the scarab ring he had recently given her. "Nothing," he whispered, "nor change, nor death, may, nor the permutations of Time, have kept me from you. And this ring, into which the power of our mutual love has entered, was returned to me by one who knew more of my fate than I guessed, so that I might put it again upon your hand, as I promised then."

She gave a stifled cry and clung to him, oblivious for the moment of the others, even of the fate which lay heavy upon them. "But I betrayed you, have you forgotten that? Have you forgiven me?"

"I betrayed my vows and my gods," he said gently. She shuddered.

"And Nikolai! What I did to him!"

But Nikolai interrupted. "Here, stop a minute, I must get this straight. Do you mean this was the memory of an actual life—that we were all in it?"

Simon nodded. "It looks like it, doesn't it? Unless, of course, you can find a better explanation. But you've got to admit that it could hardly be coincidence that we should all have an identical dream."

"No—and this wasn't an ordinary dream." He sat brooding, obviously trying to recapture more of those elusive memories. His aggressive scepticism had completely vanished. How different he was, Carol thought, from the man who had jeered at Simon in their tent a few hours ago. A few hours? A lifetime seemed to have intervened between then and now. And hadn't it done so, indeed? True, it was a life that had happened thousands of years ago, but it made so little difference in this timeless darkness which had engulfed them all. She looked at Simon; he was standing there patiently watching Nikolai, as if every moment were not of the most vital importance. He had said that. They would have to do something—soon. Yet here they were sitting around, talking. A wild surge of impatience arose in her. She wanted to jump to her feet, to tear Nikolai from his dream. That was what had always enraged her with him: this necessity to work everything out logically, slowly, methodically. "Act, act!" something cried within her, "or it will be too late."

Strange that Simon should have chosen that moment to turn and smile at her, to touch her hand reassuringly. Had he felt through that extraordinary link of sympathy which seemed, every moment, to be increasing between them, the turmoil in her mind? At any rate she was instantly calmed. He knew. If he had got some plan, as she believed, some plan for which he must have Nikolai's whole-hearted co-operation, it was obvious that Nikolai must be convinced of Simon's superior knowledge and power. And he would have to come to such a conviction in his own way, from an inner acceptance, otherwise it would be valueless.

Meanwhile, Nikolai had turned an intent gaze upon Betty as if seeking in her face the features of that woman he had loved thousands of years ago. "Anf-Kaseth," he whispered presently. "Betty, do you remember. Did you dream, too?"

"No, I don't remember anything." She looked from one to the other with frightened eyes. "What is all this about? What happened?"

"We went back to a past life when we were all together in Egypt, a life that must be connected with this place," Simon answered.

"But I didn't. Why didn't I go back, too?"

For a moment he hesitated, as if undecided whether the time had yet come to speak; then he said slowly: "I think you did, but you see you were in a trance, and as Zarov was using you, it was he who contacted the past; that's why you can't recall it as we've done."

"Zarov using me?" She began to tremble violently. "What do you mean?"

Simon put his hand on hers. "You spoke of it when you woke up. Don't you remember?" She shook her head. "All right, I'll try to explain; I couldn't tell you anything much before, because Annerly, anyway, wouldn't have believed me; but you've got to know now, for if you do, and can accept it, I think we may find some way out of here between us; but only if we face facts and shirk nothing—nothing at all."

"Go ahead," said Nikolai. He put his hand to his forehead with a weary gesture. "I'm ready to listen to anything; I confess this has me beat!"

"Do you remember in your vision a man called Apepa? I asked you just now if the name was familiar—"

"Of course," Nikolai interrupted sharply, "I know now—that magician!"

"Yes; so far as I can judge Zarov is Apepa reborn. That's why we're all caught up in this business; each of us, you see, in our own way, came under his influence in that past life. I, through my infatuation for Cheosri, let him defeat me; she, because she sold herself to him for the sake of her ambition. Betty, because she was his medium then, but even more so because she betrayed him—for one is always bound to the people one wrongs—has a special link with him now. You, Annerly, were drawn to him for much the same reasons. You, too, followed him and afterwards betrayed him, at least I suppose you did, I didn't get so much of your life in my vision."

"I did betray him," muttered the other man.

"Good; that clears up that point, anyway."

"But it doesn't," said Carol sharply, "you say Zarov used Betty now as a medium; but it ought to be me! I was worse than she ever was! Look at the end . . ." her voice trailed off.

"My dear," he said gently, "we don't know what happened between that life and the present one. No two people ever develop in the same way and at the same pace. It's possible Betty was a little slower than you; she may have given herself as a medium to evil forces in many other lives as well as in that one. There are lots of ways of doing that, you know; drink, and excesses of all sorts. She must have done something of the kind, otherwise she wouldn't have come back this time with such a negative, mediumistic, weak body. One doesn't get anything by chance. You're far too positive for Zarov to use in that way. No, you've learned some wisdom in the interim, that's what it amounts to."

But Betty was clinging to Simon again, her face stricken, terrified. "You mean Zarov can use me—now—any time, make me do what he wants, *see* for him? Oh, it's horrible! I wish I were dead! Why, perhaps even now . . ." And she covered her face with her hands, as if to shut out all possibility of sight or sound.

"Is that true, Conningsby?" asked Nikolai tensely. He had slipped his arm round Betty and was holding her close as if desirous of protecting her against this evil thing.

"Unfortunately, yes; but of course . . ." Simon broke off, he was looking at Betty speculatively.

"Of course, what?"

"I was going to say the powers of good might use her just as easily as the powers of evil, that is, if she wanted them to. Anyway I think I could protect her against Zarov, to start with."

"Oh, do it!" Betty cried, "I don't care what you do, only keep him away from me."

"I'd have to hypnotize you, put you under my will and influence for a while."

"I thought you said," broke in Carol, "you never used hypnosis."

"I said it isn't one of my methods, and certainly I'd never try it on against anyone's will. But I seem to remember that you were suggesting I should hypnotize Annerly!"

"I wish to God you had," said Nikolai gloomily, "or knocked me on the head!"

Simon grinned. "I don't believe in putting things off; we'd have to have tackled this business some time, you know."

Nikolai only stared at him, but Betty's hands were insistent on his sleeve.

"I'll let you do anything you like—if only you can keep me safe. Won't he be able to—to use me, or whatever it is, if you do this? Are you sure?"

"Almost sure—yes."

"Then why didn't you do it before?" asked Carol.

Again she saw that visionary look spread over his face. "I don't think it would have been possible then," he replied slowly; "you see, none of you quite trusted me, that makes a lot of difference. Besides I doubt if I knew enough myself; I think we've all learned a lot of things from this vision."

Then Carol remembered. Senhu-re had been hidden for years with that Secret Brotherhood. What had he been doing there, in that mysterious temple, between her betrayal of him and the moment when, armed with the power of glory and light, he appeared to bring defiance and death to all that was evil in the tomb? The tomb . . . abruptly she sat up, gazing round at those walls close-packed with menacing shadows, which hemmed them in. Hadn't Simon said just now that this was the place? Those passages, haunted and terrible, that *coulée!* Yes, it must be the same! She began to shake, icy jets of water seemed to be running down her spine, beads of sweat were on her face. She felt a tide of hysteria rising within her, she must escape from here, get away, away . . .

Then she heard Simon's voice. With a supreme effort she controlled herself.

"If you will let me do it, Betty, I think it will help us all."

Betty got to her feet. "Yes, yes, of course I will."

"Must you do it now?" Carol broke in. "I thought we were going to try and get out, and we just sit talking—talking. We must have been here hours already."

Simon looked at his watch. "Just over three-quarters of an hour, to be exact." He put his hand on her shoulder. "It's all right, darling, just be calm a little longer, and patient. If we are going to make the attempt I have in mind the talking is necessary and so is this business with Betty. It's all part of it." He turned to Nikolai: "Do you agree, too, Annerly, that I should try this hypnosis?"

Nikolai's eyes were upon the girl. "I agree to anything she wants, anything that'll make her feel safe and happy." He also stood up. "I want to tell you, Conningsby, that I didn't trust you before, I wish to God I had! I don't understand what's happened now, but I feel that the whole business is mostly my fault, I shouldn't have been so pig-headed. I'd like you to know that I know it and—and appreciate all you tried to do for us. I'm sorry . . ." He turned away with a helpless gesture.

"My dear chap," Simon replied, "it's no more your fault than mine. I realize now that it's a bigger thing than all of us; it had to happen. If you're on our side now against Zarov and his crowd it's going to make a lot of difference; it's when people are at sixes and sevens that the powers of disruption get their chance. And now to safeguard you, young woman," he continued, putting his arm round Betty's shoulders. "Come out of the light, I don't want your mind to be distracted. And if you two wouldn't mind not talking—it won't take me five minutes; just a few little passes."

He drew Betty as far away as possible, and when they had been swallowed up by the darkness which reigned outside the tiny circle of torchlight Carol made another effort to recall some more of that vision of her past, so much of which was still hazy and incomprehensible. But now she could only think of the end. That torture chamber, with Nut-Feru cursing her from the rack; small wonder there had been always this strange feeling of lurking distrust and dislike between them. Could she ever hope for his forgiveness? A surge of remorse swept over her. Not a lifetime of service and love could compensate for what she had done then. Not a lifetime! And perhaps they had but a few hours. Oh, she had never wanted life so much as now; not for herself, not even for Simon, but for the chance to repay some of those terrible debts, for the chance to help Nikolai, her chief enemy, to do something for him at last. How strange, she thought, that all suspicion, all dislike, all the friction she had felt between them should have ceased so completely from the moment she understood its cause. Who was it who had said: *And the truth shall make you free?* It was so indeed. She looked up and found Nick's eyes upon her face, and in them she saw a recollection of her own thoughts. He also understood and, understanding, could forgive. Their age-old enmity was drowned in that understanding. She stretched out her hand to him, smiling wanly, and his closed round it in a warm clasp. In that moment whatever the dark, unknown ages had held of evil between them was obliterated.

Simon appeared behind them. Betty, looking a little dazed, sat down on the ground by Nikolai, pressing against him.

"I think we've checkmated friend Zarov in that quarter, anyhow," Simon remarked.

"Does he know what's been happening here?" Carol asked.

"He was probably able to keep in touch up to the moment I came to," Simon replied rather grimly. "But directly I recovered and realized what had been happening I shut him out."

"Shut him out? How could you?"

"By drawing a mental ring around the place to insulate it—building what the Atlanteans used to call a 'wall of silence' in etheric matter. It's a method all occultists use to protect themselves from those who would like to get at their secrets; it's absolutely essential for any serious occult work."

"You mean he couldn't possibly know what's happening here—not by a crystal or anything?"

"Not possibly. He'll get nothing and presume, I hope, that we're all dead."

"But if he were using Betty at the time wouldn't he have been able to see you when you first got up?"

"I didn't get up," said Simon shortly. "I did it before, on my way back to my body." And Carol knew she must ask no more questions on that subject at the moment.

"And now—what?" put in Nikolai. "As you pointed out, the air won't last for ever. I wish you could use your occult powers and see whether anyone is coming to our rescue."

Simon shook his head. "It wouldn't be worth the effort. Even if they were it doesn't mean they'd succeed. We don't know that half the cliff isn't down further on."

"But just now you seemed pretty sure that Zarov would have a shot at getting through, though why Zarov should be here at all I don't quite see."

In a few words Simon gave Nikolai as comprehensive a sketch as possible of what he knew of Zarov and of his intentions.

"Good Lord," Nikolai exclaimed when he had finished, "he doesn't seem to have changed much, anyway. What mutts we were to be caught like that!"

"I'm not so sure. We were all linked together in evil then, so obviously at some time we've got to come back to tidy up the mess we made."

"I don't like that idea much; it means that events change so little that they reproduce themselves continually. No, it's an awful thought."

"It would be if we hadn't got the power to alter the rhythm. If events tend to reproduce themselves it's because we haven't learned anything, have gone on blindly sowing the same kind of seed, if you like to put it that way. I think the whole trouble is, we don't in the least realize the terrific power of thought, of will. If you take a certain kind of oath, dedicating yourself to a Cause—it doesn't matter whether it's a good or an evil one—you bind yourself much more inevitably than you know, to fulfil that oath, to follow that Cause to its logical conclusion. That's what we all did in Egypt. Probably nine people out of ten don't bind themselves body and soul to anything so terrific as this Secret, therefore they don't have such forces to contend with; but we did, and we can't alter that original impulse or escape from the consequences. We've got to go on now. We all vowed, in our different ways, that we would discover it; I, for the sake of my country (and to satisfy my vanity), and you for the sake of knowledge and power. We were all mistaken, but that doesn't matter; we did it, and now I feel we shall have to continue with the work we began then. We all used our powers wrongly, now of our own free will we've got to deal with those powers we conjured up to serve us, and defeat them."

"Was Father in with us?" asked Carol suddenly. They had almost forgotten the old man, so quietly was he lying in the shadows. Now Simon looked down at him. "I think he must have been the Pharaoh of that day; he was, so far as I recall, a weak and inefficient monarch; I suppose he's progressed so little through the centuries that he's not ready even for the knowledge that we've been given. Probably that's why he's been kept unconscious. It's better for him; he's too weak still; it would kill him or send him mad."

"Poor Father," said Carol softly; "but now what are we going to do about it? I mean it all leads nowhere if we die here. We don't conquer, or transmute or whatever it is—we've just failed again."

"I don't see it that way. Even if we did die now we'd die understanding at last what life means and what we'd undertaken to do with it; therefore we'd come back properly equipped next time and then we wouldn't be nearly so likely to fail. But we're not going to consider dying, anyhow. I don't think we've finished with this life yet, not while Zarov's loose outside. We've already done a spot of transmutation, to my mind, by getting to understand things more clearly. I think that when Mr. Zarov meets us again he'll find he's got a very different proposition to tackle! I'm perfectly convinced he'll make an effort to get in somehow, now that the force of the Curse has been expended. He'll want to have a shot at getting at the Secret before the catastrophe gets known."

"But is the Secret hidden there?" asked Carol. "If it was really in this place that I—I died, then it isn't: I was only trying to find out where It was hidden—at least that's what I seem to remember. And yet—in the end . . ."

She sat frowning, trying to recall that end. Hadn't she known something—had some revelation? But it had gone for ever; she would never be able to recall it now.

Simon was looking at her with a smile. "Yes," he replied in a low voice, "you did have a vision of it. I remember more of that last phase than you."

"Then you know?"

He did not reply, but picked his way across the rubble to where the fallen slab lay, while they watched him in silence. Then he turned to them and said: "Do you realize that the way into the tomb is clear?"

They all started. Somehow they had forgotten the importance they had once attached to opening up this burial chamber. Now all three of them shrank with a feeling of horror from even looking towards it.

"How can that help us?" asked Nikolai, after a pause.

Simon did not give a direct reply, instead he remarked quietly; "Don't you think it's getting very oppressive here? Aren't you beginning to feel tired—a little queer?"

"You mean—the oxygen's beginning to give out?"

"I mean we've got to get a move on, if we're to live."

"But how can we?" Nikolai stood up and stared round rather wildly; then his eyes came back to Simon. "What are you thinking of, Conningsby?"

"It was an idea," Simon replied very slowly, as if searching in his memory for words to clothe so indefinite a thought, "that came to me just as I came to, I lost it entirely when we started talking, but in the last few minutes I've been getting it back. It's terribly vague, and I can't quite see yet how it's going to help us, but I feel there's a clue there, if only I could get it." He paused and stood frowning before him. "It's about this Guardian. I've been trying to remember exactly what happened in the tomb when the Great High Priest of Egypt brought me with Him, in order to use me to combat the invocation to the Dark Ones that Cheosri and Apepa were employing in their effort to discover the hiding-place of the Secret. I know that, in the combat between the Powers of Light and Darkness, I was killed; but my memories don't end there, for my consciousness, which had, for magical purposes, temporarily become one with that of my Master, lived on. So I remember the culmination of the Great Magic. I saw Him invoke those Lords we know as Archangels, and create from their Essence a Being who was given charge over the tomb to keep it closed for ever from invaders, so that the Forces that had contended therein should remain imprisoned, since They were so powerful and *so full of knowledge*. Thus down the ages all who attempted to open this place up were either killed at once or put out of action in some way, until we came . . ."

"Why weren't we killed then?" asked Carol.

"That's what been puzzling me. Things like that aren't just luck. Perhaps it's because we've got to undo the evil we created in some way; after all this *is* our own private battleground! Perhaps we've got to conquer Apepa through our united efforts."

"But how can we," asked Nikolai, "when we can't get out; and, so far as we can see, we'll all be dead when he gets in!"

Simon took no notice, but continued, as one thinking aloud. "It's pretty obvious that after centuries even such Powers become weakened, unless they are renewed, I think Zarov was right in his assumption that, after the first violent repercussion which would inevitably fall on whoever did succeed in getting in, the strength of the Guardian would be considerably depleted. In consequence, anyone following immediately afterwards, armed with newly-invoked forces, would stand a pretty good chance of defeating It."

"Do you mean the Guardian is—is here now?" interrupted Betty, looking round nervously and clinging closer to Nikolai's side."

"Of course." He struck his hand suddenly on the rock behind him. "That's it! Don't you see? We were deliberately allowed to get in, saved from death in the most miraculous way—because it was nothing short of a miracle—in order that we should join our forces with those of the Guardian imprisoned in this place for centuries and so be strong enough to defeat Zarov."

"Yes, but how?" Carol cried.

"That's what I don't know yet; I've got to find out more about the tomb, where Zarov is, what he's doing." He paused. instinctively they all held their breath waiting for his next words. And at once the silence swooped down upon them like smothering, dark wings; but surely it was something more than silence that they felt!

Carol looked at Simon. He was facing them, his head uplifted. It struck her that he had changed a great deal since this catastrophe. He looked taller somehow, more authoritative, a strange, magnetic power seemed to emanate from him; a fantastic thought flashed into her mind. Was not he, perhaps, just as mediumistic in his way as Betty was in hers? Couldn't he be used too? She experienced an instant's confusion. Was it really Simon looming there between those two god-shapes on either side of the entrance—or the Guardian Itself, waiting to slay or to save them?

Then he moved and the illusion was shattered. He pointed to the gaping hole in the rock behind him, "There's only one place where we can find out what we've got to do"—he said,—"in there."

The other three stood staring as if hypnotized at that cavity, and a feeling of terror, so acute that it made them weak and sick, swept over them. What was down in that place? What would they find there? Was Simon right, or would some new disaster, more sinister perhaps than even the previous one, overtake them?

They hesitated. Then Betty covered her eyes with her hands and drew back. "Oh, no," she moaned, "I'd rather die!"

"We can't go," said Nikolai sharply; then, rationalizing his instinctive recoil, added: "The air will be poisoned; it's from there the danger came before. Besides, what's the good? Better stay here; at least we know where we are."

Simon turned and looked at him. "The Powers of Disruption," he said, softly.

Then Carol stepped forward. It needed all her courage; she could never have done it had it not been for her love of Simon. He must not stand alone.

"Why not?" she exclaimed. "Suppose we do die, won't it be better than waiting here while the air gives out? Nothing could be worse than that. Besides, didn't we say we'd act together? This may be the one hope." She took hold of Nikolai's hand, and at the touch it was as if something between them became reunited. His response was instantaneous.

"You're right. Come on, Betty darling; damn that fellow Zarov, we'll beat him yet!" And drawing the younger girl after him he strode up to the entrance of the burial chamber.

CHAPTER XI

PRINCIPALITIES AND POWERS

"WAIT! We mustn't go like this, it wouldn't be safe." Simon had stepped before the entrance and stood now facing the others authoritatively.

"What do you mean?" asked Nikolai.

"If we want the Guardian to help us we must invoke the Energies It represents. There's an Egyptian Ritual.... I'll use it, if you'll stand just as you are now, and try to help by—by, well, praying, if you like; praying for guidance and protection."

They remained as he bade them. In this semi-gloom, with the faint light from Nikolai's torch throwing a circle about Simon's feet and the threatening forms of the Egyptian gods looming on either side, he seemed a curiously remote yet significant figure.

Slowly he raised his arms, spreading them out, palms upward. His head was flung back, his eyes closed. And while they waited and watched, gently into the silence which already held the menace of death, the first of those mighty syllables from the Book of the Dead—the Invocation to the Bornless One—took shape, vibrating in growing thunder upon the air.

Over Carol they swept in wave upon wave of power, terrible, yet somehow familiar, fraught with mystery, yet lifting up her spirit into an unspeakable ecstasy. The past, the present and the future converged here in this magic Utterance; all significances fell into their inevitable pattern. What had been was; what would be existed already now, in THIS.

She apprehended yet she did not hear; for she herself, participating in these Elements, became a part of the mystic symbols of Power.

"*I invoke Thee, the Terrible and Invisible God, Who dwellest in the Void Places of the Spirit. Hear me ... Sothou; Modoria; Phalarthao ... Mighty and Bornless One ...*"

Again and again in that cascade of words which thundered, which drowned her, Names shone forth like blinding points of light. What were these names, beautiful as "Whirling Air," as

"Rushing Fire?" *Abrasar... Ishuré... Diarthanna Thorun... Adonaie...* Out of the glorious symphony of unfolding syllables these emerged, catching her up on dazzling pinions of colour, light and sound.

At last silence fell, but a silence that throbbed and pulsed, that was vibrant with unseen movement, with unheard voices. Her heart was thumping, fire seemed to be pouring through her veins. A current of electricity was beating upon her head, tingling in her feet.

Then once again, pealing forth now on a higher, purer Note, majestic as the sound of an organ, the Second Invocation sounded, uniting Man and Gods in the supernal recognition of the ONE.

... *"Thou who holdest in Thy right hand the magic wand of Double Power, and who bearest in Thy left hand the Rose and Cross of Light and Life, Thee, Thee do I invoke!*

"Thou, whose head is as an emerald and whose Nemyss as the Night-Sky blue, Thee, Thee do I invoke!

"Thou whose skin is of flaming orange as though it burned in a furnace; Thee, Thee do I invoke!" ...

On, on; power flowing around them. The Response swelling and thrilling:

"... I am He! The Truth!

"I am He! Who hate that evil should be wrought in the World!

"Behold I am yesterday, To-day and the brother of the Morrow! I am born again and again. Mine is the unseen force wherefrom the Gods are sprung, which giveth life unto the dwellers in the watch-towers of the Universe.

"I am the charioteer in the East, Lord of the Past and the Future, who seeth by his own inward light, and whose birth is from the House of Death ..."

There were no more barriers; there were no adversaries.

"... Behold! He is in me and I in Him!... Thoth, Hermes, Mercury, Odin! By whatever name I call Thee, Thou art still un-Named and Nameless for Eternity. Come Thou forth, I say, from Thine abode in the Silence, Unutterable Wisdom, All-light, All-Power. Come thou forth, I say, and aid and guard me in this work of Art!"

There was silence; but now it was no more the silence of death, but rather the pregnant, waiting silence of Life that trembles on the verge of manifestation.

Carol found that she had fallen upon her knees, and when she looked round she saw that Betty and even Nikolai, the sceptic, were also kneeling; but the man had abased himself and was lying with his forehead pressed against the earth.

Slowly he raised his head, looking about him wonderingly, then with a long sigh he slipped his arm round the girl and lifted her to her feet.

"We are ready," he said, but it was not to them that he spoke.

Simon's arms had dropped; he stood motionless for a moment or two, then stepped away from the aperture.

"Now," he said, "we can go."

"But what about Father," asked Carol; "ought we to leave him alone?"

"I don't think he'll come round; and if he does we won't be far away if he calls out. No, he'll be safer here."

Nikolai gave Simon a sharp look as if he considered that last remark a little sinister. "Wouldn't it be better if we went alone," he suggested, "and left the girls here, too?"

"The girls won't stay," put in Carol quickly, "at least this one won't."

"Oh, no!" cried Betty, and clung to Nikolai's arm.

"They must come," Simon said quietly, "they'll be needed. Male and female principles, you know."

They didn't know; but none of them said anything more. Simon was in absolute command.

He picked up another torch which was lying on the ground and tried the switch; as the powerful beam shone out he gave a sigh of relief. "What luck they weren't smashed."

"And had just been recharged," murmured Nikolai.

"Yes. I've got a small one here I'll leave with your father in case he comes to. Now I'll go first, the girls in the middle and you at the end, Annerly." He paused with his hand resting on the stone above that dark, gaping space. "If anything does happen, *anything*, stand firm; don't be afraid, and keep close together; hold hands if possible. Try to remember that invocation. I'll repeat the words:

" '*Come thou forth, I say. Came thou forth and make all spirits subject unto me! So that every spirit of the firmament, and of the Ether, upon the Earth and under the Earth, on Dry Land and in the Water, of Whirling Air and of Rushing Fire, and every spell and scourge of God may be obedient unto me!*

" '*IAO: SABAO!*'

"If you should forget the words invoke mentally all the Powers of Good, and you'll be helped to recall them. Try to visualize yourselves surrounded by a wall of white fire, and never forget for an instant that you *are* protected by the Invocations, and that the stronger the Forces which are called up against you the stronger automatically that protection will become."

"But what do you suppose might happen?" Nikolai asked. "I mean, it's just as well to have some idea—"

"I don't know; it all depends on Zarov."

"But Zarov is outside!"

Simon only grunted. "You forget he's a magician and a pretty powerful one at that. Besides, there are other factors . . ." He broke off. "I'm not sure, myself. I'm frankly puzzled about something, something that came to me in that vision. I think I can only get it back in the same atmosphere. Come on, we've wasted too much time already."

He turned and stooped to enter the burial chamber. Carol noticed that the shape of the opening was that of an upturned sarcophagus, and as he paused for a moment, between the figure of Maat and the evil monster which leapt up in the beam of their lights, she saw him as some new Osiris lured into the magical mummy-case by another Set. Swiftly she grasped hold of his coat. There was only room for one to squeeze through, but she was on the other side almost as soon as he.

"A step," he said in a low voice, "another; three steps."

Now there was space. She moved to his side. The other two came up close behind.

It seemed even more silent here than in the chamber they had just left. It was an oppression of silence, like a weight upon one's body and mind. And dark! They had never known such darkness. It was a Presence brooding over them.

Cutting a way through it, the clear, white ray from the torch swept the floor. And suddenly, as if at that moment materialized out of nothingness, a hand lay there, the fingers curved. Carol all but screamed. It had such a look of life. But it was just a dead hand, severed or perhaps fallen away; shrivelled, dead three thousand years; yet the sight of it brought back, as vividly as if it had happened yesterday, that scene in the burial chamber. Yes, this was the place. The light moved. The hand was gone. Instead now, almost at their feet, was a skeleton; it lay with its arms outstretched. Around its neck still were strings of beads, a golden collar; lying in the dust, a bracelet like a snake and a huge ruby ring which shot baleful fires as the light aroused it from its long sleep. At the side of the skull, as if it had fallen when the woman fell, was a head-dress of extreme beauty, the outstretched wings wrought with plowing enamels, while in the centre the Uræus serpent raised a shining crest.

And that was all that remained of the pride, the beauty, the glory of Cheosri.

And as Carol gazed at this, which once had been herself, as avid for life as now she was, her consciousness became marvellously quickened. She actually felt the blood in her veins, the breath vitalizing her body, herself as a being, alive in every particle. And yet *that* on the ground was she, and she was *that!* Death stood at her shoulder again and if he struck, then she would be Carol no more. Yet would she not, by this very token at her feet, still exist? Here at last was direct knowledge of continuity; not its mere acceptance as a theory. Cheosri—Carol; and in between, how many bodies used and cast aside like outworn garments? Yet *she* remained. Some words flashed into her mind: *Never was I lost, nor thou, nor all of these, and never shall we cease to be.* Then for a moment, again, she had the transient sensation of being lifted up beyond the limitations of time and space. Cheosri was herself; yet she, was she not already that other future self, the fruit of this eternal tree whereon the blossoms flowered, dropping their petals, yet generating another flowering through their seed?

How long that moment of perception endured she did not know, but she was brought back to the limitations of earth by a stifled cry behind her. She opened her eyes, which she was surprised to find had been closed, to see Nikolai's torch picking out of the darkness the remains of what appeared to be two charred and blackened mummy-cases lying crookedly upon the floor.

Now the whole scene came sharply into focus. Between them was a wrought-iron brazier, but the metal was twisted and melted together as if it had been subjected to intense heat. "Struck by lightning," was Carol's first thought. Here were the remains of another skeleton, a few charred bones, no more—Apepa? And on each side were the remains of the two mummies: little piles of dust, a few wrappings, a few broken fragments.

Nikolai stepped forward to examine these relics. "They look as if they'd been burned," he said. And Carol wondered how much he knew, how much he recalled, or guessed.

"Yes," came Simon's voice, "they were." Curiously enough they were all speaking in whispers; the silence had laid its spell upon them. "You don't remember anything of that, then?"

"No. You mean . . . ?"

"Your bodies, yours and Betty's. Cheosri tried to use you after death—and failed; or at least partly failed."

"Us," murmured Nikolai, staring down upon those decaying things. He accepted it now, but Carol could see that to Betty this revelation—for such it had been to both Nikolai and herself—meant little or nothing.

Nikolai stooped and touched the bones of Cheosri; they dropped to dust in his hand.

"These looked charred, too," he said.

"Yes." Simon moved the light of his torch slowly onward. "There should be another somewhere."

Towards the opposite wall the beam travelled. They all watched it. Rocks came into view. The chamber had been hewn roughly out, there were projecting cornices with inky shadows behind them, shadows which the light did not disperse.

"There!" whispered Carol, and caught her breath. It lay, this other skeleton, huddled up against the wall. A few brown shreds were all that was left of the garment which had clothed the priest. The skeleton was more intact than the others; they could imagine how he had fallen, first to his knee, then slipping sideways with arms upraised, perhaps to shield his mortal eyes from that which no mortal eyes should see. Instinctively, so projected was she once more into that past, into that moment when Senhu-re had stood glorious in power defying her, Carol looked upon the hand for the ring; and only then remembered that now it was upon her own.

She stretched out her living hand to look at it again. "But how did it get out of here?" she murmured. Simon heard and answered her. "It never was here. The High Priest took it from me; it was a sacred symbol—it had other work to do."

He left them and leant over what had been Senhu-re. "I must remember... I must remember!" Then he straightened himself abruptly, *"But how did he get here?"* he asked in a louder voice.

He seemed to expect an answer and Nikolai replied, rather vaguely: "Why, the way we came in, I suppose."

"No," Simon's voice was sharp. "Carol, think! Can't you recall what happened?" He stepped back and stood over the remains of Cheosri, glancing about him with that perplexed expression still on his face. "Try hard to think back, to get back into your vision; everything, I tell you, *everything* depends on us remembering. Now look, you and Apepa were standing here; the mummy-cases were there opposite you, *facing the entrance*; that's very important, don't forget it. You and they were making three sides of a triangle with the brazier in the centre. Now—*where did I appear from?*"

"I—I don't know; you just were there."

"Not behind you?"

"Of course not. At the side, I think. Why, no! Where the body is now."

"You're quite sure of that? I didn't come in behind you, through the doorway?"

She considered this carefully. "No, you just seemed to appear—from nowhere. Perhaps—couldn't you have materialized, used some kind of magic?"

He shook his head. "I don't think so—I don't think it was necessary."

He stood for a moment sunk in thought, then looked up.

"We've got to know the answer to this—our lives depend on it; perhaps more than just our lives. Betty," he took her hand, "will you do something for us? It is a sacrifice, for it may be a horrible experience, but if it succeeds it'll save us."

All this time Betty had been silent; now Carol saw that she had a curiously blank look, yet strained, as if she were undergoing some inner tension. But at Simon's question she glanced up smiling, the old gentle smile that Carol loved.

"Of course I will. What do you want me to do?"

"I want you to 'see' for me; to go back into the past. If you're willing I'll use you as Zarov has used you, as a medium. But this time it'll be for good, not for evil."

"Can't you use me?" Carol interposed swiftly.

"You're not a medium. If I could do the 'seeing' myself I would, but it means getting into a state of trance which wouldn't be safe at a time like this, when I must be psychically on the alert and ready for emergencies. Anyhow," he added, turning to Betty again, "I can promise that you you'll be protected, no harm will come to you."

"I'll do anything," she said softly.

"Good. Sit on the ground, just here." He drew her down close beside the skeleton of Cheosri and facing that of Senhu-re; picking up the golden snake, he fastened it upon her arm. Nikolai and Carol he placed one on either side of her also facing in the same direction; then, standing before her and focusing the light into her eyes, he began to make swift passes, intoning some invocation as he did so. Almost immediately her eyes became fixed and her body rigid.

"Go back," he commanded, "become again a part of the play which was enacted here, yet remain above it, not partaking of its pains or its penalties." Three deep, slow sighs shook her. Her lips parted; so soft was her voice at first it was hard to distinguish her words. "The evil—the evil in this place . . ."

Simon stooped over her. "Do you see Cheosri?"

A quiver passed through the entranced girl. "I stand, I invoke; Oh, I am Cheosri, the sorceress. Yet I am not her, I am the Oversoul, the spirit that watches the Play of its shadows."

"It is well. Is Cheosri alone?"

"No; there stands another by her side. They are encircled by the legions of evil and with them are the dead ready to serve."

"Light conquereth Darkness. Does not the light come?"

There was a long pause. When she spoke again it was as if her eyes were actually watching the scene she described. "The Light waits outside under the moon; but not at the entrance through which Cheosri came. The Light waits by a rock, high up, a secret place. Ah, now it passes behind the rock and goes down into darkness. It is very dark. The passage winds on. Only the few, those with vision, the Elect, know that this rock was riven asunder, and long ago, for the purposes of the Ancient Ones, was widened secretly. But I know—I and the Light."

She moved, making feeble gestures with her hands. "How close the rock is to my head! On and on. Oh, cling to the rock, there is a chasm; it goes down, down even to Amenti. Up now, so steep . . . Here it is open like a cup; above me is the sky. The blessed stars, I see them like a crown above my head." Her voice grew so faint that it was like the sighing of a breath. "I am going down again among the rocks; I am crushed by the darkness; surely no man's body can pass through so small a space! Now it is wider, more easy. Now I hear the sound—the sound . . ." She hesitated, then went on more slowly, between laboured breaths: "The sound . . . nearer . . . nearer . . . nearer . . ."

There was another long pause. They pressed close about her, hanging on her words. Then, quite suddenly, a change came over her face; the eyes grew wild, the mouth opened, her voice shrilled out: "It is not the Light that approaches, not now! It is Darkness, the Lord of Amenti, Set, Sutekh—the evil one. He comes, he comes! Nearer . . . nearer . . ."

"Does he follow the same path?" It was Simon's voice, tense and sharp.

For a moment she did not reply; then, once more, her eyes changed. It was as if a mask dropped over her face; power emanated from her, so that her frail body seemed to expand and the voice with which the answer was given was not her own. Deep it was and slow, each syllable distinct, commanding and strong.

"He comes indeed. He seeks to enter this place wherein the Secret was once invoked. For, behold, Its Power dwelleth for ever where it hath been manifested. And those who have trodden the path of Knowledge breathing this air, and thus partaking of the divine Essence, would henceforth possess the power to reawaken Its vibration within themselves. He is driven here by one greater than he, who uses him as he has used this medium, and if in the act of sacrilege the servant be destroyed—what matters it to those who See and Know? But woe unto the earth if *that one* should obtain, even for a brief moment, the Power and the Glory and the Attributes of the Word."

The Voice ceased; and instantly all strength went out of the medium. She fell forward and lay still, but when Nikolai would have sprung forward to help her Simon thrust him violently away. "Leave her alone!" he whispered fiercely, "you'll kill her if you touch her now." In a few seconds, however, she moved again and began to cry and to tremble, "Stop him!" she sobbed. "Oh, stop him! He is coming—he is coming. He is near now, so near . . ."

Instinctively they all turned at that cry towards the shadowed rock under which the bones of Senhu-re lay. Their torches flashed upward, but the shadow behind that projection remained impenetrable. For an instant both Nikolai and Carol stared at it, waiting for something to move there, to emerge, but Simon was now stooping over Betty, passing his hands over her head, intoning a *mantram* as he did so. "Wake, Betty, wake," he repeated on two rising and falling notes; "wake, Betty, wake—and forget."

Her eyes opened, she gazed vaguely round. "Come," he said, "it's over, you're all right now. We've got to be quick."

He was alert again, master of the situation. "Annerly, go back and fetch Mr. Mannering. Can you manage him alone?"

Nikolai nodded and disappeared into the darkness whence they had come. Simon turned to Carol: "Keep hold of Betty, and bring her after me." Without more ado he turned and strode across to that shadowed rock. Carol's heart was pounding; she felt sick with fear as she watched him clamber up and thrust himself into that black patch of shadow. Betty's words still rang in her head: *He is coming—he is coming; he is near now, so near* . . . Who or *what* was descending that passage? Simon, visible once more and immobile now, staring up at something she could not see, would interpose his whole force, his body, his very life between this place and whoever sought to violate its secrets.

She put her arms round Betty. "Come on, darling," she murmured and led her across the chamber. Betty's feet struck the little heap of bones and dust which might have been Anf-Kaseth, scattering them as she moved half blindly forward. When they stood behind Simon the aperture was revealed. From here it appeared to be no more than a rather wide slit in the rocks, not even worth investigation. Yet to them it showed the path to freedom, or perhaps to death; certainly to dangers and ordeals unimaginable.

At that moment Nikolai returned carrying quite easily the frail body of their father.

"Shall I give you a hand?" asked Simon without, however, taking his eyes off the entrance to the passage.

"No, I can manage; he's no weight at all."

"Right; when you want help, tell me. We'd better start. As quietly as you can. I'll lead, then Carol and Betty and you last. Don't talk. Try to think of nothing but that Invocation. It has a tremendous protective power. Nothing'll be able to touch you so long as you hang on to that. The 'Darks' can only get at us through doubt or fear; we'll be all right so long as we remain confident."

He went on ahead. The opening was bigger than it looked, but there was still only room for one at a time. Carol could not help being thankful she wasn't Nikolai, encumbered with the unconscious man and the last in the line. How horribly vulnerable one would feel, knowing that that place, so packed, so alive with evil, was behind one!

The passage continued to be not much more than a slit, or fault in the rock. It went steadily upward twisting continually, so that, despite the powerful torch, they could see but a short distance ahead. Each blind corner held a menace. At any one Simon might find himself face to face with what Betty had called the Power of Evil.

They progressed very slowly, for Nikolai was often in difficulties, being forced to prop Mannering against the wall whilst he squeezed through some narrow part and drew the old man carefully after him. And all the while they were acutely conscious that somewhere in the darkness ahead their enemy drew nearer every moment.

Then Simon suddenly stopped, flashing his torch up and down. A wall of solid rock confronted them. He frowned, and turning to the others whispered: "There must be a way out; unless, of course, there's been a subsidence. But have you noticed that the air is comparatively fresh here? Besides, Betty said . . ." He broke off abruptly and pressed his ear against the rock: "Can't you hear something?"

They all held their breath, straining every nerve; but the silence had fallen again like a cloak and they could only hear the blood beating in their ears. But Simon, using senses more trained than theirs, knew he had not been mistaken. Perhaps it was instinct rather than an oral sensation which warned him; he had felt rather than heard a movement somewhere ahead, behind this wall of rock. The silence seemed absolute, but it was not so.

He put up his hand, running it along a little cornice, but beyond this, rock again met his fingers. The torch revealed no more but its own limited area in which everything was sharply defined, unreal, shadows ink-black outlining all the irregularities of the structure of this enclosed space which threatened them, pressed down on them, close like the lid of a sarcophagus. His mind went back to Betty's words: *Surely no man's body can pass through so small a space*; then in a flash understanding came to him. He turned the torch down upon the ground and saw, what the first cursory glance had missed, a space about two feet high. He put his hand to ground level; yes, a faint but steady draught was blowing upon it.

"Through here," he said. "Hands and knees! He turned to Nick, "Annerly, are you sure you can manage? I don't want to leave the head of the line, particularly here. I think Carol had better go behind you while we squeeze through this bit, then she can help guide her father as you drag him, it'll take a bit of doing."

For a moment, then, Carol hesitated. So it had come! One always had to face things. She was going to be last after all, and in the most terrifying attitude, that on one's face, crawling. She realized what a difference the upright position makes to man's sense of security—to his ability to face things, any sort of things, mental or physical; she had never thought about that before. But Simon had said there must be no fear, no doubt or refusal. Flattening herself against the rock, she waited for Nikolai to pass.

In places the roof was lower than Simon had imagined. One had to squirm along with the rock scraping one's back and neck. He pushed the torch in front of him; the tunnel seemed endless. It would not have been so bad if he had not had that increasing conviction of the approach of danger. Supposing he met his enemy like this—face to face—literally face to face?

Well, there was nothing for it but to go on. The shadows were more than ever fantastic here; they were like threatening arms, like genii stooping down, barring one the way. Fear . . . he must not admit fear. But this sense of restriction was damnable! One's shoulders were so hampered, one felt as if paralysed from the neck down; only one's face seemed to advance, to have any power, and one's face was so pitifully vulnerable, the part one always had the instinct to shield. Where, indeed, was his power now, in such a predicament? Where his protection? Not in this helpless body, squirming its way like a snake upon the ground; not even in the mind which darted like a trapped thing between the shadows, conjured up attack where no attack might threaten, let loose man's worse foe, panic, upon him. There must be no thought, even, of that; for he knew only too well that those who followed him would be affected by his slightest change of attitude, by his faintest weakening. He must seek his power, his protection above the sphere of the trapped body, the wavering mind, in those Forces which he had invoked, which were superior to the hampering restrictions of matter.

Every spirit of the firmament: of the Ether, upon the earth or under the Earth, on Dry Land and in the Water, of Whirling Air and Rushing Fire, and every spell and scourge of God . . .

He drew a long breath and like a shield before him, as he crawled into that endless vista of darkness, he sent forth again the Invocation to the Guardians; and it seemed to him that indeed now a cloud of white radiance rose before his eyes, advancing as he advanced, cutting him off from the Unknown which lay beyond. Imagination? Perhaps; but the feeling of panic slipped from him, and, as if his courage had been a magical power lifting an illusory menace, he suddenly found that the roof was getting higher. He raised himself to his knees, then with a sigh of relief stood upright. "We're through," he whispered back to those panting, sighing noises behind him which indicated the laborious advance of the rest of the party, and he helped them out one after the other.

"We'll rest here, just for a few minutes." He switched off the torch. The darkness swooped down like a waiting thing, but out of the darkness now, high up, a faint patch of luminosity appeared. He pointed to it: "Look! the stars!"

Yes, faintly, far away, their eyes could distinguish now a chain of stars, beacons of hope in the gloom, while upon their heads, cool, sweet night air blew down. Instinctively they all relaxed, breathing deeply, but as the tension lessened, so they became aware of the full extent of their exhaustion. Nikolai, with a sigh, sat down upon a rock and felt for a cigarette while Betty dropped beside him and laid her head on his shoulder. Carol, still feeling sick and shaken after that ordeal in the tunnel, took Simon's arm and was comforted by the answering pressure. Following the direction in which she could feel, rather than see, that he was gazing, she found comfort also in the twinkling of the stars which, as her eyes grew accustomed to the gloom, increased momentarily in size and brightness. Far, far away indeed that opening appeared, yet after those hours cooped up and imprisoned in the womb of the earth, the sight of the sky and the feeling of fresh air gave renewed confidence and strength.

But it lasted for a moment only; the dream was shattered by Betty's voice raised in a scream which trailed off into a thin wail of terror.

Instinctively they drew together, peering up through the shadows.

On the opposite side of the cavern, high up, perhaps some twenty feet from the ground, in a faint aura of luminosity, hung, disembodied in a void of darkness, Zarov's face. Like a dead mask it seemed floating in space, yet it was alive: for the eyes, mocking, cruel, gazed down at them and the mouth smiled.

Without a moment's hesitation Simon stepped in front of the others. "Remember—the Names!" he whispered. "He can do nothing." Then he addressed the head in ringing tones.

"Zarov, we know you. You cannot play your tricks on us. I give you warning, you will not be allowed to pass. We are protected with a greater protection than you can ever hope to receive. Turn back before it is too late. As I succeeded in defying you before so shall I defy you again, but this time not by my strength, rather by the strength of Those whose Names I have invoked. No man can pass where we have passed—and live!"

Echoes caught up Simon's words, throwing them back and forth in sportive mockery; when they ceased the answer came.

"Speak for yourself if you will, magician, who yet escaped me only through the incapacity of my servant; but do not speak for those I perceive trembling behind you. What do they know of magic? And what protection can they invoke against my servants? They are blind, else they would know that the darkness of this place is crowded with those who, when I give the word, will advance against them, seize them, disintegrate their minds and their bodies with invisible weapons. Nothing you can do will help them in that hour against the Lords of the Dark Face."

As the echoes answered again Simon put out his hand to the others and whispered: "Take no notice, he can't do anything." But he was acutely aware of their shaken confidence, their rising panic, and knew that the issue was joined at last.

Then, rising about the little group, coming from nowhere, a sudden whispering arose, borne on an icy wind which rushed out of the darkness upon them, dropped, then arose again, stronger than before. It was accompanied by a low, humming sound and a faint, yet sickly, smell.

Simon spoke again in a ringing voice, seeking as much to calm the fears of his friends, as to impress his enemy.

"We have love," he cried. "Love is the greatest protective Force of all."

Again that laugh arose to be echoed upon all sides in a crescendo of mockery.

"Love! Are you so sure of that? Have not their hearts known hate also? Over all those who can hate—yes, and fear—my Powers have dominion."

The cold wind struck them again, the humming increased, the sickly odour was now almost overwhelming; and with these manifestations a doubt, very faint certainly, yet insidious, for the first time arose in Simon's mind. Wasn't there a certain amount of truth in what Zarov said? And were the great Beings he had invoked in the tomb to protect them, strong enough to counteract such a tremendous concentration of destructive forces as those with which Zarov threatened them now?

And, as if in response to even this inner acknowledgment of their power, these evil forces hitherto hidden from Simon by reason of his own intense concentration upon forms and symbols higher than they, began to materialize before his eyes. The darkness grew faintly luminous; he saw it now, vibrant and alive; and Shapes, invoked and formed of old through Rites which only the Great Magicians knew, appeared, ringing the cavern round, towering up in its dim recesses, blotting out the little girdle of stars. Faint at first they grew moment by moment more distinct. Their faces looked down on him, faces without hope, without light, faces of the demons who haunt the nether worlds and from which the drugged and mad flee in vain. Yet from these blind eyes shot forth baleful fires, and from the putrescent lips an icy wind issued like a pestilential breath, while their voices sounded forth the dull humming note of disintegration.

Mighty, omnipotent they seemed, in this moment of his weakening. And now the hideous doubt returned more acutely, shaking his erstwhile confidence. Was he strong enough himself? When these evil entities massed to the attack would his mind be sufficiently steady to hold the Image of mightier Principalities? Could his lips sustain the sound of the Names to which would answer the Lords of greater Kingdoms? Everything would depend upon this, upon his capacity to invoke a bulwark against which the Elements of Destruction might hurl themselves in vain. He was the focus, the sole focus which the Powers of Good could use to defeat their adversaries' purpose. If he failed it would be the end; for he believed that, bound by their own immutable Laws, no Powers could manifest on the physical plane save through some physical intermediary attuned to Their rhythm and Their will.

And in this place where, through man, Evil had first been invoked, only through man might it be ultimately defeated.

If Zarov succeeded in conquering him and passing into that chamber where, in the Astral Light, he could read the Secret of the Soul of the World, then without doubt it was these Principalities and Powers whose baleful forms threatened him now from all sides, which, for a period of time, would conquer and rule the world.

It must not—it could not happen!

Abrasar . . . Ishuré . . . Diarthanna Thorun . . . Adonaie.

What were These? Forces—Energies . . . Could they not be invoked for greater purposes even than protection? Surely protection was no longer enough. And there were Others besides, whose power could combat and overthrow these hideous legions of evil. Yes, in this capacity he must now call upon them. At all costs the Secret must be guarded; they would be his allies, would hurl themselves against the foe—and conquer.

With a supreme effort of will he shut out the vision of those other forms. Making a Sign upon the air he uttered three mighty Names. Visualizing them as glittering warriors he bade them defend their own.

The response was immediate; as the vibrations went forth, smiting upon the darkness, the humming quivered, died, arose, then died again. Even the light upon Zarov's face grew dim and the forms that filled the cavern trembled and began to fade. And when the reverberation of the Names at length died there followed a great stillness; yet it was not the stillness of peace. It was as menacing in its intensity as that which precedes the earth-shattering thunder. Then, just as Simon was about to congratulate himself upon his tactics, invisible, yet powerful as the result of an explosion, the evil force arose once more and hurled itself upon him. He found himself giving way before the malignancy of its attack. There was nothing for it now but to invoke his own gods anew. The result was similar. A recrudescence of protective might, yet followed by a recrudescence equivalent to, if not more violent than the forces of his adversary. And he soon was to discover that each time he made this evocation the ensuing repercussion increased, and the threatening Shapes became even taller, more distinct. Yet now he dared not cease these repeated efforts. Yet how would it end?

Neither he nor Zarov were, in reality, men in conflict any more; they had become rather the temporary symbols of opposing centres of force; champions of Light and Darkness they were hurled back and forth by the Energies which they had invoked to serve their purposes.

Thus, for what seemed like an eternity, the battle endured. Each man, using all the magical knowledge at his command, invoked Forces increasingly powerful and more extensive. But inevitably, at length, they both reached the limit of their capacity. Deadlock ensued. Dark and Light were equally matched.

Like wrestlers, poised in the highest pitch of tension, the adversaries were immobile, seemingly inert. Neither could advance. The pressure became like that of an overcharged battery which at any moment might explode. How long, Simon thought, how long? Everything, even the issue was forgotten now, in this tremendous effort at concentration, in this attempt to hold the swaying, contending forces in equilibrium, rather than give way. Yet the moment must come when something would happen: the scales would tip. Were they tipping now? Was he weakening? Whoever made the next move would hold the advantage. The sweat was pouring down his face and he had the utmost difficulty in keeping the essential rhythm in his breathing. Then, suddenly, he became aware that Zarov's face, which he had been using as a focus, had disappeared. He tried to pierce the gloom, to distinguish his enemy's form from among those shifting, threatening Shapes of Illusion, but failed to find even a trace of him anywhere.

Keeping his right hand upraised in the gesture of defence, with his left he felt in his pocket for the electric torch. He switched it on, but nothing happened.

"A light! Quick!" he muttered to Nikolai.

"It won't work!" came the reply, evidently through chattering teeth.

This small yet significant occurrence disturbed him profoundly. The batteries were out of action: electricity, one of the most potent of the elements, was under Zarov's control.

Despite all his efforts now he could not rid himself of that dangerous doubt which was rapidly growing to the proportions of a definite fear.

The scales *were* tipping. Zarov had the advantage.

If he were to hold Zarov at bay what must he do, what *could* he do?

One thing appeared certain, the Powers he had invoked were no longer capable of defending him. Why was this? What had happened? With lightning rapidity he reviewed his actions. Could the fault be in himself? Had he made a mistake? It must be so, why else did he have this fatal sensation of uncertainty which was already undermining the integrity of his purpose? He must not give way to any doubt. He must maintain absolute conviction as to the outcome; he must have unshakable faith. But were certainty and faith justified any more, since these Mighty Ones were no longer omnipotent?

If only he could know—could see. His mind strove blindly to thrust its way upward and transcend this welter of emotional forces that confused and obliterated every effort to perceive the truth.

And at last the effort succeeded. In a flash he knew. The fault was his. Once more, as in his previous contest with Zarov, he had endeavoured to oppose force by force. Then, however, it had been merely his own will, his own hate, his own fear that he had launched against his adversary. Yet that had nearly been his undoing. And he had forgotten! But this time the force he had used was of a far different kind; he had invoked divine, transcendental Energies. At this realization terror overwhelmed him; the confidence in his own action, which hitherto had upheld him, was shattered. And on the instant everything about him began to change, to expand, to increase. Force rushed into Force. Like a giant wave, like a vortex of whirling and roaring fire, like a hurricane, faster, faster, the Forms and Faces spun upward as a waterspout which, in an instant, will break and destroy everything beneath it.

He could do no more. But as the maelstrom converged upon him in one last, despairing effort, he launched his whole being in a supreme cry for help and for guidance.

And the answer came—as it had come once before, and in the same words—*To the Greater I submit.*

But now, at last, he understood.

The Greater—what was that but the Supreme Power, all-comprehensive, all-embracing, whereof all else, men, gods and spirits, Principalities and Powers, were but partial manifestations? What else but that *Name above every Name, whereunto every knee shall bow*?

With his whole being now he accepted the command, without condition, without reserve. Submission absolute, that was his part. Not his to will any more, to invoke, to struggle. The body was nothing, let it be destroyed; the mind and will were nothing, if THIS needed them not.

And in that act of supreme oblation, when the human, surrendering to the Divine, becomes united with It, the man lost all sense of separation, of a personal self, of a body that could move, of a tongue that could speak.

Swiftly, more swiftly now, the mighty vortex converged upon him; but he feared it no more. Nay, rather, he moved forward to meet it. His arms, guided no longer by his own will, stretched upward, as if, in love, opening themselves to receive even evil into a divine embrace. Through him, using his body as its focus, the supreme Power of Love flowed, unchecked now by any human will, pouring Itself out in wave after glittering wave towards those malignant Shapes, drawing them, uniting Itself with them. And in that fiery effluence, in which the man was no more than a whirling particle, the Shapes melted and were transformed. Colour flowed into their forms; their eyes became suffused with light; flames of supernal beauty shimmered and flashed about their towering heads and now from their lips rolled forth mighty peals of music, unearthly and transcendent. Still were they the same great Elemental Principalities and Powers, but now, released and regenerated by love from the spell of perversion man had cast upon their divine Essence, they appeared in their true, eternal, archetypal Forms.

As for that Spark of the Divine fire which, in its sojourning on earth, was known by the name of Simon Conningsby, no longer was it, either, held by the Shapes of Illusion. It escaped and dwelt for æons in knowledge and bliss amid protean Forms and Sounds of a loveliness surpassing any human imagining. For æons...

Then, piercing the empyrean, a cry struck upward like a sword of darkness, a cry of supreme human fear, yet of more than human agony. And at that cry Pity entered into Bliss; and with Pity came once again that consciousness of Separation implicit in those activities in which pity was expressed—desire to serve, to help, to save whoever uttered that despairing appeal. But to answer that cry meant to descend to the level whence it came. Love drew down its instrument in the wake of that diminishing note, which still summoned it so imperatively . . .

The light dimmed, the colours faded, the Forms withdrew, as darkness veiled them. And when Simon opened his eyes, still dazed and but half-aware, he saw this darkness and knew that the earth had received him once more into her womb.

He looked vaguely around. Darkness . . . but piercing it a sharp beam of light. And there, not far away, lit by this beam, the form of Zarov. He was kneeling with one arm over his eyes. But at Simon's almost involuntary movement forward he flung up his head. Simon saw his face, as a dead man's face with fallen jaw, and eyes that were sightless and blank.

"Zarov!" he whispered in horror and in pity.

But at the name, as if galvanized into life, the man stumbled to his feet, and swung round and in a second was swallowed up by the darkness, although the sound of his footsteps could still be heard.

With one swift glance behind to see that the others were unharmed, Simon picked up the largest torch which was now working perfectly and sending out the clear beam that had revealed Zarov a moment before.

Flashing it to right and left he followed the sound of stumbling footsteps. In a moment the light picked out Zarov's figure. The cavern was much vaster than Simon had at first supposed. He lost him again as he swerved, but the next time that the light caught him Simon paused in amazement, for Zarov was running straight forward at a wall of rock. He struck it and reeled back; righted himself and started feeling desperately along its surface. Only now did Simon realize that the man had actually lost his sight.

"Zarov, wait!" he cried, but Zarov's movements only became more hurried. Then, while Simon still watched, a strange thing happened. Zarov's body jerked upright; the groping movements ceased and like an automaton he made straight for a jagged escarpment. With lightning rapidity he began climbing the rock. Simon understood now how it was his face had first appeared so high above them, for there must be steps here. A moment later Zarov appeared on a shelf of rock. His face was turned up blindly, yet as if guided by another will than his own, with unerring precision he made for a dark fissure visible now in the torchlight.

Again Simon shouted: "Zarov!" Again a hundred echoes caught up the name as if the demons Zarov had conjured were mocking at him. Zarov . . . Zarov . . . Zarov . . . !

Simon saw him turn and hesitate.

"Wait—wait!" he called again. "I am your friend!"

"Friend . . . friend . . . friend . . ." jeered the hidden voices and Zarov, as if fleeing from them, disappeared into the opening.

Simon wasted no more breath, but sprang up the steps and into the passage after him. The thought of that blind and terrified man running through the darkness, hurtling into rocks, driven ever on and on by the furies of his own imagination, filled him with horror. Perhaps the passage ended high up on the mountain side; if so he would go hurtling to death.

And as he ran the desire to save his erstwhile enemy became almost an obsession. He did not reason any more; thus it never occurred to him that the dark forces, working on his own impulsive chivalry, might actually be using Zarov's blind and empty shell to lure him to his destruction.

The passage began to go downhill. Every moment it became steeper until it was difficult to keep a footing. Loose stones shot away under their feet and clattered from the walls as their hands scraped against them.

Zarov was running now at breakneck speed, guiding himself with outstretched arms. Whenever the passage twisted he would disappear from view, but his progress could be followed by the clatter of stones.

Flashing his torch always before him Simon saw at last a long stretch of descent, almost as steep as the side of a house. At the bottom was a jagged spur of rock; obviously the passage went off sharply here at an angle. Zarov checked at this spot for a moment, then swung abruptly to the right and disappeared. Simon hurtled on. The passage must widen here, for he could no longer see the rock wall, nor even hear Zarov's footsteps, just before he reached the outcrop of rock a piece of loose stone caught him between the feet. He tripped and lurching forward was flung against the wall; he leant there a moment clutching it for support, thankful for a breathing space in this mad descent. He dashed the light forward to see what happened to the path. Into a well of darkness it fell. There was no path. He was hanging over an abyss.

He shrank back, closing his eyes for an instant, sick with the sudden realization of what he had escaped, then cautiously he backed away from that knife-edge. What had happened to Zarov? Had he gone over? And was there no more path? Then he recalled Betty's words in her trance: *"There is a chasm that goes down, down to Amenti."* So the path must go on. Cautiously he approached the edge. Zarov had turned to the right. He dashed his torch along; yes, skirting the abyss, to be approached only by a step across a slit which also dropped into darkness, a path could be seen. So Zarov, or whoever was controlling him, had known of this, and had planned this trap for him already in the cavern! He shivered, then started with a stifled cry, for the white beam, travelling haphazard through the darkness, suddenly revealed the figure of a man, clinging like a fly to the sheer, black wall just below the pathway. There he hung, making feeble efforts to drag himself back to safety, yet probably not aware what a fall would imply. What had happened? Had he missed the path, had he slipped? Or had the Intelligence which had used him hitherto, realizing that Simon had escaped, precipitated its now useless instrument to his doom? Simon could not tell, but even as he was about to shout a warning the body swayed and tipped backwards, then with a convulsive jerk righted itself again.

Aghast, Simon watched that silent struggle. All around was blackness, above, below; Amenti indeed, waiting to receive its hierophant who, having failed, was incontinently abandoned. Simon could see that expressionless face, those eyes which had once sought to dominate his will, blinded now—by what Force he did not know—but symbolical of the spiritual state of Zarov's being—turned up, gazing at nothingness. One hand came away; for a second the other clung to the rock, then it, too, slipped. Without a word, a sound, the man's body shot downward and was received by the impenetrable shadows of the gulf.

For a few moments Simon waited, listening; but no sound came up to him.

A stone—that was all that had intervened between him and the same fate! Then he recalled the words of the Invocation to the Bornless One: *". . . Come forth . . . Spirits upon the Earth and under the Earth . . . Aid and protect me in this Work of Art."* Well, indeed, had the Spirits of the Earth served him!

He turned back. Now he must find the others. What had been happening to them while he was combating Zarov—and after? How long could that struggle have lasted? Perhaps an hour, five minutes—five seconds even . . . he would never know. But the race down the passage must have taken ten minutes, at least.

Before he had retraced his steps a few yards he heard running feet, then Carol's voice calling faintly: "Simon, Simon!" He laughed softly to himself. "What courage!" he muttered. "And I'll bet she's alone!"

She was; her torch was giving out too. He shouted up to her: "Stop, Carol, try to stop! I'm here, I'm all right!" But all the same her impetus was so great that she was flung full against him as he braced himself across her path.

"I thought he had killed you," she moaned, and clung to him trying to stifle her sobs.

"I'm very much alive," he murmured, and hugged her close.

"Did you kill him?"

"No, thank God, I didn't have to . . . but he's dead. Don't worry, I'll tell you later. Now we must go back for the others."

Exhausted as they now were this was perhaps the worst part of the journey. Simon got them over the narrow slit somehow, leading them one by one and lifting the old man across with Nikolai's help. The narrow path where Zarov had fallen was a nightmare, but fortunately it was short, and from here onward matters improved. Simon carried Mannering as Nikolai obviously was at the end of his tether. The path became comparatively easy, slanting upward again; but wide, with plenty of foothold. They went slowly now, with long pauses during which they sat without speaking, resting their aching limbs as best they could.

Once Nikolai, who was supporting Betty, by this time in a half-fainting condition, said tentatively: "I'm about all in, Conningsby, don't you think you'd better leave me and come back for me later?"

"You'll do it," Simon encouraged him, "it can't be far now. Listen, what's that?" Simon held up his hand, and they all roused themselves to listen.

From somewhere, not very far away, they heard the long-drawn-out, rhythmical call to prayer and the monotonous chant of voices in the eternal cry of man to the Unknown:

"*Al-la-hu, Al-la-hu . . . Akbar . . .*"

"Not far to go," said Nikolai with a sigh.

A moment later Simon cried: "Come on, we're nearly out. Look!"

Before them, where the passage gave one of its abrupt turns, there was a faint grey gleam upon the rock. "Daylight!" he announced. They hurried their flagging steps. As they came round the corner the rock narrowed again, but now the light was brighter; the next corner was even more narrow, but as Simon squeezed past with his burden he called back: "We're through!"

They pressed after him and found themselves on a narrow ledge of rock. On all sides rose barren mountains, but from where they stood a kind of landslide led down to a dried-up w*adi*; between two shoulders of rock the desert lay bathed now in a sea of rose and gold, herald of the rising sun.

Beautiful—unearthly, that glory meant only one thing to them—freedom!

"I think—I'll stay here," murmured Carol and sat down abruptly, closing her eyes as if the radiance hurt them.

Only Simon was standing now, staring down that long, dry, difficult track. He turned and looked at his party, all of them lying at his feet in attitudes of collapse.

"I can see I'll have to get help," he remarked, "or I'll never get you down at all."

"Give me half an hour," said Nikolai. "What's the hurry, anyway?"

"I could do with a nice, long drink," Carol said sleepily.

At that moment the figure of a man appeared in the gap below. He was strolling along, examining, through a pair of field-glasses, the rocks on either side.

Simon leant forward. "It can't be . . ."

He got up and shouted. The man swung round and sent out an answering call. Simon turned to the others; his face was alight. Carol had never seen that look upon it before.

"It is! It's my friend, Weyland! This is a miracle!"

As if Weyland's proximity had provided him with renewed energy, running and slipping he set off down the hillside.

Nikolai stared after him. "Miracle!" he snorted, "he calls *this* a miracle—after last night!"

EPILOGUE

"But what beats me," said Carol, "is how you knew that Simon needed you!"

They were seated outside one of the tents, Carol, Simon and Weyland. Betty was lying down and Nikolai was with Mannering who had not yet shown any sign of returning consciousness.

Weyland smiled. "Oh, I had a hunch."

"But to act on it! And arrive just at the right moment!" She leant forward and said persuasively: "Tell me—how *did* you really know?"

"I was in the garden after dinner when I distinctly heard him call. So I went in at once and—er, went to sleep."

"To sleep?"

"Yes, it's as good a name for it as any other. As a matter of fact it's not sleep, exactly; it's a method of projecting your consciousness out of your body. I made a powerful thought of going to Simon and so was enabled to get in touch with him. I found him in that room of Zarov's, and showed him the best way of tackling the situation. If you wanted proof of such things this would be quite convincing. He remembers it clearly. We've compared notes and not only the time tallies—that is so far as he can reckon it out—but the instructions we gave him tally too, and the description of the other man who was with me and whom Simon has not yet seen in the flesh. Of course, I realized that things were pretty serious; I would have left next day, but there was sudden trouble in the clinic. The next thing was a frantic cable from Ahmed."

"He never told me he wired you, the scoundrel!" muttered Simon.

"No, he knew you would have been furious; but, of course, he was quite right. I started off by aeroplane at once, but half-way something went wrong and we had to stop for repairs. I chartered another, but there was a series of mishaps with that one, too. I've got a pretty shrewd suspicion who was responsible for all those hold-ups. When I eventually arrived in Cairo Simon had just left. Another hour or so and I'd have been with him."

"And I wouldn't have had the chance of making every kind of fool of myself," Simon commented bitterly.

Weyland sent him an affectionate glance: "Nor the chance of learning several invaluable lessons."

Carol looked from one to the other in amazement. "A fool of yourself? You saved us! You were marvellous!"

Simon gave a short laugh. "Marvellous! I very nearly put 'finish' to all of you."

"Don't be absurd! Zarov did, you mean."

"Zarov couldn't have touched us, my girl, if I hadn't lost my head." He regarded her sombrely. "You might just as well know the worst. To all extents and purposes I'm nothing but a black magician myself."

She turned to Weyland in despair. "What is he talking about? I suppose he's been telling you some silly modest story. But I can tell you what really happened, I was with him. I repeat, he was wonderful."

"But *do* you really know what happened?" asked Weyland gently.

A troubled look came into her eyes. "No, as a matter of fact, I don't. I was going to ask you to explain, Oh, a lot of things. It's queer, but when Betty and Nick and I came to talk it over we found that there was a kind of blank none of us could fill in. We were all three simply dithering with fear one moment, it was just like the worst kind of nightmare, there aren't any words to express what one felt; then—well, I suppose we must have all fainted, because the next thing we remember is that the torches were alight and the cavern felt fresh and clear, and Simon was running after Zarov. Whatever he says he must have done something extraordinary. Why he should call himself a black magician I can't think."

"I oughtn't to have fought Zarov," said Simon, rather in the tone of one repeating a disagreeable lesson.

"What!" She turned to Weyland who was looking at them both with that faintly ironical yet kindly smile. "Not fought Zarov? What else should he have done? Sat down meekly and said: 'Please go anywhere you like, don't mind us!' Shouldn't he have invoked the—the Guardians or whatever they are, to look after us, either?"

"He had a perfect right to do that," Weyland replied gravely. "Everyone has the right to invoke divine protection, but when you have the knowledge and the power to call upon such Beings you've got to have the faith necessary to leave the issue in Their hands, not try to use Them in your own way. Fighting is not one of the divine methods, nor is interference with free will."

"Then you really do mean he should have let Zarov pass?"

"If he had continued quite calmly and fearlessly to invoke the protection of Those Whose Names he knew, there wouldn't have been any need for attack, nor would Zarov have got past. He would merely have exhausted himself hurling defiance at an imperturbable and immovable barrier. You see," he continued, as she appeared still unconvinced, "there's a well-known law in Nature that opposition creates resistance. To meet force with greater force is to generate a nucleus of ever-growing energy. You can go on like that *ad infinitum*. To battle with any adversary on his own level and with his own weapons, merely spurs him on to greater efforts. The art of Judo is founded on this principle. One must give way in order to conquer. But giving way doesn't mean, necessarily, giving in; it means refusing to use the same weapons and calling to one's aid Wisdom instead of brute force; in other words, submitting the wrong to a higher Tribunal altogether, which, manifesting in a sphere above action and reaction, good and evil, positive and negative, can therefore perfectly adjust the balance between such opposing forces. That's what 'turning the other cheek' really means; not a negative act of non-resistance, but a positive aspiration to something higher, an acceptance of the truth that only by being prepared to give up everything, by losing his life, can a man really contact the greatest life force of all."

"You mean no one ought to resist attack of any kind, from people or countries either?"

There was a remote look in his eyes when he at length replied. "In reality, no; not, that is, if they have got beyond the primitive stage which learns through blood and conflict and misery. A man—or a country—having once learned how to invoke these divine Protectors of mankind and acquired the courage and the faith to rely absolutely upon them, would never need to fear anything. For, as I told Simon a long time ago, Force is like a boomerang; unless it meets resistance it recoils upon the sender." He tapped Simon on the shoulder: "You've got the living example before you. The moment he started using the Powers destructively, hurling his armies against Zarov's, his enemy was bound to call more and more forces to his aid. Therefore it actually is a fact that Simon, as much as Zarov, was to blame for that terrific convocation of the Lords of the Dark Face. So he wasn't as far wrong in calling himself a black magician as you thought."

"But he didn't go on!" she cried.

"No; fortunately he realized in time what he was doing."

"And then what happened?"

Weyland did not answer directly. "What you've got to realize," he said after a moment, "is that in *reality* good and evil are relative, they are just forces used wisely or foolishly. So, in actual fact, there's only one fundamental difference between a black magician and a white one—that is *motive*; change your motive, your goal, and you change even the appearance of your energy. When Simon realized that his motive was no longer pure, that it was actuated by vanity—yes, he's recognized that too, now—and fear and hate and desire to conquer, he did what he ought to have done long before, gave himself up to the Greatest Energy of all, and let It act through him in Its own way and for Its own purpose."

"It was love," said Simon in a low voice.

Weyland smiled. "You call it that," he replied, "but some would call it wisdom, or harmony, the name doesn't really matter."

There was a long pause. Simon looked up. "You remember that first experience I had in Zarov's room. This, in the cavern, was much the same, and yet entirely different. Both times I went right out of my body, consciously, but I certainly didn't find the same conditions. Why not?"

"Because you weren't focusing your attention on the same plane on both occasions. It's like the after-death states; people go to the sphere they are attuned to in their life. The first time you were thinking of Carol and of me—so you went to her and to my laboratory. The second time—well, you were appealing to something rather higher than either of us, I fancy!"

Simon said nothing and after a moment Weyland added: "On the whole you didn't do too badly. The Test of the Cavern always was counted upon to show up a man's weaknesses."

"It showed up mine all right—vanity! When I think how busy I was doing God's job for Him! It turns me cold! But what do you mean by the 'Test of the Cavern,' by the way?"

"In the old Mysteries the Neophyte actually did undergo very much the same sort of trials of courage, endurance and power as you have done. But usually in these modern days the tests have to take other forms."

"Why did I have to go through the old methods, then?"

"Because in Egypt you broke the Seal of the Mysteries. This child," he tapped Carol gently on the cheek, "had to go through this recent terrifying experience for rather different, although similar reasons."

Carol looked from one to the other. "I feel I'm out of my depth again," she murmured.

"Simon will teach you—many things," said Weyland, and added with a sly smile, "but I don't fancy the teaching will be all on one side, by any means!"

Simon grinned. "It will not! By the way, did you know, when we talked that day at Skilworth, that I was going to find Carol?"

"I guessed something of the sort might happen. You see, it was in your horoscope. But I'm sorry to say you are still a bit slap-dash in your astrological readings, so you overlooked that pleasant Venusian aspect. Or perhaps you just misread it because you had a conviction that women were not worth troubling about," he added mischievously.

"Most women," said Simon, but Carol had grasped his arm in excitement.

"Betty's horoscope!" she cried.

Simon nodded. "Yes, you'll find they usually vindicate themselves, my dear; and if they appear to be wrong it's the slap-dash astrologer—like me—who's at fault, not the science."

"I'd like you to find out what else is in my stars," she said thoughtfully.

"A lot of hard work," put in Weyland, "that is, if you intend to follow Simon's path—and I think you do. You're not likely to find it easy going, we haven't done with our friends, Zarov and Co., yet, for one thing, I fancy."

"But Zarov's dead," said Carol.

Weyland leant back, stretching his arms behind his head. "Zarov!" he repeated, with an air of faint scorn. "He and Hafiz are only tools. There's someone much bigger at the back of them, and he won't stop because they have failed. He wants the Secret and he'll never rest till he finds it."

"But this must have checkmated X., surely, so far as the tomb is concerned?" said Simon, recalling a certain moment when, after the others had been safely despatched with the natives to the camp, Weyland and he had turned back and climbed to the entrance of the passage on the mountain side. Weyland had put an invisible Seal upon it and had invoked a Name of far greater protective power than Simon would ever have been able to contact. He knew also that Weyland had come to the camp armed with a charge of dynamite, calculated, the moment their party had left, to finish the work the "Guardian" had begun and bury the tomb itself too deeply for anyone ever to dig through to it.

"Yes," Weyland was saying, "we can call it checkmate, I think. But I don't believe X. would have had another shot at getting in here anyway. However, this isn't their only line, you know."

Simon sat up. "You mean you've got an inkling of his next move?"

"No; but now we realize what their game is we'll have to keep an eye on them. Not easy, but it can be done. Of course there will be a next move by both sides. My personal belief is that Egypt isn't the best place to look for a clue or even a trace of this Crystal."

"Where, then?" Simon was leaning forward eagerly. It was obvious that he was ready for fresh adventures.

"I'm—not—sure. And even if I were, young man, I'd not be fool enough to tell you here and now, without any kind of protection; I can feel our friend, X., quite busy around us, even if you can't. However," he added after a pause during which Carol looked rather nervously about them, "there's no doubt this Crystal has got to be found—and by us, if only to keep it out of the hands of those who would use it as X. intends to do."

"But what would they do with it?" asked Carol.

"You'd better ask Simon; Zarov gave him a very extensive lecture on the subject. He wouldn't have done it had he known Simon's abilities, but like all vain people he suffered from overconfidence and didn't trouble to make sure that his deductions were founded on fact. It was very useful to us, anyway; it's given us a line to go on in the future."

At that moment Nikolai put his head out of the tent.

"Carol, can you give me a hand. I want to shift him a little."

She got up; as she passed Simon he caught her by the arm and drew her to him.

"You are with us, aren't you, darling?" he whispered.

"Always, always with you, Simon," she murmured back, and, stooping, rubbed her cheek against his, "you'll have an awful job to get rid of me now!"

His eyes followed her as she passed into the tent. Then he turned with a half-sigh. "The old man won't live, you know. The shock was too great, with all that dragging about."

Weyland nodded. "All the better, it'll release her. We'll have the sister over to the clinic; not that I think there's much more to be done—she's almost cured. She's worked through a lot of bad *Karma* in the last week or so."

Simon nodded, then, glancing sideways at his friend, said rather tentatively: "And what about—us? I suppose we'll have your paternal blessing?"

Weyland hesitated. "Is there all that hurry?"

"Why not? What's the point in waiting? A couple of thousand years seems long enough for any engagement!" As Weyland only smiled, but did not answer, he leant nearer. "Why? Is there anything to stop us?"

The other put his hand on the young man's arm. "Nothing, nothing; if she's content—to stand aside."

"To stand aside?"

Instinctively both men had risen. "My boy," Weyland answered. "You heard what I said just now. There will be no rest for any of us until we have got this Crystal in safe keeping. At present I am convinced *no one* knows for certain where it is, but we have got to find out. What you have just been through has proved you fit for greater work. I have been instructed to tell you so. But there is no doubt that if you undertake this search much of your time will have to be spent where no woman can go; you will both of you have to work alone. Of course you and she are free agents, you must make your choice."

For a moment Simon hesitated. While they had been speaking Carol had come up behind them; now she stepped to his side and put her arm round his shoulder.

"I think I can answer that for both of us," she said. "Together or alone—the Work goes on . . ."

THE END

RAMBLE HOUSE's
HARRY STEPHEN KEELER WEBWORK MYSTERIES
(RH) indicates the title is available ONLY in the RAMBLE HOUSE edition

The Ace of Spades Murder
The Affair of the Bottled Deuce (RH)
The Amazing Web
The Barking Clock
Behind That Mask
The Book with the Orange Leaves
The Bottle with the Green Wax Seal
The Box from Japan
The Case of the Canny Killer
The Case of the Crazy Corpse (RH)
The Case of the Flying Hands (RH)
The Case of the Ivory Arrow
The Case of the Jeweled Ragpicker
The Case of the Lavender Gripsack
The Case of the Mysterious Moll
The Case of the 16 Beans
The Case of the Transparent Nude (RH)
The Case of the Transposed Legs
The Case of the Two-Headed Idiot (RH)
The Case of the Two Strange Ladies
The Circus Stealers (RH)
Cleopatra's Tears
A Copy of Beowulf (RH)
The Crimson Cube (RH)
The Face of the Man From Saturn
Find the Clock
The Five Silver Buddhas
The 4th King
The Gallows Waits, My Lord! (RH)
The Green Jade Hand
Finger! Finger!
Hangman's Nights (RH)
I, Chameleon (RH)
I Killed Lincoln at 10:13! (RH)
The Iron Ring
The Man Who Changed His Skin (RH)
The Man with the Crimson Box
The Man with the Magic Eardrums
The Man with the Wooden Spectacles
The Marceau Case
The Matilda Hunter Murder

The Monocled Monster
The Murder of London Lew
The Murdered Mathematician
The Mysterious Card (RH)
The Mysterious Ivory Ball of Wong Shing Li (RH)
The Mystery of the Fiddling Cracksman
The Peacock Fan
The Photo of Lady X (RH)
The Portrait of Jirjohn Cobb
Report on Vanessa Hewstone (RH)
Riddle of the Travelling Skull
Riddle of the Wooden Parrakeet (RH)
The Scarlet Mummy (RH)
The Search for X-Y-Z
The Sharkskin Book
Sing Sing Nights
The Six From Nowhere (RH)
The Skull of the Waltzing Clown
The Spectacles of Mr. Cagliostro
Stand By—London Calling!
The Steeltown Strangler
The Stolen Gravestone (RH)
Strange Journey (RH)
The Strange Will
The Straw Hat Murders (RH)
The Street of 1000 Eyes (RH)
Thieves' Nights
Three Novellos (RH)
The Tiger Snake
The Trap (RH)
Vagabond Nights (Defrauded Yeggman)
Vagabond Nights 2 (10 Hours)
The Vanishing Gold Truck
The Voice of the Seven Sparrows
The Washington Square Enigma
When Thief Meets Thief
The White Circle (RH)
The Wonderful Scheme of Mr. Christopher Thorne
X. Jones—of Scotland Yard
Y. Cheung, Business Detective

Keeler Related Works

A To Izzard: A Harry Stephen Keeler Companion by Fender Tucker — Articles and stories about Harry, by Harry, and in his style. Included is a compleat bibliography.

Wild About Harry: Reviews of Keeler Novels — Edited by Richard Polt & Fender Tucker — 22 reviews of works by Harry Stephen Keeler from *Keeler News*. A perfect introduction to the author.

The Keeler Keyhole Collection: Annotated newsletter rants from Harry Stephen Keeler, edited by Francis M. Nevins. Over 400 pages of incredibly personal Keeleriana.

Fakealoo — Pastiches of the style of Harry Stephen Keeler by selected demented members of the HSK Society. Updated every year with the new winner.

Strands of the Web: Short Stories of Harry Stephen Keeler — 29 stories, just about all that Keeler wrote, are edited and introduced by Fred Cleaver.

RAMBLE HOUSE's LOON SANCTUARY

A Clear Path to Cross — Sharon Knowles short mystery stories by Ed Lynskey.
A Corpse Walks in Brooklyn and Other Stories — Volume 5 in the Day Keene in the Detective Pulps series.
A Jimmy Starr Omnibus — Three 40s novels by Jimmy Starr.
A Niche in Time and Other Stories — Classic SF by William F. Temple
A Roland Daniel Double: The Signal and The Return of Wu Fang — Classic thrillers from the 30s.
A Shot Rang Out — Three decades of reviews and articles by today's Anthony Boucher, Jon Breen. An essential book for any mystery lover's library.
A Smell of Smoke — A 1951 English countryside thriller by Miles Burton.
A Snark Selection — Lewis Carroll's *The Hunting of the Snark* with two Snarkian chapters by Harry Stephen Keeler — Illustrated by Gavin L. O'Keefe.
A Young Man's Heart — A forgotten early classic by Cornell Woolrich.
Alexander Laing Novels — *The Motives of Nicholas Holtz* and *Dr. Scarlett*, stories of medical mayhem and intrigue from the 30s.
An Angel in the Street — Modern hardboiled noir by Peter Genovese.
Automaton — Brilliant treatise on robotics: 1928-style! By H. Stafford Hatfield.
Away From the Here and Now — Clare Winger Harris stories, collected by Richard A. Lupoff
Beast or Man? — A 1930 novel of racism and horror by Sean M'Guire. Introduced by John Pelan.
Black Beadle — A 1939 thriller by E.C.R. Lorac.
Black Hogan Strikes Again — Australia's Peter Renwick pens a tale of the 30s outback.
Black River Falls — Suspense from the master, Ed Gorman.
Blondy's Boy Friend — A snappy 1930 story by Philip Wylie, writing as Leatrice Homesley.
Blood in a Snap — The *Finnegan's Wake* of the 21st century, by Jim Weiler.
Blood Moon — The first of the Robert Payne series by Ed Gorman.
Bogart '48 — Hollywood action with Bogie by John Stanley and Kenn Davis
Calling Lou Largo! — Two Lou Largo novels by William Ard.
Cornucopia of Crime — Francis M. Nevins assembled this huge collection of his writings about crime literature and the people who write it. Essential for any serious mystery library.
Corpse Without Flesh — Strange novel of forensics by George Bruce
Crimson Clown Novels — By Johnston McCulley, author of the Zorro novels, *The Crimson Clown* and *The Crimson Clown Again*.
Dago Red — 22 tales of dark suspense by Bill Pronzini.
Dark Sanctuary — Weird Menace story by H. B. Gregory
David Hume Novels — *Corpses Never Argue, Cemetery First Stop, Make Way for the Mourners, Eternity Here I Come*. 1930s British hardboiled fiction with an attitude.
Dead Man Talks Too Much — Hollywood boozer by Weed Dickenson.
Death Leaves No Card — One of the most unusual murdered-in-the-tub mysteries you'll ever read. By Miles Burton.
Death March of the Dancing Dolls and Other Stories — Volume Three in the Day Keene in the Detective Pulps series. Introduced by Bill Crider.
Deep Space and other Stories — A collection of SF gems by Richard A. Lupoff.
Detective Duff Unravels It — Episodic mysteries by Harvey O'Higgins.
Diabolic Candelabra — Classic 30s mystery by E.R. Punshon
Dictator's Way — Another D.S. Bobby Owen mystery from E.R. Punshon
Dime Novels: Ramble House's 10-Cent Books — *Knife in the Dark* by Robert Leslie Bellem, *Hot Lead* and *Song of Death* by Ed Earl Repp, *A Hashish House in New York* by H.H. Kane, and five more.
Doctor Arnoldi — Tiffany Thayer's story of the death of death.
Don Diablo: Book of a Lost Film — Two-volume treatment of a western by Paul Landres, with diagrams. Intro by Francis M. Nevins.
Dope and Swastikas — Two strange novels from 1922 by Edmund Snell

Dope Tales #1 — Two dope-riddled classics; *Dope Runners* by Gerald Grantham and *Death Takes the Joystick* by Phillip Condé.
Dope Tales #2 — Two more narco-classics; *The Invisible Hand* by Rex Dark and *The Smokers of Hashish* by Norman Berrow.
Dope Tales #3 — Two enchanting novels of opium by the master, Sax Rohmer. *Dope* and *The Yellow Claw*.
Double Hot — Two 60s softcore sex novels by Morris Hershman.
Double Sex — Yet two more panting thrillers from Morris Hershman.
Dr. Odin — Douglas Newton's 1933 racial potboiler comes back to life.
Evangelical Cockroach — Jack Woodford writes about writing.
Evidence in Blue — 1938 mystery by E. Charles Vivian.
Fatal Accident — Murder by automobile, a 1936 mystery by Cecil M. Wills.
Fighting Mad — Todd Robbins' 1922 novel about boxing and life
Finger-prints Never Lie — A 1939 classic detective novel by John G. Brandon.
Freaks and Fantasies — Eerie tales by Tod Robbins, collaborator of Tod Browning on the film FREAKS.
Gadsby — A lipogram (a novel without the letter E). Ernest Vincent Wright's last work, published in 1939 right before his death.
Gelett Burgess Novels — *The Master of Mysteries*, *The White Cat*, *Two O'Clock Courage*, *Ladies in Boxes*, *Find the Woman*, *The Heart Line*, *The Picaroons* and *Lady Mechante*. Recently added is A Gelett Burgess Sampler, edited by Alfred Jan. All are introduced by Richard A. Lupoff.
Geronimo — S. M. Barrett's 1905 autobiography of a noble American.
Hake Talbot Novels — *Rim of the Pit*, *The Hangman's Handyman*. Classic locked room mysteries, with mapback covers by Gavin O'Keefe.
Hands Out of Hell and Other Stories — John H. Knox's eerie hallucinations
Hell is a City — William Ard's masterpiece.
Hollywood Dreams — A novel of Tinsel Town and the Depression by Richard O'Brien.
Hostesses in Hell and Other Stories — Russell Gray's most graphic stories
House of the Restless Dead — Strange and ominous tales by Hugh B. Cave
I Stole $16,000,000 — A true story by cracksman Herbert E. Wilson.
Inclination to Murder — 1966 thriller by New Zealand's Harriet Hunter.
Invaders from the Dark — Classic werewolf tale from Greye La Spina.
J. Poindexter, Colored — Classic satirical black novel by Irvin S. Cobb.
Jack Mann Novels — Strange murder in the English countryside. *Gees' First Case*, *Nightmare Farm*, *Grey Shapes*, *The Ninth Life*, *The Glass Too Many*, *Her Ways Are Death*, *The Kleinert Case* and *Maker of Shadows*.
Jake Hardy — A lusty western tale from Wesley Tallant.
Jim Harmon Double Novels — *Vixen Hollow/Celluloid Scandal*, *The Man Who Made Maniacs/Silent Siren*, *Ape Rape/Wanton Witch*, *Sex Burns Like Fire/Twist Session*, *Sudden Lust/Passion Strip*, *Sin Unlimited/Harlot Master*, *Twilight Girls/Sex Institution*. Written in the early 60s and never reprinted until now.
Joel Townsley Rogers Novels and Short Stories — By the author of *The Red Right Hand*: *Once In a Red Moon*, *Lady With the Dice*, *The Stopped Clock*, *Never Leave My Bed*. Also two short story collections: *Night of Horror* and *Killing Time*.
John Carstairs, Space Detective — Arboreal Sci-fi by Frank Belknap Long
Joseph Shallit Novels — *The Case of the Billion Dollar Body*, *Lady Don't Die on My Doorstep*, *Kiss the Killer*, *Yell Bloody Murder*, *Take Your Last Look*. One of America's best 50's authors and a favorite of author Bill Pronzini.
Keller Memento — 45 short stories of the amazing and weird by Dr. David Keller.
Killer's Caress — Cary Moran's 1936 hardboiled thriller.
Lady of the Yellow Death and Other Stories — More stories by Wyatt Blassingame.
League of the Grateful Dead and Other Stories — Volume One in the Day Keene in the Detective Pulps series.
Library of Death — Ghastly tale by Ronald S. L. Harding, introduced by John Pelan
Malcolm Jameson Novels and Short Stories — *Astonishing!* *Astounding!*, *Tarnished Bomb*, *The Alien Envoy and Other Stories* and *The Chariots of San Fernando and Other Stories*. All introduced and edited by John Pelan or Richard A. Lupoff.
Man Out of Hell and Other Stories — Volume II of the John H. Knox weird pulps collection.

Marblehead: A Novel of H.P. Lovecraft — A long-lost masterpiece from Richard A. Lupoff. This is the "director's cut", the long version that has never been published before.

Mark of the Laughing Death and Other Stories — Shockers from the pulps by Francis James, introduced by John Pelan.

Master of Souls — Mark Hansom's 1937 shocker is introduced by weirdologist John Pelan.

Max Afford Novels — *Owl of Darkness, Death's Mannikins, Blood on His Hands, The Dead Are Blind, The Sheep and the Wolves, Sinners in Paradise* and *Two Locked Room Mysteries and a Ripping Yarn* by one of Australia's finest mystery novelists.

Money Brawl — Two books about the writing business by Jack Woodford and H. Bedford-Jones. Introduced by Richard A. Lupoff.

More Secret Adventures of Sherlock Holmes — Gary Lovisi's second collection of tales about the unknown sides of the great detective.

Muddled Mind: Complete Works of Ed Wood, Jr. — David Hayes and Hayden Davis deconstruct the life and works of the mad, but canny, genius.

Murder among the Nudists — A mystery from 1934 by Peter Hunt, featuring a naked Detective-Inspector going undercover in a nudist colony.

Murder in Black and White — 1931 classic tennis whodunit by Evelyn Elder.

Murder in Shawnee — Two novels of the Alleghenies by John Douglas: *Shawnee Alley Fire* and *Haunts*.

Murder in Silk — A 1937 Yellow Peril novel of the silk trade by Ralph Trevor.

My Deadly Angel — 1955 Cold War drama by John Chelton.

My First Time: The One Experience You Never Forget — Michael Birchwood — 64 true first-person narratives of how they lost it.

Mysterious Martin, the Master of Murder — Two versions of a strange 1912 novel by Tod Robbins about a man who writes books that can kill.

Norman Berrow Novels — *The Bishop's Sword, Ghost House, Don't Go Out After Dark, Claws of the Cougar, The Smokers of Hashish, The Secret Dancer, Don't Jump Mr. Boland!, The Footprints of Satan, Fingers for Ransom, The Three Tiers of Fantasy, The Spaniard's Thumb, The Eleventh Plague, Words Have Wings, One Thrilling Night, The Lady's in Danger, It Howls at Night, The Terror in the Fog, Oil Under the Window, Murder in the Melody, The Singing Room*. This is the complete Norman Berrow library of locked-room mysteries, several of which are masterpieces.

Old Faithful and Other Stories — SF classic tales by Raymond Z. Gallun

Old Times' Sake — Short stories by James Reasoner from Mike Shayne Magazine.

One Dreadful Night — A classic mystery by Ronald S. L. Harding

Pair O' Jacks — A mystery novel and a diatribe about publishing by Jack Woodford

Perfect .38 — Two early Timothy Dane novels by William Ard. More to come.

Prince Pax — Devilish intrigue by George Sylvester Viereck and Philip Eldridge

Prose Bowl — Futuristic satire of a world where hack writing has replaced football as our national obsession, by Bill Pronzini and Barry N. Malzberg.

Red Light — The history of legal prostitution in Shreveport Louisiana by Eric Brock. Includes wonderful photos of the houses and the ladies.

Researching American-Made Toy Soldiers — A 276-page collection of a lifetime of articles by toy soldier expert Richard O'Brien.

Reunion in Hell — Volume One of the John H. Knox series of weird stories from the pulps. Introduced by horror expert John Pelan.

Ripped from the Headlines! — The Jack the Ripper story as told in the newspaper articles in the *New York* and *London Times*.

Rough Cut & New, Improved Murder — Ed Gorman's first two novels.

R.R. Ryan Novels — Freak Museum and The Subjugated Beast, two horror classics.

Ruby of a Thousand Dreams — The villain Wu Fang returns in this Roland Daniel novel.

Ruled By Radio — 1925 futuristic novel by Robert L. Hadfield & Frank E. Farncombe.

Rupert Penny Novels — *Policeman's Holiday, Policeman's Evidence, Lucky Policeman, Policeman in Armour, Sealed Room Murder, Sweet Poison, The Talkative Policeman, She had to Have Gas* and *Cut and Run* (by Martin Tanner.) Rupert Penny is the pseudonym of Australian Charles Thornett, a master of the locked room, impossible crime plot.

Sacred Locomotive Flies — Richard A. Lupoff's psychedelic SF story.
Sam — Early gay novel by Lonnie Coleman.
Sand's Game — Spectacular hard-boiled noir from Ennis Willie, edited by Lynn Myers and Stephen Mertz, with contributions from Max Allan Collins, Bill Crider, Wayne Dundee, Bill Pronzini, Gary Lovisi and James Reasoner.
Sand's War — More violent fiction from the typewriter of Ennis Willie
Satan's Den Exposed — True crime in Truth or Consequences New Mexico — Award-winning journalism by the *Desert Journal*.
Satans of Saturn — Novellas from the pulps by Otis Adelbert Kline and E. H. Price
Satan's Sin House and Other Stories — Horrific gore by Wayne Rogers
Secrets of a Teenage Superhero — Graphic lit by Jonathan Sweet
Sex Slave — Potboiler of lust in the days of Cleopatra by Dion Leclerq, 1966.
Sideslip — 1968 SF masterpiece by Ted White and Dave Van Arnam.
Slammer Days — Two full-length prison memoirs: *Men into Beasts* (1952) by George Sylvester Viereck and *Home Away From Home* (1962) by Jack Woodford.
Slippery Staircase — 1930s whodunit from E.C.R. Lorac
Sorcerer's Chessmen — John Pelan introduces this 1939 classic by Mark Hansom.
Star Griffin — Michael Kurland's 1987 masterpiece of SF drollery is back.
Stakeout on Millennium Drive — Award-winning Indianapolis Noir by Ian Woollen.
Strands of the Web: Short Stories of Harry Stephen Keeler — Edited and Introduced by Fred Cleaver.
Summer Camp for Corpses and Other Stories — Weird Menace tales from Arthur Leo Zagat; introduced by John Pelan.
Suzy — A collection of comic strips by Richard O'Brien and Bob Vojtko from 1970.
Tales of the Macabre and Ordinary — Modern twisted horror by Chris Mikul, author of the *Bizarrism* series.
Tales of Terror and Torment #1 — John Pelan selects and introduces this sampler of weird menace tales from the pulps.
Tenebrae — Ernest G. Henham's 1898 horror tale brought back.
The Amorous Intrigues & Adventures of Aaron Burr — by Anonymous. Hot historical action about the man who almost became Emperor of Mexico.
The Anthony Boucher Chronicles — edited by Francis M. Nevins. Book reviews by Anthony Boucher written for the *San Francisco Chronicle*, 1942 – 1947. Essential and fascinating reading by the best book reviewer there ever was.
The Barclay Catalogs — Two essential books about toy soldier collecting by Richard O'Brien
The Basil Wells Omnibus — A collection of Wells' stories by Richard A. Lupoff
The Beautiful Dead and Other Stories — Dreadful tales from Donald Dale
The Best of 10-Story Book — edited by Chris Mikul, over 35 stories from the literary magazine Harry Stephen Keeler edited.
The Black Dark Murders — Vintage 50s college murder yarn by Milt Ozaki, writing as Robert O. Saber.
The Book of Time — The classic novel by H.G. Wells is joined by sequels by Wells himself and three stories by Richard A. Lupoff. Illustrated by Gavin L. O'Keefe.
The Case in the Clinic — One of E.C.R. Lorac's finest.
The Strange Case of the Antlered Man — A mystery of superstition by Edwy Searles Brooks.
The Case of the Bearded Bride — #4 in the Day Keene in the Detective Pulps series
The Case of the Little Green Men — Mack Reynolds wrote this love song to sci-fi fans back in 1951 and it's now back in print.
The Case of the Withered Hand — 1936 potboiler by John G. Brandon.
The Charlie Chaplin Murder Mystery — A 2004 tribute by noted film scholar, Wes D. Gehring.
The Chinese Jar Mystery — Murder in the manor by John Stephen Strange, 1934.
The Cloudbuilders and Other Stories — SF tales from Colin Kapp.
The Compleat Calhoon — All of Fender Tucker's works: Includes *Totah Six-Pack, Weed, Women and Song* and *Tales from the Tower*, plus a CD of all of his songs.
The Compleat Ova Hamlet — Parodies of SF authors by Richard A. Lupoff. This is a brand new edition with more stories and more illustrations by Trina Robbins.

The Contested Earth and Other SF Stories — A never-before published space opera and seven short stories by Jim Harmon.
The Crimson Query — A 1929 thriller from Arlton Eadie. A perfect way to get introduced.
The Curse of Cantire — Classic 1939 novel of a family curse by Walter S. Masterman.
The Devil and the C.I.D. — Odd diabolic mystery by E.C.R. Lorac
The Devil Drives — An odd prison and lost treasure novel from 1932 by Virgil Markham.
The Devil of Pei-Ling — Herbert Asbury's 1929 tale of the occult.
The Devil's Mistress — A 1915 Scottish gothic tale by J. W. Brodie-Innes, a member of Aleister Crowley's Golden Dawn.
The Devil's Nightclub and Other Stories — John Pelan introduces some gruesome tales by Nat Schachner.
The Disentanglers — Episodic intrigue at the turn of last century by Andrew Lang
The Dog Poker Code — A spoof of *The Da Vinci Code* by D.B. Smithee.
The Dumpling — Political murder from 1907 by Coulson Kernahan.
The End of It All and Other Stories — Ed Gorman selected his favorite short stories for this huge collection.
The Fangs of Suet Pudding — A 1944 novel of the German invasion by Adams Farr
The Finger of Destiny and Other Stories — Edmund Snell's superb collection of weird stories of Borneo.
The Ghost of Gaston Revere — From 1935, a novel of life and beyond by Mark Hansom, introduced by John Pelan.
The Girl in the Dark — A thriller from Roland Daniel
The Gold Star Line — Seaboard adventure from L.T. Reade and Robert Eustace.
The Golden Dagger — 1951 Scotland Yard yarn by E. R. Punshon.
The Great Orme Terror — Horror stories by Garnett Radcliffe from the pulps
The Hairbreadth Escapes of Major Mendax — Francis Blake Crofton's 1889 boys' book.
The House That Time Forgot and Other Stories — Insane pulpitude by Robert F. Young
The House of the Vampire — 1907 poetic thriller by George S. Viereck.
The Illustrious Corpse — Murder hijinx from Tiffany Thayer
The Incredible Adventures of Rowland Hern — Intriguing 1928 impossible crimes by Nicholas Olde.
The Julius Caesar Murder Case — A classic 1935 re-telling of the assassination by Wallace Irwin that's much more fun than the Shakespeare version.
The Koky Comics — A collection of all of the 1978-1981 Sunday and daily comic strips by Richard O'Brien and Mort Gerberg, in two volumes.
The Lady of the Terraces — 1925 missing race adventure by E. Charles Vivian.
The Lord of Terror — 1925 mystery with master-criminal, Fantômas.
The Melamare Mystery — A classic 1929 Arsene Lupin mystery by Maurice Leblanc
The Man Who Was Secrett — Epic SF stories from John Brunner
The Man Without a Planet — Science fiction tales by Richard Wilson
The N. R. De Mexico Novels — Robert Bragg, the real N.R. de Mexico, presents *Marijuana Girl, Madman on a Drum, Private Chauffeur* in one volume.
The Night Remembers — A 1991 Jack Walsh mystery from Ed Gorman.
The One After Snelling — Kickass modern noir from Richard O'Brien.
The Organ Reader — A huge compilation of just about everything published in the 1971-1972 radical bay-area newspaper, *THE ORGAN*. A coffee table book that points out the shallowness of the coffee table mindset.
The Poker Club — Three in one! Ed Gorman's ground-breaking novel, the short story it was based upon, and the screenplay of the film made from it.
The Private Journal & Diary of John H. Surratt — The memoirs of the man who conspired to assassinate President Lincoln.
The Ramble House Mapbacks — Recently revised book by Gavin L. O'Keefe with color pictures of all the Ramble House books with mapbacks.
The Secret Adventures of Sherlock Holmes — Three Sherlockian pastiches by the Brooklyn author/publisher, Gary Lovisi.

The Shadow on the House — Mark Hansom's 1934 masterpiece of horror is introduced by John Pelan.
The Sign of the Scorpion — A 1935 Edmund Snell tale of oriental evil.
The Singular Problem of the Stygian House-Boat — Two classic tales by John Kendrick Bangs about the denizens of Hades.
The Smiling Corpse — Philip Wylie and Bernard Bergman's odd 1935 novel.
The Spider: Satan's Murder Machines — A thesis about Iron Man
The Stench of Death: An Odoriferous Omnibus by Jack Moskovitz — Two complete novels and two novellas from 60's sleaze author, Jack Moskovitz.
The Story Writer and Other Stories — Classic SF from Richard Wilson
The Strange Case of the Antlered Man — 1935 dementia from Edwy Searles Brooks
The Strange Thirteen — Richard B. Gamon's odd stories about Raj India.
The Technique of the Mystery Story — Carolyn Wells' tips about writing.
The Threat of Nostalgia — A collection of his most obscure stories by Jon Breen
The Time Armada — Fox B. Holden's 1953 SF gem.
The Tongueless Horror and Other Stories — Volume One of the series of short stories from the weird pulps by Wyatt Blassingame.
The Town from Planet Five — From Richard Wilson, two SF classics, *And Then the Town Took Off* and *The Girls from Planet 5*
The Tracer of Lost Persons — From 1906, an episodic novel that became a hit radio series in the 30s. Introduced by Richard A. Lupoff.
The Trail of the Cloven Hoof — Diabolical horror from 1935 by Arlton Eadie. Introduced by John Pelan.
The Triune Man — Mindscrambling science fiction from Richard A. Lupoff.
The Unholy Goddess and Other Stories — Wyatt Blassingame's first DTP compilation
The Universal Holmes — Richard A. Lupoff's 2007 collection of five Holmesian pastiches and a recipe for giant rat stew.
The Werewolf vs the Vampire Woman — Hard to believe ultraviolence by either Arthur M. Scarm or Arthur M. Scram.
The Whistling Ancestors — A 1936 classic of weirdness by Richard E. Goddard and introduced by John Pelan.
The White Owl — A vintage thriller from Edmund Snell
The White Peril in the Far East — Sidney Lewis Gulick's 1905 indictment of the West and assurance that Japan would never attack the U.S.
The Wizard of Berner's Abbey — A 1935 horror gem written by Mark Hansom and introduced by John Pelan.
The Wonderful Wizard of Oz — by L. Frank Baum and illustrated by Gavin L. O'Keefe
Through the Looking Glass — Lewis Carroll wrote it; Gavin L. O'Keefe illustrated it.
Time Line — Ramble House artist Gavin O'Keefe selects his most evocative art inspired by the twisted literature he reads and designs.
Tiresias — Psychotic modern horror novel by Jonathan M. Sweet.
Tortures and Towers — Two novellas of terror by Dexter Dayle.
Totah Six-Pack — Fender Tucker's six tales about Farmington in one sleek volume.
Tree of Life, Book of Death — Grania Davis' book of her life.
Triple Quest — An arty mystery from the 30s by E.R. Punshon.
Trail of the Spirit Warrior — Roger Haley's saga of life in the Indian Territories.
Two Kinds of Bad — Two 50s novels by William Ard about Danny Fontaine
Two Suns of Morcali and Other Stories — Evelyn E. Smith's SF tour-de-force
Ultra-Boiled — 23 gut-wrenching tales by our Man in Brooklyn, Gary Lovisi.
Up Front From Behind — A 2011 satire of Wall Street by James B. Kobak.
Victims & Villains — Intriguing Sherlockiana from Derham Groves.
Wade Wright Novels — *Echo of Fear, Death At Nostalgia Street, It Leads to Murder* and *Shadows' Edge*, a double book featuring *Shadows Don't Bleed* and *The Sharp Edge*.
Walter S. Masterman Novels — *The Green Toad, The Flying Beast, The Yellow Mistletoe, The Wrong Verdict, The Perjured Alibi, The Border Line, The Bloodhounds Bay, The Curse of Cantire* and *The Baddington Horror.* Masterman wrote horror and mystery, some introduced by John Pelan.
We Are the Dead and Other Stories — Volume Two in the Day Keene in the Detective Pulps series, introduced by Ed Gorman. When done, there may be 11 in the series.

Welsh Rarebit Tales — Charming stories from 1902 by Harle Oren Cummins
West Texas War and Other Western Stories — by Gary Lovisi.
What If? Volume 1, 2 and 3 — Richard A. Lupoff introduces three decades worth of SF short stories that should have won a Hugo, but didn't.
When the Batman Thirsts and Other Stories — Weird tales from Frederick C. Davis.
Whip Dodge: Man Hunter — Wesley Tallant's saga of a bounty hunter of the old West.
Win, Place and Die! — The first new mystery by Milt Ozaki in decades. The ultimate novel of 70s Reno.
Writer 1 and 2 — A magnus opus from Richard A. Lupoff summing up his life as writer.
You'll Die Laughing — Bruce Elliott's 1945 novel of murder at a practical joker's English countryside manor.

RAMBLE HOUSE
Fender Tucker, Prop.   Gavin L. O'Keefe, Graphics
www.ramblehouse.com   fender@ramblehouse.com
228-826-1783   10329 Sheephead Drive, Vancleave MS 39565

Printed in Great Britain
by Amazon